BEYOND THE REALM

Compiled & Edited by
Ben Thomas & D Kershaw

Also available and coming soon from Black Hare Press

DARK DRABBLES ANTHOLOGIES

WORLDS
ANGELS
MONSTERS
BEYOND
UNRAVEL
APOCALYPSE
LOVE
HATE
OCEANS
ANCIENTS

BHP WRITERS' GROUP SPECIAL EDITIONS

STORMING AREA 51
EERIE CHRISTMAS
BAD ROMANCE
TWENTY TWENTY

OTHER VOLUMES

DEEP SPACE
WHAT IF?
KEY TO THE KINGDOM
DEEP SEA
BEYOND THE REALM

Twitter: @BlackHarePress
Facebook: BlackHarePress
Website: www.BlackHarePress.com

BEYOND THE REALM title is
Copyright © 2020 Black Hare Press
First published in Australia in August 2020 by Black Hare Press

The authors of the individual stories retain the copyright of the works featured in this anthology

All characters and events in this publication, other than those clearly in the public domain, are fictitious and any resemblance to real persons, living or dead, is purely coincidental.

All rights reserved. No part of this production may be reproduced, stored in a retrieval system, or transmitted, in any form or by any means, electronic, mechanical, photocopying, recording or otherwise, without the prior permission of the publisher and copyright owner.

Paperback : ISBN 978-1-925809-77-0
Hard cover : ISBN 978-1-925809-78-7

Cover design by Dawn Burdett
Formatting by Ben Thomas

The stranger began then to vomit forth fire,
To burn the great manor; the blaze then glimmered
For anguish to earlmen, not anything living
Was the hateful air-goer willing to leave there.
The war of the worm widely was noticed,
The feud of the foeman afar and anear,
How the enemy injured the earls of the Geatmen,
Harried with hatred: back he hied to the treasure,
To the well-hidden cavern ere the coming of daylight.
He had circled with fire the folk of those regions,
With brand and burning; in the barrow he trusted,
In the wall and his war-might: the weening deceived him.
Then straight was the horror to Beowulf published,
Early forsooth, that his own native homestead,
The best of buildings, was burning and melting,
Gift-seat of Geatmen. 'Twas a grief to the spirit
Of the good-mooded hero, the greatest of sorrows:
The wise one weened then that wielding his kingdom
'Gainst the ancient commandments, he had bitterly angered
The Lord everlasting: with lorn meditations
His bosom welled inward, as was nowise his custom.
The fire-spewing dragon fully had wasted
The fastness of warriors, the water-land outward,
The manor with fire. The folk-ruling hero,
Prince of the Weders, was planning to wreak him.
The warmen's defender bade them to make him,
Earlmen's atheling, an excellent war-shield
Wholly of iron: fully he knew then
That wood from the forest was helpless to aid him,
Shield against fire. The long-worthy ruler
Must live the last of his limited earth-days,
Of life in the world and the worm along with him,
Though he long had been holding hoard-wealth in plenty.
Then the ring-prince disdained to seek with a war-band,
War-thane, when Hrothgar's palace he cleansèd,
Conquering combatant, clutched in the battle
The kinsmen of Grendel, of kindred detested.

'Twas of hand-fights not least where Higelac was slaughtered,
When the king of the Geatmen with clashings of battle,
Ecgtheow's bairn o'er the bight-courses swam then,
Lone-goer lorn to his land-folk returning,
Where Hygd to him tendered treasure and kingdom,
Rings and dominion: her son she not trusted,
To be able to keep the kingdom devised him
'Gainst alien races, on the death of King Higelac.
Yet the sad ones succeeded not in persuading the atheling
In any way ever, to act as a suzerain
To Heardred, or promise to govern the kingdom;
Yet with friendly counsel in the folk he sustained him,
Gracious, with honor, till he grew to be older,
Wielded the Weders. Wide-fleeing outlaws,
Ohthere's sons, sought him o'er the waters:
They had stirred a revolt 'gainst the helm of the Scylfings,
The best of the sea-kings, who in Swedish dominions
Distributed treasure, distinguished folk-leader.
'Twas the end of his earth-days; injury fatal
By swing of the sword he received as a greeting,
Offspring of Higelac; Ongentheow's bairn
Later departed to visit his homestead,
When Heardred was dead; let Beowulf rule them,
Govern the Geatmen: good was that folk-king.

Beowulf: An Anglo-Saxon Epic Poem

TABLE OF CONTENTS

The Cloak of Kings by Nicola Currie 11

Atmus Fear by A.L. King 61

Ziyad the Blasphemer by Abigail Linhardt 113

The Last Dragonrider by Raven Corrin Carluk 159

Midnight in Autumn by Cindar Harrell 193

Dragomancer by Elizabeth Montague 231

Reign Delay by John H. Dromey 261

Vanya's Necklet by Rich Rurshell 307

The Seventh Soul by Carole de Monclin 333

Seeker by Stuart West 385

Vestal Scarlet by Jacqueline Moran Meyer 421

A Knight of Many Pieces by Derek Dunn 469

Acknowledgements 499

BEYOND THE REALM

THE CLOAK OF KINGS
By Nicola Currie

Rysario is only a humble dressmaker but when the Mage Councilman to the broken line of kings knocks on her door, she faces dark alchemy, warrior witches and hellish infernophids as they journey to find a legendary cloak and the king it will reveal.

It was three months until the Festival of Kings, yet fireworks already sparked in the sky some nights. Rysario allowed herself a pause from her sewing. She stepped out the back door of their lonely cottage on the lakeside opposite the city, to watch as the baubled heavens reflected their brief treasures in the water below. Even a king, if they had had one, could have no such view as she did.

Rysario looked at the castle too. It was a stunning fortress of white stone. The many towers were topped with silver spires that glinted from the gate tower to the high turrets where princesses used to live. How strange that hundreds of servants laboured there to maintain its regal perfection with no royal master to enliven it.

As the fireworks dwindled, Rysario returned to her labours. The festival brought a rush of orders. It was the highlight of every citizen's year and those who could afford it would have new garments. For ten days and nights, Rysario had toiled over an intricate gown of velvet and satin for a rich merchant's wife. Her fingers were weary and her neck sore from long hours leaning into the firelight, but it was almost finished. Tomorrow, she would take her payment gladly. The price for this dress alone would keep them fed for a month.

"Rysa?"

Rysario's little sister, Serene, descended the stairs in her nightgown, rubbing her eyes so sweetly it belied her thirteen years.

"Hungry, Rysa." Serene had been gifted with a sweet heart and few words, content to observe the world in silence, fascinated by details. She could replicate the pattern of a spider's web in stitch but could not say the word spider. She was happiest sitting on the lakeside grasses, making daisy circlets for their heads. She would gaze at the castle and say the phrase she always repeated. "Princess someday."

Perhaps she hoped to meet a prince, like the ones in mother's stories. Serene was fair, with golden hair and eyes of sparkling green but would be unlikely to find even an honest labourer willing to marry one so different. Rysario had promised her parents as they died of fever that she would take care of Serene. She could not give her castles or crowns, but she would give her what she could.

"Hungry," Serene said again. Rysario had rationed their food well and tomorrow she would buy them all a breakfast of cinnamon porridge. Still, she had not eaten her own supper in case either of her younger siblings asked for more. With a kiss on Serene's cheek, she placed an end crust of bread and a rind of cheese on the table. She smiled as she watched Serene eat then nod off in father's chair. Rysario spent her final hours on the dress knowing she was blessed to have such fine company.

***

Rysario rose with the sun and lay the dress on the table for wrapping. It was a beauty, of deep vermillion with a golden brocade of fleur-de-lis. With a little sadness, she thought of how well it would have complemented her chestnut curls. She would never wear a gown so splendid.

"Is there any breakfast yet?" Olgaf said as he came down the stairs, rubbing his eyes not quite as adorably as Serene but with her same golden hair.

"Soon," Rysario said. "I am taking the dress now and will bring a feast back with me. Watch over Serene until I return."

Olgaf nodded. "I will take her to the turnpike on the road from the sea. I heard the King's Council left Valanda a week ago and should reach the Capital any moment. Serene will like to see their banners flying."

"I am sure she will." Rysario smiled. Olgaf spent hours regaling Serene with heroic tales and epic poetry. He wanted nothing more than to join the council as a new recruit, to search for the rightful king. There could be no greater crusade.

With a warning not to linger too long on the road lest he be robbed of a warm breakfast, Rysario left their cottage for the city. The lakeside quiet was quickly replaced as she joined the main road, by the whiney of horses and the trundle of carts as traders from the outskirt villages headed for the market. Already, their number had grown ahead of the festival, their wares more exotic and strange by the day.

She headed for the busiest shop in the city, filled with spices and confectionaries. Two city guards stood at the door; their blue and white tabards were emblemed with the empty throne that was the city's crest. She had never purchased anything from the shop for herself, only bolts of fabric for her most expensive dresses. The merchant's wife had sold the material for her dress to Rysario herself, insisting that it was the perfect weight and colour for the dress she wanted.

When there was finally a gap at the counter, Rysario filled it.

"Madam, I have bought your dress," she said with a smile.

The woman ignored her. "Here you are, Sir," she said, handing a package to a grey-haired man next to Rysario. "Arrived two weeks ago and has been kept safe and private until you could collect. That will be ten golden crowns."

"Ten crowns!" the man said, his already weather-chapped cheeks reddening further.

Rysario wondered if the man was poor. He wore a simple hooded robe of cream hemp, with a scratched leather bag across his body. He was old, reliant on a staff of twisted blackwood. He was perhaps one of the penurious monks of the Southland monasteries, that studied the ancient annals of the lost kings. Ten crowns would be a princely sum to such a man.

"Ten crowns!" the old man repeated, slapping the money down on the counter. "To receive a package? You rob your fellow man, Madam."

"I have kept it safe and untampered with, as promised, Sir," the merchantess said snootily. "I ask for fair reward. Though I am uncertain why you would care about a bit of old fab…" The woman bit her tongue.

"Indeed, it is a mystery, Madam, one almost as unfathomable as how you know its contents, if you have kept it as secure as you claim."

The merchantess collected her money and moved on to another customer, the matter dismissed.

The man tutted and walked away. As he reached the door, the paper of his package opened at one end, as though it had been poorly resealed. A bundle of fabric fell to the floor.

"Sir!" Rysario shouted, sacrificing her position at the counter to follow. The man turned in the door as she picked up the cloth with her free hand. She gasped. When it lay on the floor, it looked like grey wool but as she touched it, she felt it soften, silken, its colour started to bloom to rich purple. She had never seen cloth like it.

The old man stared at her, clutching his chest. This strange fabric has startled him too, Rysario thought, and the poor gentleman is quite overcome.

"Here you are, Sir," she said

He stared at her, bewildered, before his eyes dropped to her hand.

"In...in here," he said, holding his bag open. Rysario obliged and he quickly sealed the clasp. "Than...thank you." He scurried out of the shop, clutching the bag to his side, glancing back at her every few steps until he was gone.

What a strange man, she thought. With such strange wares.

Rysario waited for another place at the counter. Eventually, the merchantess looked at her.

"I have brought your dress, Madam, as ordered," she said.

"Dress?" The woman scoffed. "What dress?"

"The...the dress you ordered, Madam. The vermillion velvet."

The woman looked at Rysario with eyes of sharp stone. "I sold you velvet, yes, but I ordered no dress. What scam is this? Guards!"

"But you did, Madam. You insisted you sell me the velvet so I could make this elegant dress for you. Here," Rysario said, starting to unwrap the paper. "Let me show you and you will remember."

"Guards! Get her out of here, she's pulling a fast one. Trying to sell my own product back to me, at ten times the price I am sure."

"No, Madam, not so much as that. We agreed. I bought the velvet for twenty crowns and you would pay me fifty."

"See, she admits it. Swindler! Check your pockets everyone. She's probably filled her bodice with your coin."

"No…I…"

Rysario could say nothing more. As the crowd called her thief, the guards dragged her from the shop. They threw her into the street and the dress after her. As she fell mere inches from a fresh pile of dung, the crowd jeered. She wept and ran until she was clear of the city and back by the lake. Only its quiet did not comfort her now. Her cries never sounded so loud.

***

When Rysario returned home, Olgaf glanced at the dress slung over her arm. His face fell.

"You did not sell it then?"

"No," Rysario sniffed. "It seems the order was a cruel fraud all along." Serene came and buried her head in her shoulder in comfort, but it only reminded Rysario of how poorly she provided for one so deserving of more.

Olgaf's face turned red with rage. "Tell me where I might find the villain responsible and I will collect their debt. I am strong enough for father's sword and will use it if I must."

That was the last thing Rysario wanted. She had seen Olgaf train and he was a fearsome swordsman for one so young. She had no doubt he could take on the merchant, but he was not yet a match for the city guard.

"If you want to help, there is something you can try."

"Anything for my sisters."

Rysario knew he would not be so noble once he knew what she meant.

"We have nothing but offcuts from the dress. I can fashion a small purse or two that will sell for a few crowns and buy material to begin again. Our only hope in the meantime could be the mill where father worked. There will be many who remember him, who might give us flour to…"

Olgaf's eyes flew wide in dismay. "You want me to beg?! How could I live with honour?"

"You would have the honour of knowing you family did not starve."

"I would rather starve then…"

Their sudden squabble ended with a loud knock on the door. How surprising it was to open it to find the old gentlemen she had aided, with a trio of warriors resplendent in patterned doublets of blue and gold. A brooch of a golden crown was pinned to their navy berets. The emblem of the King's Council.

Stunned, she ushered them inside. She glanced at Olgaf and almost laughed. As he struggled to speak, his mouth opened and closed like a breathless fish. Serene simply waved at them shyly.

"Forgive me, Sir, but I do not understand."

The old man saw Rysario look at his pauper's robe and the grand uniforms of the others and gave her an apologetic smile.

"Forgive me," he said, removing his robe to reveal a long surcoat of brightest gold. "I had business of a sensitive nature in the city so felt it best to go in disguise. I did not mean to deceive one as kind as you, my dear. Please, allow me to introduce myself. I am…"

"Garner Veridicas," Olgaf said. "Mageman to the King, and leader of the King's Council. It is an honour to meet you, Sir."

Rysario introduced her siblings and Veridicas, his knights. Loret was tall and broad with a beard of black curls. His face was badly scarred, but his gentle eyes glistened like the brown pebbles of the lake. Graston was thin and twitchy, as though he had too much energy to spend in audience when battles awaited elsewhere. Nylena was fierce-faced and serious—her hair cropped to a jawline that could cut paper. She did not smile like the others as Rysario welcomed them.

"We are honoured, Sir," Rysario said. "May I ask the purpose of your visit?"

Veridicas gestured to Loret who passed him a covered basket.

"I wanted to thank you for your assistance earlier. I always visit Sumpkins Pie Shop whenever I am in the city. There is no match for it in any a land in which I have journeyed." Veridicas took three large pies from the basket —one boar, one chicken, and one salmon— and laid them on the table. He had brought bottles of sweet cider too.

"Through many years and expeditions, I have learnt to value those who will step out of the crowd to help others. I offer this feast as thanks for the aid you have given me."

Who was she to accept gifts from the Royal Mageman? But the kind man did not know how much he had saved them.

For the next hour, their cottage was reminded of a warmth it had not known since their parents' passing.

Loret was gentle despite his tough appearance, serving Serene slice after slice until she could eat no more. She reminded him of his own sweet sister, he said, god rest her soul. Graston, one of the newest Councilman in his inaugural year, answered Olgaf's questions about his adventures, how he had earned his station.

It was clear that Nylena did not agree with their presence there and questioned Rysario as if to show Veridicas that she was someone on whom Council time should not be spent. When she asked how Rysario earned her coin, she even smirked.

"Pretty dresses?" Nylena snorted to Veridicas. "What has that got to do with the rightful king?"

"Well, now you mention it… Olgaf, my good man," he began. "Your questions suggest that you are most knowledgeable about the King's Council. I assume you must know its primary purpose."

"Of course!" Olgaf said, flush-faced with enthusiasm. "The King's Council is tasked with restoring the line of kings that was lost long ago and to oversee the Kingdom until the true king is found again. Each year, on the night of the Festival of Kings, they present their strongest candidate for the secret ceremony. If the ceremony is successful, the new king is presented to the populace. Only that last part has never happened. The King's Council…"

"...has failed. Or at least," Veridicas said, "We have not yet succeeded. But this year, we have found our missing piece. Something that will enable us to finally find the answer and complete the line of kings. Or should I say, someone."

"Princess someday," Serene said, nodding.

Veridicas looked long into Serene's eyes until his own beamed.

"Astonishing," he muttered to himself.

"But who?" Olgaf asked, leaning forward in his chair, his mind already joining them on their quest.

"Why, your eldest sister, of course."

Rysario spluttered on the last drops of her cider.

"M...me, Sir? What use am I to the Council?"

"My thoughts exactly," said Nylena. "It is not as though this year's candidate will have any better chance of completing the ceremony if we dress him in a fancy tunic."

"I do not speak of tunics. I speak of a cloak."

There was a moment of confused silence until Olgaf spoke.

"You don't mean the Cloak of Kings?"

"Truly excellent. You would make a prodigious scholar." Rysario knew Veridicas said this in compliment but the soldier in Olgaf scowled. "The ancient annals tell us it is a cloak that is worn by a king who is worthy, a king who lives by the virtues of sacrifice, bravery, and compassion. In Rysario, we have found our Mistress of the Cloak. She will come with us to the farmlands of Sheraq, on the far side of the easterly mountains. There we will find our candidate and his cloak. There we will find our king."

"You flatter me, truly, but why me? There are many dressmakers in this city alone and I cannot claim to be the best of them."

"You do not need to claim anything, my dear, you have already shown me. This whole year past I have studied rare fabrics that exhibit strange and unusual qualities, to investigate how the cloak might be identified. It was to such a purpose that I visited our friend the merchantess this morning. When the she rifled through the parcel, she saw nothing but grey cloth. When I look at it, I see something more, a deeper hue, a slight softening of the texture. But when you saw it, it was quite transformed, was it not?"

Rysario nodded tentatively.

"I am still unsure what you expect me to do."

"Six months ago, I heard about a young man in the region of Sheraq, an orphan boy of unknown origin, with no knowledge of his family except the strange cloak in which he was swaddled when an old farmer found him at his door. A young man known by his neighbours for his compassion, kindness, and fearlessness. Our task is to travel to Sheraq to claim our candidate. Yours is to come with us and verify the cloak."

How could Rysario answer such a request? Whatever Veridicas said about her suitability for this Mistress of the Cloak, she knew she was no one special. And she could not leave her family. How would they survive?

"I see I have added a certain gravity to the evening," Veridicas said apologetically. "The fireworks have been lit again. We have much to think on. A stroll by the water is in order, no?"

Rysario could not enjoy the fireworks as she had the night before and walked with Serene behind the rest of the group. She did not want to disappoint Veridicas but wanted to leave Serene even less. No, she would not go.

Rysario had always noted how Serene could look intently at the smallest detail and wondered if she gained some insight that she could not share.

"Go," Serene said. "Princess someday."

Veridicas dropped back to join them but Serene ran off to skim stones on the lake with Loret. Veridicas and Rysario walked in silence for a time, neither knowing how to ask and answer.

"I do not make my decisions blindly," Veridicas began eventually. "I know you take care of both of them. If you do not trust in my decision in choosing you then trust in the care I can ensure for your family in your absence. They will be wards of the Council and will want for nothing. However our mission fares, you will be well-rewarded, all of you."

She watched Olgaf up ahead, nattering with Graston still, and Serene giggling with Loret, as Nylena followed behind. Perhaps this was the answer to saving her family's future once and for all.

She turned to Veridicas and nodded.

***

The next morning, Rysario rose before dawn song. She had not rested well, rolling over in the bed she shared with Serene to watch her sleep. She kissed her as she slept on, whispering a promise to see her soon.

She tiptoed into the hallway where Olgaf waited, rising from a slump against his door.

"I knew you would try to slip away," Olgaf said, grumpy with fatigue. "Will you not even bid us farewell before you run off to your adventures?" He looked at her like she had stolen his dreams.

"You must know I do not wish to leave you.

Would you deny your duty to the king if it were you?"

Olgaf shook his head but his expression did not soften.

"I will return to help you on your way to your own adventures. Having an acquaintance like Veridicas can only be of benefit. Just be patient, Olgy."

Olgaf smiled reluctantly. "No one's called me Olgy since Mother died, since I stopped being a boy."

"You are still a boy," Rysario said, kissing him. "Cherish your time with Serene. The Gods know I wish I could stay here with you. Now rest. Dream your dreams. I will pray for a dull journey so as not to live too many of them for you."

With a hug, she left him, with a dull ache that felt like she was leaving her heart upstairs with them. She collected her cloak, turning at the front door to take one last look at the cottage. She had a feeling that when she saw it again, she would not be the same Rysario anymore.

Veridicas and his trio of knights were waiting outside, with a young brown stallion for her, ready to be mounted. Rysario's tears fell silently to the clop of horseshoes for some time and did not ebb before the sun had climbed. When they reached a stream and stopped to water their steeds, Veridicas came and sat beside her.

"Are you alright, my dear?"

"I am well," she said. "I have never been so far from home. It is strange."

"I understand. I must warn you, we have much farther to go. This little distance will feel like the edge of your back garden in comparison to the distances we must cross. I wonder, how much do you know about our Kingdom beyond the Capital?"

Rysario knew little beyond basic geography. She knew the farmlands and vineyards lay to the east and the monasteries of learning and history to the south. Northwards lay the sea and the rich port city of Valanda, known for its silks and jewels. She knew little of the west, only that few lived there.

"I have not told you about the dangers that lie ahead. Did you know that a sacred protection lies over the Capital, and the villages that immediately surround? It protects its citizens from any evil incantation or assault. It will hold as long as the King's Council continues to ensure the castle is maintained. Without a rightful king on the throne, this protection does not extend to the lands beyond however, and they have suffered. Foreign conquerors assault our country on all sides, razing border towns and slaughtering the innocent. The western lands were completely overrun until I rallied every sorcerer in the Kingdom to force our enemies back. The surviving sorcerers still guard the border, watching from their spell towers along the boundary, with only the charred and desolate westerlands beneath them."

Rysario felt strangely guilty, to have been privileged to live in peace and safety, while others suffered and died.

Veridicas reached into his pocket and pulled out a golden pin. It was a small crown. The brooch of the King's Council. He pinned it to Rysario's cloak.

"The protection of the King extends to all who bear the symbol of the King's Council. It is not only war that afflicts our rural countrymen. Foreign mage man summoned dark clouds to carry foul diseases into our territories. You must wear this at all times to ensure you are not touched by malevolent plagues that even I may not be skilled enough to cure."

Miles later, Rysario wondered if Veridicas had known what they would find as they journeyed on. They passed into a shabby hamlet, silent as a grave although it was now noontide. The small market square was deserted; the cobbles were strewn with rotting cabbages and broken crates. A cry came from a window.

"The Mageman! The Royal Mageman!"

Doors opened. Pale-faced men, woman, and

children walked weakly into the square. Some sweated heavily. Others cloaked themselves in every piece of cloth they owned yet still shivered. Most coughed. Some, carried by their loved ones, could do no more than rasp.

"Help us, High Wizard! Help us!"

Veridicas turned to Rysario.

"There has been word of enemy armies swarming through villages like this one once their dark sorcerers have weakened any who could fight. Lingering here would put you at risk of extraordinary danger."

Some of the faces in the crowd were already as pale as her parents had been in the end. A girl, about thirteen with golden hair, waved sweetly, even as she coughed.

"We have to help them!" Rysario did not wait for Veridicas to agree but dismounted and rushed into the crowd.

The afternoon flew away as they cradled crying babies, cooled fevered brows, and built fires. After they had settled everyone back inside their homes, Rysario looked into the square. Veridicas stood by the well. He dipped the tip of his finger in the bucket and dabbed it on his tongue. The taste of it made him grimace. Rysario could not hear his words, but saw his lips moving as he held out his staff. A purple light shone into the water. A sudden bang of greenish smoke exploded from the well, knocking Veridicas to the floor. The purple light went out as the smoke settled back into the well.

"Please, miss," a middle-aged man said. "The wife of my cousin, the Gods give him rest, is sick in her chamber with the last of her babes. She has lost five already. Can naught be done?"

By the time the man had led Rysario to the house where the woman lived, Veridicas and his knights had joined her.

"Perhaps the infant is better," the man said, as they entered the silent house. "All night it did scream so."

The woman did not look up when they entered the bedroom. A girl of three played with a doll by the cold fire. Her mother rocked in a chair, singing softly to the sleeping baby in her arms. Except, Rysario realised, the infant was not sleeping. The poor grey child was dead.

"Curse the Gods!" the man said, angry tears falling down his cheeks.

The pale mother stirred, eyes sparking with hope as she saw Veridicas.

"Oh joy, Sir! You have come to save my children." She stood and brought the baby to him.

Veridicas gently took him. The mother's face flitted from hope to confusion as Veridicas passed the silent infant to her cousin.

"Will you do nothing?" the woman cried.

"I will give you herbs to bless the burial of your baby," Veridicas said, taking the woman's hand in his. "That will summon good spirits, to guide him to the arms of his father."

Loret caught the woman as she screamed and collapsed.

"Not another!" she cried. "All taken now apart from my Alyssa!" The name of her last child shocked the woman into a strange quiet. "My Alyssa," she said softly, looking to the child now crying by the fireplace. "You can help Alyssa, Sir. Look, she is red-cheeked and bonny."

The child looked like the sickness that afflicted the village had not yet found her. The rush of hope Rysario felt evaporated when she looked at Veridicas. He promised to examine the child while the woman went with her cousin to care for her departed baby, but Rysario saw the grey sadness in his eyes. The woman placed Alyssa into Loret's arms and took the herbs Veridicas offered. As weak as a shadow, she followed her babe to his final resting place, trusting her last daughter to their care.

"Can nothing be done?" Graston asked, having noticed Veridicas's look of defeat too.

Veridicas sighed.

"The well is infected with a poisonous alchemy that cannot be undone." He turned to Rysario. "You have given these people much comfort, which will ease their passing. But pass they will."

"But Alyssa doesn't even look sick," Rysario said. "Surely we can help her?"

"How exactly?" Nylena snapped. "What do you expect us to do with her? There are a hundred villages like this one. We've seen thousands die as we've travelled across the Kingdom and we couldn't help any of them. I wouldn't expect a shallow Capital girl with her head buried in taffeta to know that, but that's the situation."

As unfair as she thought Nylena was, she could not deny the truth in what she said. How could she have ever bemoaned her own hardships? She had not seen hardship until this day.

"I could take her," Loret said. "My birth town is far from here, but there is a good woman there who cared for my sister until she died from such similar a malady. There has been no disease there now for several years and the town rallies. I know if I can bear Alyssa there, she will find a warm home waiting," he said to Veridicas but turned to Rysario at the last moment, as though it was her permission he sought.

"You have a loving heart, Loret," Veridicas said, "But the child would not survive the journey. Too many dark diseases lay across the land. Besides, your duty is to find and protect the king. And protect our Mistress of the Cloak, of course."

That could not be the answer, Rysario thought. That could not be the way of the world.

"I would have thought a true king would care about nothing so much as the safety of his people," Rysario said. "A true king would not abandon the innocent."

A glance passed between Veridicas and Loret that Rysario did not understand. It left Loret with a hopeful gleam in his eye as he looked at her.

"I suppose you are right," Veridicas said, rubbing his chin. "But what of your innocence? A true king would care for your protection also, no?"

"I still have the rest of you," Rysario said, "But even if I did not, I would still bid him go. Even the poorest amongst us deserves a chance. It is what is right."

The matter was settled. The woman, weaker still as the shadows of the day grew long, shed many tears as she said goodbye to her last daughter, with a hundred kisses, a thousand sweet words. Rysario kissed Loret and Alyssa goodbye too and hoped with all her heart that they would make it.

They had travelled some miles further on their journey when Veridicas noticed.

"Where is your brooch?" he asked Rysario.

As she rode with Loret in the opposite direction, Alyssa played with the little crown pinned to her dress. She liked how it shined.

***

For weeks they passed through villages, offering what comfort they could. Eventually, they passed under the boughs of the great Red Forest, which led to the slope of the easterly mountains, five days hence. Rysario welcomed the solitude of the forest's shadows. She could face no more death, even if woodland spirits and miscreations lay ahead.

Graston, Nylena, and Veridicas shared the watch each night without incident, and by the third night, Rysario was at ease as they stopped to rest in a wide clearing. It was quiet when she woke some hours later. Graston was on watch but his head lolled forward on his chest.

"Girl," a woman's voice said from the tree line at her back. "Come here, girl."

Rysario snapped around. The snow-pale face of a

woman glowed from the dark of the forest like a strange moon. As she stepped out into the starlight, Rysario saw she was dressed in a hooded gown of black leather that had hidden her in the shadows. She was middle-aged but strong and muscular, with an ornate bow of greenish wood in her hand, carved with strange symbols. A quiver of black arrows with green fletching was tied across her shoulders.

She beckoned to Rysario with a black-nailed finger.

"Come here and I will tell you how your friends deceive you."

"Stay back," Rysario whispered as she got to her feet. She wanted to scream but knew a sudden panic could set the woman to her bow.

"No need to fear, beauty. I have come to liberate you. You do not know the peril you are in. Come, let my women protect you."

As the stranger spoke, twenty other dark-gowned women with bows stepped out of the forest from all sides.

"From what?" Rysario asked. The woman was so close now Rysario could see her vivid green eyes. A green flame moved in them as the light from the fire danced there.

"From Veridicas and all who serve him. You do

not know that he means to sacrifice you to save the kingdom, sweet innocent. Join us. We will protect you always." The woman held out her hand, smirking.

A new uncertainty filled Rysario's mind. There had been strange looks between Veridicas and his knights. There was something they were not telling her. She did not believe they would want to harm her but if one life could save the whole kingdom…one Rysario, to save all the Olgafs, and Serenes, and Alyssas…

"Will it work?" Rysario asked. "Whatever Veridicas has planned?"

The smirk fell from the woman's face.

"Did you hear what I said, girl? Stay with Veridicas and your life will no longer be your own."

"It has never been my own," Rysario said. "I have lived for my family. I would die for them too. Veridicas said they would always be cared for. I will follow any plan that ensures that. So, I ask you to tell me, if you are my friend, will it work?"

She had not heard them stir but suddenly, Veridicas and the others were beside her.

"Yes, child," Veridicas said. "It will work."

"Such a sweet girl," the woman mocked. "If she is so willing, we will take her sacrifice for ourselves."

The woman and her companions drew their bows. They formed a perfect circle around them, the sharp tip of an arrow wherever Rysario looked.

"Stay back!" Veridicas said. "She is a fletcherwitch of Zurgog, a great enemy of our lands, a bringer of pain and poison. Quickly now, close to the fire!"

The witch roared as she and her coven rushed forward. Veridicas spun his staff and held it horizontally in both hands. As the first arrows flew, a band of purple light burst from each end of the staff, forming a boundary of protection around them. The arrows bounced off the air in front of them like dying birds. The witches roared and drew again.

They were not ordinary arrows. The air puffed with a greenish smoke as they hit the boundary. Soon, Veridicas shook as he held on to the staff, its light starting to sputter.

"You can't hold them off forever," Graston said, his face flushed with righteous anger. "I can take them!"

"No, you can't!" said Nylena. "They have us surrounded. I will clear a path through them and keep them distracted while you take the girl. Your horse is swift, and you can lose them in the night."

Rysario was struck by how Graston looked at Nylena. It reminded her of the way Olgaf had looked at her when she asked him to sacrifice his honour.

Graston said nothing but stepped away from the fire. He instantly took down a witch with a single swipe of his sword, but it was only seconds before the first arrow found his upper arm. The poison was powerful and quick, the veins on his neck starting to spread a throbbing thick green. He gasped as he fell, his mouth opening and closing like a breathless fish.

"No!" Rysario yelled, rushing to his side. As she dropped to her knees beside him, she saw long nails reaching for her. The witch screamed as a burst of purple engulfed her with a vaporising flame. She was nothing but scraps of leather as her women turned and fled.

Graston's eyes started to go dark.

"The poison is too quick," Veridicas said, distraught. "There is no cure I can give him."

Nylena draw her sword.

"Hold him and I'll take his arm. I'll cut the poison out."

"It is too late!" Rysario said. The green veins spread across Graston's jaw and onto his face. He looked at her with little boy eyes that reminded her of what she must do.

She ripped the cloth at his shoulder and placed her lips to the wound. Olgaf had been bitten by a grass viper once. She had seen her brother writhing in pain, wishing she could take the poison from him. So, she had.

The poison from Graston's shoulder tasted like iron and rotting fish. She gagged as she spat it out but could not stop yet. It was some time before the green disappeared from Graston's face and she was sure the light in his eyes would not go out.

Veridicas gave them herbs to chew on, to counter any lingering trace of the poison, but Graston was pale and needed more care. Nylena settled him by the fire until morning but Rysario knew his journey with them was over.

Rysario would not go back to sleep. She sat silently with Veridicas around the fire as Nylena prepared their horses for an early departure. It was some time before he spoke.

"I find myself quite astonished. The witch told you your life would be sacrificed and yet you chose to stay to save others."

Rysario nodded and asked, "Is it true?"

"There is a sacrifice I will ask of you, at our journey's end, but be assured no harm will come to you. Your life will be far from over."

They did not talk on it further but watched the sky brighten to morning. It was hardly an unwelcome thought to learn that her death did not necessarily lie ahead but her uneasiness had not shifted.

As Veridicas joined Nylena, they glanced towards her as they whispered. Rysario knew that in one thing, the witch had spoken true. Somehow, her friends deceived her.

***

Two days later, when they left the bounds of the forest and started to climb the mountains, Graston left with their affection, heading for a village at the base to find rest. Rysario would miss him. She had passed the journey so far in conversation with him and before that, Loret, listening to tales of adventure. Veridicas spent much of his time lost in thought, often travelling a little way behind them.

Nylena was a colder companion. Their ascent took a week and they spent many hours in silence as the weather chilled. She was a proficient huntswoman and kept them well fed on mountain hare and goat. Each night, Rysario thanked her and tried to talk but Nylena would only scowl and move away.

It was not until they reached the summit that Rysario asked a question Nylena could not ignore. The Kingdom spread out beneath them was glorious: immediately below, the Red Forest, so much wider and longer than the narrowest point they had passed through—the green fields beyond, stretching back towards the Capital far away and lost from view—even a line of subtle blue, painted across the northern horizon, hinting at the distant sea.

"Which way lies your homeland?" Rysario asked Nylena.

Nylena turned to the west. Her face fell.

Rysario followed her gaze and shuddered. The western lands were nothing but charred ash as far as they could see, as though a fire the size of a country had burned every trace of life away.

"I knew, of course," Nylena said quietly. "After all those we lost, after the flame we had to flee. But to see it like this…" Nylena looked like something inside was broken and Rysario wished she could fix it.

"I am so sorry," she said. "I wish I had known."

Nylena scoffed and looked at her with contempt.

"What difference do you think you could have made, dressmaker? Tell me, what hope could you have brought them, as you lay safe under the castle's protection while the westerlands burned?" Angry tears formed and Nylena grunted in fury, turning away, back to the east.

"We will shortly reach our destination," Veridicas said after a time. "We must be friends and work together for our common purpose. I know what you have lost, Nylena, but Rysario has come on this journey to help us discover the one who will protect the Kingdom, so others will never suffer as you have suffered."

Nylena laughed a bitter laugh.

"Then she should have come sooner."

The next days were the coldest Rysario had ever known until, at last, they came to the lush lands of Sheraq.

***

The town reminded Rysario of home. A lake bordered one side of the town, surrounded by cherry blossoms. A white church provided the town's centrepiece, opening onto the market square. Farmers' cottages lined the outskirts. Golden fields of wheat and bountiful vineyards filled the fields beyond.

Their arrival at one such cottage marked the end of their outward journey. Rysario held her breath as Veridicas knocked on the door.

The man Veridicas believed to be king was barely a man, within a year of Rysario's own age. She blushed. Despite the poverty of his farmer's shirt and breeches, he was as handsome as any girlish fairy tale could imagine: tall, muscular, and dark of hair and eye.

"Veridicas!" The stranger cried in joy, pulling the mage into an embrace. Veridicas returned it but awkwardly and Rysario caught the secret glance he shared with Nylena as they parted.

What were they hiding? They had led Rysario to believe that the future king was an unknown stranger—his identity not yet confirmed. Wasn't that why she had come?

"Is this her?" the excited man said as he turned to Rysario. She blushed again as he looked at her and smiled.

It seemed the stranger somehow knew of her too.

"Yes, your grace," Veridicas said slowly, emphasising the title. "This is Rysario. Your Mistress of the Cloak."

The man's brow furrowed until something in Veridicas's expression provided clarity.

"My Mistress of the Cloak, of course," the man said, stepping aside to kiss her hand. "Charmed to meet you, Rysario. I am Deneki."

"It is my honour, your grace," Rysario said with a curtsey, her face scarlet now.

A little baffled laugh escaped Deneki, but he quickly stifled it and bowed in return.

"Please come inside. You must be weary after your

journey."

The home Deneki ushered them into was a humble one. Still, the room she was given to share with Nylena would provide comfort like she had not known for weeks, her nights of late offering nothing but the grassy earth for a bed. She was grateful when Veridicas bid them rest until supper and she slept the afternoon away gladly.

At dusk, they supped on a simple meal of bread and cheese, but with local wine finer than any she had tasted. Afterwards, Veridicas stood.

"Follow me outside into the moonlight. It is time. Deneki, your cloak."

Deneki disappeared and returned with a common burlap cloak. Was this the fabled Cloak of Kings? Rysario could not help but be disappointed.

The night was bright under the full-mooned sky. The stars were sharp and plentiful, as though they too knew the significance of the moment and stood in audience. Veridicas took the cloak from Deneki and turned to Rysario.

"Take this now, Mistress, and cloak your King. Should its appearance change, declare it so and we will know the cloak has found its master."

Rysario felt like a fraud. She was certain she would see nothing but burlap and would anger them all. Could it even be considered treason, to deny the cloak and thereby the King? But as she tied the cloak to Deneki's shoulders, it started to soften, to smooth. By the time it lay down his back, it had turned to a cloak of brightest gold, glinting in the moonlight in its brilliance.

"It has transformed," Rysario confirmed. "It has found its master."

"I see it too," Veridicas said, "And I declare it so."

"Aye," said Nylena.

Deneki laughed and turned to Rysario, beaming.

"Thank you, your…Thank you, Mistress."

Veridicas's grey eyes danced silver with joy.

"Come!" he said. "I call for another glass of that wine before we rest. Tomorrow, we return to the Capital."

Rysario and Deneki followed but Nylena did not. Instead, she stared back towards town. As she turned back towards them, Rysario saw the horror in her eyes.

"Fire," she whispered. "The town burns. The town burns!"

An angry orange light filled the sky as screams sounded and the church bell began to chime. Snakes of fire with flaming wings writhed in the air, igniting tree and timber.

"Infernophids," Veridicas spat. "Servants of the armies of Exfilian, our enemies to the east. These simple townsfolk cannot withstand them. Deneki, we must save as many as we can. Nylena, I trust our Mistress of the Cloak to your care. Flee now and see her safe back to the Capital."

"Wait!" Rysario shouted after them as they mounted their horses and rushed towards the town. "What about the King? She should take Deneki not me."

Veridicas rushed on. Deneki turned back for a moment.

"What kind of a King would I be if I fled? What kind of a King would I be if I let them burn?"

Nylena gave her no further opportunity to protest. She grabbed Rysario and flung her onto her horse, jumping up beside her. They galloped towards the town. The screams got louder as the flames spread. As they passed the edge of the square, a platoon of soldiers in armour of black and red were herding terrified citizens into the church. As they passed it in the shadows, they realised why. The commander of the army, his seniority signified by a blood red pauldron studded with vicious spikes, gathered a swarm of infernophids around him as his troops barricaded the church door. At his word, they shot forward. Their flame was so hot the church windows started to shimmy and melt. The stone spire started to liquidise and would soon collapse in on itself, drowning everyone beneath in molten rock.

Nylena halted as they reached the edge of the woods behind the church. Her whole body shook as she heard the cries of torment, the wailing of children, as she watched the earth turning to black ash. Rysario knew she must have wanted nothing more than to rush to their aid.

Nylena shook her head at herself. "They are doomed, and I must get you away."

"Wait!" Rysario said. "There!" A small door at the back of the church was barricaded with wooden planks but unguarded. "If we can get it open, the people can escape into the woods while the soldiers hold the square."

Nylena looked at her and, for the first time, there was no trace of disdain or annoyance. "We will stay, whatever the danger to your life, if that is your command. If your will is to save them before yourself, as is mine, that is an end I can accept."

Who was she to command Nylena? But she could not run while others burned.

"Let us help them. Hurry!"

They made it to the back door without challenge, the soldiers fighting in the square with citizens rushing in from the outskirts, choosing to fight back. Bolts of purple lit up the air and Rysario knew Veridicas fought there too, Deneki surely at his side.

They heard banging and scratching on the other side. Nylena handed her a knife and together they started to pry off the boards. They were almost done when there was a shout. Four soldiers turned the corner and ran towards them.

"I'll hold them off," Nylena said, drawing her sword. "Get them out and into the woods. Then run, and do not stop until you are on the path homewards."

She ran away before Rysario could reply. As she heard the clash of metal on metal, the last board came loose.

"To the woods, away through the woods!" Rysario guided the citizens as they spilled out like water. She looked for how Nylena fared. One guard already lay dead at her feet but the other three surrounded her. She was quick and ferocious and met each assault with her own.

"Come, miss, away," one of the old town mothers said, grabbing a hold of Rysario's hand. But as she looked back again, Rysario saw how Nylena tired. One of the solders went for the back of her calf and Nylena fell to her knee. The soldiers tightened around her, their swords ready to deal three fatal blows.

Rysario's body decided for her and she rushed

towards them. She picked up a rock and threw it, hitting one of the soldiers in the face. It could not have hurt him much, but it turned his attention towards her and distracted the other two soldiers enough to give Nylena the chance to rise and fray with them once more.

Only now, as the soldier approached, his blood-smeared sword pointed towards her, Rysario's body no longer knew what to do. As Nylena killed one of her pair, Rysario's soldier raised his blade. In what she thought was her last moment, she raised her hands in defence. She watched as the world between her fingers turned purple and the soldier's sword dropped at her feet; its bearer, vanquished, would challenge her no more.

As Nylena ended her final foe, Veridicas called from the square, firing more streams of purple at circling infernophids, who blew away like smoke.

"Now Nylena, away! You must save her!"

As they galloped away, Rysario bid Nylena to pause at the edge of the trees once more and looked back. As the people ran west to neighbouring towns for refuge, the red army ran to the east, retreating as a massive shock of mage light erupted in the sky. Except this time, it was blue.

***

They had returned to the other side of the mountains when Rysario saw Deneki again. Her days alone with Nylena passed with more friendship now but she had spent every hour worrying about her King. As they entered the great forest once more and looked for the night's resting place, they found him, fire lit, waiting for them.

Rysario pulled him into an embrace, quite forgetting her station and his. "How? When? What of Veridicas?"

"All is well, Mistress," Deneki comforted. "Veridicas lingered to help fortify the town for those who wished to remain but urged me follow you, so we might return to the Capital together. He says that is the only way to ensure true protection, that the coronation of the true King would extend the protection of the Capital to all the Kingdom."

"Then we must hasten. The festival begins within the month."

Their journey home was swift and demanding, as they rested only a few hours a night. That was long enough for a deeper warmth to grow between Rysario and Deneki. She did not blush now but felt herself glow when he looked at her. They told stories of their lives and journey around the fire. When Rysario told him of how she had aided Graston, he pulled her into his arms.

"You are brave, indeed," he said, his eyes swimming with love.

The day of the Festival of Kings came as they passed the stream at which they had first watered their horses. Veridicas had been right. She had had no idea of how far she would go, how much she would face. How entirely she would be changed. As she started to recognise the land of the Capital outskirts, Nylena said something that shocked her to her core.

"Do you have a pretty dress?" Nylena said.

Rysario smirked. "Pretty dresses?" She laughed. "What has that got to do with the rightful King?"

Nylena scowled but this time, it did not last, replaced by a smile.

"Veridicas wants me to see you to the castle for the ceremony. You will be seen in attendance with the King when he is presented. The Kingdom's Mistress of the Cloak should look the part."

How fortuitous even our upsets can be, Rysario thought, as she thought of a dress of velvet vermillion. But as she saw the roof of her home in the distance, it was not thought of the dress that quickened her pace.

"Serene? Olgaf?" she called as she burst through her front door. The cottage was as she had left it. Still the same, still beloved but a smaller part of the wide world she knew now. She ran upstairs but her siblings were there neither, nor at the lakeside.

"Do not worry," Nylena said. "I imagine Veridicas has arranged for them to join you at the castle after the ceremony. Which I must remind you is due to begin shortly. We must deliver our King. Hurry!"

As evening fell, Nylena rode ahead to form a path through the crowd streaming into the city. Deneki and Rysario rode side by side. People turned to stare at them as they passed. She realised they made quite a spectacle together, she in her velvet, he in his golden cloak.

"What a handsome couple," an old woman gushed as they passed. Rysario glowed once more.

They reached the castle gates. A salute of Council Knights lined their path to the door. As they dismounted, they raised a collective cheer as Rysario and Deneki entered the castle.

"Long live the King!"

If Deneki was nervous, he did not show it as they climbed the grand staircase to the ceremony chamber above. Instead of thinking of his crown, he looked at her again, with joy in his eyes. Her heart skipped a beat at the words he spoke.

"It will be my joy to spend my days beside you," he said, as the ceremony chamber door opened.

The room was a perfect white circle, except for an alcove at the front with two silver doors. It was skirted by columns, with banners of the city's blue and white hung high between. The floor was silver except a raised circle in the centre, of white stone engraved with a celestial chart. As Rysario glanced upwards she saw why, understanding the importance of the Festival's timing. A round skylight was carved into the ceiling. As the moon rose to fill it perfectly, it shone down to the white circle, creating a column of silver light.

Members of the King's Council lined the chamber. She smiled as she saw Loret and Graston amongst them, smiling back at her. Only Veridicas stood in the centre, before the circle.

Nylena moved to the sides to join her fellow knights and to Rysario's surprise, Deneki did too, joining Graston. Feeling out of place, she followed.

"I must stop you, my dear." Veridicas halted her. "That place is not for you. Only the King's Council may observe the ceremony by forming a sacred circle around the chamber."

Rysario felt mortified. Perhaps she was not meant to enter the chamber until after the ceremony had been completed. She mumbled an apology and turned towards the door.

"It is quite all right, Rysario," Veridicas said,

holding out his hand. "There is another place for you." He gestured towards the stone circle. "This place has always been destined for you. I knew it the moment I saw you in that swindler's shop, when you touched the Cloak of Kings." He gestured to a knight who brought a cloak of grey wool forward, that remained grey wool as Veridicas took it in his hands.

Rysario remembered how shocked Veridicas had been when she picked the cloth up and it had transformed. As Veridicas placed it around her shoulders, the cloak changed once more, from the most common grey to the finest regal purple.

"But the cloak has already found its master," Rysario said. "I placed it on Deneki's shoulders myself."

Veridicas grinned.

"There is lore that is lost even to King scholars as eager as your brother. The Cloak of Kings is but one of a pair. The Cloak of Mages is what you gave to Deneki, identifying his destiny as your Royal Mage. Deneki has been my apprentice for many years now. When I left him in Sheraq almost a year ago, he knew the next time I came to him, I would bring the rightful heir to the throne. But my missive to him, of the deception I felt was necessary, was lost, so our arrival caused some confusion when he was thrown into the role of playing

King."

"But why?" Rysario said, sure Veridicas mocked her, deceived her still.

"I will confess now that, as the fletcherwitch knew, I deceived you. Somehow, our enemies knew I had found something significant and sent their spies, increased their attacks. Your councilman companions, too, I deceived at first when we visited your home. I revealed the truth to them on the day our journey together began. As you know, some of them had their…uncertainties."

Nylena held her hands up in silent apology.

"Uncertainties you would have shared had I told you the truth. You who did not know the parents who raised you were not your blood. It did not take me long to question your father's old colleagues at the Mill to learn how they had found you, abandoned at their door. How would I convince you that you were destined to be Queen, someone who lived by the virtues of compassion, sacrifice, and bravery? Virtues your sister always recognised in you, as she heard stories of the nature of the King from your brother. She has always known who you are. She always knew someday she would be our princess."

"I knew you would not believe it until you could see who you are for yourself. I knew the dangers of our journey would provide ample opportunities and you embraced them all with Kingly honour. The cloak confirms your identity. All that remains is the ceremony, to complete the coronation. Step into the light, Rysario, and sacrifice the life you have for the one you are meant to live."

In a daze, Rysario took Veridicas's hand and allowed herself to be led to the circle. As she stepped onto it, she felt a weight form on top of her head. A crown.

Around the room, the empty thrones on the blue and white banners disappeared as golden crowns appeared there too. The Queen's Council erupted.

"Long live the Queen!"

Rysario's heart thudded in her chest but when the chamber door opened, it skipped a beat. Olgaf and Serene rushed into her arms. Serene wore a golden crown of her own. She spun around to show off her fine pink dress. "Princess," she said, as she twirled.

Olgaf wore the blue and gold, the navy beret of the Queen's Council. He hugged her again. "It is my honour to serve you, your grace."

The chamber filled with excited chatter. Deneki, Graston, Nylena, and Loret came to her side.

"It is my honour also, my Queen," Deneki said.

Rysario's blushes returned as she realised her

foolishness.

"When you said you would spend your days beside me, you meant as my mage, not…" She was not sure how to end such an awkward question but Deneki blushed also.

"I am afraid not, your grace. I am spoken for." He took Graston's hand.

When Deneki's eyes had filled with love as she told him of Graston, she had thought that love belonged to her. Yet when she looked at Graston, safe and well by Deneki's side, she was happy that it did not.

"Come, your grace," Veridicas said. "With my last act as Royal Mageman, I will present you to your people."

When Veridicas opened the doors and led her through to the balcony, the sea of people below fell silent in surprise until Veridicas spoke.

"I present to you Queen Rysario the First, protector of the Kingdom. Blessed be the Kingdom! Blessed be the Queen!"

Deneki pulled a silver wand from his cloak and filled the sky with fireworks of brilliant blue.

BEYOND THE REALM

NICOLA CURRIE is a multi-genre writer from Cambridge, England. She writes fiction and poetry for both children and adults and her work can be found in various anthologies and magazines. She is a Bath Children's Novel Award longlistee. Nicola loves singing, nature and her Syrian hamster, Chonka.

Bibliography
Bad Romance, Black Hare Press, 2020
Bath Children's Novel Award Longlistee, 2016
Beyond the Realm, Black Hare Press, 2020
Dark Drabbles (*Beyond, Unravel, Apocalypse, Love, Hate, Oceans, Ancients, Quietus 13*), Black Hare Press, 2019/2020
Envy, Black Hare Press, 2020
Greed, Black Hare Press, 2020
Lust, Black Hare Press, 2020
Pride, Black Hare Press, 2020
Sloth, Black Hare Press, 2020
Starlings, Sarasvati Magazine, 2019
The Bedroom Cupboard, Mother Ghost's Grimm Volume 1, NBH Publishing, 2019
The Border Wall, Mslexia Magazine, 2014
The Shadow, Mother Ghost's Grimm Volume 2, Nocturnal Sires Publishing, 2020
The Tides, Sarasvati Magazine, 2019
Tickle, tickle, burn, burn, Midnight in the Witch's Kitchen, Alban Lake Publishing 2020
Twenty Twenty, Black Hare Press, 2020
Vixen, Sarasvati Magazine, 2019

Connect
Website: https://writeitandweep.home.blog/
Twitter: @Speculative_Nic
Amazon:https://www.amazon.com/Nicola-Currie/e/B07YYHZFKY/5

BLACK HARE PRESS

BEYOND THE REALM

ATMUS FEAR
By A.L. King

Surrounded by a cursed woodland, the Indmeire Empire is a dangerous place to live. Young orphan Atmus knows this painfully well. He vows to atone for past mistakes by entering Trepidon Forest and ending the threat it poses once and for all.

1-Folly in the Fist

Giants towered across the grounds of the Indmeire Empire. Although made of wood, stone, and mortar, from a distance they seemed a gathering of colossal men. The people of the kingdom resided within these enormous, manlike statues.

Hiding beneath the floorboards of the left fist of one such abode, Atmus listened to the family that called the hand their home.

"Toss me a spud!" the poppa yelled at one of his children. There was a sudden knock on the board just above Atmus's head, and dust fell into his eyes. He breathed in and struggled not to sneeze.

"Milbrook!" the man's wife shouted. "That spud nearly spilled over the light and started a fire. What would we do should this place burn? Mind that we share this Oni with other families."

Floorboards creaked as the man of the household—man of the hand rather—stood and walked across the room to pluck the food off the floor. The spud's hot aroma wafted between the cracks and greeted Atmus. He hoped his stomach would not growl.

"Aye, Effica, but I shan't shoulder all blame. Our Elena throws like a gimp-armed knight in a suit of armour-rusted stiff."

There was a mousy *oomph*. From the sound of it, a spud splatted against the wall behind Milbrook.

"Better try," he said.

The whole family laughed, or at least it sounded that way to Atmus, who could only listen. The mother, Effica, must have seen otherwise.

"Something a bother, Gilly?" she asked.

He hesitated, then said, "I don't understand why we live inside Oni."

The matriarch's voice was soft and comforting as she explained. As Atmus listened, he missed his own mother.

"Long, long ago, this land faced countless assaults. Enemies used the forest that surrounds this kingdom as cover to attack. This empire always prevailed, but it wasn't worth the loss of life. King Indmeire the Third was desperate, so he sought help from a witch."

Atmus could hear the kid's feet nervously tapping the legs of the chair above. The little guy was likely not yet tall enough to reach the floor.

"A witch?"

"A powerful witch. She made the king a deal. For the right price, she would cast a spell that stopped any enemies travelling through Trepidon Forest dead in their tracks."

"Did he agree?"

"Yes. His soldiers delivered riches to Yuckberry Heights, where she lived in a cave. She then used magic to open a portal to the netherworld in Trepidon Forest. From that realm came scores of fearful creatures to call the woodlands home. They devoured most of the kingdom's enemies before they could get here and attack, but they proved to be a far worse threat to this place. When the soldiers returned to Yuckberry Heights to capture the witch, the cave—the entire rockface—had disappeared. King Indmeire the third also vanished shortly thereafter."

"But Ma...that doesn't explain why we live in a house that looks like a giant person."

"I'm getting there. As you know, Gilly, horrid things live in that forest to this day, and not everything stays in the forest. Do you remember the giant snapping turtle you once saw crawling towards the lake and how badly it scared you?"

Atmus heard no response, so it was likely that Gilly only nodded. The boy's father, however, eagerly recalled the encounter. "Aye, glad ya spotted it, son. Thing put up a fight, but that was the best turtle stew I ever ate."

"There were countless creature attacks in the years following the witch's betrayal," Effica continued. "Foul owls were the worst. They emerged from the woods as soon as the sun went down and attacked homes and tore off roofs and plucked people from their beds and either ate them immediately or flew them back to their nests in the forest. It was Indmeire the Sixth who offered a solution. Using what resources our kingdom could muster up, he set about having the first Oni built."

BEYOND THE REALM

Gilly's feet tapped the chair legs, faster and faster. He had gone from anxious to excited. "Oh! I get it! The foul owls stay away now because they're afraid! The Oni are like giant scarecrows! People live inside and don't get attacked no more!"

The boy beneath the floorboards felt sick from more than hunger. The kid above was right, and yet he was wrong—because the foul owls still attacked on occasion. Not every structure was built equally. Atmus knew that painfully well.

If the birds saw the Oni as fierce giants, the one in which he and his family once lived had been a dwarf giant by comparison. Set too near the tree line, a distance from any other homes, the winged demons had picked it apart one night.

A shiver ran up his spine as he recalled the loss he suffered. At least…he took it as a shiver at first, until the furry spider crawled around his neck and onto his cheek.

Under the family's feet, Atmus let out a startled cry.

He went silent. So did things above. They had no doubt heard him.

He swept the spider off his cheek and scurried towards the spot where he entered the crawlspace just hours ago. Escape was important. He might remain hungry now that his plan to sneak out and claim their leftovers after they went to bed was ruined, but fleeing unfed was far better than being captured and starving in a dungeon or facing exile.

Large, stomping footsteps overhead—no doubt issued by Milbrook—seemed to follow his movements. Falling dust covered Atmus and clung to his sweat. The apparently burly man was heading to the hatch that served to access the cubby. It was also the only exit, meaning he was trapped.

The young intruder wiped grime from his eyes. There was enough room for a turnabout, so he went back to the space beneath the table. When directly under the boards that held up the giant slab, he caught a whiff of something musty. He raised his nose and sniffed. The planks smelled primarily of grog, yet heavily mildewed.

Atmus grinned in the darkness below, picturing all the times the man drank while eating, sloshing drink over his chalice as he conversed with his family, drunkenly unaware that little spills were splashing the floorboards, rotting them over a period of many days, weeks, months, and years.

"Come out and I won't hurt ya!" Milbrook called. "But if I have to squeeze my arse down there to fetch ya, I won't be as friendly!"

Atmus touched the softened wood above his head. The father remained at the other end of the dining room, expecting the intruder to exit through the hatch there. Now was his chance. He rolled onto his back and sent his tattered shoes into the boards above. It took three strikes to break through the floor. Splinters tore at his ankles and drew blood, but he kept kicking apart the soggy planks.

He peered through the hole at the bottom of the table above and understood why no one had noticed that the floor softening. The large table likely never moved, and there was little chance a pair of feet would come to rest on that spot.

Effica, Gilly, and Elena called out in panic. He could make out some of what they said.

"Over here, Pa! Under the table! He's breaking the floor!"

"What should we do?"

"Back away from the table! It's sinking!"

Atmus heard wood groan. The weight of the table was indeed sinking through the floor, about to finish what he started.

The table base would have pinned him down had he not immediately rolled away. Half the slab fell through the floor, creating a larger passage than needed for escape. The half remaining above the hole sent much of the contents catapulting, including an oil lamp. The glass encasement shattered, spraying the floor with fire that caught quickly.

Atmus saw faces above staring at him in perplexed shock, but it was not until later that he could stop and allow himself to feel pity for them. He climbed out of the crawlspace, ran from the room, and climbed the steps up the hand. He continued up the arm of the Oni, to the chest, and then practically spilled down the spiralling steps that ended at the bottom of the building's left boot.

He fled the structure and did not stop running until he reached Yuckberry Heights, from where he watched the giant burn. Although it appeared everyone made it out safely, words he could never outrun reeled in his head.

"What would we do should this place burn?" the mother of the family had asked.

Watching from a distance as she cried with her husband and children, Atmus wondered the same.

2-The Corpse of the Cave

As far as Atmus could see, there was no cave at Yuckberry Heights. Whether it had ever been there did not seem to matter. The people of Indmeire Empire—even the bravest of soldiers—kept away. According to rumour, disappearances occurred around the hilltop.

He assumed he would continue to elude capture if he stayed there. Surviving, however, was another matter. The only food was those nasty berries that gave the hilltop its namesake. *Yuck!*

Gross as they were, he squashed the tiny fruits together into different shapes and pretended they were spuds, hog legs, and drumsticks. Unfortunately, his body didn't play along with these imaginings. The berries made him sick.

Around his fourth day there, dehydrated from sickness and despite the rainfall he was able to gather, the hallucinations started. The clouds turned pink like uncooked meat. The mostly full moon at night was a head with a ghastly smile and then a few days later, a skull with the same, sinister grin.

A week into his outdoor retreat, rain poured what looked like miniature javelins. As he ran for cover for fear of being impaled, a towering stone edifice appeared before him. So suddenly it manifested, he feared that he could not slow himself in time and would collide with the rocks. Fortunately, this seemed a hallucination within a hallucination. Instead of his face striking a hard surface, it was greeted by cool air as he entered a sudden opening.

It took until the next morning, finally waking from a restless bout of sickness, to accept that the cavern was not a fever dream. It was real, and a voice within was calling his name.

"Atmus. Atmuuus. Atmuuuuus."

Every time he turned towards the light at the mouth of the cave, the walls appeared to extend. He feared they would grow infinitely if he attempted to run. So, he waited. He listened to the voice crawling out of the darkness, towards him.

"You've been a bad boy, young Atmus. Your greed got people killed."

Despite weakness and fear, he scoffed at the disembodied voice. His protests echoed into the cavern, down the hole that housed the wicked harasser.

"If you're the witch I've heard about, then you have some nerve calling *me* greedy! You took riches from the third king to make things better, but you made them worse instead. You're also a liar. I've been watching the kingdom from the hilltop. I saw no burial carts since the fire."

BEYOND THE REALM

There was ugly laughter, and then the witch followed up with further taunting. "They don't use burial carts for people reduced to ashes. They would be indistinguishable from charred ruins of the Oni they lived inside. But they're good as dead, young Atmus. They were blamed for the fire you caused and banished to Trepidon Forest, where they will most assuredly die. Perhaps young Gilly will go first, since he is already such a weak lad!"

Atmus, in his outrage, failed to notice that he was walking deeper into the cave.

"How might you know they were banished?" he asked, although he assumed she must be psychic by the way she knew his name.

In response, everything went black. Darkness beyond darkness surrounded him.

"This cave is my grave," the witch said. "I cannot travel elsewhere physically, but I am free as a ghost is to haunt this empire. I've seen into your head. Now would you like to know some of the things I've seen while alive and dead, young Atmus?"

"No," he answered immediately, still walking towards the voice despite the darkness.

She answered anyway, flooding his head with sickening visions. He bore the mental pain as he travelled into the seemingly infinite blackness. He would later reflect on that moment with a single, stark thought.

Things can always get darker, and often they do.

He saw hands—not his hands, but ones with long red nails—drop apples into a barrel of poison. He saw a plump boy staring up at him in disbelief as a hatchet came smashing into his face, and next he saw cooked meats on a plate before him. He saw an unfathomably handsome man above him, thrusting in pleasure as large wings splayed out behind him.

"That last is the Devil," Atmus said, fighting delirium. "What he was doing to you… you really were his bride."

"Still am." Snickered the witch. "One of them, anyway."

Images continued cycling through him, too quickly to decipher them all. That was surely for the best. If what he witnessed remained as still pictures in his mind, he doubted he would ever be the same. Yet inscribing the visions into him was not her intent. The rapid collage was meant to strike a tone. In a way he supposed it was as much sound as sight, composed of a myriad of visuals.

He told himself to be angry rather than fearful. She had opened the portal that allowed creatures like foul owls to arise, making her responsible for what happened to his family.

"The ghastly things you've shown—the horrors you've committed—are merely echoes of the dead."

"Aye, but echoes are everlasting," replied the witch. "Were someone to string them together…"

It occurred to Atmus that the experiences still assaulting him spanned more than a single lifetime. Her haunting of the mystic cave was thus a hibernation of sorts. She waited out death as a bear waits out winter.

Her flashing memories slowed so that he could focus on but one. He—she—was falling from great heights, but he—she—survived the fall. Soon after, a pack of dogs bearing fangs lunged at him—her—and began tearing away his—her—flesh.

He could hear this scene as well. The woman the witch used to be screamed in sheer agony.

Atmus opened his eyes and swallowed back his own screams. His reaction brought great joy to the witch, who appeared as dancing smoke in the blackness.

"Such a tough guy you are," she jived, then began laughing, unaffected by the memory of her death. Was that her first death? There was something familiar about it. Biblical. Could she be…

"Jezebel," he said.

The face of that billowy ghost smiled. The smoky

form vanished, and an ethereal light bloomed in the cave. This mysterious illumination was dim yet heightened as it reflected off the witch's treasurers. Gems and coins lined the floors and were even embedded in the walls. The heads of small statues representing several deities were buried mockingly in the softer ground of the cavern floor. It seemed odd a being powerful enough to open portals between worlds and live multiple lives had the slightest use for such trivial possessions.

Beyond the space where the wisp of a woman had danced before him stood a throne, perhaps delivered by King Indmeire the Third's soldiers long ago. A skeleton was seated there.

Atmus realised in horror that there were more bones. Skeletal remains were scattered on the ground behind the witch's posthumous pose of mock sovereignty.

"Do you figure to kill me like all those who disappeared from Yuckberry Heights?" he asked.

The grinning skull remained still as she spoke from somewhere beyond. "You're mistaken, young Atmus. I did not kill them. They were food for my familiar, Oborus."

From the passage behind the throne, something large moved over scatterings of bone. It was not visible to him until it opened two green eyes with black diamonds at centre and hissed a single word.

"Hello."

The snake's hot breath stank of decay, as if the meat from all the bones it shat were still rotting in its guts.

"Go ahead and kill me," said Atmus, hoping his mistakes would be forgiven in death so that he could be with his parents.

The evil Jezebel cackled. Although the skeleton's mouth remained still, he heard the clattering of bones. Perhaps it was Oborus sliding closer, preparing to strike.

"Kill you? I'm not going to kill you. Not yet!"

"So be it," he said, shaking despite the bold words that followed. "If you don't kill me now, I vow to save the banished family and close the portal you opened. I shall also rid the world of you and your familiar."

Blackness drenched the cave again, and something rustled about. He thought it was Oborus coming for him, but it was the witch. Before, when she spoke, the voice had sounded disembodied. What she said next sent hot breath into his ear.

"Yet, young Atmus. I said I didn't want to kill you *yet*."

Atmus screamed in response.

3-Enter the Forest of Fear

He didn't know he had passed out again until he awoke on the still-drying grass of Yuckberry Heights. He sat up and looked around. There was no cave. Only the hilltop and the rest of the kingdom below.

The legend suddenly made sense to him. Too much sense. The witch had tricked the king into giving her riches because she could live, and spend her stockpiled loot, during multiple lifetimes. He briefly wondered what a magical being would want with treasure, but it wasn't all that strange. Everyone adored wealth, he supposed, even supernatural beings.

That explained the first thing, but he still wondered why she had opened a portal to the netherworld, unleashing monsters upon the Indmeire Empire.

He thought back to the night he watched his parents pecked apart by the beaks of several foul owls, while he hid beneath the wreckage of the pitiful Oni they had called home. He'd never been more afraid.

Was her wicked spirit watching me back then? he considered.

No matter the answer, he determined that he would no longer provide a show for her, at least not one she liked. He would do as promised. He would destroy the witch and her familiar. First, however, he would make good for the family apparently banished because of him.

Atmus stood up and began his descent from Yuckberry Heights. Soon, he would leave the Indmeire Empire behind for the trees of Trepidon Forest.

He was aware of Oborus following him as he walked. It had shrunk to the size of a normal snake, but he could hear it slithering.

There was a psychic nature to the witch, for she had read much of his mind as she toyed with him. Did her snake possess the same abilities?

I'm going to remove you from this realm, Oborus! he thought, imagining that mental thread floating back to the creature.

The response was a sudden hiss behind him. Had it heard his threat? Was it laughing at him?

Atmus paused when he saw the current King Indmeire's Oni. He stared in its direction and felt a glint of purpose. The largest and strongest structure of the land, it was built like a castle as well as a giant man. He wished he could reside within its walls—not to be protected by them—but to have his chance to make things better from behind them.

He made another vow. "I will be king of this land someday. I won't be perfect, but I'll do my best, and I won't let orphans go hungry."

He thought he heard another mocking hiss. He fought back a shudder and marched onwards.

Entering the forest was as terrifying as the idea of walking into fire. So long had he watched the space where the empire met the woodlands that the border became his greatest fear. On countless nights, he had stared out of an Oni eye—his bedroom window—waiting for something dreadful to crawl out from between the trees. In reflection, he wished he'd been looking up instead.

He held his breath upon entering the trees, expecting various creatures to attack at once. When nothing happened, he breathed a sigh of relief.

Don't get too comfortable, he told himself. *Anything here can be dangerous. The plant life, the air, and the ground itself.*

As he considered this, he dodged a marshy space that resembled quicksand. He walked faster when a section of it solidified into an arm that reached after him. Thankfully, the earthy appendage came up short.

How far has the family gotten? he wondered. *If they got far at all.*

As his father once relayed to him, the woodlands between the Indmeire Empire and other territories were quite a journey long before the witch opened a portal to the underworld and unleashed all manner of monsters.

BEYOND THE REALM

Atmus figured the truest measure of distance accounted for the perils of the terrain. If those harsh spans were applied to his situation, he might be walking for ages. Even if he survived this journey before his body reached manhood, his mind could be worn by the time he returned.

"You really think you'll make it out of here alive?" a voice asked, causing him to jump. He first thought Oborus—still following—was taunting him. However, the voice was too small, even for a shrunken version of the snake. He then worried that his own thoughts were sinking into self-doubt.

Those concerns fell away to new ones as the voice spoke up again. There was a sudden tickle in his left ear, and he understood that something was inside his head. Whatever it was, it had a physical form, but rather than speaking, it directed its words directly into his mind.

"I'm not doubting you, young man. I'm hopeful you can make it out alive. I'd like to leave this forest as well." Atmus was about to respond when it stopped him. *"Bite your tongue and think to me instead, as I think to you... unless you want the snake to know I'm here."*

"Oborus can read minds," Atmus thought back to the mysterious voice. *"So, I'm pretty sure it already*

knows you're here."

"I assure you that the basilisk behind us knows nothing but its own panic. I am blocking it from reading your thoughts. The serpent cannot understand how such a barrier has gone up. This gives you an advantage!"

"*Who are you?"* Atmus asked.

"I am a friend, and my name is Erwin."

"What are you?"

The thing in his head snickered. *"I am an earwig!"*

Atmus had heard about the small insect species. According to his dad, they crawled into ears and either laid eggs or milled about until there was little left of the brain.

"Relax!" said Erwin. *"Those tales are false. I'm sure your father only told them to you as a joke. Earwigs are relatively harmless. My presence in your head is a matter of convenience. I'm a thinker, not a fighter. As for my telepathic abilities, I gained them from living in this magically imbued forest."*

Atmus took a deep breath and attempted to calm himself.

"How long have you lived in this forest?" he asked.

"Too long," Erwin said.

He wondered how long that could have been since

most insects had short lifespans. It was strange to think that any amount of time could be too long for the earwig. Then again, to Oborus behind him and the oft-reborn Jezebel, human lifetimes might seem just miniscule.

"We can get philosophical about life and death when we're not trying to avoid the latter," said Erwin, no doubt reading his mind.

"Any idea how we can throw Oborus off our trail?" he asked.

"Yes." Another snicker from the bug. *"We find bigger monsters."*

4-The Puppet Show

Atmus asked his new friend if he had maybe seen a family enter the forest. Then, in order to show Erwin their appearances, he conjured up how they had looked just before he fled their quarters and the burning Oni.

"I have not seen them," said Erwin. *"But I have seen from a distance those goofy statue homes you think of as Oni. They protect your people from the giant owls that also plague this forest—foul owls is your name for them. Sadly, the Oni aren't impervious. Sometimes the people who live inside them are attacked. Oh Atmus…you're now thinking of what*

happened to your parents... I'm so sorry."

Atmus thanked the sentimental insect for his condolences and continued walking. He didn't get much farther before he felt wetness drip on his head and run through his hair. He took a step back and paused, hoping more drops would come down all around him, proving to be rain. Another drip landed in the spot where he had previously been standing. Even on the dark, dirt ground, he recognised the colour red.

More crimson fell around him. He glanced up to see bodies hanging from tree branches. There seemed to be a hundred corpses, maybe more. Some fresh and keeping flesh; some old and little more than bone. Above those bodies were gargantuan forms he wished he didn't recognise.

"We're here," Erwin said. *"Remain calm. The spiders above are friends, not foes."*

"What kind of friends would do something like this?" asked Atmus.

"The kind we need. Do not fret about them reading minds. They lack that ability."

The corpse closest to him began descending slowly. Atmus saw that the hanging body had not broken free of its bindings but was instead being lowered. At first glance, it appeared as if the line of suspension were merely frayed. He soon understood, however, that it was not rope.

Webbing held up the body now before him, whiteness travelling in separate strands along a busted-up jawline. As the eight-legged puppeteer above flexed a section of string, the puppet-like bundle of decay moved its mouth.

A voice rang out from the treetops, speaking through the dead, "Who are you? What are you doing here?"

"My na-name is At-muh-mus," he said, struggling to hide the fear in his voice. "I come as a friend…to make an offer."

There was cackling in the treetops. He pictured the source of that sound as thousands of large fangs clattering together.

Another flesh-and-bone puppet descended until it was beside him. The webbing bobbed, moving an almost entirely rotted-off jaw. A few teeth collided together and flew out of the makeshift marionette's mouth. "And what might you offer other than your corpse as a new doll?"

He started to speak before realising he still didn't have an answer. He looked at the slack jaws of other descending *dolls* and clamped his own mouth shut. Just what did the spiders want?

Something stirred, not from above but behind.

Thinking of Oborus filled him with rage.

"Don't do anything rash," Erwin advised. *"We need to gain their trust."*

"You don't eat people," Atmus said to the spiders after a moment of consideration. "Or you don't *prefer* eating people. I think you find the bodies and keep them around as bait, to draw in other tasty creatures that do like human meat."

Laughter rang out once more from above. The humour was portrayed on the faces of corpse puppets.

"You are wise for your size," a new voice said. It was a domineering voice, sort of feminine. "But you still haven't stated your offer."

Unlike the bodies dangling around him, he didn't need webbing to help him grin. He smiled at his friends in the branches. Friends, not foes.

"I offer your kind a seat at the table in what shall one day be my kingdom."

More laughter from above.

"And what might earn us this seat?" asked the apparent arachnid leader.

Erwin squirmed in his head. *"Are you sure this is the best approach?"*

Atmus ignored the earwig's question and answered the one posed by the giant spider above.

"There's a portal to the underworld located

somewhere in this forest," he said. "I need help getting there. As a peace offering, I present my enemy as a gift. The snake hiding in the bushes behind me appears small, but I assure you he conceals a larger form. A serpent his size will provide plenty of meat."

The morbid puppets were yanked back to the forest rafters, and the eight-legged puppeteers quickly descended.

Oborus expanded in size and skittered away as arrow-like shots of webbing landed around it. It grew even larger than it had been when he met it inside the cavern on Yuckberry Heights. As it slithered past, several trees toppled completely over, exposing ancient roots.

Perhaps two hundred yards away (for the giant creatures covered ground quickly), the snake came to a stop, seemingly surrounded. Twenty arachnids pounced at once, but Oborus was ready. It sprang up on its tail and began spinning like a cyclone. Its serpentine form thinned and sharpened, becoming a giant, rotating blade.

The spiders that had launched themselves at the snake were instantly dismembered. Arms, fangs, and thoraxes flew in all directions. Three eyes, still connected, landed just before Atmus. He watched the life fade out of them, then glared at the witch's familiar.

The reptilian damnation wore several scratches, most likely caused when fangs briefly permeated the living tornado.

"You meddle too much, you bastard," hissed Oborus. "Why can't you be a good little sacrifice?" The giant snake appeared as if it might slither back to kill him, but then it froze. "Why did I just say that? I wasn't supposed to tell you that you're a sacrifice. What's going on?"

"Yeah..." Atmus thought to Erwin. *"What's going on?"*

Erwin's chuckles echoed in his head. The earwig waited for the resonance to die down before explaining. *"I knew the spiders could help us, but I forgot entirely about their venom. It acts as a truth serum in small doses."*

"So, what Oborus just said is the truth? The witch plans to use me as a sacrifice?"

"It would seem that way."

Although terror gripped Atmus at the thought of being a martyr, he was no longer afraid of the spiders. He was thankful for them as they continued to pursue Oborus despite the risks.

The tips of their fangs dripped venom as the army of spiders pursued. To keep from further sharing its secrets, Oborus clamped its jaw closed and slithered away.

5-Echoes

There was a clearing. Atmus could not recall how he and Erwin ended up there. All he knew was that the spiders were not with them. He and the insect were alone.

"Where are we?" he asked the bug inside his left ear.

"We've reached the portal," said Erwin. *"Do you see how it darkens for you?"*

Atmus squinted. It was night time, but the mass at centre of the clearing appeared to be darkness beyond the mere absence of light. And it was getting even darker. There was dusk, and then there were things that crept beneath the cover of dusk. He could only imagine what was hidden within that orb-like portal.

"There are all sorts of things hidden in the underworld," said a voice coming from the shadow core. "Like you were hidden under the floor before you caused a fire."

He shuddered. It had been some weeks since he heard her speak, but the voice belonged to Effica, matriarch of the banished family.

"It was an accident," he tried to explain, walking towards the pulsating black mass. "It was my fault, and I take responsibility. I've come here to shut down the portal to the netherworld, but I've also come to find you and your family. I want to make things right. When my business is done here, I'll return to Indmeire Empire with your lot and confess that the fire was my fault."

"My family is dead!" Effica screamed.

The orb suddenly shone with light and colours, playing out the deaths of her husband, son, and daughter in Trepidon Forest. Not a single, gruesome detail was spared.

"Do you see what you've done, young Atmus?" asked Effica, who had also become the witch that was now standing behind him, slinking her bony hands around his neck. "You're going to Hell sooner than later. You should enter the portal and begin your eternity of suffering now."

He woke up breathing harder than any time in his life. He was relatively warm, resting on the back of a giant arachnid, but his thoughts were cold. Something had been in his head.

"I'm sorry, Atmus," Erwin said. *"I saw every moment of your nightmare. Truly horrible. I can keep Oborus and the witch out of your mind, but there are fragments of her evil in this forest that sneak in unexpectedly. I don't think they're still attached to her or that they can haunt more than dreams, but they certainly do her will. Like echoes."*

Atmus recalled something the witch said while he was inside her cave. *"Aye, but echoes are everlasting. Were someone to string them together..."*

Was that what she wanted? Someone to string together the echoes? Her echoes? Was that why she needed a sacrifice?

He fell back asleep, wondering just that.

6-A Moving Target

"Where are we going now?" Atmus asked Queen Vindica from his seat on her back. It had been days since they began hunting Oborus, and he was beginning to worry that his new friends were skittering around in circles. They had travelled on the ground and through the highest branches, but there was still no hint of the snake's whereabouts.

"We lost the scent yesterday," the queen answered "We are decent trackers, but there are better. We are going to find them."

"Who—*what*—are we going to find?"

"Lycanthropes."

"You mean like people who transform into wolves under a full moon?"

Vindica laughed. It was a dry sound, like dehydrated leaves rustling in the wind.

"Not quite," she said. "They were born more mongrel than man, so their human forms are merely for show. They are incredibly loyal, and a debt of gratitude is owed to us for protecting them from the birds."

Birds? Atmus thought of the foul owls. Is that what she meant? If so…

"Don't be distracted," Erwin advised. *"We can focus on that later, assuming there is a later."*

He didn't like the sound of that. Dusk was approaching, further darkening the already gloomy woodlands. Luckily, the spiders had excellent night vision. The horde of them—some hidden, and some in plain sight—marched onwards.

Finally, a light flickered in the distance. It was fire, Atmus realised with a longing shiver. His senses were so frayed from being constantly on edge, he failed to realise how cold it had gotten until he saw the pulsing glow. Growing closer, he made out forms gathered around the flames. They resembled people, and for a moment he hoped it was the banished family. He knew better, however.

Their seemingly human physiques appeared meek, but he suspected such forms were a façade meant to lure in predators who thought they were targeting easy prey. As he considered this point, the lycanthropes turned their heads in unison. Surely, they could hear the spiders approaching.

Limbs elongated and fur grew rapidly, so much it seemed to sprout from every pore. Muscles swelled beneath these sudden pelts, and fingers stretched and sharpened into claws. While the noses flattened into short black nostrils, the mouths remained surprisingly flat and human, only extending far enough to allow for two curled rows of fangs. All of these occurred in a matter of seconds.

"Settle!" announced the royal spider carrying Atmus on her back. "It is I, Queen Vindica. My clan has remained in these parts to protect you from birds of prey. I have come with more of my kind, as friends, to collect a return favour."

The largest of the wolves—the alpha, perhaps—let out a growl that was somehow welcoming. He spoke with a sharp-toothed smile. "Pleasure to finally meet you, Your Highness. How may we help you?"

There were far less lycanthropes than arachnids. Atmus suspected their low numbers were the result of foul owl attacks. He discovered that the wolf people had a different name for the birds.

"Legend says the horror hoots came from the portal many moons ago," a pup named Carver told him. About the same age as Atmus, he remained in his human form during their conversation. The spiders had retreated to the branches while most of the hybrids had gone on their nightly hunt, so it was just the two of them, boy and pup-boy, by the fire.

"The people of the Indmeire Empire call them foul owls," explained Atmus. "We live in buildings that look like giants to scare them away, but it doesn't always work. They destroyed the one my family lived in, and then they…they…"

Carver interjected, "I lost my family as well. Now the pack takes care of me. Used to be we could fend off the birds on our own, but lately we need help from the arachnids. Something about the portal has stirred up the horror hoots."

"You know where the portal is?"

"No," Carver said. "And if I did, I wouldn't for long."

Had Erwin not been sleeping, Atmus figured he would have chimed in and explained. However, he needed no explanation. It was obvious what the wolf-boy was saying.

"You're telling me the portal doesn't stay in one spot?"

Carver nodded. "It moves. I think it's moving a lot more lately. It would explain the strange behaviour of the—I'll use your word—foul owls."

He lowered his head in disappointment. The portal

was a moving target. How would he close it off if he couldn't get to it?

"Keep your spirits up," his new friend said. "And get some rest. Tomorrow is a big day."

Carver took his wolf form, circled a few times, and laid on the fallen-over tree where the two had been sitting. He was nocturnal like the others in his pack, so he was obviously just resting rather than committing to slumber.

Atmus, on the other hand, was almost snoring before he closed his eyes and stretched out on the long log. This time, basked in the warmth of a fire, he slept without dreaming.

The alpha's grumbly voice greeted Atmus the next morning, just after he opened his eyes. He was pleased, at least, to see that the leader of the lycanthropes was wearing human skin—as well as a loincloth.

"My name is Orion, and I serve as head of this pack. Queen Vindica said that you will help us if we help you."

"Say you will," Erwin practically shouted, startling Atmus, who played off his slight surprise with a yawning stretch.

"What is it I can do for your people?" he asked.

"We wish to join the Indmeire Empire. We are not entirely monstrous, and we would never harm people…seeing as we are partly human."

Atmus offered a smile without showing his teeth, afraid doing so would come across as a challenge. "If we can work together to slay Oborus and shut down the portal, the king should do more than welcome your people. He'll probably throw us all a parade."

Orion gave toothy grin. Although his teeth were currently flat, Atmus didn't want to test just how much the wolf-man valued human life. He hoped he could deliver on his end when the time came.

It seemed a parade a few minutes later when Orion signalled the spiders with a whistle. They came forward in uniform rows, except for Vindica, who remained poised in the branches just above the centre of the camp. The pack-leader addressed only the queen.

"We shall assist your mission," he said. "Bring forth your fallen soldier…the one upon which the snake's scent lingers."

Three thinner-looking spiders came forward. Each one had a cord of white extending from its thorax. The cords joined in a large ball of webbing that had been dragged behind them. Orion stepped to the cocoon and used his claws to tear it open. Instead of a butterfly coming out, only flies flew up from the husk. Erwin pointed out the irony of flies feasting on a dead spider, but there was no humour to this observation, for the creature had died fighting on their side.

The mongrels advanced one at a time. They sniffed the fallen arachnid soldier.

"Well?" asked Vindica.

Orion practically howled. "We have the scent. Let's be on our way."

7-Penance in the Portal

They moved quickly. Atmus was riding on Carver's back now rather than camping out on a thorax the size of a jousting arena. The young lycanthrope informed him that the wolves had caught a scent and that's why they were picking up speed.

Atmus was struggling to keep his arms locked around Carver's furry neck when he glimpsed her from the corner of his right eye. He had only seen her once—and quite briefly, after he crawled out from under the floor—but he recognised her purple shawl instantly, even from his periphery. When he turned his head, he saw that she was standing perhaps thirty yards away. Floating before her was a large, black, undulating mass.

He returned his attention to the wolves ahead. Their necks were bent towards Effica and the portal, but only for cursory sniffs. Atmus wondered how it was they didn't see her. Then he glanced back to his right and discovered that he had also lost sight of the banished matriarch.

"I didn't just lose sight of her," he thought to Erwin.

"Agreed," the earwig replied. *"We're moving fast, but not that fast. It's like Carver touched on last night. Even if you know where the portal is, you won't for long."*

An idea formed. Erwin, of course, read his mind and fretted over it.

"I hope you know what you're doing," said the earwig in his head.

"Signal the others," Atmus told the pup carrying him. "Then follow me."

The young lycanthrope barked his compliance. Atmus tipped over and fell to the forest floor.

Atmus stood and ran against the blitz of werewolves and spiders still heading in the opposite direction. He reached a rather gnarled tree near where he'd seen her, and for a moment nothing happened. That was to be expected, at least for a few seconds. If his theory was correct, then the portal moved in a quick cycle and would soon return to that location. Effica would hopefully be there with it.

He was about to give up on his theory when the

space around him suddenly changed. The temperature dropped, and the air dampened with a sparkling, almost crystalised coolness. The tree branches above became bare and hung down like the limbs of hanging victims. Massive roots jutted up from the ground, resembling giant earthworms (which existed in Trepidon Forest as far as Atmus knew).

And there the portal was, hovering about one hundred yards away. Effica had returned, as well.

Atmus dodged low-hanging branches and jumped over exposed roots, making his way towards the woman.

"Effica!" he called. "Effica, it's me, Atmus! You don't know me, but I know you. I've come to shut down the portal and help you and your family escape this forest!"

Her back remained to him. She appeared to be wearing the same garb she'd worn on the night he sprang up from her floor. The purple cover was still quite beautiful despite bits of mud and blood smeared upon it.

"Blood! She's covered in blood and she's alone!"

"Now...don't do anything rash," warned Erwin. *"Our allies are turning around now. Let's wait for them."*

But he wasn't listening to the earwig. He had

reached Effica. He wanted to know what he could do to help her, to make things right.

"Effica…" he managed despite being out of breath. He was now close enough that she must have heard him.

She pulled the shawl over her head and spoke. Her words reflected off the black orb's cascading surface, twisting her voice into something far darker than grief.

"Atmus, did you say? So, you're the one responsible for my family being out here. You got them killed. My Milbrook. My Elena. My…boy…Gilly. There's only one way to fix what *you* did."

"I'll do anything," he said.

Effica began bawling. The sound of it made him shiver.

"There's nothing *you* can do," she croaked. "The snake has shown me the way. Only I can bring them back. The netherworld needs a sacrifice. It's blood for blood."

She sprinted towards the orb. Atmus followed despite the screams in his head insisting otherwise.

Entering the portal felt like diving into a cool pond if it were infested with scum. There was no time to react to the physical sensation, however. It required his entire focus just to keep his eyes on Effica. Although he had entered just behind her, she was somehow far ahead.

And he wasn't the only one attempting to reach her. Although it was cold, dark forms were bubbling up from a ground that appeared to boil like water. Some of them separated themselves from the grimy earth they just crawled out of, while others were too large to crawl out completely. Instead, their giant arms and tentacles stretched towards Effica…and Atmus as well.

He recalled what she said just moments ago: *"It's blood for blood."*

"Maybe I'll let these things take me," he thought as several dark forms seemingly made up of only arms and a mouth crawled toward him. *"And maybe my family will return as a result."*

There was a faint rustling in his ear. The noise even in his own head was partially drowned out by the force of the psychic energy around them, but still he made out what Erwin had to say.

"Oh Atmus…that's not Effica ahead of us. I'm afraid you've been tricked."

He watched as the purple shawl slid away, revealing snakeskin as black as the otherworldly sky around them. Seeing that it was of their ilk and not a human woman after all, the creatures turned their attention away from Oborus and began—all of them, now—towards Atmus.

Oborus cackled, "You were a troublesome pawn, but you served a pawn's purpose no less. Your great grandmother will be so pleased."

"You mean?" Atmus asked.

"Yes," hissed Oborus, slipping behind him to block off the exit.

The horde of abominations covered Atmus. Countless claws pinned him down. The heat from several hung-open maws basked him in putrid warmth.

Teeth tore into his left arm, and that's when utter blackness took him.

The moment Atmus saw clean castle walls, he knew that he was dreaming. He assumed his body was back in that wicked realm, getting slowly torn to shreds. This reverie, or hallucination, was likely his mind's way of protecting him from the pain of death.

Or that's what he believed until the person whose eyes he was seeing through began speaking. The voice was one he recognised, although it now sounded much larger.

"We cannot do what you're suggesting," Erwin said, rolling over. Atmus realised that he was now in the earwig's head. Only, the earwig was no longer an earwig…or *not yet* an earwig. There was a glimpse of hands as the body turned in bed.

There was another person—a naked woman—

there with him. She was beautiful, almost too beautiful, like a skilled painter's artistic rendering of a person. She reached over to caress Erwin's chest, and Atmus was shocked when he felt the stroke of her fingertips.

"It's not wrong if we never die," she said. "Think about it. With your wealth and influence and my magic, we can rule this land for ages. We can rule the world if we choose!"

Erwin turned to the witch. He placed his hand on her abdomen. As he did this, Atmus could feel the swell of love in his great grandfather's chest. The third king of the Indmeire Empire knew what she was, but he loved her anyway. Damned as it made him, he loved her. *Had* loved her, at least.

"The cost is too great," he said. "I already feel badly enough for the havoc the things from your portal are causing my kingdom."

Jezebel's face shifted, hinting at her truly ancient age. There were some things magic couldn't hide. Her legendary wrath was among them.

"Sacrifices must be made. Besides, it's not like we're tossing unwilling virgins into volcanoes. Our offspring have free will and must choose to enter the portal on their own."

"Living endlessly after surrendering our children for the sake would be worse than an eternity in Hell," the king protested.

"Wait until you've clawed your way out of Hell," she said. "You'd do anything to keep from dying again. I won't go back!"

He kissed her forehead. "You'd do anything to stay out of Hell? Does that include repenting?"

She pulled away from his lips and threw her head back in a nearly violent fit of hysterics. She didn't need to say anything. Her laughter said it all.

Atmus opened his eyes for real this time and found that he was immediately gazing back into the eyes of a demon. Its face appeared human, but somehow it had fit his entire left hand and most of his arm in its mouth.

In horror, he understood that his fist, which had been tightly balled as the beasts approached, was no longer attached. The wretched thing staring into his eyes—into his soul—was sucking the meat off what was left of his wrist.

He screamed out loud, but his mind raged at Erwin.

"It's not what you think," said the insect that used to be a man, a king. *"My memories were locked away until you ran into the dark sphere with me inside your head. She turned me into this bug, and she made me forget. I didn't know who I was."* He paused, then added, *"I didn't know who I was to you, Atmus. If I*

knew that, I wouldn't have led you to this portal to be her sacrifice."

Atmus felt as if his head were literally spinning. He figured some of the dizziness was from blood loss. Still, he managed to stammer his defiance.

"I s-s-say no. I wo-wo-won't do it. I wo-won't sacrifice myself."

"Oh Atmus," his cursed relative said from inside his head. *"I wish it worked that way, but the ritual has already begun. I'm afraid the witch has won."*

The creature staring into his eyes seemed to sense his distress and take delight in it. Despite its full mouth, it managed a smile. As it grinned, Atmus felt himself draining. He wasn't just joining its gut. His devoured flesh and blood were going somewhere else, appeasing something else—Jezebel's true lover.

He passed out again. He wasn't sure how long he was gone. There was, however, a faint and almost distant gnawing sensation that told him the shadows had moved to his right leg. Wherever his awareness lingered, he could still hear their gnashing teeth and smacking lips.

His eyes tried to flutter open, but this time they would not. Instead, he was resigned to listening, as he had done when he waited under the floorboards in the fist of an Oni, hoping to sneak out and steal leftovers.

That mistake seemed like an eternity ago, but being on the verge of paying for it with his life, he found himself hoping that he would be able to rest easily in death.

That's when he heard the wolves calling for Carver. Either they had returned to their human forms and were speaking or his fading mind was deciphering words from the subtle variations of their howls.

"Stay away from there!" they warned the pup-boy of the portal. "Atmus is as good as dead!"

But Carver would not listen. Atmus heard a hiss from Oborus and prayed for his own death before he might hear the snake rip the pup-boy apart. Except, that didn't happen. The young werewolf's paws continued padding towards him.

A muffled cry sounded like it was coming from the snake. The orphaned boy still being devoured did not need to look to know what was happening. A spider had followed Carver into the portal and used the distraction to clamp the snake's mouth shut with webbing.

A few seconds later, and the weight of the shadows eased off Atmus. He felt one with the air around him, seeming to float. Now he could open his eye—his left eye, for the right had been plucked out and devoured.

As the hazy sky above seemed to rock, he understood that he wasn't floating. He was on the back of a spider, being carried away from the entrance of the netherworld. Tree branches appeared overhead, and a sliver of sky beyond them shined as blue as his mother's eyes had been.

Atmus closed his eye in a prayer that was equal parts wishful and thankful.

8- The Corpse of the Cave (Part II)

Something was wrong. Although she was dead, her lingering spirit had always been able to see through Oborus. However, the last glimpse through those snaky eyes had been that of a giant arachnid approaching as the serpent blocked Atmus from leaving the portal.

But the sacrifice must have worked! If it had failed, why was flesh returning to her bones?

"Oh, but not enough flesh," said a voice. *"Because not enough flesh and blood was given."*

Who said that? The voice was familiar. It came from inside her now-functioning ear. Could it be…

"It is indeed I, King Indmeire the Third."

"Erwin!" she sputtered, her mouth actually moving now that a few sinewy stretchings had returned to her jaw. "You've reclaimed your memories, then. Was it you who blocked me from reading Atmus's mind? What a fantastic trick! I should have crushed you instead of turning you into a bug after you crept into my cave that last time, pretending to still be my lover just to get close and strike a fatal blow. I should have used my fading energy to destroy you rather than wiping your mind and turning you into an earwig. I guess this is where sentiment gets me."

The royal earwig laughed.

"No matter," she said out loud. Although she knew he could read her mind, she was pleased to speak using a physical mouth. "I'll remove you from this world soon enough. And for good. No more games."

"I agree," said Erwin. *"That's why this is checkmate."*

Her fresh flesh began to sweat. Something was coming her way through the cave. Her former lover wouldn't have the last laugh, after all. Her familiar was there to save her.

"Oborus! You've returned! Oh, how I've missed you! You gave me quite the scare."

Her snake—or rather, the husk of its skin—continued towards her, carried on the backs of large arachnids, babies of the giant spider clan she once welcomed through the portal.

"Betrayals," she muttered. "Betrayals everywhere."

That's when she saw the boy through the dim glow

her powers granted the cave. Riding on the back of a lycanthrope pup, he was brutally maimed but no less threatening.

The witch stood and made to flee her hiding place. She would get out and seal the entrance, leaving her enemies stuck in the mystic dwelling. Her riches would be lost, but she would find a way to complete her resurrection.

Yet her legs were not yet strong enough. She took a few steps and fell, fracturing her still partially exposed skull against the cave floor. Her last sight was the rest of the wolf pack entering her den. They surrounded her. They dug into her.

She pleaded in her mind for Erwin to help her. It wasn't too late yet. She could repent. They could start a family and live happily ever after. They could—

"Erwin, where did you—" she started to think, but it didn't matter where he went. Her former lover had left her ear. Rightfully so, because teeth were digging into her head.

For a second time, Jezebel was torn apart by a pack of canines; for the final time, she died.

9-So Long, Scarecrows

At first, the current king did not want to believe the

earwig that had crawled into his head and professed to be an early ruler over the empire. Erwin, however, convinced him to trust Atmus. That trust served him and the entire kingdom well.

It was Atmus who arranged a pact with the werewolves and spiders. In the days that followed his summit with the wounded boy and his band of creatures, the king found himself nervously glancing out the eye of his own majestic Oni, especially at night. Each time he looked, he marvelled at what was taking place.

Atmus, riding on a lycanthrope as if it were a majestic stallion, had borrowed some of the king's soldiers and corralled them far away from any of the Oni, where they would be seemingly susceptible.

Howling in the distance let everyone know that the foul owls were on their way.

When the giant shadows began flying overhead, the king balled up his fist and bit nervously into it. Yet he soon discovered that he had no reason to be worried. As the boy had promised, the spiders protected them. They caught the birds in their webbings when they swooped low enough and pulled them to the ground and pumped them with venom until they seized and died.

With the portal closed (apparently as the result of

the witch's death) and the foul owls seemingly brought to extinction, the Oni were steadily replaced by real homes, structures intended for each family. Using the protection of their new animalistic allies, Atmus travelled through Trepidon Forest and brought back supplies from other kingdoms. Somehow the boy had come by a great deal of treasure, and he used it all to improve Indmeire Empire.

The king soon found himself tipping his crown in Atmus's direction. Now a formidable young man despite his wounds, he led negotiations with kingdoms near and far, even helping them to alleviate the burdens caused by Trepidon Forest.

He was a born leader. He was indeed of the family.

And although Atmus Indmeire had a literal iron fist—matching an iron leg—the current king trusted that the empire would be in good hands when it came his successor's time to inherit the throne.

10-Happy

Even with his new standing, he never forgot about the family whose home he destroyed. He asked that Erwin check up on them frequently, seeing as they were all still alive.

Despite what the witch had wanted him to think,

they were never banished to Trepidon Forest in the first place. Their exile was only a story Jezebel concocted as a means of coaxing Atmus into the woods—to the portal—like a lamb heading to slaughter.

"Are they all happy?" he asked the earwig.

"Very," said Erwin. *"Are you?"*

Atmus considered. Despite everything he'd been through, his answer always remained the same.

"Very."

A.L. KING is an author of horror, fantasy, science fiction, and poetry. As an avid fan of dark subjects from an early age, his first influences included R.L. Stine, Edgar Allan Poe, and Stephen King. Later stylistic inspirations came from foreign horror films and media, particularly Japanese.

He is a graduate of West Liberty University, has dabbled in journalism, and is actively involved in his community. Although his creativity leans toward darker genres, he has even written a children's book titled "Leif's First Fall."

He was raised in the town of Sistersville, West Virginia, which he still proudly calls home.

Bibliography
BEYOND, Black Hare Press, 2019
Deep Space, Black Hare Press, 2019
MONSTERS, Black Hare Press, 2019

Connect
Facebook: @alkauthor

BLACK HARE PRESS

BEYOND THE REALM

ZIYAD THE BLASPHEMER

By Abigail Linhardt

Returning home from war, Ziyad finds another man has taken his throne, wife, and swayed his people against him. Turning to dark magic to exile the usurper, the mysterious price might just break the hardened eastern soldier.

The aureate domes of Moshav glinted in the high sun, nestled like golden eggs in the vibrant sands. The minaret's spire flashed like a clean blade, the priest calling his prayer to the city in trembling high and lows. Gauzy curtains and thick silky banners fluttered in the hot wind off the desert sands. It was market day, and camels and horses lined the docks, winding up the path into the small village.

Ziyad trained his eyes on the domes and the white marble balcony where white silks waved. The ship he stood on the prow of had taken him across the world and now brought him home. Scars from the war mapped out across his body the terrible journey he had suffered over five years. The green lands across the sea had been foreign to him. The battles had been bloodbaths. His fellow lords, called to aid by the king, had fallen. He alone returned to his village. He had been lord of the village with serfs under him. Market day was his favourite before the war. His land provided everything that kept Moshav alive. It was small, but it was his.

No one stood on the balcony, looking towards the sea. He had sent word ahead to his wife, Reza, that he was alive and coming home. His son, Sahir, would be a man now. He had dreams of coming home and seeing Sahir in his council chambers, managing his land, profits pouring in. Moshav singing praises of his valiant bravery in the war. The last lord had returned.

He leapt from the ship's side before it even pulled into port. He could not wait to see Sahir and Reza. He thanked the crew as they tossed him his leather satchel and curved sword. Smiling, his brown eyes sparkling

BEYOND THE REALM

with joy and anticipation, he made his way through the coloured stalls of market day. Very few paid him any heed. Perhaps he looked too different. Moshav was the same, it seemed. Except the melons that were normally harvested this time of year from the nearby mountains were missing.

When no one cried a salutation to him, he asked one merchant selling oil, "Is Ziyad's estate well maintained? Does Moshav still prosper under its rule?"

The man, his tongue out at an angle while he cleaned a lamp, eyed Ziyad carefully. "The lord went to war. Left us for some holy war in the west. Dead. His memorial was some years ago."

Ziyad grew accustomed to hiding his emotions in the heat of battle, but this was his home. Moshav was his. Concerned, he thanked the man and made his way right for the golden roofs of his house.

The guard at the gate stopped his pacing when Ziyad approached. Ziyad recognised him as the captain of his guard, an old friend and combat teacher.

"Malil!" Ziyad called out.

The guard's face turned pale. He glanced back and forth as if to check for spies. "My lord Ziyad?" His tone was thunderstruck. After a few moments' hesitation, he knelt on one knee and bowed his head, only to look up again in disbelief. "Is it really you? We were told all the lords within a horses ride were killed! How are you back?"

It was not the greeting he had expected. He pulled Malil to his feet, no longer smiling. "I am surprised at the doubt Moshav has shown. Would I really die in a western war?"

"The stories we heard…" Malil said, trying to pardon the misunderstanding.

"It was hell," Ziyad confirmed. "Where is my wife? My son? Where is Reza?"

Malil swallowed. "They are commanded to stay inside the walls when the lord is at market."

Ziyad's spirit grew dark. His face clouded over. "I am not at market. Apparently, I am dead." His eyes roamed the white walls of his home. All the windows were closed with wooden shutters. "Where is Reza?"

***

Malil took Ziyad inside the gates and into the entry way where the fountain still sang its gurgling music and the foliage blossomed over the walls. It was just as he remembered it. The colourful flowers were in their full beauty and birds nested in the branches of the trees with their long leaves.

"Bring me Sahir," Ziyad said. "Do not tell Reza I

BEYOND THE REALM

am here yet." He had to do this right. He did not know the way of things any more. Another man in his home? In his throne? With his wife…

"We cannot have visitors during market," a strong, young voice said from the second floor above. "Inaam will have your hands for this, Malil."

"Inaam is it?" Ziyad called up, recognising what must have been his grown son's voice. "Come and face me like a man!" He smiled.

A tall, broad-shouldered youth appeared at the top of the steps. His skin dark from working in the sun but his eyes cunning and sharp: her eyes, his body.

"Gods!" Sahir whispered, emotion strangling him. "Father?"

Ziyad held his arms out to his son. Sahir flew down the stairs and into his embrace. His arms were strong and his hands rough where he pulled a bowstring and wielded a sword. Good. He held him out at arm's length and could not help but beam.

"You were dead, they told us!" Sahir's voice echoed joyously. "Wait until mother sees. Inaam will be furious."

"Yes, tell me about him," Ziyad said, signalling for the servant to bring a pipe and tea. This was his home and he would be obeyed. "But first, let us sit."

He went to his favourite garden, which was

blessedly untouched. Sahir told him stories about growing up, hunting with Malil, and even a girl he knew in the village he fancied. A part of Ziyad ached as Sahir spoke and told his stories. They were so different from his own. It was his childhood and Ziyad had missed it. He had left behind a boy too scared to ride a camel and had come home to a warrior.

"Then there was Zeva," Sahir said, his face losing some of its vibrance.

"Zeva?" Ziyad asked. "I wanted to name my daughter Zeva once. Long before you were born." He smiled.

Sahir turned his gaze away from his father's. His jaw clenched. "She was my sister."

"What?" Ziyad gasped.

"Not long after you left. But…" He swallowed. "She got sick."

Even though he had not known her, a stone seemed to settle in Ziyad's heart. He'd had a daughter. A princess to love, protect. It would have made the war worth it. But he had his son.

"What was the war like?" Sahir asked, after he was nearly hoarse from telling his own tales.

"Another time," Ziyad said, waving his hand and drinking his tea. "Who is Inaam?"

Sahir took a long draw on the pipe and blew a

perfect ring into the bright blue sky above, contemplating his answer carefully. His son was wise to not immediately slander the man who took his inheritance. Ziyad was glad to see this.

"He was a merchant from the far east," Sahir started, measuring his words. "I suppose mother met him in the market the summer after you left. She was pregnant."

Curse the war and curse the kings who fought for land in the west. Ziyad swallowed hard. "Is he a good lord? A good father?"

"A father?" Sahir cried out, finally showing some emotion. "He takes everything we have here and gives it to the temple. He says our wealth is Moshav's wealth and we must give it back."

Ziyad frowned. "Charity is not above us, Sahir."

His son composed himself, trying to remain under control. "We give what we always have, we are not tyrants. But Inaam is! Father, our stores are empty. He takes from all of Moshav and then redistributes it as he sees fit. He pays our serfs in supplies and very little gold. He has lost all my inheritance!"

There was a point Ziyad could see now. Inaam was driving his family legacy into nothingness. Making a lord into a peasant. Giving away what was not his to give. Taking what was not his…

"And your mother?" Ziyad asked his son. "She sees no wrong in this?"

"She says we must do away with the lords and all earn what we desire." Sahir relaxed into the colourful cushions. "She is blinded by how he lusts after her. I can hear them at night…"

The warrior—the killer—in Ziyad checked himself. He laid his hand on the hilt of his long, curved sword and breathed to steady himself.

"I built this city," he said softly. "From sand and sea, I created Moshav brick by brick!"

Sahir said, "He promises protection from the nomads."

"Nomads?" Ziyad asked. There had been no nomads when he was lord.

"The heretics to the south of Moshav," Sahir explained. "They defiled the temple, tore the mihals from the doorways."

Ziyad's eyes travelled to the mihals, holy words wrapped and stored in a clay pot above his own lintel. He had forgotten to touch them when he entered. He had lost a lot of traditions while crusading for another man's war. The religion seemed silly now.

"Inaam gives how much to the temple?" he asked simply.

"Most," Sahir replied shortly. He glanced around

as though afraid of what he was about to say. "Temple is corrupt," he whispered. "I am sure. What they do with our money is wrong."

This was news. "How so?" Ziyad asked.

"They have so much wealth now. They make new laws—they have an army now!"

Strange, Ziyad thought. "With Inaam's wealth, they have changed. As most would. Perhaps too powerful? Why?"

Before he could consider more, a cry arose from outside his gate. Malil shouted up to a watchman in a turret who rang a bell.

"What is this alarm?" Ziyad shouted, standing up, hand on his sword again.

"The nomads!" Sahir cried. "Moshav calls for our aid!"

***

Five years before, Ziyad would have given his life for Moshav if bandits had invaded, harming his people. It was a small village, known for its temple pilgrimages and its market days, but it was his. Now he wanted to watch. To see what Inaam would do now that he had taken the seat of lord.

"Where are you going?" Sahir asked, when his

father did not follow him to the stables to fetch a mount.

"Go," he ordered. "Do not tell Inaam I have returned."

He quickly hid his face in the wrappings hanging around his neck and made his way into Moshav where the people were screaming. The desire to fight made his palms itch and sweat as he clenched them. It was his nature now to draw the sword, defend the weak. These were his people. But he had to watch and learn.

He found the raid party in the market. They seemed to be soldiers, armoured and wearing helmets with red and black trimmings. Their bodies seemed odd. Their gait was awkward, almost limping. Perhaps they were all wounded? They swung with no regard to their surroundings. One temple guard shot a raider in the eye socket. The raider twitched backwards but still advanced. He had never seen such discipline. These were soldiers to be proud of.

He scanned the madness and followed the line of raiding soldiers up to where they seemed to be coming from. Sahir was right; it seemed they must have a camp in the east, beyond the dunes. Then he spotted it: a human figure, wrapped in black and face covered, was watching the soldiers march. Almost like it was giving them orders. This had to be the leader. Maybe a general of some sort. Then he saw three more, standing in formation. They were all making signs with their hands. He could not see their mouths if they were speaking. He pulled his glass out and peered in their direction. There were pale, blue eyes looking out over the face covers. He had only seen eyes like that in the west. None in Moshav especially had pale skin and blue eyes.

Just as he was deciding to chase them or not, a great horn shouted into the streets of Moshav. A war cry, the likes he was familiar with, broke the screams of his people. From the temple poured out the familiar scarlet and red of his own guards and more clad in black and green that he had not seen before. These must be the temple's new army.

Leading the charge was a man about eight years his junior. He was handsome in red and gold, holding a spear poised to throw above his left shoulder. Ziyad recognised the white war horse he was riding—it had been his. He had purchased it just before he was called to war. He couldn't remember what he had called it, he just remembered it because it was a true white: a pink nose and hooves. It had been a great find.

This had to be Inaam. Donning his colours, riding his horse, coming to the aid of his people. He led the armies in, slaughtering the strange soldiers. While reliant, the invading soldiers fell like stacks of hay. It took little time for Inaam to fight them off and push them back.

Inaam rode into the centre of the village where the people praised him, thanking him for his protection. Some fell to their knees and prayed for thankfulness right in the streets. A strange feeling crept into Ziyad when he saw the love the people had for Inaam. He was doing good, perhaps.

While being praised, Inaam ordered the removal of the corpses and help for the wounded. Ziyad decided to meet him. But not here, among his adoring people. In his own home. Covering himself again, he made his way back to his home, stealthily, and went into the accepting hall, a small chamber where he had heard the needs of his people once upon a time. The sandstone chair, a trifle of a throne, was still there. He sat in it, feeling its familiar embrace, threw his long cloak over one of the arms, and waited.

He had left the door open, a clear indicator that someone was inside as it was not custom to have it opened. He waited longer than he expected but was ready when he heard them returning. The first sound to reach his ears was Reza's adoring laugh. He loved that laugh because it was often accompanied by her squeezing his arm and then leaning in for a kiss. She was no doubt kissing Inaam.

"Malil, what is this?" her voice broke off. She had seen the door. When Malil did not answer, Inaam took sure, long strides and threw the doors open, sword in hand.

Ziyad did not smile. He glared at the pair through his dark brows. Inaam did not advance when Reza gasped, holding her heart. Her surprise stayed his hand but not his tongue.

"Ziyad," Inaam whispered.

"Has my wife mentioned her husband?" Ziyad asked, putting on a lazy aura. "Because she never mentioned you in all those letters she wrote to me in the west." He fixed her with a pointed stare. "Oh yes, there were no letters."

"You were dead," Reza said in a strained tone. "Moshav mourned you. We all did."

Ziyad leapt up from the chair. "I was alone in the west, Reza!" he shouted. "We were forbidden to write home but you could have reached out to me!"

Inaam put out his arm, shielding Reza from his berating. "Even the king died, Ziyad. We knew the west was lost."

"Who are you?" Ziyad asked him at last. "How do you know my name?"

Inaam frowned, half smirking. "All in Moshav

know you, my lord."

"And you thought you'd just step into my shoes? Take my land, supply the temple with an army using my gold? Taking my wife!"

Swords were drawn.

"I stepped up when no one else would!" Inaam shouted in his defence, backing a few steps away. "Moshav was berate with cursed soldiers once we knew the king's ships had landed on the western shore. Moshav needed a saviour."

Ziyad put his sword away. There was no point in drawing blood now. He noted Inaam did not retaliate. "I have returned. I am prepared to take my seat as lord back."

Reza's eyes simpered. "My husband. You are unwell. The Ziyad I knew would not be so quick to anger. The war has unsettled you."

She stepped out from behind Inaam and came to him, taking him in her arms and running her fingers through his long, black hair like she used to do.

He let her touch him. Her pale, long fingers in her hair was something he had missed. Her hands on his face. She was slender and delicate compared to his dark, rough skin and knotted muscles. He gently grasped her hand with mild urgency and kissed her palm. She smelled of flowers and myrrh. His eyes were heavy as he made eye contact with her. He saw her desire for him there.

"Let me come home," he begged her softly so the others could not hear.

"You cannot take back what you lost," she whispered, just for his ears. "You cannot take it by force. Inaam has use of the temple's army. And yours." She cleared her throat and said to the room at large, "Go to the guild of serfs. Speak with them to see what can be done."

"I am not giving up what I have fought for and protected," Inaam said sternly.

"What you took from me," Sahir hissed from behind.

"Not now, son," Ziyad chided quickly before Reza could retaliate. To Reza he said, "I will visit my serfs. So they may see their lord has returned."

***

The guild hall was just a walk from his golden-domed home. It was market day so they should be in session until prayer at sunset. It was close. He took his white horse, stripping it of all its pompous bridles and frills and road bareback to the guild hall.

The servant at the door was shocked to see him and

announced him with great enthusiasm to the serfs who were all sitting on cushions on the floor around a round table. Ledgers were out before them and the clear pot of tea on the table was empty; it was almost time to depart.

Various cries and oaths went up as Ziyad entered. A few of the serfs called him "my lord" and bowed their heads to him.

"Inaam has taken my seat as your lord," he addressed them. "I see in my absence he has done well to sustain your lives. How do you fare?"

A few of the serfs looked around, unsure who was going to speak first or what they should say. Ziyad did not sit down among them. He focused on one who managed a large orchard on his land.

"Tell me about Inaam," he ordered her.

She caught her breath before addressing her lost lord. "We all maintain a share of what we make," she started. "But…" she cast her eyes around, fearful of what she was about to say. "He takes it all and then divides it equally among us."

"This is not a bad thing!" an older serf interjected.

"Not for you!" she shot back. "You thrive under this rule. You have more than you ever have had. If you managed the wool as well as you should, this would never have been an issue."

"Stop, what do you mean?" Ziyad asked his serfs. "Equally?"

The woman nodded. "You know how much I bring in for your land. The orchard, the winery. I am organised and work hard. I do most of the tasks myself!"

Ziyad remembered. She was a magnificent worker and a genius when it came to the distillery. He had paid her accordingly. "And now?"

"And now all I do is for naught! I can work hours every day, sell at a magnificent profit and Inaam takes it all, giving me only a fraction of what I earn. We all earn the same, no matter the work we do."

The tyranny was obvious. If Inaam paid each serf the same, if it was low enough, he would have more resources to give elsewhere. Like to the temple.

"And some of us are happy with this," the older man said.

"Because you make more now than you ever did," the woman replied.

"And you're angry because you make less," he scoffed.

"Yes!"

A small argument broke out while Ziyad contemplated. Inaam was playing it as he had never thought to. The temple and the priests were the ones who dictated the morality of a people to the people. Moshav was deeply steeped in its faith. He was a faithful man himself to his god. He prayed every day. Worshipped when the call came. This could not be his god's will. Once Inaam had the temple in his debt, he would be the most powerful man in Moshav. In the kingdom perhaps. It was genius.

"Inaam is using you," he said over the ruckus that was growing. "Each man shall be given what is owed." He stepped up onto the table so they all could see him. "This is not how a fair man runs his lands. My lands will not be treated thus! I answered our king's call just to come back to my home—my wife—taken by another man who would use it for ill intent."

"He turns the temple into his own private army. Takes our god and makes him his slave! Heresy, I say! This is not his will. This," he pointed to the mihals above the door he had come through, "is not our god any longer. This is allegiance to Inaam. We must remove it from our homes.

"Come with me into Moshav and tear down the heretical symbols. Take back our god and show Inaam he is just a man who took what was not his. And I will see to it that every serf who serves under me is given back tenfold what he is owed. Come with me once more so we may live together and prosper!"

"Aye!" the woman shouted, standing up. She turned to her fellow serfs. "It is not a battle, but a crusade. Ziyad is our lord. Has he ever led us a stray?"

The serfs whispered among themselves. It was not a madman's idea, they said. Inaam had profaned the temple and the priests had let him. It needed to be cleansed. He had taken what was not his.

"But he protects us," the old man said out loud.

"As if I will not?" Ziyad cried. "Five years I have been gone. What is that compared to the lifetime I had served you in return. I will find the nomads and stop them from ever entering Moshav again. But I cannot if Inaam controls my army. Let me be your lord again."

***

The following days were a rush for Ziyad. He visited his home only to take some of his belongings while planning the sacking of the temples, shrines, and mihals on the people's doors.

"Let me do this with you!" Sahir begged on the third day while he was packing.

He did not want to leave things like his father's armour in the home of a man who would no doubt sell it. He took his mother's quilt and his older brother's sword, who had passed away when he was still just a boy.

"Absolutely not," he quipped. "I need you safe inside our home."

"This isn't my home," Sahir argued. "Inaam has made it his own. I have been living in a stranger's house. I have fought the bandits; I have trained like you taught me. I am not a boy any longer, father."

Ziyad was wrapping his brother's sword when Sahir said this. He stopped and looked up into his son's dark eyes.

"Perhaps I could use someone I know is loyal to me. But I fear for your soul."

Sahir scoffed, "It is as you said, this is not our god's will. We will owe no penitence or prayers for the destruction of the temple. Inaam has destroyed their meaning already. Taken them for his own banner."

A smile shifted across Ziyad's face like the sands on the dunes. He was proud of his son.

"I look forward to drawing swords with you," he said.

"What is this?" Reza said, appearing in the silks that dropped across the door. She was wearing red. He loved her in red. "Finished?"

Her figure was perfect for his eyes to roam. "Yes," he said, stifling his feelings. He had to push past her, eyes trained on the floor to avoid her alluring gaze.

***

BEYOND THE REALM

The day of the plan arrived, and dozens appeared outside the temple. The waiting serfs attracted more crowds and word began to subtly spread of what was about to happen. Ziyad was perched above the temple entrance, waiting. But when a small disturbance alerted him, he called to Sahir.

"Someone spoke!" he called up to his father. "They are calling Inaam!"

There was no time to lose.

"Do not stop us!" he shouted at those not among his raiding army. "I wish you no harm. I only wish to remove the man who would take from you what is yours. Who would defile your god and use him to control Moshav. You are a free people and should not live in fear of a man who snuck in during the night and took my place as your lord while I fought a hostile nation. You know me! I have fought when our king called. I have brought prosperity to Moshav."

"Inaam is a good man!" a priest shouted. "He has given to the temple like you never have."

"And in return what have you given him? A whole new military." Ziyad scanned the crowd, trying to judge the peasants of his village. They seemed to be waiting. "Do not defend him. Turn Inaam over to me and I will be lenient when I return as your lord."

There was a stir at this. The other peasants began

to whisper and his serfs seemed to be getting restless.

"Inaam has done nothing wrong," the priest said again.

"Taking your religious freedom is not wrong?" Ziyad shouted.

"What has he done?" the priest shouted back.

"Forced us to give," the woman serf screamed. "Taken when we do not. He takes everything!"

"Silence!" the priest screeched.

The uproar had maddened the crowd. Ziyad had seen mobs before. A person was easy to counsel, but a mob wanted to take action. A mob craved violence. And they would follow whoever struck first, no matter the reason behind.

Ziyad stood up, all eyes on him. "You cannot silence us."

He drew a bolt and shot so quickly no one gasped until the priest's blood spattered their nearby faces. The priest's head jerked back and was followed by his body. There was silence for just a moment.

"Destroy the corrupt symbols!" he screamed to his people. With a roar like a wave in the ocean, the mob moved out, smashing the mihal on the doorways, clogging the temple doors on their way to topple the statues and symbols.

Ziyad leapt down from his perch, drew his sword,

and marched to the shrine in the middle of the market. He saw the temple's new army marching up from the other side. He glared at them across the square, unblinking. He had fought in a holy war before. They were pointless. But this was his village and his people. If Inaam would use his gold to turn their god into a war machine, then it had to be destroyed.

He took the mountain goat horn flask from his belt and heaved it with all his might at the tall shrine. The liquor splashed down it, covering the entire side. Grasping the eternal fire that burned in the centre, he pulled the torch out, poising it for a strong throw.

"No man can own god! No man should use our god as a reason to enslave his people!"

"Stop!" one of the temple guards shouted.

With all his might, Ziyad threw the torch at the doused shrine. It caught instantly, erupting in a flame that devoured the old structure in seconds. The people screamed, some women cried, screaming prayers to the smoke-filled sky. They were praying for him. He had defiled the temple, burned the shrine.

"Arrest Ziyad! Arrest the blasphemer!" the temple guard ordered.

His work was done. He called for his serfs to fall back and for Sahir to follow him. Mounting his bridleless horse, he galloped away, out of Moshav and into the sandy wilderness.

***

"What will the serfs do?" Sahir asked as they finally slowed to a walk. "They will hate you for leaving, they will be arrested by the temple guard and their lands seized for this heresy."

"Is that so?" Ziyad asked, cocking an eyebrow. He smiled at his son.

"You wanted this?" Sahir asked. "Why?"

Ziyad knew his son was smarter than that. "All of Moshav is in Inaam's gilded pocket. My serfs needed just one more reason to hate him. This should do it."

Sahir pulled his hood up to block out the scorching sun. "That seems like an awfully big risk. What if they do not see it the same way you do and hate you now?"

"They won't. Inaam will see to that."

They climbed over the sandy hills for some time before Sahir spoke again.

"Are these tracks?"

"Just noticing now?" Ziyad stopped his horse and scanned the dunes. "I need an army to outlast Inaam's. And my serfs would not do." He pointed to the mountains that were closer now than Sahir had ever seen. "It is the rain season in the mountains. It is called the Moshav monsoon. Once a year it rains and floods the mountains."

The boy trained his eyes on the mountains in the distance. "I wondered why they called it that. Those melons grow there."

Ziyad laughed gently and smiled at the memory. A small Sahir marvelling at the large, pink melon he had bought at market during the monsoon. Only a few farmers and merchants went that far into the mountains to get the melons and it was always well worth the trip. The people in Moshav paid handsomely for the sweet things. As far as he knew, Sahir had not eaten one since then. He had eaten so much, so fast that he had gotten sick and hated them ever since. He loved that his boy had an appetite for more than just the melons.

"The bandits are there this year," Ziyad explained. "I knew it the moment I saw them. There were no melons in the market, and this was the best explanation. Their tracks lead right to it."

His boy pressed his lips tightly. "But won't they kill us?"

He shook his head. "They just wanted a quick plunder. They are probably already preparing to leave. I hope we haven't missed them."

"How will you convince them to fight Inaam?"

"They are lawless men already. All I have to do is

bargain with them."

***

The jungle was teeming with sounds uncommon to the village of Moshav. A kind of black and white monkey screamed in the dense foliage above. Hidden birds cawed and screeched across the roaring river where it fell far into a cold basin of clean water.

"I've never been up here after the monsoon," Sahir said in awe, his eyes taking in all the colours. "I had no idea anything could be so green. Or that water cried so loud."

Ziyad held up his hand to silence his son. He had spotted them. They were not far into the jungle or trying to hide themselves. They were so sure no one would follow. There were four figures, wrapped in black, hoods up. They had uncovered their faces. They had a camp set up around a black wagon with a roof. They seemed to be doing something oddly normal: eating around a fire.

Sahir and Ziyad crouched down and slinked through the underbrush to get close to them. When they rounded to the backside of the wagon, they could see inside the formidable structure. It was barred closed, humming with the buzz of a million flies feasting on dozens of bodies. Ziyad squinted at the steeds pulling the grotesque thing; they seemed like horses but their skin was leathery and their bones shone white in places that were missing the black skin. They were not panting or grazing. They stood perfectly still, eyes covered.

The four figures around the fire seemed unaware of their presence still. Ziyad inspected them closely. Two men and two women. His trained eye could see that they only had daggers around their ankles. Their hands were covered in silver rings with runes etched on every surface. He froze: magic users. There was no going back now.

He strode out of the green, drawing his sword. Sahir followed him in perfect rhythm.

One of the women leapt up and reached for the cage door where the corpses laid. Ziyad didn't know what she was going to do, but it couldn't be good.

"Do not move!" he shouted, pulling out a small, concealed crossbow. He hadn't pulled it back to fire yet but maybe they didn't know that.

"Stay, Shiva," one of the men said. He stood up, removing his hood. His skin was pallid, almost a lavender shade, and his hair was white. All across his skin were tattooed similar symbols as were on their rings. He seemed old but there was not a wrinkle on his face. His blue eyes were steady, unafraid.

"You are the ones who attacked Moshav?" Ziyad inquired, pointing the bow at the man now. "I am not here to kill you," he added quickly.

A shared smile passed between the four robed people.

"Then how can I help you?" the man asked. "Do you care to share in our meal?" He smiled darkly and motioned to the stew hanging above the fire.

"I have a business proposition for you," Ziyad said cautiously, taking one step closer, keeping his eyes on the woman called Shiva who had not moved her hand from the gate on the wagon.

The man calmly tented his fingers. "Do you know who I am?"

"Does it matter?"

The man frowned. "Do you know *what* I am?"

At this, Ziyad gave pause. "*What* you are? Are you not a man?"

"There are many kinds of men in this world. What kind are you?" the man asked.

The riddles were frustrating. Ziyad pulled the bow back and locked it in place, aiming it at the other two who had not yet spoken or moved. This made them rise, the second man putting his arm protectively around the woman.

"I will kill you," Ziyad warned them. "*All* of you."

They didn't smile this time.

The first man lowered his hands. "I find you are a man of persuasion and desperation. Though you should know we do not fear death. But I must warn you—"

"What are you?" Sahir spat out since he father would not. "We fear nothing. We have lost all we have; do not think we are wary of dangerous men."

The man nodded. He lifted his hand and slowly motioned for Shiva to step away from the wagon of corpses. "We can talk. Please sit."

Not releasing the bow, Ziyad sat, facing all four of them. Sahir stood behind him, hand on the hilt of his sword.

"Who are you?" Ziyad hissed. "But I cannot see how it matters. You have the armies to sack Moshav again and again. I need that army. I cannot pay you now, but I can promise you whatever you desire once we have overtaken the lord's house."

"Overthrowing the lord?" the man mused. "Seems to be taking more than you need."

"I am that lord!" Ziyad shouted. "My home was taken while I was away, fighting another man's holy war. So I am here to wage my own and take back what is mine."

The four all shared a glance.

"I need your oath before I speak," the man said.

The markings on his skin seemed to shift as he spoke. It made Ziyad's skin crawl.

"I'll promise you anything."

The man's face was grave. He had expected these bandits to be snide, excited to be hired mercenaries, but they seemed far more hesitant than he was. Almost like they were afraid for him. The unknown was grating his nerves.

"Remove your glove," the man said. He held out his own.

Exasperated, Ziyad threw his glove off and grasped the other man's over the fire. He cried out as a million needles pierced his palms. He tried to pull away but the man held his hand tightly and glared at Sahir as he drew his sword. The other three stood up, ready to defend if the boy came at them.

Looking down, Ziyad saw the runes on the silver rings adorning the fingers that clutched his bloody hand, were turning red. They seemed to be filling up the longer he held on. It was his blood.

"Promise me one thing in this oath," the man said. This time, the symbols on his skin really were moving. His veins pulsed black under his pale skin. "Give me the first thing to leave your doorway once you have reclaimed your land. Do you agree?"

His entire arm was throbbing by now. It was like

something from the mysterious man was flowing into him and back out through the painful incisions.

"I can give you gold," he said through clenched teeth.

The man narrowed his lips. "What comes out the door of your reclaimed home."

"It'll be fine," Sahir whispered from behind him.

Trusting his son, Ziyad nodded. Even though he didn't understand, he said, "Fine. But you have to tell me how you plan to do this."

The man released his hand and flexed his fingers several times. "I am Tarkan, the archmagian of our tribe. You have met Shiva, my apprentice. This is Ashkan and his wife Elahel."

"You are not from Moshav," Ziyad mused. "Your names are Porshian. The tribes of Porsh were wiped out by the invading armies of Alahar a decade ago, I thought."

"We were." Tarkan didn't smile but a kind of joke underlined his reply. "We still travel together."

Ziyad's eyes travelled to the wagon of bodies. "Necromancers."

Tarkan half-smiled at the knowledge Ziyad showed. "I am honoured you know of our people. You seem unconcerned. Alahar murdered my people, overthrowing our tribal ways and establishing his own government because we broke mihal law."

"It is condemnable by death," Sahir said, his face twisted in disgust. "We have sought the wrong men for aid, father."

Ziyad's heart was conflicted; it was true. His face collapsed into a deep frown as he weighed his options. He had made an oath. It was wise of Tarkan to make him swear before revealing his ways. His soul might be damned if he weighed himself with the necromancers. He might be lost, but he could save his family.

"I am already damned," he said finally. "But so is Inaam. He has turned the temple in Moshav into his own private army. I have desecrated the shrines, defiled the temple, and torn the mihal from my neighbour's homes. I have nothing left to lose."

Tarkan studied the man before him carefully. "Men with nothing to lose are dangerous. They tend to ignore the needs of those who follow them. Often people with much to lose. They follow an ideal, not a man."

"What harm can befall you?" Ziyad glared at Tarkan. "I saw you the day you ransacked Moshav. You stood back while your dead army did the work."

"And if we fail, will you come for me and my tribe?" He motioned to the other three. "Are we safe from you?"

Ziyad scoffed, cocking his lips in a dangerous smile, "Then don't fail. Or you'll be resurrecting each other."

***

"I need you to let me in tonight," Ziyad said to Malil at the gate.

It was a cool desert night and the moon was hanging low, orange and too large as if warning the village of the impending doom.

"She hasn't even asked to see you," Malil replied apologetically.

Ziyad clutched the bars and pressed himself against the gate as if he could pass through by the power of his desire. "I need to speak to her!" He couldn't tell Malil about the attack. It would be his sworn duty to raise the alarm. Even though he trusted the older man, had ridden with him into battles, had learned to wield a sword from him.

The guard sighed and looked down at the sparkling sand. "Very well, my lord."

Sprinting through the gate, Ziyad crouched, covering his face, and ran soundlessly around to the side of the house that faced the ocean. Her balcony was softly glowing in torches with citrus oil in them to keep the bugs away. He could smell them from where he crouched in the garden. She always smelled of citrus and the vanilla plant. The tall tree he had planted when he built the house for her was still there, just grazing the white railing around the balcony.

With a short running start, he leapt up and began to climb the slender tree using his hands and feet. His right hand pulsed as the bark irritated the wounds on his palm and fingers. Pushing through the pain, he climbed up and peeked over the railing.

Reza was sitting just inside the white silk curtains, brushing her hair, wearing only a cotton robe over her bronze figure. She was facing the mirror before her but wasn't really looking. Her eyes were glassed over and a slight crease rested between her elegant brows. He smiled. It was just as fiery the first time he had seen her, when he was a boy and she was locked away in her father's house. He had to build Moshav from the ground up, win civil battles, and make himself a lord before the man even thought to let Reza see him. But what her father hadn't known was they spent many nights in each other's arms before he consented to let them marry.

He pulled himself up onto the balcony, scanning for anyone else. No one, not even a handmaid, was present. He leaned up against the wall, took a breath, and spied around the corner. Reza stood up, her legs visible and bare shoulders soft over the cotton. Ziyad sighed and prayed. Her body always made him lose control. But now he saw her differently. She had been touched by another. He needed to remove those caresses. Those kisses.

He slipped into the white silk and stood just over her shoulder in the mirror. Reza saw the black shape and gasped, standing up, pulling the robe closed.

"What do you want?" she cried, fear closing her throat. "I'll scream and my husband—"

"Inaam will do nothing," Ziyad said, removing the covering from his face. "Because your husband is here."

"Ziyad." She exhaled sharply.

He strode cautiously to her. When she didn't back away, he took her wrist in his hand and pulled her hips against his. Her breath panted against his face. Her eyes whipped back and forth between his. They were no longer innocent as he remembered them. They were sharp, cunning, dangerous. He liked it and pulled her into a deep kiss. She returned the kisses fervently, their breath intermingling as they desperately fell into each other's arms.

The passion came and he picked her up, dropping her onto the bed they once shared. She gasped for air as he ripped his robes off and untied the sash around his waist.

As he ran his fingers over her skin, he knew Inaam had touched her. He kissed her neck, shoulders, face—everywhere he could to remove any affection left behind by Inaam. He needed her to forget him.

***

They lay together, wrapped in the white silk—the huge, orange moon visible outside the balcony where the torches had gone out. He pulled her harder against him in the glow and inhaled the scent of her deeper. It had been just as he remembered. The night before he had left, they had stayed together from dusk till dawn and the sands turned orange, heralding his departure.

"Come with me, Reza," he whispered, his voice dry and husky after their ferocious, overdue lovemaking. "Leave him. If he wants to be lord of Moshav, he can be."

She traced his jawline slowly, making the hair on his arms stand up. "Can you leave? Walk out on Moshav, leave it all behind? Not take back what was stolen from a man you hate? Is this something you can do?"

Never.

He took a steadying breath and looked over her at the moon. She always had to make things more complicated. "I need you to leave. To be safe."

"You will keep me safe." Her voice was dewy, sweet.

Ziyad pushed away, up onto his elbows now, meeting her eyes. "I cannot promise that. I am coming with an army tomorrow. You are right. I cannot just leave, letting him take what is mine. No matter how much the people love him, he is a thief."

Reza pushed herself up, modesty suddenly overcoming her as she clutched the silk to her chest. "He is a good man, Ziyad. Just because you do not agree with how he chooses to provide for Moshav. He has done much good."

"Did I not as well?" His voice strained to shout but he knew he had to keep quiet. "Was I a bad man?"

Her brown eyes simpered innocently. "No. You were a good man." She laid her hand on his bare chest. "But…you are different now. I need you to see that."

He stood up. She was under Inaam's spell. He could never make her understand, but maybe she could see. Taking up his robes, he dressed quickly. "I am attacking Moshav with an army. I have found a tribe of Porshians."

Reza gasped. "Ziyad, they are heretics!"

"I have made an oath with them." He wrapped his sword on.

"What have you promised them?" Her voice quivered.

He looked around for his last boot. "Nothing. A trifle. The first thing that comes from my house upon our victory." He fixed her with a hard gaze. "You see why I need you to leave."

She breathed a curse into the cool night, almost glaring at him. "What has the war done to you?"

The last boot slipped on with a great force. He growled and made his way to the balcony and the tree. "Promise me. Sahir will be with me. Leave tonight."

There she was, an amber jewel among white silk, quivering in the orange moonlight. "I promise," she whispered.

***

Tarkan's mutant blue eyes did not leave the back of Ziyad's head as they waited in the twilight. The sun rose a vicious pink and the sky was still a dark purple.

"Will you stay back?" he asked.

"No," Ziyad replied without hesitation.

Tarkan's brows twitched in amusement. "You attack your own home? A most intriguing man."

Ziyad bent his bow, knocking the string. "You are not a soothsayer, Tarkan. Do not speak as one." He glanced over his shoulder at the now empty wagon. Dozens of corpses littered the dark sands. "Is this enough?"

The necromancer smiled sardonically. "Your village is not so large. And my warriors cannot die. They do not mind an arrow to the eye. Or a missing leg."

Ziyad remembered that. He had seen one take an arrow all the way through the eye and out the back of its aging skull. This hadn't stopped it then and he hoped this wouldn't stop it now.

The other three had been chanting for near an hour. Tarkan had said the ritual was long. They had used a kind of sacred blade to draw blood from each of them, mingling their blood in the fire. He had turned away, unwilling to watch a heretical ritual. Soon, the sound of dozens of feet shifting in the sand came to him.

"You may lead my army," Tarkan said slowly. "They will not harm you or your son. But I cannot guarantee your protection."

"You only promised me an army," Ziyad sneered. "You have delivered."

Sahir spoke up now. "They will hate you, father. Perhaps we should stay back."

No. Inaam was going to die by his blade alone. "Do not touch that man who took your mother," he instructed Sahir. "If you find him, tell me. He is mine."

The sun struck a sharp blade of light across the sky, slashing over the sands.

"They have risen," Tarkan said. He kicked his black horse gently and began a trot towards Moshav. He covered his face so just his blue eyes glinted above the black coverings. He turned his icy eyes to Ziyad who met them. "Best of fortune in your battle, Ziyad."

With Ziyad in the lead, Sahir, Tarkan, and the others marched towards Moshav. The three necromancers split up at an angle, reaching out with their magic to control the undead horde. They stopped on the dunes overlooking Moshav.

Ziyad took out his curved sword. "Make them run!" he screamed.

With a terrifying, guttural cry, he led the mass of undead down the dune at a terrifying gallop. He could see as he approached, the people running in terror, crying out, ringing the village bell. They broke into the village perimeter easily, the dead soldiers doing their duty, ripping, tearing, killing. The mix of hot sand and blood gave off a familiar iron-forge scent.

Ziyad did his part too, not wanting his sword to go unbloodied before he plunged it into Inaam.

"My lord Ziyad!" one man screamed when he recognised his once lord.

With a swift and unforgiving thrust, Ziyad stabbed the man with one sword then lopped his head off with the curve of the other. The violence was familiar, making him feel safe and in control.

He scanned the pathway that led to his home. That was where Inaam would come from. Beside him, Sahir lobbed a spear with admirable strength into the skull of a temple guard.

It was an ill-balanced fight. The people of Moshav fell to the undead army easily, confused and frightened of Ziyad and his son. It was true what they said: it is far more easily to be killed by someone known than a stranger. They didn't run. They cried, confused, standing their ground.

"Ziyad, you blasphemers!" a strong, high voice rang out. "You slaughter your own people, desecrate your own temple. For vengeance on me?"

Turning, Ziyad saw the man he had been waiting for. Inaam came for a fight: he wore golden armour, wrapped in red silks on a white horse: Moshav's hero.

"I was beginning to think you wouldn't come," he shouted to Inaam.

He kicked his horse in the side and galloped up to meet the man. He didn't wait to strike but Inaam was ready. He swung with his curved sword and Inaam parried the blow. With Ziyad slipping past on the horse, Inaam made a daring stab with a dagger he had up his sleeve.

A sharp pain touched Ziyad's side and his robes stuck to him. Turning his horse, he saw Inaam had gotten him with the little blade.

Leaping off the cumbersome horse, Ziyad shouted, "Fight me with your feet on the ground. No!" he shouted when Sahir charged up on his own horse. "Stay back, my son."

Inaam leapt lightly off the horse and twirled his sword to relax his grip. "That's right, Sahir, let the soldier spill the blood of his people alone."

They circled each other, each one weighing the other. Ziyad had to find an opening in the armour. He had none. But Inaam was right: he was a soldier. A fighter. If he came at Inaam from above, he'd raise at least one arm to block the blow. But that would leave Ziyad's unarmoured middle open to a stab. He was faster though.

They spun, swords sparking as they blocked, stabbed, slashed. The people gave them a wide berth. Ziyad worked his way in circles around Inaam, judging his reactions and speed. Without knowing it, they clashed their way close to his home's gates. The sandy pillars on either side presented themselves and Ziyad was backed into them. It was a risk…

Inaam kicked one sword from Ziyad's hand and stabbed with his. Seeing this, Ziyad ran the last two steps to the pillar, took three steps up it, and flipped behind Inaam. He saw his opponent turn to greet him on his landing and pulled a knife from his ankle. Spending just one second longer in a crouching position when he landed, he dodged Inaam's initial attack, rose, and put the blade through his eye socket.

The people didn't scream yet, too shocked at the speed with which their lord was killed. Panting, Ziyad turned to face the frightened people. Too soon, he realised, when he felt Inaam fall into him and a sharp pain plunged into his mid back. When he turned, the man was dead but he had gotten one last attack in.

"Father!" Sahir cried, running to him. "A healer, please!"

A man in white robes came forward but was blocked by the formidable form of Tarkan and his three necromancers.

"Call your wife," he said softly.

Looking to his house, even in his pain, he could see Reza in the doorway. She had not left. She had lied. But something else caught his eye. Beside his wife was a small girl of about five. She had her mother's hair but his fierce eyes.

"Zeva?" Sahir breathed. "Sister?"

Remembering Sahir mentioning the sister he had lost during his absence, Ziyad's heart rose. This was her. Reza was smiling, tears in her eyes as she nodded.

"I'm sorry, I lied." Her eyes went to Inaam. "He told me that…" But she couldn't finish. Her voice broke and she wept. "Do you want to see your daughter, Ziyad?"

Struggling to stand and Sahir helping him, he rose to his feet. Around him, all of Moshav waited to hear what their reinstated lord would do. Some whispered for forgiveness. Some spoke pledges to support him again. Others confessed that Inaam had promised them too much to turn away. Realising he had done it, he motioned Zeva to come to him.

He had slaughtered the man, overtaken the village, and ruined his people's places of worship. He had won.

Cautious, Zeva took a few steps towards Ziyad.

"Where has she been this whole time?" Sahir asked his mother. "Why did you hide her?"

"With a family," was all Reza whispered, fresh tears spilling down her cheeks.

Before Zeva made it out of the gates, a swirling of black robes intercepted her. She screamed as Tarkan grabbed her arm, pulling her from the path to her home.

"Leave my daughter be!" Ziyad shouted, brandishing Sahir's sword.

Tarkan smiled slowly. "You took an oath, my lord. That which is first from your door shall be mine." He raised his other hand where his rings still glowed vibrant red with his blood. "You cannot break this oath."

There was no way to attack the necromancer. His undead army was around him and Ziyad had witnessed twice their devastation to Moshav.

"Tarkan, please!" he begged.

The necromancer turned his icy eyes onto the wounded lord. "If you follow me, I will kill you, raise you up, and force you to kill your son." He smiled at Sahir. "Consider the oath fulfilled. Enjoy your seat as lord."

Mounting their horses, the necromancers galloped into the dunes, Zeva screaming, and their undead army in their wake.

ABIGAIL LINHARDT has been a gamer all her life but is a teacher at heart. When she is not writing, you can find her slaying enemies online or teaching in a college classroom. She has published works of fiction, poetry, college essays, and even won two literary awards for her short stories in science fiction and horror. Abi lives and writes in the sunflower state of Kansas where she is a proud mother of ferrets.

Bibliography
Apocalypse, Black Hare Press, 2019
Autom's Grandfather, Upliterate, 2017
Clockwork Dragons, Zombie Pirate Publishing, 2020
Coffins and Dragons, Dragon Soul Press, 2019
Lost Love, Dragon Soul Press, 2020
Old Family Recipe and D.E.F, From the Writer's Kitchen, 2014
Revary, Dragon Soul Press, 2019
Season of the Runer: The Trial of Two, SummerStorm Press, 2020
The Inspector's Last letter, Mind's Eye, 2009
These Darker Streets, Dragon Soul Press, 2020
The Camelot Project, Dragon Soul press, 2020
Unravel, Black Hare Press, 2019

Connect:
Website: abigaillinhardt.com
Facebook: https://www.facebook.com/abilinhardt
Twitch: twitch.tv/promthanius
instagram: @promthanius

BEYOND THE REALM

THE LAST DRAGONRIDER

By Raven Corrin Carluk

Princess Cailleach and her dragon, Zarryn, hunt for an ancient sword that will grant them the power to overthrow the Empire, setting the enslaved races free.

"You think this is the one?" I looked up from the map to glare at the nameless swamp. Skeletal trees clawed up from the fetid waters, sharp hills creating a hard border between life and death. Grey clouds loomed overhead, but I doubted there'd be much life even on a sunny day. The closest village was a half-day's ride away, and nothing but scrubby brushes and sparse grass grew between us and the unnamed swamp.

Zarryn rumbled low in his throat, claws digging into the turf beside me. I was tall, like all Tuatha, but the black dragon always made me feel small and frail. One fore talon was nearly as long as I was tall, his body larger than a barn, and wingspan twice his length. His clan were all long, lean, with spiralled horns and spikes; their nimble strength used for stealth attacks.

The dragon's head wove back and forth as he scanned the landscape. *You didn't expect it to actually be called Swamp of Doom, did you? Sword of Ultimate Power This Way?* His mental voice was sharp and sarcastic, as were most of his sendings. He'd served in many campaigns before eating his last commander and being sent to the gladiator pits, from which I rescued him. He didn't hide his contempt for the world anymore, nor did I expect him too. We had much in common.

I smirked, rolling up the vellum and sliding it back into its carrying case. I didn't worry about Zarryn trying to eat me, because I never *demanded* he risk his life for something foolish. "Thank you for your thoughtful insight. As astute as always." I attempted to hide my humour behind my sharp retort, but our connection made hiding anything from each other near impossible.

The obsidian dragon rumbled again. *Is that not why my Princess Cailleach picked me over all others?*

He shifted to loom over me, wings spread wide, then tipped his spiked head to stare at me with one jewel-like eye. Humour tinged our connection. *Or was your cousin right, and it's just because I match your hair?*

"Still not letting that go, are you?" I met his gaze with my shoulders back and spine straight, though my bitterness was directed at the catty women of my family, at the weak men they married.

The Tuatha had created a vast empire from the backs of dragons, then fell into decadence, and neared collapse. The empire still held dragon slaves, forced them to battle in gladiator pits, threw their lives away in pointless wars, and treated them as pets. There was no respect for the mighty people, nor for any whom chose to ride them anymore.

They'd show respect once I reclaimed Heartflame.

Zarryn turned his snout to deliver a short blast of air. His spicy breath enveloped me, eased my tension. *Only because it irks you so. I wouldn't be your loyal companion if I let you lose that passion for this quest.* Then he lowered himself, extending his foreleg for me to mount.

I grabbed the harness and stepped onto his leg, though I didn't climb fully into the saddle. I stared off across the swamp, leaning against the thick scales of his shoulder. "There's no guarantee the sword is here.

There's every possibility that it's just another clue sending us somewhere even more remote." With a sigh, I finished climbing into the thin saddle, settling my riding leathers and goggles.

The dragon rose, spread his legs, but did not launch himself into the sky. He snaked his head around to look at me with both eyes, wings spread out at his side. *I never expected that freeing my people from slavery would be easy. Did you? I will carry you as far as possible to get that fucking sword.* Muscles bunched as he straightened his neck then leapt to the air.

Zarryn was right. We quested for more than just a family heirloom that had become misplaced. Heartflame was one of a dozen celestial swords, crafted in a previous age by aspects of the gods themselves. Each one had untold powers, god-like in their own way.

The Tuatha had used the great sword to enslave multiple races, including the dragons, and only I knew that the Emperor no longer had it.

I stroked one of the scars on Zarryn's neck, other hand loose on the harness. I rode in the old way, with neither reins nor muzzle, only a thin saddle to protect me from sharp scales, and simple rigging to hold onto during quick manoeuvres. I showed him respect by giving him his head and leaving his forepaws unbound, offered my trust that he wouldn't eat or impale me.

Quartering the swamp for signs of the temple would take some time, and I let my thoughts wander as my eyes wandered the approaching terrain. We had a righteous mission to fulfil and would do anything to succeed.

Before here, we'd been to the Eversong Forest. The fae and dryads had resentfully helped a Tuathan princess and her dragon. I was certain they'd feared me more than Zarryn. When my ancestors had conquered in the previous millennia, the tactics had been so brutal that few were willing to risk our wrath, even generations later.

We'd been at the Southern Seeress before then, the Library of the Keepers before her. A dozen stops in the last five years, hunting for the tiniest scraps of information. Anything that could lead us to the real Heartflame, not the replica the Emperor wore.

Zarryn growled beneath me, echoing my frustration. I stroked the scar again, calming myself. The closer I got to the sword, the more easily it frustrated me. Impatience was not a desirable trait when hunting a legendary item of such enormous power.

We'll get it. Zarryn growled again, and the sound rumbled through my body the way his presence rolled against my mind. *And if we die, remember this was all your idea.*

I chuckled, frustration fading to a manageable level. We flew low enough that my voice wouldn't whip away when I spoke. I wasn't a strong telepath, even with our bond. "Neither of us said this was a good idea." He rumbled a laugh of his own.

He crossed the border into the swamp and my stomach plunged. Zarryn roared, wings buckling, and we fell from the sky.

"Zarr?!" I clung to the harness. Would I need to use my powers to soften the blow? The dragon was a lot of mass for me to account for, and the ground was rushing towards us.

I think…trying to…hold on long— He snarled and strained, head up and wings stretched out, but I heard the weakness in his voice. We were going down, might be lucky to hit a mossy hummock and not one of the enormous trees.

Closing my eyes, I summoned magic to me. The wind screamed in my ears, trying to distract me, but I focused on my task. Needed to slow us down, soften the blow, prevent Zarryn from breaking his wings. Dragonriders were expected to perform this kind of emergency spell, but it wasn't something that could really be practised.

The spell wouldn't respond, as though there wasn't

enough power in the air. I sensed the rough makings of a magical cushion, but we fell too fast. It wouldn't hold our weight. I tried not to tense up, needing to roll when we hit. There wasn't even time to feel fear.

Zarryn shrieked just before impact.

I was thrown from the saddle onto a dry patch of land, then rolled into a mossy log, where the wind was knocked from my lungs. Water splashed across me, into my gasping mouth, and down my throat. I shifted onto my side, stars in my eyes, and gagged, still unable to draw breath.

The first waves of pain spiked across my nerves, adding to the building panic. My lungs didn't want to work, my eyes wouldn't open, and my thoughts spun in maddening circles. If I wasn't dead, it might be better if I was.

My training took over, and I stilled my mind. Push aside the panic, ignore the pain, and relax my struggles. Don't fight to breathe, just let my lungs reset themselves. This *was* something I'd practised with my weapons master, though I'd yet to need it on our quest. Another heartbeat passed before I was once more in control.

I stretched onto my back, drew a deep breath, and opened my eyes. I was definitely alive. Nothing seemed broken, despite the burning ache in my spine.

The spell had cushioned my fall just enough for survival.

But how had Zarryn fared? Our connection was still there, thus he was alive. I sat up, unable to tell anything else about his current condition.

Zarryn knelt nearby in his elven form.

I stared, speechless, and slumped my shoulders. My head rang, spun. This had to be a hallucination brought on by the trauma. The dragon hadn't shifted forms since I'd purchased him and set him free. No dragon wanted to be anything but themselves, though they could take a bipedal form when ordered to by their slave masters.

He groaned, one hand to his forehead, one to his shoulder, and managed to look at me. The same uplifted eyes I remembered, the same missing ear point and scars, the same suede armour. His frown softened, then became a smile. "Could have been worse."

I laughed. A tiny noise at first, disbelieving, then a full peal, and finally great gales of laughter. Leave it to my sardonic companion to downplay what could have been a devastating crash.

Zarryn rose to his feet, slow and careful, and closed the distance between us. "How is my Cailleach?" He offered me a hand up.

I allowed him to help me to my feet, and I took a

moment to stare at him. He was only a handspan taller than myself in his elven form, with alabaster skin and unkempt raven's wing hair, and solid black eyes. All dragons preferred an elven form; elves were our smaller cousins; thus, they could look like a Tuatha without showing disrespect.

"What happened?" I finally asked. My back hurt, but the pain was already fading now that I was on my feet. The bond with the dragon buzzed, and I probed it mentally as best I could. Something felt off, but I couldn't figure it out.

Zarryn released my hand, wiping mud and debris from his armour. Thin and strong, same as his scales. "There was a force. A barrier. We crossed over it and all the power was sucked right out of me. I couldn't prevent the change, though I held it off as best I could." He sighed, more like a growl, and clenched his fists. "It's like wearing that damn necklace again."

A chill passed through me. Tuathan mages had long ago laid spells upon crystal pendants to lock dragons into their elven forms. The second thing I'd done upon taking Zarryn as my own was to destroy his. "So, you're stuck like this?"

He did growl then, turning away from me. "It would appear so." I knew he'd lash his tail with agitation if he could. Instead, he kicked something into the closest pool of water.

I gave him a moment to himself while I looked over our gear. Saddlebags and harness had tangled amongst the brush, and the map roll rested at the base of a dead tree. Best to gather them while I figured out a plan.

Zarryn joined me after only a brief time, stooping for the saddle. He said nothing, jaw clenched, focused on working. Without being asked to, he gathered everything to the highest dry land nearby.

On the strength of his silent intent, we soon had all our gear in a neat pile atop the hill. "Everything seems to be here," I said, kneeling by one of the saddlebags. "Though I think the food's ruined." Pulling out one of the oiled wraps, I shook off swamp water. "And we only have the one sword."

Zarryn stood close by my side, less obviously angry, though our connection still buzzed in the back of my head. Whatever trapped him as an elf must be affecting that as well. "We'll manage without it, though I think you need to draw yours. The natives have come to check on us."

I rose, hand on the hilt of my sword, though I didn't draw it yet. I followed the direction of his gaze, spotting the approaching figures immediately. Short, small, covered in moss and twigs, they looked like some variant of water goblin to me.

The lead goblin gave a shrill cry, then the pack charged us.

My blade sang free of the scabbard and I took up a defensive stance. Zarr did the same thing, but with bare hands crooked like talons. I trusted his ability to fight weaponless, though a lash or two of his tail could crush the approaching goblins with minimal effort.

Several of them threw tiny spears, which we easily dodged. More of them gave shrill cries, and the first reached us. I thrust and slashed, killing two, then kicked a third away from us. The goblins jabbed with crude weapons, mostly pointy sticks, none of them strong enough to pierce my reinforced riding leathers.

Zarryn kicked one, then grabbed another and bashed the little thing into the remaining goblins. Cries went up from our tiny foes, and they attempted to surround the dragon. He broke the neck of the squirming goblin before continuing to batter its friends with the corpse. Being locked out of his native form didn't seem to slow the warrior down.

Between my sword work and his creative brutality, we made short work of a score of water goblins, taking no damage to ourselves. The attack was more annoying than dangerous, but that didn't mean I wanted to spend our entire search facing more of them. I said as much while I cleaned my sword.

"Sorry to hear that," Zarryn said, kicking corpses into the water.

"Why?" I asked, voice tight, glaring at him. I knew he wanted to say more, but he wanted me to draw it out of him.

The dragon pointed towards a nearby hill. "They came from that direction." I nodded, narrowing my eyes. "I'm pretty sure that's a building of some kind." I rose, hands on my hips. "It looked temple-like when I was still airborne."

I looked at the hill in question, noting details. It wasn't round like a natural hummock and was both taller and broader than most of the surrounding hills. Neither trees nor bushes grew on it, only moss and wispy grasses. There was a black cave on the near side that looked squarer than any natural formation should.

"Could it really be this close to the border?" I asked, turning to look back the way we'd come. Further words died as I stared at the mountains on the distant horizon. Zarryn swore, scanning our surroundings as I did. From the outside, the unnamed swamp had been no more than a few hours of flying across, the hills sharp but not tall.

From here, craggy mountains scraped the bellies of the clouds, and it would take most of a day to fly to them. "Might be safe to say we're in the right swamp," the dragon finally said.

I shifted the sheath on my hip, drew my shoulders back, and looked at what we hoped to be the temple. "Nothing for it but to go inside," I said.

Zarryn started towards the cave, leaving our stuff in piles on the hill. I snatched up the map tube and tucked it into the back of my belt, then followed. Everything else could wait until we returned and figured out how we were getting out of here.

If Heartflame were inside, I'd have more than enough power for us to leave.

Foul-smelling mud sucked at our boots, even when we avoided the deepest pools. There were no insects, though the stench was nearly as annoying. Brushes snagged at us, grasses cut at us, and every step took far more effort than it should have. By the time we got to the entrance, I had to stop and rest. Zarryn said nothing, but he certainly didn't complain while standing beside the black hole.

"It smells like goblin," the dragon said, touching the stone lintel. Mud and moss had disguised the original shape and decorations, piling up around the base. There was no judging how long the temple had been sinking into the swamp, but I would have believed centuries.

"Surprisingly better than out here." I knelt beside him, peering into the darkness. There was the suggestion of stairs, but mud and debris had turned it into a messy ramp. Though the ceiling was not as tall as a Tuathan, at least it wasn't goblin sized. I didn't look forward to slogging through even more muck, but thankfully we wouldn't be crawling.

Zarryn stepped inside, one hand on the wall as he tested his footing. "What was that cryptic thing the soothsayer said to you?" He glanced back at me, eyes sparkling in the shadows. A splash of goblin blood stained his forehead, dried green beside black flecks of swamp dirt.

"My fae language skills are a little lacking. Something about a warren and desires." I tried not to let excitement rise. She could have been telling a prophecy, or she could have been cursing my people for eternity. "Nothing we should be taking literally."

"Of course not. Not when we're about to make our way into underground tunnels after the sword that could change the course of history. Shouldn't give them any serious thought." He smirked, gesturing into the dark. "Would you like to lead the way, Princess?"

I glared and pulled a light crystal from a pouch on my belt. Crystal in one hand, sword in the other, I led the way down. I had to stoop slightly to fit beneath the ceiling and wasn't surprised to find Zarryn awkwardly crouching. He simply shook his head, daring me to say anything. I studied the walls, ignoring his discomfort.

Time and goblins had removed all pigments from the stones, worn most of the carvings away. Roots dangled between seams, snagging at my hair, and sickly moss clung wherever it could. The stench grew stronger as the air grew more humid, until I could taste goblin filth on every breath.

We continued for at least a quarter of an hour, mostly downwards with a few level spaces, but no branches. Zarryn cursed and grumbled after a while, and I gained several scratches from overzealous roots. My legs began to burn, and I was ready for a break when the dragon laid a hand on my shoulder.

"Stow the crystal," he whispered in my ear, looming close behind me. His presence wrapped around me like wings, protective, and I went immediately on guard. Slipping the crystal back into its pouch, I tightened my grip on the sword and listened for whatever had spooked my companion.

Warm orange light outlined the end of the tunnel.

Zarryn pushed past me, shoulders stiff despite his crouch. I followed close behind, listening for more goblins. This narrow hallway would favour them, but perhaps we could get into the chamber below before they attacked.

There was no attack.

We stepped out of the tunnel into ankle-deep water and an empty room. I frowned, examining everything, and Zarryn stood on guard before me, the faintest growl rumbling in his chest. Somehow that noise from elven vocal cords was more intense than his normal one.

A vaulted ceiling was lost to shadows and straggly roots, high overhead. Branches of dead trees formed goblin lean-tos throughout the space, mounds of mud and leaves peeking above the water level at various locations. Moss covered the walls of what I assumed to be the main worship hall, reflecting the orange flames on the altar.

I gasped to behold the altar. My blood chilled, and I let my sword dip into the water. The longer I looked, the more my nerves hummed with power, the more I wanted to cross the chamber and claim the sword.

Heartflame hung suspended amidst magical flames.

The dragon pressed a restraining arm against me when I stepped forward. His touch brought me out of my daze, made me question what I'd been about to do. "Something's here," he warned, voice low, eyes scanning the entirety of the chapel. Nothing moved, but he had senses designed for the hunt, for finding the unseen.

Several heartbeats passed and nothing happened. Heartflame pulsed, calling to me on a soul-deep level, though it didn't put me in the same trance as before. I wanted to hold it, and it very much wanted me to hold it. Wield it. Carve my name into the flesh of history.

"I'm going for it," I told Zarryn. We could handle whatever guardian waited for us. Better to fight them than cower with our goal so close.

I stepped around the dragon and the water came alive.

Zarryn yanked me behind him, standing between me and the surging swamp. Waves pulled at our feet, threatening to steal our balance, then surged towards the centre, carrying debris with it. Magic pulsed in the air, sour on the back of my tongue.

Before our eyes, a swamp golem formed. Branches became the skeleton, mud and muck the muscles, and leaves the armoured skin. Fetid water puddled around its stocky feet and filled out its form.

It reminded me of a simian, though with no mouth, and a scorpion tail made of goblin bones. Although it was the size of a hut, it had room still to manoeuvre. The first thing the golem did was impose itself between us and Heartflame.

"We're going to need to work together," I said

lowly, staring at the golem. The control glyph pulsed on its forehead, surrounded by a wall of thorns and brambles. Watery eyes watched us, the magical creature weaving back and forth as our standoff continued. "I need to get to its head."

Zarryn growled, fingers crooked at his side, feet braced but prepared to move. Our connection hummed and burned, still somehow blocked yet tighter than ever. I sensed his readiness, felt his muscles tremble with need, but had almost nothing of his actual thoughts. "What do you need, my princess?"

The golem charged forward, wooden limbs clattering against the stone floor. We dodged right, moving as one, and its tail snapped towards us, forcing us apart.

Zarryn ripped several bones free of the tail, and murky water splashed him in the face. It turned on him, and I rushed behind it, looking for a way up to its back. "Keep it distracted!"

I sheathed my sword, eyes constantly scanning. The weapon wouldn't do me any good against this creation, was only an unnecessary burden when I needed my hands free. It shifted, and I grabbed its back leg to begin my climb.

Slimy leaves clung to my hands and feet, hampering my movements. Thorns pricked at my skin, trying to work beneath my armour, and I swore. Tuathans practised sorcery and necromancy, not alchemy and wizardry. If the Emperor had purposely hid Heartflame here, he would have needed someone else to cast the ritual to give the golem life. Our people would have left an elemental as guardian, or some other creature of more chaotic origin.

I understood, then, why a golem had been placed to protect the sword.

An elemental, I could have dealt with. Even a djinn, or a bevy of demons. My magic was not the strongest, but at least they would have been in the same sphere. We'd have been on level ground, able to bargain and communicate, instead of me clambering up a back leg in desperate hope of reaching the control glyph.

The golem didn't appreciate my efforts. Swamp water sloshed at my face, trying to clog my mouth and sinuses. Leaves and slime pulsed beneath my hands, loosening my grip, and the entire creature thrashed as it attempted to dislodge me.

Zarryn shouted something I couldn't hear, but I felt his rage. He wanted to set it afire, use his real strength, but all he could do was pull ineffectually at the debris that formed the golem in an attempt to give me an opening. He dodged heavy blows and shouted again, keeping its attention as best he could.

I cried out when the tail slammed into my left shoulder blade. The point managed to penetrate my armour and cut flesh, just barely, but the force of the blow was more than enough to dislodge me. A whip of the tail and a shake of its leg, and I went flying against a mossy wall. It didn't hurt, but stars danced in my vision.

The dragon's fury filled my senses, adding to the disorientation I suffered. I couldn't let him fight alone, but I couldn't get my eyes open yet. There was still no pain, though I'm sure there would be.

I drew a deep breath, gathering every string of magical energy I could. Zarryn's anger added to the meagre amount, though it buzzed against my control like a hive of furious hornets. I soon had a glowing ball of force awaiting my commands. Opening my eyes, I saw my target and unleashed the power.

The golem didn't see it coming, was unable to dodge as the mage bolt flew through the air and hit the ground at its feet. Light pulsed silently, blinding, throwing a shockwave across the chamber. Heat washed over me, then various swamp debris, and I heard the golem land on its side.

Not waiting for my vision to recover from the magical flare, I rose to my feet and stumbled towards our fallen foe. It surely wouldn't stay on its side long, wouldn't let me walk up and simply wipe its glyph out.

I blinked the last of the blurriness away, just in time to avoid the lashing tail. Muddy rocks robbed me of my balance, and my dodge turned into a fall. I rolled away from another strike, heart in my throat, and stopped just before a back foot caught me in the face.

"Keep doing that," Zarryn shouted. "I'm almost there."

So long as the golem was stopped, it didn't matter which of us destroyed the glyph. I jumped to my feet, drew my sword, and stabbed at the closest limb. There was no hurting it, but I only needed it to think I was trying, that it had to defend against me.

The golem thrashed, kicking at me. I dodged both feet and the tail, attempting to gather strands of magic to me. Another burst of power would help, would keep the golem from regaining its feet. There wasn't much, but I threw another blast at it, closing my eyes against the flare.

Zarryn gave a triumphant cry. The golem flailed a final time, then collapsed in a pile of debris. Water gushed across the floor, knocking me to my knees, but my sense of elation was too great to care. "Are you alright?" I called, regaining my feet.

The dragon stepped around the former golem.

Muck covered his armour, blood ran down his face, and his hair dripped with water. Despite the signs of combat and his wounds, Zarryn grinned, revealing sharp teeth and immense pleasure. "Hale and whole, verily. How be you?"

I didn't need our connection to tell me how pleased he was. The dragon only spoke with such strange cadence when he rode high on massive success. In another person, I might call it giddy. "Just fine." I sheathed my mundane sword and turned towards the magical one.

"You bleed." He sloshed closer, concerned.

"I'll be alright. I've had worse…" My voice softened, trailed off as I stared at Heartflame. I felt neither pain nor triumph, only a rising heat that pulsed in time with the sword. I took a faltering step, then another, hand extended towards the magical blade.

Zarryn stood behind me, touched my wounded shoulder. His concern overrode his high spirits. "Maybe it should wait until we get you patched up. Might not even be the one."

"It's the one." I took another step, barely aware of speaking. Couldn't be certain I'd actually said the words out loud. Another step, and I was awash in power.

The dragon said something to me, but all I heard was the low humming of Heartflame. It longed to be used, to cut and kill and slay, and would give me more strength than I could imagined if I would but pick it up. Heartflame promised to give me an empire.

My hand slipped over the pommel, down the hilt, and settled against the cross guard, all in one loving caress. I moaned to myself, and Heartflame moaned in response. Warm like a lover, like a fever. Soft like silk, light as silver. It rang with a chiming note, and my soul replied.

Power arced up my arm, wringing a cry from me as pain ate at my nerves. My hand clenched tighter around the hilt, though part of me wanted to let go. But if I let go now, I'd never get another chance. I held tighter, refusing to let go.

The bonding continued, moving faster now that I'd passed yet another test. I had the strength to wield it, proven with the golem's defeat. I had the will to wield it, proven when I continued through the electric wards on the hilt. Did I have the heart to wield it though?

Flurries of images crossed before my inner eye, giving me a history of the sword: its birth, its life, its murders, and its triumphs. It wanted me to know more and more about it, and all I could do was open myself to the tumult, give myself over to it.

Epiphany struck. *Not* a neutral, inanimate object. A living being with a semblance of sentience. She lived and desired and hated and loved, but she needed a companion to do so. Everything I experienced, she would as well.

A single cry rose from my aching lungs, a long note that echoed through the world and beyond. The very walls of the temple rattled with the sound, and I opened my eyes to a much brighter world.

I saw flows of energy, but like bright afterimages, sensed more than seen. I tasted life and death, growth, and decay. Felt the tides and the stars and the clouds and the wind and the rain. Everything moved around me, through me, and I moved through and around everything.

Zarryn whispered my name, but I didn't respond at first. "Princess Cailleach?" he said louder. I looked at him as if from a great distance, unsure of what I saw, then everything came sharply into focus.

The dragon knelt before me, my sword reflected in his inky eyes, his expression deeply awestruck. Scars and wounds stood out on his silvery skin—the finest detailing of scales highlighted by Heartflame. Dirty, bloody, fierce, loyal. He watched me closely, waiting to enact my commands.

I grinned, a crooked twisting of my lips, and offered him my free hand. "Shall we depose an emperor?"

He laid his hand in mine and rose, a feral grin of his own forming. "I thought you'd never ask." He longed for battle almost as much as he longed for the freedom of his people. "But I'll need to rest before I return us home."

Heartflame pulsed in my grip, and an idea formed. An understanding of what she would allow me to do, the magic she possessed. I glanced down at her, then back to the dragon. "We don't need to fly. *I* can take us home."

Zarryn quirked one brow, grin fading. "Just like that? Cut straight to the end?"

She moaned, pulsing through my entire body. I sighed and shifted, riding the wave of energetic bonding. She was as hungry for conquest as I, restless and tired of being locked away from the world. "It would appear so."

The dragon drew his shoulders back, jaw set. "They'll never see us coming."

I closed my eyes and focused on the Emperor's throne room. The columns carved to look like naked bodies. The vaulted ceiling and stained glass windows. The polished floor and silk carpets. The courtiers, the guards, the servants.

The man himself.

Emperor Talasar. Lord of the Savage Isle. Master

of dragons, fae, and elves. Decadent, drugged, deranged. Warrior on the way to pot, charismatic and respected. Cruel and callous, hiding behind a facade of power, wearing a replica of Heartflame.

She was angered by his lie, disrupted my focus for a heartbeat. She had languished in her cradle for the last hundred and fifty years, with no partner, unused, while Tuathan emperors claimed power in her name. All of them unworthy. Liars. False gods.

Power surged from my core and through my sword. Zarryn swore, and I opened my eyes to find a glowing portal waiting beside us. Sounds came from within the golden light; the Emperor was holding evening court.

"It'll be crowded," Zarryn said.

"Mostly the fops and courtesans, the pleasure slaves. Few warriors." I faced the opening Heartflame had created for us. "Very few capable of stopping us."

Zarryn moved into position before me. "Many will come to our side once they see you." He glanced over his shoulder; eyes narrowed. "Are you ready for this?" I nodded, and he stepped through.

Heartflame pulsed once, then I stepped into the throne hall.

Voices dropped in volume at Zarryn's appearance. Complete silence fell when I appeared behind him. All eyes upon us, we stared back with hardness and determination. We were the exact opposite of everyone here, covered in dirt and blood, armed and armoured, ready to kill.

"Who are you?" Talasar shouted, leaning forward in his alabaster throne, but not bothering to stand. He wore the flimsiest of kilts, a golden torc, and an emerald in his left nipple. The Emperor had gained weight during the last five years; all signs of the warrior were lost beneath a layer of fat.

"I'm not surprised you don't remember me. I was presented when I came of age, then sent back into exile with the rest of my family." I stepped around Zarryn and lifted Heartflame. "But do you remember this?"

Gasps and murmurs travelled through the court. Guards stepped forward and courtiers stepped back, but no one did more than stare. Heartflame glowed with a suggestion of fire, drawing all attention to her.

Zarryn growled behind me, remaining in elven form. There was room for his true shape, but he would be hampered if he tried to fight. Better to wait until he absolutely needed to.

Talasar frowned, touched the hilt of the sword behind him. The replica Heartflame that kept the enslaved bound to an emperor that had no power over them. The entirety of the Tuathan empire had become a hollow shell, continuing its existence through habit instead of strength.

"Who *are* you?" he asked again, rising to his feet. He drew the fake sword, and a colourful riot of flames erupted along the blade, eliciting gasps and cheers from those closest to him. Several of the noble courtiers murmured, staring at me.

"Princess Cailleach of House Veron." I took another step towards the throne, Heartflame singing softly.

Guards closed in; spears levelled at my heart. Servants whispered excitedly, glancing at each other. Nobles let their gazes move between the Emperor and me, eager for the conflict to come. This wasn't the first time a member of House Veron had attempted to claim the throne, but it would be the last.

Talasar had no choice but to meet my unspoken challenge. Our eyes met as he descended from the throne, and I saw acceptance in them. He knew this would end one way.

Not that the Emperor was going to make it easy.

He gave a silent command and the guards lunged and thrust. I slashed with Heartflame, and she created a wave of force that halted the spears. I glared at Talasar. "Coward. Honourless rat." Sharp exclamations rose from the gathered; they were always hungry for violence, especially if lives were on the line.

Talasar was a fool and a fop, but he had still been a warrior in his younger years. He was taller than I, with more muscle, and combat magic I had no skill for. It would be a tough fight, but I couldn't let myself doubt when I was this close to the end.

Zarryn roared, his voice mutating as he transformed into his true form. Screams filled the hall, though his echoing cry was louder than most of them. The dragon's tail whipped through the air, knocking guards aside like they were made of paper.

Heartflame dropped her barrier so we could focus on the Emperor while Zarryn handled potential interlopers. I trusted the dragon to watch my back, closed everyone but Talasar out of my attention. Flames spouted from the dragon, engulfing men in sticky death. They screamed and I joined with Talasar.

Our blades clashed, flames danced together, and we glared at each other from close distance. His eyes had hardened for the fight, revealing nothing of his emotional state. I snarled and spat at the Emperor, letting all my anger and frustration rise to the surface.

He wasn't the worst of the Tuathan emperors, by far, but he was the current one. He was the monster in my path, the only one stopping me and Heartflame from acting upon our destiny. Talasar was cruel, decadent, shallow, and loveless. Quite deserving of death, especially when it would free multiple races from slavery.

I shoved him back, then took a swing. Talasar blocked my blow, took another step back, and attempted an attack of his own. Heartflame guided my moves, countering the Emperor and lashing out, drawing blood. She sang, encouraged me to let her take control, and I did.

My sword controlled the fight from then on, matching Talasar's moves, whispering to my subconscious where to put my feet, when to lean, how to make use of her skill. The fight became a dance of death that I was all too happy to participate in.

The Emperor and I traded blows, drew blood on each other, but showed no signs of advantage over the other. Heartflame could only do so much to enhance my skills, but it was enough to keep the fight even, allowing me to observe the rest of the fight from the corner of my eye.

Courtiers screamed as Zarryn dealt with the guards. Flames licked at rugs and hangings, filling the air with rancid smoke. Armed men entered the throne hall, bringing weapons effective against dragons with them. He roared, buffeted them with his wings, and lashed out with his tail.

I scored a massive blow, slicing deep into Talasar's left thigh. He grunted in pain, stumbling back, and barely fended off my follow-up attack. Blood poured freely down his leg and his emotionless facade began to crack. This wasn't just a fight to *the* death, but a fight to *his* death.

Pressing the advantage, I let my sword harry him with multiple quick attacks. Talasar moved slower with each flick of Heartflame, leaving more of himself open. We drove him back towards the throne, drawing blood a half dozen more times, a cry of triumph and rage rising from me.

Nobles fled the hall. Servants attacked the newly arrived guards. Flames grew higher, raising the temperature all around us, adding to the chaotic scene. Zarryn growled and snarled, attacking anyone of Tuathan blood, killing and maiming whomever he could reach.

Talasar stumbled on the lowest step of the dais, falling at the foot of the throne. I was upon him in a flash, Heartflame plunging into his chest. The Emperor gurgled, eyes wide, but couldn't lift his sword as I leaned on mine. The enchanted blade seemed to laugh as I drove her the rest of the way home, taking the Emperor's life.

It was over. As easy as that.

Unbelievable. After the years and struggles and all the worthless clues and hard living, it was finally over. I stared down into his face as the light left his eyes, and I simply couldn't believe it. Heartflame purred in my grip, happy for me, for us, but I still couldn't comprehend that it was finally over.

Zarryn bellowed a cry of triumph, long and loud, shaking the windows behind the throne. I pulled Heartflame free and turned to face the remains of the court. Blood and flames were everywhere. The courtiers that hadn't fled cowered in the corners and behind pillars. Slaves beat guards to death, feral in their exuberance.

Silence followed Zarryn's roar. I stood before the throne and watched as all eyes turned towards me. Their expressions varied between awe and fear, and all of them waited for me to speak.

I'd had years to plan this speech, but the words wouldn't come. Not in the heat of the moment, not with fresh blood dripping from my wounds and my sword. I opened my mouth and hoped to say the correct things.

"The Emperor is dead, and the policies of slavery and pointless wars with him." Cheers went up as I drew a breath. "I shall take the throne and the title. I will treat my people fairly." More cheers, and stunned murmurs from the nobles.

I settled onto the throne, and a sense of belonging washed over me. I laid Heartflame on my lap, and she sang happily. Courtiers moved forward, speaking my name. Zarryn tossed his head and trumpeted. I smiled at all of them and gave my first proclamation as Empress.

"The Tuathan Empire will spread farther than it ever has in history, but on the strength of free warriors. Join me of your own will, and we shall rule as never before."

Every voice lifted in howls of support. My reign was born of blood and fire.

BLACK HARE PRESS

RAVEN CORINN CARLUK writes dark fantasy, paranormal romance, and anything else that catches her interest.

She has authored and self-published five novels and one novella, where she explores themes of love and acceptance. She has also self-published two collections of short stories, ranging from the lustful to the horrific, the darkly humorous to the tragic. Her shorter pieces, usually from her darker side, can be found in several Black Hare Press anthologies, at Detritus Online, with Fantasia Divinity, and through Alban Lake Publishers.

Bibliography
All Hallows Blood,2011
ANGELS, Black Hare Press, 2019
BEYOND, Black Hare Press, 2019
Deep Space, Black Hare Press, 2019
Martyrs (The Birdman Project), 2019
Midsummer's Unveiling, RCC Tales, 2012
MONSTERS, Black Hare Press, 2019
Nomycha, RCC Tales, 2018
Saint Valentine's Clash, RCC Tales, 2011
stories with bite o,.,o, 2010
WORLDS, Black Hare Press, 2019

Connect
Website: RavenCorinnCarluk.Blogspot.Com
Amazon: amazon.com/author/ravencorinncarluk
Smashwords: smashwords.com/profile/view/RavenCorinnCarluk
Twitter: @ravencorinn
Facebook: RavenCorinnCarluk

BEYOND THE REALM

MIDNIGHT IN AUTUMN

By Cindar Harrell

Amaranth will call upon all the magic at her disposal to stop a banshee from taking the one she loves the most, but will it be enough?

I had heard tales about them but had never witnessed one myself. Once I did, I wished that I never had.

When I was a little girl, I had a morbid fascination to see one, the women who warn the coming of death, silver hair like moonlight, eyes dripping rivers of blood, skin like cracked porcelain, beautiful in their dark fashion. A banshee. Back then, I had no one I really cared for enough to mourn if I saw her lamenting beneath a weeping tree, but that changed, in the most unexpected ways.

During my darkest hours, *she* came into my life, like a solar flare to help bring me out of the dark abyss. Two years younger than me, she had the innocence of a child, but the regal bearing and cunning of a queen. I loved her immediately. It was the single most happy and sorrowful moment of my life up until then; for even though I had found the one deep inside I knew to be my soulmate, we would never be allowed such happiness.

Years later, on the autumnal equinox, long after I had forgotten my dark desire to see a banshee, I got my wish. The dark fae was sitting beneath a dying tree next to the river, she met my eyes and her soft, mournful whining turned into a screech that pierced my soul like a shard of glass. In her cry, I heard the words meant only for me: "The one you love the most will die at midnight on the autumnal equinox next year."

The next moment she was gone, and I sank to my knees, blood pounding in my ears. It wasn't until my coven ran outside that my mind slowly began to return to me.

"Amaranth! What has happened?" one said.

"Oh my, your ears my dear! They are bleeding!"

said another.

Sluggishly I lifted my hand to my ear. Indeed, there was blood. Another omen of the dead.

But when I saw *her*, Liana, kneel in front of me, I felt the life inside me return. She was everything. She was vibrant and beautiful, so full of energy. There was no way she would die within a year's time.

"Are you all right? You look like you've seen a ghost!" She touched my cheek and I held my breath.

"I…I'm fine. I'm not sure what came over me," I managed to say softly.

"Well, you better get to feeling better, the ritual is about to start! This is my favourite time of year, but it won't be perfect without you!" She smiled, so beautiful and pure. I couldn't help but smile back and take her offered hand.

She was my world; I *would* protect her. No matter what the cost.

"Are you ready to start, Amaranth?" the eldest of our number asked.

"Yes, of course," I replied.

The ritual was a sacred rite, one of the most important of the year. We made an altar in the meadow at the very edge of the enchanted forest. Only those specifically chosen to carry out the will of the Goddess were allowed entrance into that hallowed place. This year, I would be one of the chosen.

We carried the bounty of our harvest and placed the best on the altar and encircled it with gleaming red apples. The leaves on the trees were still the green of summer; but by the time the sun sets on the equinox, they would be the hues of autumn.

Our coven gathered in a circle, just inside the protective ring of apples. We closed our eyes and began by harnessing and blessing the power of the elements, asking them to imbue us with their gift. We turned in unison, facing each direction until we were once again facing the altar. Eyes closed, we raised our right hand, the one in which we harnessed the power, holding it up to the sky. I knew each of us could feel the presence of the Goddess growing.

After a few minutes, the elder said, "The one among us who is pure and bright, who represents the long days of summer and the light of this world, step forward."

I wasn't allowed to look, but I knew that Liana stepped from the circle to stand in front of the altar.

Once again, the elder spoke; hers were the words of the crone and sacred. "The one among us who is stained with shadow, who represents the long nights of winter and the dark of this world, step forward."

I took a deep breath, heart pounding, opened my

eyes and walked forward to stand behind the altar, directly across from Liana. Our eyes met and a faint blush dusted my cheeks. I prayed to the Goddess that she wouldn't notice. She simply smiled sweetly.

Pure and bright indeed.

"These two of our sisters have been chosen to represent the Goddess and to fulfil her wish. They will be the ones to say farewell to the warmth and light of summer and to usher in the cool and darkness of autumn in preparation of winter. May the Goddess be pleased with their performance and bless this season and our new harvests. Blessed be."

"Blessed be," we all replied in unison, although my voice shook with anticipation when I spoke.

Silently, we were guided to the edge of the forest; we had been prepared earlier for our task once inside, for none of the others could follow us, not even the elder.

We stepped past the treeline and everything became quiet; there was no longer the sound of the wind rippling through the green trees, no scurrying coming from the underbrush, no birds chattering overhead. Just silence. As we walked farther in, I noticed that not even our footsteps made any sound. I wondered if I tried to speak, if Liana would even hear me, but I knew to do so would be an ill omen. We were not supposed to speak until we reached the final ritual site.

Eventually we came to what appeared to be a shimmering ripple in the forest, glistening in the dimming sunlight.

I gasped and had to bite my tongue to keep from speaking. Instead, I looked at Liana, we locked eyes and I saw the wide-eyed wonder on her face.

We walked through the barrier and suddenly the forest came alive; fairies fluttered amongst the leaves and animals frolicked in the lush brush without fear of us. Bubbles of mystic light seemed to glimmer down from the canopy overhead. Without thinking, I reached out my hand and caught one. It was intoxicating, holding the light in the palm of my hand, but then shadows engulfed it and it became a pocket of darkness. I gasped and dropped it, letting it float to the ground, shattering like glass upon impact.

That's when I remembered, this wasn't my time, my realm. I was chosen for darkness. I looked at Liana again and saw the balls of light circling her, fairies braiding bright flowers into her hair. She was the light. I smiled despite my inner turmoil.

When the fairies were done preparing Liana, she bowed her thanks and we continued to our destination.

Soon enough, we arrived in a small clearing with

what appeared to be a fairy circle in the middle. We stood in the centre of the circle and waited. We were told that the Goddess's acolyte would appear before us and give us further instructions.

In what felt like both an eternity and a single breath, movement caught the corner of my eye. I looked to see a large oak that stood on the outer ring of the clearing move. My eyes narrowed, thinking maybe I had imagined it, but it did so once again before a beautiful girl stepped out. Her skin was a dazzling shade of brown and her hair was the verdant colour of the leaves around us, her eyes a deep forest green. She was bare before us and smiled sweetly.

A dryad! I thought.

I had only heard of them in legends. This forest truly was blessed by the Goddess!

She tilted her head down and spoke, "Welcome, chosen ones, to the forest of the Goddess. Yours is a sacred task set before you today. Are you ready to begin?" She looked to each of us as we nodded in turn. "Good, now bare yourselves before the presence of the Goddess."

My hands went hesitantly to the laces of my corset. I glanced back to the dryad who nodded. With a sigh, I began untying it, trying not to think of Liana doing the same right in front of me. I discarded my clothes piece by piece, entirely focused on my task, eyes staying down. Before long, there was nothing left to remove, and I was forced to look up.

Liana's face was dusted in a striking pink blush as she glanced around anxiously.

Looks like I am not the only one nervous. I thought with a sigh of relief, although I wasn't sure what she had to be nervous about. Her flawless skin glistened in the sunlight and I had to force myself to focus on her face for modesty's sake. But I already knew she was perfect.

Silently, the dryad, bowl in hand, anointed our foreheads with essential oils.

"To give the Goddess a path to use you as her vessel," she explained once she was done.

She then wove crimson cords around our arms and middle, tying us together, the dark and light as one. I blushed, feeling Liana's breasts pressed against my own, and turned my head in the hopes that she wouldn't see.

The dryad chanted over us and my vision began to blur. It was like I was floating in water, weightless and unable to breath. I couldn't open my eyes, even though I didn't even remember closing them. I tried to focus on Liana's skin against mine, but even that became fainter.

Falling, falling. No longer held by the water.

My eyes were closed, I was sure, and yet light appeared, clear as day, not the shaded view you get behind closed eyelids. No, I wasn't seeing it with my natural eyes, my *human* eyes, but with my mind's eye or through the Goddess herself. Like a lucid dream I still couldn't control, images began to appear, and I felt myself pulled to another time, another place—a memory I never wanted to go back to.

***

The room was stuffy. Hot. The smell of incense was so prominent in the air that it was enough to make me gag. It was dark and I wondered why until my fog-laden brain realised that it was because my eyes were closed. I opened them and everything was blurry. Images danced in front of me, but I couldn't make them out.

Dark figures.

Smoke.

Fire?

No, candles.

I tried to speak, but I couldn't make my vocal cords work. I heard an agonised croak and realised a second later that it was me. I tried to raise my arm, but it felt heavy, something was holding me down. I turned my head to look and realised that I was being held down by large leather straps.

"The demon is awake!" I heard from somewhere off to my side.

"Sister Agnes! Please, control yourself," a male voice said, one unfamiliar to me.

Other voices in the room were chanting in a language I didn't understand. Someone moved on top of me and I screamed as hot liquid splashed my face. It burned like candle wax and clung to my skin.

"Stop! Stop it please! Why are you doing this?" My ragged voice screamed, and I felt a painful tear in my throat from the effort.

"Enough of this! She is just a little girl!" A third voice.

"That is no little girl! That is a demon! Listen to how it howls, Sister!"

I must have blacked out soon after that because my next memory was of the day after. When I woke up, I was no longer tied down, but my wrists and ankles bore the evidence from the day before, telling me that it wasn't a dream. I was in my own room, sparse in furnishings and decorations and there was no longer any heavy smoke or incense clogging the air.

The door opened and a girl with sunshine hair, a

little younger than me, walked in. She walked up beside my bed with a small glass in her hand.

"Here, I brought you some water," she said with a warm, if somewhat timid smile. I took the glass, grateful to have something for my parched and sore throat. I was expecting her to leave again, but she sat down in the chair beside my bed. No one ever stayed with me; most couldn't wait to leave me alone. Her constant smile comforted me even though I had never met her before.

"My name is Liana. What is yours?"

"Amaranth."

"Let's be friends, Amaranth! Ok? We will be together forever!"

Friends?

It was such a foreign word to me. But I never forgot that. How easily she accepted me, not even knowing who I was. But moments later, she was pulled from my room.

"Don't ever speak to her! She is a witch, a demon! She is far too dangerous for a precious young girl such as yourself." I recognised him as the male voice from before.

Apparently whatever process they had tried to rid me of the evil they thought was inside me had failed.

The memory faded and shifted. Dark wisps

clouded my vision again before I was thrown into another memory of despair. I was screaming, tearing at my hair. It was a few years later and the pastor at the orphanage had finally broke me. Instead of ridding me of the dark magic, they had inadvertently released it.

Only a girl with sunshine hair was able to calm me.

***

A tingling sensation was the first thing I noticed when I woke up from the strange visions, followed by something coarse tickling my nose. I opened my eyes, still heavy, and pulled the object from my face.

A leaf?

I blinked against the sun, shining far too brightly amongst the cloudy blue sky. A canopy of colour danced above me, falling like rain.

It worked! We ushered in autumn! The Goddess must have been pleased.

I looked beside me and saw Liana, still asleep curled on her side. Her naked form was still covered with the red cord along with a thin layer of freshly fallen leaves. Her long blonde hair was splayed around her and down her back like angel wings. She was like a princess waiting for her prince to kiss her and save her from her slumber.

I wanted to be that prince, the one to save and protect her, but unfortunately, that was not the role that was given to me. I resisted the urge to kiss her sleeping lips just once.

I knew once would never be enough.

***

The next day, our coven went into the woods that surrounded the clearing where the enchanted forest began. It was another tradition where we fed the animals and blessed all of nature as it began to drift into sleep, preparing for winter.

We split up into groups, Liana and I naturally breaking off on our own.

For several long moments, we did our duty in silence.

"Did…did you have any strange dreams? During the ritual, I mean," eventually she asked.

Hesitation stayed my answer, and she must have noticed.

"It's all right if you don't want to tell me, I understand," she said quickly.

"I don't mind, it's just…they weren't exactly very pleasant."

"I see…" she paused before continuing, "I was

afraid of that."

"Well, I was representing darkness, I suppose it is only natural that my dreams would be filled with darkness as well." I picked some bird seed from my pouch and tossed it to a couple of robins standing on a low hanging branch from a nearby tree. "What about you? What did you dream about?"

She smiled brightly and her cheeks reddened. "I had beautiful fantasies," she said wistfully.

"Fantasies? Of what?"

"I'll never tell!" she shouted as she ran off deeper into the forest.

"Wait up, Liana! You can tell me!" I sprinted after her, nimbly dodging roots as I went. "Besides, we are supposed to be doing this together!"

"We are together!" I heard her shout from somewhere to my right, even though I had just seen her slip into an undergrowth ahead of me.

She's using her magic for such a simple game?

Her voice shifted to my left, whispering in my ear, warm as if she were really there. "And we always will be."

***

When October came, I had an urge to visit the

orchards. I walked through the village, alive with colour and activity until I reached my destination. At the centre, one tree stood taller than the others and I plucked the reddest apple I could find from its branches.

Just as I was about to take a bite, something hit me from behind. I gave a surprised shout and turned to find my attacker.

A whirl of skirts quickly vanished behind a thick trunk, a ghost of a giggle dancing on the wind. I smiled.

"Aren't we a little old to be playing games, Liana?" I asked, even though there was nothing I could imagine that would be better than doing just that as long as it was with her.

She poked her head out from behind the tree. "Perhaps. But that doesn't mean we can't."

The mischief in her sparkling eyes told me to prepare for another attack. I raised my arm just as I was pelted with another apple.

"At this rate, there won't be any apples for the festival tomorrow." I laughed.

"Aw, you're no fun," she said with a mock pout. "But I suppose you're right." She bounced over to stand next to me. We sat at the base of the nearest tree, leaning on each other in comfortable silence. I held out the apple I had picked, and she took it in her gentle fingers, taking a small bite.

"Do you remember how we use to do this when we were kids?" she asked.

"Of course, I do. You saved me when I was in the pastor's orphanage, and again when I…" I paused. "Well, you're always saving me in some way. And then we would meet here, under the apple trees, where we thought no one could hurt us."

"And no one did, this orchard is blessed by the Goddess!" She cheered happily.

Not long after the incident at the orphanage, Liana had convinced her mother to talk to the coven. She told them of my power, and they agreed to take me in.

I owed everything to her.

***

We spent the rest of the year in peaceful bliss, as we always had. But nothing lasts forever, and the harder we try to hold on, the sooner it falls apart.

"Amaranth, have you heard what they are saying in the village?" Liana ran into my cottage, gasping for air, her whole body thrumming in nervous excitement, or so I thought.

I laughed. "Breathe, Liana. Since when do you care what those old ninnies have to say?" I placed my

BEYOND THE REALM

herbs back into the cabinet and looked into the bubbling cauldron before me.

"No, you don't understand." She grabbed my arm hard and wheeled me around to look at her. That's when I saw the panic in her eyes. "There are witch hunters in the village, and they are coming for us."

"Witch hunters? Here? But they have always let us be, we are protected in this village by the Goddess and the forest."

She shook her head. "Not anymore. They are waging a war against the Goddess herself now. They seek to obliterate us all. We have to flee!" She grabbed my face with both hands, forcing my eyes to lock with hers. I had never seen her so scared. Her touch calmed my outward nerves, but inside I felt lost and confused.

"But where would we go?" I asked quietly, despair slowly rising within me like a disease. "Our coven has been here for centuries; this is the only safe place for our kind!"

"Don't you see? It's not anymore! Everyone in the village knows all of us by name and where we live. They will find us in no time! They have even recruited some of the local men, claiming that if we remain unchecked, we will turn their wives and daughters against them!"

"But that's ridiculous! We don't take people

against their will!"

"You don't know these men. I heard one of them speaking. He is charismatic and handsome and the whole village is hanging on his every word. If we stay here, we will be persecuted and burned at the stake like our ancestors before us."

"Have you spoken to the elder about this?"

"I…" She stopped, releasing me and looking down. Sorrow filled her beautiful blue eyes.

"She has already been taken. They have hung her in a cage at the village square. They said they are going to burn her at dawn."

My breath froze and my heart stopped. I clumsily fell back into the nearest chair I could find. "That's impossible… Surely, they must give her a fair trial, or something!"

"There is no reason for a trial, everyone knows who and what she is. There is no use for her to deny it, for any of us to. She has already confessed." Her voice wavered, but she carried on. "I stole a minute to speak with her once they had moved on. She said that she would rather die with her dignity, serving the Goddess, than to run like a coward and be killed anyway. She would never deny who she is. But she did tell me to convince the others to run, not from cowardice, but to continue to serve the Goddess and to find a new haven for us all."

"But where would we go," I asked again. I didn't doubt the need to leave, but if they were that determined to come after us, then nowhere would be safe. No place would be any better than here. The cruel fact was that there was nowhere for us to run. Nowhere to hide.

Liana thought for a moment before she spoke. "The forest."

"It's forbidden! No one is to go in there except to…"

"Serve the Goddess, and that is what we are doing. In order to serve her we must survive." She leaned down in front of me and took both my hands in hers. "I know you are scared, Amaranth, I am too." She smiled and I saw immeasurable strength in her eyes that belied her frail frame. "But we need to do this. I won't lose you."

What? What could she mean? We are friends, sisters in the coven, she could not possibly think of me any other way. Could she? Pink stained my cheeks. Unable to speak, I looked away and simply nodded.

"I've already packed what little I need. You have more herbs than me, you pack those, and I will get some clothes and food together. We need to leave before the sun sets. Once they burn the elder at dawn, they will be coming for us."

***

We only spared a moment to warn our sisters before leaving for the enchanted forest. True to their word, the hunters were fast on our trail. I looked back when I heard the shouting over the ridge and was shocked to see someone I knew leading the pack, crossbow and torch in hand.

"Liam?"

"He was one of the villagers taking a stand with the hunters yesterday, convincing the others that we were their enemy."

I found it hard to believe. I never really had friends until Liana and my sisters, but if I had to choose one person among all others, it would have been him. He had been my neighbour and was always kind to me, especially once my parents had died, right before I was whisked away to the orphanage. Although I wouldn't have said I knew him well, I thought I knew him better than this. But the fear and hatred I saw in his eyes was completely foreign; a stranger stared back from the once familiar auburn orbs.

"Amaranth, we don't have time! Let's go!" Liana pulled me along and I snapped back to the present. I never was one for sentiment, so what was with my hesitation? The whole thing seemed surreal, but one look into the sky blue of Liana's eyes and my stormy mind calmed. I had no need for the past, I had her. I needed to protect her. Whether or not she cared for me in return didn't matter, I would make sure she made it through safe.

"Stop! Amaranth, you can't run from this! Your time has come! The reign of witches is at its end," he bellowed across the open field.

I closed my eyes and blocked out his words.

Keep running, I just have to keep running!

The sound of horses followed us, and panic seized my heart.

No, no, no… We can't possibly outrun horses!

"Keep going Liana! I have to buy us some time! Don't look back!" I called out.

"What? No!" She stopped and looked at me.

"Keep going!" I turned towards our pursuers. If they wanted a witch, then they would get one. There was a reason I was chosen to represent the coming of darkness. I was one of the most powerful practising witches in our coven. And now it was time to show them.

"Why are you doing this, Liam? This isn't like you." I stood my ground and watched them closing in.

"We have no choice, Amaranth, the world must be saved from evil."

"And you think I am the cause of this evil?" I crossed my arms, showing more confidence in my stance than I felt. It had been a very long time since I had to use my magic for offensive purposes. The last time, things didn't go well—I lost control; I had no idea what I was doing. That was before the coven took me in. Whether they agreed to in order to train me or control me, I wasn't sure. I'm still not.

Closing my eyes, I unleashed a spell strong enough to daze and confuse them, but not to kill. I never wanted to do that again.

I managed to hold them back and buy Liana enough time to escape. I circled around, making sure none of them followed me before entering the woods. Liana was a little ways ahead.

"What are you doing? You were supposed to be in the enchanted forest by now!"

"I couldn't leave you." She grabbed my hand and warmth filled the increasingly cool air from her touch. She raised it up, our hands centimetres from her face. Was it my imagination or did she look like she wanted to kiss me?

A sound like a hummingbird flying past drew my attention back. Liana's eyes widened at the sound as well. It was another moment before I understood why. Red blossomed from her ivory cloak like the petals of a rose, but a rose it was not.

"Liana?" I asked before her knees buckled.

I caught her before she hit the ground. Moving her cloak out of the way, I saw the arrow piercing her shoulder. I forced myself to look away, in search of where the danger came from. Another whoosh and an arrow grazed my cheek before landing in the tree behind me.

Without thinking, I picked Liana up and carried her, running as fast as I could, my deep violet skirts tearing on the brush of the forest floor. There was a back way into the enchanted forest through these scraggly woods; I just had to make it there in time. There she would be safe. There I could heal her with the Goddess's help.

Finally, we entered the enchanted forest and the same silence fell around us. I kept running; I needed to get her to the place where I knew the magic was the strongest. I dashed through the glimmering barrier and into the same clearing where we had performed the ritual the year previous.

Kneeling on the ground, I gently sat her in front of me.

I need to get this arrow out.

"Hold still, I'm afraid this will hurt."

"It's all right, Amaranth, I'm not afraid of a little pain." She smiled weakly. It was less than reassuring.

I broke off the arrow's tip and held her tightly to my chest. Her body tensed against mine in preparation for what was to come. Squinting, I grabbed the arrow and pulled it through as fast as I could. She screamed and twin rivers fell from both our eyes.

"I'm sorry. It's all right, you're all right," I whispered soothingly to her. I leaned her weak form up against a tree and began tearing strips of fabric from my skirt to use as bandages. I mixed up a healing salve form the herbs I had packed and applied it before wrapping her wound.

"Why are you doing this?" she whispered, eyes barely staying open.

I looked up, caught off guard by the question.

"What do you mean?"

"Why would you risk your life to stay with me? We know that was no ordinary arrow. You should keep moving, they already know we were planning to come here. We may not be protected for as long as we thought."

She was right, both of us knew but had stayed silent. The tip of the arrow was dripping with a thick purple liquid. Poison, one we knew all too well, and had been warned against from the dark ages of the witches. It was a special witch hunter's poison targeted to use our innate magic against us. It killed slowly, but it was still always fatal. No one yet had been able to come up with an antidote.

"Don't be ridiculous, you'll be fine."

"I wish I could believe your pretty lies, Amaranth." She laughed lightly before it turned into quiet coughs. "Do you want to know a secret?"

"If you wish to tell me."

She looked up to the greying sky before she spoke. "I hadn't even realised. The equinox is tonight, but there is no one to perform the ritual. Who will usher in the autumn and bless the villagers' harvest?"

"The equinox? That's not a secret, Liana." I smiled at her, although worry creased my brow.

Is she already becoming delusional from the poison? Wait the equinox... My chest tightened as I remembered the frightful warning I had received last year. My stubborn hope of somehow healing Liana seemed to drift farther and farther away.

"The one you love the most will die at midnight on the autumnal equinox next year."

"Do you remember last year's ritual?"

I nodded; how could I forget? "Yes," I choked out through my ever-growing tears.

"You know when you asked me what my dreams were about?"

Again I nodded. "You said they were beautiful fantasies."

"They were. They were about you."

My heart stopped beating and my mind went blank and before I could think of anything to say, she pulled me down in a gentle kiss.

This can't be real…

Everything I had ever wanted and feared were happening all at once and all I could do was cling to her like my only lifeline. I held her face in my hands, bringing her closer when she tried to pull away.

I will never let you go…

***

Once I was certain Liana was asleep, I sneaked away.

Forgive me, but there is something I need to do.

It was time for the hunters to pay.

I waited at the edge of the forest, traps set, as prepared as I was ever going to be. Part of me just wanted to kill them all, but I needed answers, about the poison, about why, about everything. So, I waited.

I didn't have to for long.

I heard the trap engage from my hiding spot and I lunged towards my captives. There were five in all.

The crystals surrounding them formed an impenetrable barrier, holding them in place.

"It's good of you to fall so neatly into my trap. Now, if you'll simply answer my questions, then we can make this brief and all be on our way."

"We'd never answer questions from a witch!" one said. I imagine he was the young and charismatic leader that Liana had mentioned before.

"I may be a witch, but you are all under my spell. Now, it can be a harmless spell or a fatal one. The choice is yours." I let my power course through me for a moment, allowing my eyes to darken to a deep indigo, consuming even the whites.

They all shuttered in fear, moving farther back inside their crystal cage, cowering like dogs.

"What do you want to know, Amaranth," Liam asked, resignation written on his face.

"Why?" I hissed. "Why did you shoot her? Why not me?"

He sighed. "It wasn't anything personal." He turned his head, looking to the ground. "Well, perhaps that is a lie. It was personal, but not against her. I did it because I didn't want to shoot you." There seemed to be an unspeakable sadness in his eyes.

Hesitation stunned me into silence for a moment.

No, I can't get distracted by his lies! If he cared for me then he would have never joined up with these witch hunters!

"Why would it matter if you shoot me now or burn me tomorrow? Isn't that what you said you wanted? To kill all the witches, to kill the evil?" My eyes narrowed, glaring daggers into his very soul.

"I…" Before he could say anything more, the charismatic leader stepped up, shoving him aside in the small prison.

"Because I made a deal with him. It was absolutely necessary that I take this village under my control, but I knew an outsider would never stand a chance to turn the others. We needed someone the people trusted on our side. So, I asked what he wanted. Apparently, it was you, unharmed."

"Why me?" I asked.

"Does it matter?" Liam replied.

"I suppose not." I turned to leave, but then something he said triggered in my head. "Wait, you said it was absolutely necessary that you take the village. Why? Witch hunters have never tried to desecrate this village. They have left those of us here in peace. So why now?"

"Well, I guess there is no harm in telling you now.

We were told to, by a creature more powerful than any of you witches."

"Who?"

His next words turned my blood to ice.

"The banshee that lives in the fairy mound outside of this village."

***

I wasted no time in going to the banshee's dwelling. Why would she want to eradicate us? Why Liana? She came to me and warned of her death, but if she orchestrated all of this then she was stepping outside of her domain. Banshees weren't meant to cause the death of others, just to serve as a warning so that the loved ones may prepare. So why?

I didn't know, but I was going to find out.

By the time I reached the mound, my power was surging, glowing in dark circles around me. I unleashed a blast at the mound, creating my own entrance.

I took pleasure seeing the surprise on her haunted face.

"What are you doing here?" she sneered.

"You took everything from me," I said quietly, glaring at the banshee who had foretold Liana's death.

"She isn't dead yet. But I warned you. You can't

change fate. I only bring the message; I don't carry it out."

"That's what banshees are supposed to do, but not you. You acted as both messenger and executioner."

"And why would you think that?"

"You underestimate my abilities. I'm a witch remember?" I walked farther inside her home, still never taking my eyes off her.

"Barely one of note. You are the only one of your coven that uses herbal remedies only, never spells."

I smiled, darkly. "That's because my power is far greater than theirs. And should I use it, well, why tell you, you're about to find out."

She looked around, knowing that she had been found out, no doubt looking for somewhere else to cast the blame.

"Did you honestly think I wouldn't figure it out? Your hunter friend gave you up. So, tell me, why attack us? Why go after Liana?" I asked.

"If you got this far, I would think the rest would be obvious." She began to circle me, probably looking for an opening, but my magic still swirled around me, acting as a protective barrier.

What could she want that she would need the coven out of the way to get? Like a lightning strike, realisation dawned on me.

"The enchanted forest. It's protected by the coven and the Goddess. You want to control its power."

"Very clever." She smiled, cruel and wicked. "For centuries, your kind has protected it and used it to fulfil your purposes and rituals. Well, it's time that someone put all that mystical energy to good use. I waited patiently for the right time to strike, consulting every seer and oracle I could find."

"Why now?"

"Why, the equinox of course. The perfect day, when the world's light turns to darkness, when living things begin to wilt and die. Just as the leaves fall, so shall you and your coven. So shall the enchanted forest. Its light shall be corrupted with my darkness!"

She lunged at me with amazing speed and a shrieking howl. I barely had time to dodge her attack, rolling out of the way and crouching, facing her once more.

"I won't let you do this. The enchanted forest belongs to the Goddess. Besides, I'm betting that you are the one that gave the witch poison to the hunters, which means you probably have an antidote as well."

"Is it really the forest you care about or your precious sister witch?" She bared her teeth, preparing for another attack. "Your focus seems split!"

I struck first this time. I fired a spell of pure energy

that flew from my fingers in a single straight line. The magic hit the banshee and coiled around her like a rope. I smiled.

Perfect.

"How do I heal her? If you tell me, I may consider letting you live. Of course, you would need to find a new home, far away from here."

"You can't. There is no cure. She will die at midnight just as I foretold."

"There has to be a way!" I screamed, tears streaming down my face.

"Even you know that it is beyond my power to heal. I am a harbinger of death. She will die any minute now; there is nothing you can do to change that." She laughed, the sound echoing around the mound dwelling.

It filled me with an untold rage, stronger than any I had ever felt before. I raised my hands and sent a pulse of dark energy towards the death fae. Even as she died, I could still hear her laughing.

As midnight struck, my grief overwhelmed me. My screams merged with the angry winds of autumn, rivalling that of the banshee herself. The power around me was out of control, swirling in shades of black and demonic purple, crackling like a lightning storm.

"Amaranth, stop!" Came a voice somewhere

beyond the howling of magic. It was familiar but my mind was becoming more and more consumed by the magic coursing within me.

"This isn't you, Amaranth! I know you; you are not this person! You can control it! Please, come back to me! You swore to stay by me, that you would never let me go, so don't leave me now."

I struggled to make sense of the words. I finally recognised the voice as belonging to Liana, but that was impossible, midnight had come and gone.

"I'm right here! Just look at me!"

The voice said as if in response to my thoughts.

"I can't!" I screamed. "If I look and you aren't there, I won't be able to handle it."

"It's got to be better than what you are doing right now. Amaranth, please, I can't let this consume you. I love you!"

My eyes snapped open and everything grew still. There was no way that I had heard her right. She couldn't love me. A single tear ran down my face.

"What?"

"I said I love you."

A hand wrapped around mine. I glanced down at it and slowly looked to the face it belonged to.

"Liana…" The magic storm came to a complete stand still, surrounding us as if it were our own barrier, sealing us from the outside world. "But you died."

She shook her head. "No, the dryad called upon the Goddess to help sustain me long enough for you to defeat the banshee. I came as soon as I could, the winds and spirits of the forest helping me. I wish I could have been there with you to fight her."

"It wasn't your fight. I had to protect you." I looked down to the floor before asking the question that burned in my mind and heart. "Did you mean it? What you said?"

"That I love you?" she asked, and I nodded slowly. "How about I show you?" She leaned in and captured my lips with hers. The kiss was filled with all the longing I had felt all those years and I knew hers reflected mine. I wrapped my arms around her slim waist and gave in. I didn't deserve her love, but somehow, I had gotten it anyway.

Is it really possible for the light to love the darkness?

I decided I didn't care any longer as she deepened the kiss. Light and dark. What does it really mean, anyway? Why must they always be at odds. After all, they need each other, you can't have one without the other. They are the perfect duality.

***

"Are you nervous?" Liam asked me with a smile.

I shook my head, crowned with autumn flowers. "No, in fact, I have never been more at peace."

"Good. I wanted to thank you, by the way, for inviting me. Even after everything I did."

"Well, to not forgive is to turn your heart to darkness, and although I now know that both are needed, I think I would prefer to stay in the light for a while." I looked up and saw Liana approach, causing my breath to still. She was more beautiful than the morning sun, wearing a dress of flowing white with a matching crown of flowers in her sunshine hair, gently blowing in the cool autumn breeze.

"I'm happy for you, Amaranth." There was that same sadness in his eyes that I saw that horrible day with the hunters, but his smile was genuine and I knew he meant it.

"Thank you."

I walked forward, meeting Liana in the centre of the clearing in the enchanted forest, our friends and sisters gathered around us. Although the banshee had evil intentions, she was right about one thing, the forest could be used for so much more. To protect and heal, to celebrate life and renewal.

The trees around us were bright with the reds and oranges of the season, the leaves falling in a beautiful shower, as if blessing us.

I took Liana's hands in mine and the dryad appeared. She tied our hands together to symbolise our eternal bond, to bless us and to unite us by the will of the Goddess. It reminded me of the first time we came here for the ritual of the equinox. Even though we were fully clothed and people were watching, this somehow still seemed more intimate, more magical. I didn't hear much of what she said, too focused on Liana as she blushed sweetly, tears of joy misting her eyes. I was sure they mirrored my own.

When the dryad was finished, we kissed and those gathered cheered. The little balls of light that we had witnessed on our first visit here gathered and joined the parade of falling leaves. When we broke apart, Liana looked back to me, our eyes locking together.

"I told you we would always be together."

I couldn't help but to laugh. "You were right, I never should have doubted you." I kissed her once more. "And I never will again."

BEYOND THE REALM

CINDAR HARRELL loves fairy tales, especially ones with a dark twist. Her writing is often fairy tale inspired, but she also loves mystery and horror. Her stories can be found in various anthologies from publishers such as Black Hare Press, Iron Faerie Publishing, Dragon Soul Press, Blood Song Books, Soteira Press, Fantasia Divinity and more. Traveling is a passion for her as it inspires her imagination to run wild. She regularly moonlights as another human, but no matter who she is, she is always writing. Her debut short story collection *Descent into Madness* was published in March 2020.

Bibliography
100 Word Horrors vol. 3, KJK Publishing, 2019
Apocalypse, Black Hare Press 2019
Beneath Yggdrasil's Shadow, Fantasia Divinity, 2018
Beyond, Black Hare Press, 2019
Coffins and Dragons, Dragon Soul Press, 2019
Curses & Cauldrons, Blood Song Books, 2019
Divinity, Iron Faerie Publishing, 2019
Fable, Iron Faerie Publishing, 2019
Forest of Fear vol. 1, Blood Song Books, 2019
Galactic Goddesses, Fantasia Divinity, 2019
Midnight Masquerade, Fantasia Divinity, 2018
Spring's Blessing, Fantasia Divinity, 2019
Storming Area 51, Black Hare Press, 2019
Stuff of Nightmares, BMR Promotions
Summer's Splash, Fantasia Divinity, 2019
The Evil Within, Fantasia Divinity, 2017
Unravel, Black Hare Press, 2019

Connect
Amazon: amazon.com/Cindar-Harrell/e/B07W8W3CV7
Facebook: CindarHarrell

BLACK HARE PRESS

BEYOND THE REALM

DRAGOMANCER
By Elizabeth Montague

In an age dominated by war, dragons and their riders are valuable commodities, and now with witchcraft on his side, one king has found the most powerful of them all.

The skyline dipped from red to pink, the fires below the ridge igniting the sky, augmenting the dawn, and highlighting the swirls of smoke that curled up from the battlefield. The sounds were muted but not enough to quiet them entirely. The clash of swords and the screams of the dying were so familiar that they failed to register with those gathered around the plans laid out upon the oak table. Wooden figures and coloured flags littered the map; the contours of the battlefield below set out in miniature as the generals that surrounded it played out their plans in wood before they did so in the flesh of their soldiers.

Arguments and bitter words were traded more than strategy, point scoring more important than the survival of the cannon fodder especially when they were being watched from the throne set on the raised dais at the far end of the tent. King Mormoth's fingers tightened on the carved arms of his chair, nostrils flaring as he sucked in a ragged breath before he released his grip and slammed his hands down onto the chair.

"When you all have quite finished!" he roared, the room before him silenced in the time it took for him to rise to his feet. "Four years. Four years we have been relying on you imbeciles to control your counties, and this is the result."

"The most recent uprising came from the north. Firenze should have subdued it before it crossed the Inwa River,' said General Rovi. "The bridge should have been brought down before any of the rebels could cross it."

"And leave us without supplies or support," countered Firenze. "My people are not cannon fodder to keep your lands fat and free."

"No, your people are rebels."

"Enough!" snapped the King, waving a hand. "Get them out of our sight."

Two guards left their stations by the door, their height dwarfing the squabbling generals, and neither gave any fight when they were disarmed and led to the doors. The royal guard had been enhanced with the blood of both giants and the water of the Sacred River; their strength only controlled by the binding charm that kept them loyal to the King's will.

"Does anyone else want to continue the argument or would you prefer to fulfil the role we generously gave you and put down this rebellion once and for all?"

The remaining generals turned back to the map, pretending not to hear the sounds of fists meeting flesh or the pained groans of their colleagues beyond the open flap of the tent. With quieter voices, they began to move the wooden figures around the board, suggesting various strategies for dealing with the latest uprising as the King paced around them.

"The time for answers is now unless you wish to join those outside," he snapped, all three of them standing to attention even though it had been years since they had last been drilled. "Well…"

"Sire!"

The cry preceded the figure that ran through the door—uniform tattered and helmet long forgotten; the blood dry around the cut above his eye. He stumbled the last few paces, falling towards the table and scattering the figurines as he planted his hands to hold him upright.

"Sire! News from the lines. The rebels have a Fire Wraith; he is taking out line after line of infantry."

"Then have the dragon riders strike his lines in return. Their fire will soon quench his," said the King. "Farmers' and blacksmiths' boys the lot of them, they'll run at the first sight of the dragons."

"Sire, the dragons," said the young soldier, eyes wide. "They are growing harder to control. With their riders being killed, they are not forming bonds with the new ones. There are instances of them refusing to fly at best and attacking their handlers at worse. Several have even been taken by the rebels; they are using our own mounts against us."

"Then kill any that will not follow commands. They are not stupid beasts; they will soon realise where their loyalties lie when they are counting the bodies. Have the masters activate the obedience collars to maximum effect."

"Sire, they have been…they…"

The table broke the King's fall as the ground beneath their feet shuddered. The noise of the battlefield rose as the red light grew fiercer, smoke and ash swirling through the sky. He was on his feet before his remaining generals, using the young messenger as a prop as he ran out of the tent to survey the battle below.

Bodies littered the valley that had become the theatre of war; the red of the fires augmented by the gore that seeped into the ground, and the white grasses forever tarnished it seemed. Dragon bodies lay with the other beasts of burden amongst the dead, many wearing the King's colours though there were many that could have turned on their masters. The rebel soldiers, their uniforms a conglomeration of whatever they had been able to beg or steal, far outnumbered the living of his own ranks, the Fire Wraith at their head.

"Order reinforcements," he cried over the din. "Send out more troops and strike them down."

"Sire, our forces are diminished. If we send out more now, there will not be enough to hold the city. We should retreat behind the walls and prepare for a siege. We do not have the strength to fight this."

Mormoth wanted to argue but he could see the bodies before him, too many to count, too many dead to mount a significant defence. He could not risk the rebels taking the city, the very bones of their civilisation based on the notion that whoever held the city held the crown, and he had no wish to relinquish all he had been born for.

"Order the retreat," he said, "and make ready the city for a siege; all men capable of bearing arms will make our defence."

"Your Majesty," said the young messenger with a bow, turning to follow the generals as they scrambled to obey their new orders.

"A moment more, boy," said Mormoth. "We have further work to do."

"I am your servant, Sire."

"Make ready our horse and find us fifty good men to ride as guard."

"Your Majesty cannot mean to ride apart from the army as we retire; we do not know what lies on the roads between here and the city. Let me at least gather two hundred men to Your Majesty's defence."

"We do not ride to the city yet," said Mormoth. "We are riding to her. It is time that we saw what my treasury has laboured for all these years."

***

The Dragon's Nest was not a mountain to be climbed lightly; the weather known to change without any warning. Within moments, the sun that had been beating down for the entire day could change to freezing rain and fog that meant you could see little more than two inches from your nose. King Mormoth had only followed the path a handful of times in his long reign, preferring to send his soldiers to bring Mistress Libelle to the court. Drag would be a better word as she had never come willingly. The insubordination she offered would have resulted in punishment for anyone else but Mormoth could not risk angering her—her work too precious to be interrupted by her wrath against him.

They had reached the first ridge when they were met by two of her creations: the great hulking beasts, more bear than man, that acted as her guards blocking their path with their bulk alone.

"Who goes?" snapped the great teeth of one, barely able to form the words.

"Your King," said the soldier who had been thrust ahead of his fellows, his only defence the King's seal, which he waved in the faces of the guards. "You will step aside."

"You follow," growled the towering guardian, not waiting for acknowledgement as he and his companion turned and headed up the mountain.

The climb was steep and hot; the ground beneath their feet warmed by the sun and the magic that was at work in the chasms beneath. It was two hours before they reached the summit and the single door carved into the rock face. To the untrained eye, it looked like any other wooden door but the closer they got, the more the atmosphere bore down on them. It was as though physical hands were forcing them to their knees with each step they took, the runes carved upon it pulsing in rhythm with their thundering hearts. Only the beast guards were unaffected, striding towards the door before circling their arms in a gesture that quieted the press of the magic upon the King's guard.

The door opened, creaking on hinges that flaked rust as though the door had not been opened for many years.

"Mormoth alone," snapped the guard.

The soldiers that surrounded the King immediately came to arms, but he waved them down even as he scowled at the beast. He dismounted his horse—the animal shifting nervously on the rock as sweat foamed across his once pristine coat.

"This is expected," he said as his soldiers parted to let him approach the door. "Await me here and remain on your guard. Captain, you have our full authority to use whatever punishment you see fit for any soldier that does not keep to his orders."

Despite the sun and the longing for rest and refreshment after their long march, no one dared let their displeasure at the King's command register on their faces, knowing the punishment would be far worse than heat exhaustion and dehydration caused by waiting at attention in the sun.

Mormoth cast a final look over the waiting troops before he followed the hulking guards through the door. The passageway beyond nondescript, chiselled out of the rock face, the walls rough and glittering with the minerals that most others would have taken for their own gain, but they meant nothing to Libelle. Mormoth had once tried to mine them, sending the best miners his kingdom offered, but every stone they struck resisted their tools, and they returned speaking of hearing laughter in the walls every time they failed. He cursed the witch and her enchantments, but he dared not do so to her face, her powers greater than any other and he needed her cooperation to keep the rebels in check.

He grimaced as the guard pressed a little too close to his back, the stale scent of meat on the creature's breath turning his stomach as it mingled with the sweat and sulphur that hung in the air. The ground beneath his feet trembled as he walked, rocked by the deep, guttural roars from the chasms beneath. He had seen Libelle's pets twice since he had charged her with their creation almost two decades before; the magic surrounding them, she had said, was too delicate to be approached by humans too often whilst they were maturing. He would see them now though, and he would put them to their intended use.

A cruel smile split his lips as he thought of the rebels and their two-bit magicians cowering before the true might of magic; Mormoth's army rendered obsolete, replaced by the dragons and their riders that had been bred for battle alone. He did not know how Libelle had achieved all she claimed and did not care to ask; her methods not important, it was the results that mattered. It had been she who had concocted the potion that gave the current dragon riders a link with their mounts, but it was a fleeting connection, lasting only hours. If the rider died, another could take his place, but every new connection weakened the dragon breed until they were too damaged to fly.

Mormoth had charged Libelle to do better, bought her allegiance by promising to turn a blind eye to her experiments: the witch feared across the land for her rumoured torturous splicing of humans with animals to create new breeds. She had promised him that she could breed an army that could not be defeated—an army of only six to hold the entire land. He had scoffed at the idea; but she had persuaded him, and he had given her leave to begin her work. She had taken six breeding pairs of dragons, the strongest Mormoth had had, along with six of his strongest riders. She promised him dragons bred alongside their riders; their bloods mingled so much that they existed as both their minds one. He had been there for the birth, if he could call it that, the overlarge eggs hatching before his eyes to reveal not just a dragon in each but a human as well, curled around the dragon and connected by the horrific approximation of an umbilical cord. He had not shown his revulsion at the sight, the prospect of their power soon overcoming any other sensation. His dragon army—quick, intelligent, and unbeatable.

"Move!" grunted the guard as Mormoth's pace slowed, the smell wafting from below reminding him of days long since passed.

"Need we remind you who is King here?" he snapped, drawing himself tall, though it was nothing in comparison to the beast's height.

"We have no king here, only Mother."

Mormoth didn't waste his breath arguing, the guards strong but stupid, in thrall to their mistress and bred only to guard her more precious creations.

The heat increased as they finished their descent, and Mormoth cursed his armour, sweat beading down his back as the corridor widened, opening abruptly onto a large cavern that twinkled with the mineral deposits, which reacted with the fire from the lanterns illuminating the room. Various creatures Mormoth dared not name, let alone guess the mix that bred them, worked at various tasks. Large wooden tables laden with artefacts and experiments, each more potent and complex than the next.

It took him mere moments to locate Libelle amongst the busy throng—the woman petite and altogether too human against her charges. Her long grey hair was arrayed with colourful ribbons, wrapped around the ratty braids she had fashioned it into. She wore the breeches and tunic of a man, a wide leather belt hung with tools, and a knife strapped to the side of her boot. Mormoth shook his head as he regarded her, unchanged in the decades since she had first come to his attention.

"Mother!" barked the guard at his side, the voice cutting through the din of the chamber and catching the attention of everyone below.

Libelle looked up and grimaced. "Mormoth," she said, her voice carrying easily in the newly quiet room. "How disagreeable. Bring him down."

"Woman, you will remember to whom you speak," said Mormoth, but the room had already returned to its activities and his words were lost in the din.

The guard led him to the table Libelle was working

at, the woman not looking up from the books in front of her as she twisted her hair up and secured it with a well-worn scarf. "You've grown fat in your dotage. What do you want, Mormoth? I have not summoned you."

"You would do well to try," he said, ignoring the insult. "We have come for our dragons."

Libelle waved a dismissive hand. "Not ready yet. Twenty years, I told you, and not a day sooner. You are a year too early."

"They should have matured by now. You said the rate of a human; by our count that makes them old enough to fight. We have younger ones in our ranks."

"And I am sure their mothers thanked you for it. Twenty years, Mormoth; come back in twelve months."

The long scarf did nothing to obscure the handful of hair Mormoth quickly gripped, yanking Libelle from her seat and onto the floor, bringing his boot down onto the slim column of her throat as she lay on the stones.

"Call them off," he said as several of her beast guards ran towards them. "Call them off or you're dead before they can kill me."

Libelle raised a hand, the move regal despite her place on the floor. The guards ceased their approach but continued to growl as Mormoth took a knife from his boot, cutting off several of Libelle's braids before he removed his foot from her neck. The woman sat up, rubbing at the reddened skin; but her eyes remained cool, not sparing a glance to the hair that littered the floor.

"Now then, shall we see our dragons?" said Mormoth.

"As you wish," said Libelle.

"As you wish…?"

"As you wish, Your Majesty," said Libelle, leading him towards a gap in the cavern wall, pausing only to stroke the coarse hair of one of her guards to calm his growls. "Peace, my loved one, peace."

The beast backed down but Mormoth kept his knife in his hand all the same, following Libelle as she headed through the gap and into another corridor as roughly hewn as the last. The sulphur was stronger here than in the cavern, the heat further increasing, and he was forced to swipe a gloved hand over his face to rid himself of the sweat. His body yearned for water, but he would not ask for it, nor take it if it was offered, pride and fear equally weighing down the need.

The next cavern they entered was quieter than the last but the sight of it filled Mormoth with satisfaction. Six large war-bred dragons sat upon their nests, iridescent scales catching the firelight. Sulphurous smoke curled from their nostrils, each breath ruffling the fine hairs around their overlarge muzzles. The humans, if he could call them by such a name, that attended them matched each perfectly; their own skin covered by fine, snake-like scales of the same colour as their beasts. All twelve figures, human and dragon alike, looked up in perfect unison, a dozen pairs of golden eyes staring up at their mistress and the man next to her.

"Mother?" said one young warrior, his movements smooth as his dragon raised its head in an unspoken question.

"Children," said Libelle, laying her hand against the cheek of the speaker before she spread her arms wide as though to encompass them all. "This is King Mormoth. He is king above us, in the world beyond. He has come for you to serve him, though I have told him you are not ready."

Another warrior stepped forward, her hand coming to Libelle's neck before she hissed, another dragon shrieking in anger, fire licking at its lips. "Mother is hurt," she said, her nose pressed to the mark. "Him. Mother is hurt."

The room shook with the roars and hisses of the warrior pairs. Mormoth's knife felt insubstantial in his hand, the six dragons standing as their riders ran to their sides, the young female pulling Libelle along with her. The witch grinned at Mormoth but then she held up a slim hand, silence descending though the dragons remained on their feet.

"Peace," she intoned, her voice echoing around the cavern. "It was an error. You must remain calm, my children. This is the man who bid me to breed you to serve him. Though you are yet young, the time has come; you are now to serve the purpose you were bred for. You will fly. We must all fulfil our part in the world, precious jewels."

"Serve, Mother?" said the smallest of the warriors, her tongue catching on the "s" of her word, drawing it out into a hiss. "What are we to do?"

"You will know," said Libelle. "You see my dragons and warriors are young, Mormoth. They have much to learn. Do you wish to take them now?"

"They are our dragons, witch," said Mormoth. "Ours and they will serve. We don't need them to be grown, just strong, and these are by far the finest beasts we have ever seen. We did ask for only males though, yet two of these are female."

"Nature only bends so much," said Libelle. "And how are they to breed on with only males. Even you know that there must be mothers for you to steal their sons."

Mormoth sniffed, swiping at the sweat on his brow. "Get them ready to leave. They are needed on the field before sundown."

"It is time, my children," said Libelle, reaching out to stroke the snout of the closest dragon as though it were a lap dog rather than a beast of war. "You were bred for a purpose. I have not hidden that from you. It is time."

The human warriors exchanged worried looks for a moment before they stood tall, bowing to Libelle with a deference borne out of more than obligation before they headed towards their dragons, mounting them without the need for a saddle or reins.

"They are ready," said Libelle to Mormoth before she turned back to the six warriors and their riders. "You are ready."

A hiss and a single shriek were the response, all six warriors making the noise at once as the dragons rose in unison towards the ceiling. Mormoth watched as they increased their speed towards the solid rock, seeing nineteen years of time wasted as he imagined Libelle had sent them towards some dramatic suicide just to spite him. Another shriek preceded the blinding flash, six channels of flame aimed at the glittering rock which split apart, pulverised so that it rained down like dust upon Libelle and Mormoth as they watched the dragons rise up into the sky beyond.

"You'd best hurry if you want to catch up with them," said Libelle. "Not much of a victory if you are not there to see it."

Mormoth squinted in the sunlight that flooded the chamber, barely able to see the tails of the dragons. He turned and hurried back along the corridor, Libelle's laughter following him but he did not turn to chastise her. He would witness his victory even if he had to run. He broke into the cavernous workroom but not even a single head was raised, all of them ignoring him and working on their tasks. The corridor to the surface seemed endless; twists and turns of glittering rock were all he saw for several minutes before he reached the wooden door. He set his shoulder to it, grunting under the effort of opening it and barely keeping his feet as it finally gave in.

The soldiers he had left on the mountain side snapped to attention but several of them were too slow; their eyes trained on the six dragons that flew in circles above their heads, sunlight reflecting off their scales. Mormoth swung up onto his horse, staring up proudly at the dragons.

"The tide has turned in our favour. We must return for our victory," he said before he pointed to three soldiers who had failed to come to attention at his appearance. "Captain, make sure to leave their entrails for the rooks."

The captain snapped a salute and nodded gruffly, though his eyes revealed his hesitation. Mormoth did not move, waiting as the captain unsheathed his sword with a trembling hand. Several of the other soldiers, knowing the inevitability of the King's commands, helped their condemned comrades from their armour, stepping back as they knelt on the floor by their captain.

"We would tell you to make it last," said Mormoth. "But we will not be delayed. Strike, Captain, it is your duty."

The captain gritted his teeth, the soldiers before him nodding their silent assent before bowing their heads. He struck, hard and swift, their heads soon rolling in the blood that pooled before their bodies.

The King smiled. "Spill them and then follow. You won't want to miss the celebrations."

The rest of the guards followed the King, hooves and feet beating a rhythm as they descended the mountain, leaving the captain alone to follow the King's wishes and spread the guts of his comrades against the mountainside.

***

The battle was quieter than it had been when Mormoth had left it, his own troops having withdrawn to a more defensible position, allowing more to return to secure the city. The rebels waited them out, the cover of night serving them better than trying to go against the war machine of the King in the daylight. Little skirmishes flourished and were extinguished just as quickly, rebels or soldiers victorious but neither good enough to turn the battle.

Mormoth stepped into his tent; the table put to rights and the maps set back in place, his generals surrounding it. He strode forward, sweeping an arm across the careful plans and placements until they all clattered to the floor. The generals said nothing, not daring to even look at one another. The two still sporting injuries from their previous beating took a tentative step back as the King smirked, pointing to the entrance.

"Step out and watch our achievements."

The generals did as he bid, exiting into the late afternoon sun to see the same sight they had left; the lines barely moved on either side. A stalemate that would be broken at sundown they were sure when the rebels found their courage and strength. A shriek came as a prelude to the screams, and they looked up to see six huge dragons bearing down on the rebel lines. Fire spilled from their mouths, torching the ground in front of the rebels, moving in unison as they pushed them back. None of them offered any resistance as even the dragons they had brought over to their cause cowered before those that had returned with Mormoth.

"Beautiful, aren't they?" said Mormoth. "Our greatest creation."

"I thought Mistress Libelle said two decades until they are ready," said General Firenze, his lips swollen, one eye tightly shut and blackened.

"She likes to play her power games; but we informed her we would be taking our dragons, and she had no choice but to relinquish them. They are ignorant, both rider and dragon it seems; they talk like the rest of her beasts, but they are strong. Look at that, they don't even have to draw blood. We are almost disappointed but never mind, things like that are easily changed. Have your men round up the rebel leaders and prepare a scaffold. A little more demonstration of our might won't go amiss, and it has been months since we have seen a proper hanging."

The generals began their descent, keeping the dragons as best they could in their sight.

"Rovi!" barked the king, the other generals abandoning their comrade as he turned back, "Your daughter must be sixteen by now, is she not?"

"Not so old, Your Majesty, just fourteen."

"What is two years' difference when it comes to honour? Send her to me; I would like to meet her. Her mother and chaperones need not accompany her. This is a great honour for you, Rovi, and what a day to celebrate on, when our dragons have brought peace."

Rovi cast an eye back over the hulking beasts that still stalked the rebel lines, turning back with a bow even as he forced a fist against his own stomach. "Your Majesty," he said before turning to follow his colleagues down to their troops.

***

The rebel leaders were led under their dragon guard to the palace; their followers forced to march alongside them in columns that often felt the bite of a whip. Mormoth watched them file into the gates, having travelled ahead once he had been assured the leaders had been secured. He curled his hand into the long blonde hair of Rovi's daughter, the child stifling a whimper as he pulled too tight. Her obedience pleased him, even her trembles suppressed when she had been left alone in his chambers. She would be a welcome enjoyment after the hanging, his reward for his victory over the foolish rebel cause.

The scaffold was crude, swiftly erected with ten nooses prepared for its first wave of victims. He had already instructed the executioner to keep the line of prisoners swinging until the ropes themselves snapped, even those who had surrendered to be punished for their crimes. Mormoth smiled at the thought, wondering if he should force the court to place bets on how many they could execute before the ropes gave in. Whilst the rebels were dealt with, he had instructed the dragons and their riders to remain on display; the great beasts perched on the perimeter walls, and their riders seated on their backs clicking, hissing and shrieking at each other in their strange approximation of a language. He had considered sending for Libelle, but he did not want those loyal to him giving her any praise. They were his dragons now, his victory.

He dragged the girl to her feet as the drums began, the first of the rebel leaders being marched up to the scaffold. "Time to witness our victory, pet," he said. "Your father will be proud to see you at our side."

He led her out onto the balcony, looking up as the familiar sulphurous smell wafted passed him to see a dragon perched on the parapets above—the rider, one of the female pair, the one who had smelled him on her former mistress' neck and hissed like her great lizard at him. He had not forgotten the slight, perhaps the child warrior would prove useful once Rovi's daughter had served her purpose. Libelle had said the females were there to be bred. The thought in his mind, he stepped out farther, forcing the young girl back to her knees as he waved to the crowds gathered below; the generals squashed onto one of the smaller balconies next to his own.

The executioner in his black hood slipped the ropes over the heads of the rebels perched on the small wooden stools, tightening them until their eyes bulged even before the ground was knocked out from under them. He looked smaller from a distance, and Mormoth giggled that even the hulking figure he employed to mete out justice looked to be a little more than an ant. When the last noose was secured and the executioner stood at his post, Mormoth raised his hand. He took a moment to scan the crowd, silent with anticipation and fear for the dragons that would now keep all rebellious thoughts in check. When he was sure all eyes were on him, he dropped his hand.

Nothing happened.

He raised his hand again, dropping it swiftly, but still the rebels remained on their stools—the ropes around their necks lax.

"Executioner, is there a problem?" he shouted, glad for the silence. He waved a hand in front of his face with a quiet curse as the stink of dragon breath wafted over him again. "Executioner! What is the problem? Those rebels should be dancing."

"Indeed, Sire, they should," called the executioner, pulling off the black hood to reveal a tumble of grey hair, shorter in places than others. "They should be dancing in celebration over the dethronement of a corrupt king."

"Libelle!" cursed Mormoth. "What is this? Where is my executioner?"

"Amongst the crowd, I am sure," replied Libelle from her place on the scaffold. "He wanted to watch this. I think it will help, at least in part, to ease his soul for the crimes you have forced him to commit in your name."

"He has performed his duties as we have commanded, what is there in that to torture his soul? He has done his King's bidding."

"Yes, he has," said Libelle. "And you freely admit, Sire, that it is your bidding he has done. The executions of children, hanged for their birth, or the men and women who have dared to question your taxes and theft of their sons for your armies that you then turn against their own people with the threat of the lash and the noose. There is no end to your crimes, yet you stand there rather than here."

"Prattling old woman! You are determined to sign your own death warrant. Take her," he said, frowning as none of the soldiers moved. "Did you not hear me? Take her, string her up. I don't even need to try her for witchcraft. Take her or I shall feed my dragons."

"My dragons," said Libelle, her eyes moving to the roof above Mormoth. "My children, all of them."

Mormoth looked up; the lone female dragon and her rider joined by the other five of her brethren. "What is this? You should be at your posts, defending the walls. You were bred to serve me. Do as I say."

"Bred to serve," said the young female. "Bred by Mother to serve. Serve the people, the country, the cause we were born for. Stupid man. We serve Mother. We serve Mother."

"Did you truly think, Mormoth, that I would give you such jewels as they to continue your barbaric ways? They are bred to serve and serve they shall. Mind the girl as you take him, my children. She is innocent."

Mormoth pulled Rovi's daughter in front of him, placing his back against the balustrade as he retreated from the descending dragons. The female rider that he had admired with such pleasure, left her seat on her dragon's back, the beast lowering her to the balcony on its foreleg. She pulled a sword from her belt: the dark blade fashioned from a dragon's claw and sharpened to a point, and the handle carved to fit her grip perfectly. She swung it through the air with ease, slicing a path over the head of Rovi's daughter until it came to rest against Mormoth's throat.

"Let the child go," she hissed, pressing the blade just close enough for Mormoth to feel its bite.

He released his grip, the child tumbling to the balcony floor before she gathered herself and ran for the interior, doors slamming and voices rising as she screamed for her mother. Mormoth looked up as the dragons came closer; the lattice work on the window frames crushed in their claws. The sulphurous stink nearly overwhelmed him, but he refused to swoon. He stood, defiant, staring down the warrior who held his life in thrall.

"I will not beg," he said, voice raised to reach the still silent crowds. "You may as well order her to kill me here and now, witch, for I will not beg."

Libelle laughed, the silvery sound alien in the silence of the palace grounds. "They will not kill you, Mormoth. They will not allow a new era to begin bathed in blood even if it is yours. You will be imprisoned for your crimes once they are heard by a court of the Republic."

"Republic, that rabble?" said Mormoth, his voice

trying for mirth but achieving desperation.

"They have been well prepared for years. The council is already in place and has been meeting for months right under your nose, guarded by the dragons you thought were yours."

"They will throw you down, witch, throw you down and beg for my return."

"No, they won't." It was General Rovi's voice that answered, rather than Libelle's. "No one will ever want you back."

"Even your generals are sick of you, Mormoth," said Libelle. "Take him inside. I'm sure there will be many who are happy to show you the way to the dungeon."

The warrior lowered her blade, pointing it towards the door—the snap of jaws above Mormoth's head preventing any hesitation. He stepped back into his suite, the door to the interior corridor opening to reveal several of his generals, his insignia on their uniforms ripped away. Outside the dragons shrieked, the palace shaking with the volume but it was nothing in comparison to the cheers of the people—cheers that Mormoth had never heard during his reign. Above it all though one sound stood out, Libelle's laughter carrying over every other sound as Mormoth was led to the dungeons below.

BEYOND THE REALM

ELIZABETH MONTAGUE is a short story author from Hertfordshire in England.

Her debut collection, *Dust and Glitter*, was published by Clarendon House Publications in May 2019 featuring short stories spanning several genres including fantasy, science fiction and hyper-realism. She has featured in several anthologies from Clarendon House Publications, Black Hare Press, Scout Media and Iron Faerie Publishing. She is currently working on a new collection of short stories inspired by her story *The Mystery of Lydford Gorge* and also her debut novel, *Soul Less*.

Bibliography
Beyond, Black Hare Press, 2019
Blaze, Clarendon House Publications 2019
Divinity, Iron Faerie Publishing, 2019
Dust and Glitter, Clarendon House Publications, 2019
Enigma, Clarendon House Publications 2018
Fireburst, Clarendon House Publications 2018
Flashpoint, Clarendon House Publications 2018
Gleam, Clarendon House Publications 2019
Maelstrom, Clarendon House Publications 2019
Monsters, Black Hare Press, 2019
Tempest, Clarendon House Publications 2019
The Best of Iron Faerie Publishing 2019, Iron Faerie, 2020
Window, Clarendon House Publications 2018
Worlds, Black Hare Press, 2019

Connect
Website: elizabethmontagueauthor.wordpress.com/
Amazon: amazon.co.uk/Elizabeth-Montague/e/B07BGZ3DTN
Facebook: elizabethmontaguewrites
Twitter: @lizzymontwrites

BLACK HARE PRESS

BEYOND THE REALM

REIGN DELAY
By John H. Dromey

Heir to the throne from an early age, a young prince endured the apparent indifference of the regent. Benign neglect or something far more sinister? Just when his royal future seemed most in doubt, help came from an unexpected source.

With surefooted confidence, the solitary knight approached his fearsome opponent without hesitation or trepidation. Up close, he thrust his sword with uncanny accuracy through a narrow space between two massive scales. The point penetrated deep into the breast of the fire-breathing beast. For several heartbeats, the young warrior stood motionless with his arm extended. In his mind's eye, he fantasised about the accolades he should reap from his feat of derring-do. Surely his admirable accomplishment would garner nothing but fulsome praise.

"You're holding your sword wrong."

"Who said that?"

"I did."

"Who are you?"

"I'm Alex, and you're Edwin, the Inept Swordsman."

The lad glanced down at the stick cupped in his hand. A slender branch he'd taken from an ash tree. He tightened and loosened his grip a couple of times. With a puzzled expression on his face, he said, "I think you're mistaken."

"I am not. When you slew the dragon with an upward thrust, you held your elbow away from your body."

"How do you know I was fighting a dragon?"

Alex pointed. "I only have to look at yon carcass with tendrils of smoke snaking out of its nostrils."

The would-be knight turned his head. Sure enough, he also saw the supine form of a massive dragon. He shook his head and his vision cleared. Only the bare ground of the courtyard was visible. Something was amiss.

"You told me *who* you are, Alex. *What* are you?"

"I think you've already guessed. I'm a witch."

"You can't be."

"Why not?"

"Alexander is a man's name. Witches are exclusively of the fair sex."

"I'm Alexandra."

Edwin was flustered.

"Your face is turning red. Were you perhaps touched by the heat of the dying dragon's exhalation?"

"You know I was not." His blush deepened.

"I have the distinct impression you're embarrassed because you failed to distinguish my gender. You shouldn't be."

"I agree with you on that point, at least. I had good cause to mistake your ilk. Your appearance is deceptive."

Alex tilted her head and fluttered her eye lashes. "In what way, pray tell."

"You are wearing breeches, your hair is short, and you move like a…I don't know what. Besides, you caught me off-guard by making a sudden appearance. How did you find this place? It's my secret hideaway."

"Mine, too. At any rate, it was until you intruded. No one else in the palace seems to know about this clandestine enclave. Perhaps we can share it."

"Why should I agree to that? I come here to practise, not to be made fun of. What do you know about swordplay?"

"More than you might imagine. In a pretend fight I could show you a thing or two."

Edwin raised his stick. "Why don't you then?"

"Since I recognise you as the heir apparent to the throne of Gastonia, I can approach your highness only by your leave. You have the royal right to refuse my standing—and I might say generous—offer to instruct you in the finer points of fencing."

"I accept. When do we start?"

"There's no time like the present." Alex put her right foot forward and brandished a stick of her own. A tapered, highly polished wooden shaft.

"Is that a magic wand?"

"It's whatever I want it to be. *En garde!*"

The witch kept up a running commentary as they engaged in mock combat.

Feint, lunge, recover.

Edwin disengaged. "Of a sudden, my stick feels heavy. I can barely lift it."

"Your arm is tiring. Do what I do. Switch hands." Alex deftly flipped her wand from her right hand to her left.

Edwin's attempt to mimic her actions was

unsuccessful. He retrieved his stick from the ground and the faux fight continued.

Attack, parry, riposte.

Although a subsequent switching of sword hands was accomplished with increased finesse, Edwin's overall awkwardness was readily apparent. He flailed first one arm and then the other, but he persevered. The encounter continued without interruption.

"Let's take a breather," Alex suggested.

Edwin did not object. He noisily gulped in oxygen and expelled carbon dioxide with an open mouth. When his respiration returned to near normal, he proclaimed, "I believe I demonstrated rather effectively who is the teacher and who is the pupil."

"You did indeed. I'm pleased to meet a future monarch who's modest enough to acknowledge his shortcomings."

"You mistook my words. I consider myself the superior fighter."

"How could you draw such a benighted conclusion? Had our contest been in earnest, I could have slain you a dozen times over."

"I don't believe you."

"Would you like a demonstration?"

Edwin said nothing. The intensity of his concentration produced a frown as he considered his options.

"You're deeply concerned by my proposal, aren't you? Despite your self-proclaimed prowess with an ersatz sword, you think I might by pure chance strike you with the pointed end of my wand and do you some bodily harm."

"Did you somehow read my thoughts?

"There was no need. Your face is an open book. You're wary of my powers and rightfully so. What if I promise not to use lethal force?"

"Mayhap that will suffice, but how can you convince me your claim is not an idle boast?"

Alex held out her left hand. "Draw the tip of your blade across my palm."

"Do what?"

"Touch my hand with your stick."

Alex complied. A gentle swipe of his twig left a visible line through which red fluid welled up. "You're wounded."

"So, it would appear," Alex said. As her wand hovered over the scratch, she muttered an incantation. The blood receded, and the witch's skin closed in from either side to seal the gap left by the incision. "Good as new, if not better."

"How do I know that wasn't an illusion with no more substance than the dragon you showed me earlier?"

"Look closely at the tip of your weapon. What you see there is real. Test it with your finger. Taste it."

He did.

"Coppery would you say? A bit salty perhaps?"

He nodded.

"Now, all I need is a drop of your imperial blood and our bond will be complete. Take off your tunic."

"What?"

"You heard me."

"Why?"

"I don't wish to reduce your garment to tatters and then spend the remainder of the day trying to mend it."

"Couldn't you use your wand?"

Alex shook her head. "It's only effective on organic matter with a lifeforce. Your woollen surcoat is too far removed from a sheep for me to animate it."

Edwin stripped to his waist. "Your turn."

"I'll take my chances. If the need arises for me to cover myself, I have a cloak nearby" She raised her wand.

Edwin put up a spirited defence to her vigorous onslaught and then counterattacked with brio.

"Enough!" Alex said, a short time later.

"Why do you yield so soon?"

"I have what I wanted." She touched the point of

her wand to her tongue. "Now, we are bonded."

"I don't ken how that's possible. There's not a scratch on me."

"You think not? Look down."

Edwin lowered his head. His chest and abdomen were covered with bloody cuts. "How is this possible? I felt no pain."

"That's easily remedied." Alex waved her wand.

The young prince let out a prolonged mournful cry, bent nearly double, and then slumped to the ground where he lay motionless.

The witch sealed his wounds. Afterwards, she waited patiently for him to stir.

Edwin sat up. "My head is spinning. What happened to me?

"You swooned."

"Nonsense. That's what ladies at court do when their corsets are drawn too tight."

"It's plain to see you're not wearing one of those. Since, however, we're through fighting for the day, why don't you cover yourself? That way both courtiers and commoners alike will have to guess what lies beneath your outerwear."

"I don't want to get my tunic all smeared with blood."

"You won't. Look down, once more, and you'll

see your torso is again as it was when we first met."

With a sheepish grin on his face, Edwin got dressed. "Your skill exceeds mine. I could learn from you. Will you teach me?"

"I will."

"Why do you agree so readily?"

"I want something from you in return."

"I have very little to give."

"You have access to the royal library, do you not?"

"I do. The keeper of the ancient tomes is one of my few true friends. I will not betray his trust by stealing books for you."

"Nor would I ask that of you. The risk of discovery is too great. Besides, I doubt you could carry the volumes of greatest interest to me more than a few paces, anyway."

"Why must you insult me at every turn? I'll grant you some of the books are quite large, but I'm no weakling."

"Forgive me, Edwin. I did not mean to belittle your physical prowess. With a little extra effort on your part, I'm certain you could carry a tall stack of folios over a great distance, if that were your wont. In contrast, there's a comparatively small sheepskin bound codex that *no* ordinary human can remove from the repository—not even someone with the strength of a giant."

"I think I know the worthless item of which you speak."

"Why do you describe it thus?"

"The title is written in a dead language that the Keeper cannot identify. With the prospect of finding illustrations inside, I picked up the so-called codex. It was light as a feather."

"Yet you were unable to open it," Alex said.

Edwin nodded his head. "Try as I might, I could not pry open the cover and the leaves were sealed together. How did you know?"

"The book has a protection spell. Two, actually. One to keep its contents safe from curiosity seekers like you. The second—an even more powerful spell—is to prevent the codex from being carried over the threshold of the repository."

"I told you it's worthless."

"Not entirely. I know a counter spell for the first enchantment which restricts access. I can teach it to you."

"A waste of time. I can't read the dead language."

"I'll teach you not only to read the language of the codex, but to speak it as well."

"When?"

"Between practice bouts of fighting, while you're

resting your tortured muscles, we can work on the reading and writing part. There's a patch of sand where I can draw the appropriate hieroglyphs with my wand. Once you've mastered the written language, you can describe the contents of the codex to me and copy designated passages that might be useful to us both."

"What about speaking?"

"You'll have dual lessons. We'll practise speaking as we practise fighting. It should help improve your concentration."

"What if it doesn't?"

Alex held up her wand. "Then you'll learn a painful lesson—the consequences of failure."

***

Weeks and months went by. Seasons changed.

As soon as Edwin mastered the language of the codex, his tutor proceeded to instruct him in all the tongues spoken within his future kingdom and in nearby lands.

In exchange for information extracted from the codex, Alex rewarded Edwin with an amulet to wear beneath his tunic. The talisman strengthened their already strong bond. For all intents and purposes, he became a sorcerer's apprentice.

Alex introduced additional wooden facsimile weapons and new fighting techniques. Except for daggers, she avoided bringing steel armaments to the secret courtyard. The sound of clashing metal could betray their location and make known the belligerent nature of their clandestine meetings. At the witch's insistence—although he could conceive of no need for it—Edwin carried a concealed dirk for personal protection. In response to intermittent demands for proof he indeed had the weapon on his person, he became adept at producing the short dagger on a moment's notice. After much repetition, the manoeuvre became second nature. Shielded from view by one hand, the blade was so expeditiously extracted from the confines of his clothing, it often appeared in his other hand as if by magic.

With almost daily practice, Prince Edwin developed skills worthy of a true knight, yet his progress was not noted by the regent, nor his henchmen. The head of the palace guard shielded the heir to the throne from participating in, or even watching, any activity which involved a hint of violence, however slight. Military manoeuvres were especially taboo.

In addition to developing his fighting skills in private, Edwin also grew in wisdom. He was allowed, even encouraged to be bookish. His hours spent in the library relieved others from the burden of having him underfoot. As a result, the regent could openly speak his mind to his cronies and freely hint at his own ambitions which included one day assuming the throne. First, he would have to rid the kingdom of its rightful heir, but that should prove a minor obstacle, at most. How much trouble, after all, could an indolent bookworm generate?

The prince was oblivious to the plotting that went on behind his back. Alex was not. She had a bevy of reliable informants among the palace staff. Even so, she did not immediately share her knowledge of palace intrigue with her pupil. She did, however, take precautions.

"If your apple tastes bitter, Edwin, it's because I put a pinpoint size drop of oil on it—extract from a highly toxic herb."

"Why would you do that?"

"Monarchs are susceptible to such attacks. If I measured the dosage correctly, in the future you will be immune to many poisons and venoms. For the nonce, you may experience a temporary weakness in your limbs."

"On that subject, I've noticed something curious, Alex. No matter how much my muscles grow, my wooden stick still feels unnaturally heavy each time I pick it up. From my perspective, I'll wager it's now equal to—or of even greater heft—than an actual sword. You've placed an enchantment on it, haven't you?"

Alex nodded her head. "I trow you are the finest stick fighter in your kingdom."

"Think what you like, but your opinion counts for nowt as far as my situation is concerned. The kingdom is not yet mine."

"That will change soon. Just as your voice has changed. You'll soon be old enough to lead your subjects in peace or in war."

"How would I fare in battle without the aid of your wizardry?"

"Rather well, I should imagine. I daresay I've trained you well. Should you desire my continued support, however, you could make me your squire. That way I could accompany you wherever you go."

"That's a foolhardy notion if ever I heard one. My voice has changed, but yours has remained much the same as the day we first met. You'd be found out in a trice."

"Are you sure about that? After all, I have a witch's glamour at my disposal."

"You have what?"

"The ability to project an image of my choice into the minds of the people around me. I'm older than you are, Edwin, yet you perceive me as a little girl. Would you like to see me otherwise?"

"How? As a wizened old hag?"

"If that's what you want." As Alex hunched over, her face wrinkled, and her hair grew long and scraggly. She held her wand like a walking stick.

Edwin looked on in disgust. "That's not what I want. Change back!" He shut his eyes. "How old are you anyway?"

"I was in my third summer when you first saw the light of the world."

"What does that mean?"

"I'm two years older than you. Why don't I show you my true form?" Alex didn't wait for an answer. She blossomed into a young woman. "You can open your eyes now."

The prince first squinted and then opened his eyes wide. "I may know little of what constitutes true beauty, but I'd say your pulchritude far surpasses that of the ladies in waiting I've seen."

"What are they waiting for?"

"I don't know… Why did you not reveal yourself earlier?"

"I didn't want you to be distracted."

"Why would that matter to you?"

"I'm planning for the future. I want you to take your rightful place on the throne. When you oversee the kingdom, I will ask you for a boon."

"A *what*?"

"A favour you will be honour bound to grant."

***

Alexandra had a sombre expression on her face when she announced, "There are widespread rumours a legendary armoured creature long thought extinct is terrorising the Northern Provinces."

"Do you believe the gossip?" Edwin wondered.

"I do. With some reservations. Details are sketchy, but the description matches that of an herbivorous dinosaur. A threat to crops, but not to people. My greatest fear is a wizard has used black magic to shapeshift a large living animal, a pachyderm perhaps, into a veritable monster. One instilled with an insatiable craving for human flesh."

"Similar to the dragon you showed me?"

Alex shook her head. "No. I created an illusion. The shapeshifted scaly beast I envision has substance and poses a real danger to anyone in its path."

"Is it likely to come our way?"

"Eventually, unless it's stopped."

"Is there anything we can do to prevent that?"

"I'm glad you asked, Edwin. Why don't you join the hunt for the beast?"

"I'm sorely tempted to do just that. Such an undertaking would genuinely test my mettle. Alas, I foresee several difficulties, some of which may be insurmountable. If I go, I won't be missed at court, but how can I explain a prolonged absence from the library, the dining hall, and my bed chamber?"

"I may have a simple solution for that. Would you agree the court physician is a bit of a charlatan?"

"Verily. He has a pronounced aversion to sick people."

"What would he do if you took seriously ill?"

"I suspect he would toss an analgesic balm in my direction—from a safe distance, of course—and then run for the hills."

"What if I were to assume the guise of an itinerant apothecary? I could use berry juice to put some ugly red blotches on your hands, face, and neck. Then, if I mentioned the possibility of a pox or a plague within his hearing distance, how do you think your resident quack would respond? Peradventure, would he endorse a recommendation on my part that you be taken to a remote location of my choosing and placed in quarantine?"

"In a heartbeat."

"Shall we proceed on that assumption? You'd be free to join the Tariq tribesmen when they ride out to hunt the beast."

"How could I accompany them? I have no horse."

"Although many of the Tariq are nomads, they have a permanent settlement in Tarnia. I suggest you go there and seek employment as a groom or a hostler. That way, you can befriend a horse and arrange to have it available for you to borrow on a moment's notice."

"How would I go about such a thing?"

"First, you must dress the part. I'll help you with that. Although your face is not tanned by prolonged exposure to the desert sun and winds, use the dialect of the common people and they'll disregard your skin tone. If asked, tell them you're accustomed to working indoors."

"Why would they hire me if I have no equine experience?"

"For the most part, mucking out stalls is not a pleasant occupation. You can't hold a pitchfork and your nose at the same time. Don't fret about being accepted. They'll welcome you with open arms. Once you're in place, seek out the meanest, most unruly steed in the stable. A horse the other grooms keep as far away from as possible. Preferably, one the foolhardiest of knights would refuse to mount, even if it meant going into battle in an ox cart."

"Suppose I'm successful in finding such an animal, what do I do next?"

"Whisper in the horse's ear in the language of the codex."

"What should I say?"

"If it's a mare or filly, compliment her on her flowing mane."

"A stallion?"

"Ingratiate yourself by emphasising his finer points. Perhaps he stands several hands taller than his stablemates. Or you can use flattery. Tell him he reminds you of Pegasus only he's better looking."

"A gelding?"

"Commiserate with him over his loss and offer him an extra ration of oats."

"Does such an approach really work?"

"More often than not," Alex said. "What you say is less important than how you say it. The tone of your voice is crucial. Also, your comportment. Show no fear."

"I'll do my best. How soon can I leave?"

"In three days, at the soonest. First, I need to make some delicate, but necessary, arrangements. One more thing. This very night, I'll fashion a pliable leather helmet for you to wear while in pursuit of the monster. It will mask some of your features and serve as a partial disguise. To further distinguish yourself from the grooms, you can switch to the language of Tariq aristocrats. Have you selected a *nom de guerre*?"

"I have. Everyman."

"That's a curious choice. What do you mean by it?"

"Those who unite to battle the beast are equals. I am no better, and no worse, than any of them."

Alex nodded her approval. "How will you refer to yourself among the grooms?"

"As Nemo. A nobody."

***

Alex delivered the leather helmet, as promised, on the following morning. It fit perfectly.

She also brought ill tidings. "I fear your life is in imminent danger."

"Why? Is the beast moving faster than anticipated?"

The witch dismissed that notion with a wave of her hand. "There are other threats. They are deathly serious ones, and much closer to home."

"Tell me more, if you dare, but—fair warning—I am in no mood for jests."

"Nor am I. I'll tell you all I know, but one question first. Are you willing to forfeit your claim to the crown to save your life?"

Edwin thought hard before answering. "It is not my choice to make. In my estimation, the regent is an inferior ruler. I believe the people are depending on me to do better."

"I concur in your opinion, Your Highness. Regarding the source of my knowledge, I have an extensive web of spies inside the palace. Some of them are knowingly complicit—strong supporters of your cause, one and all—while others are unwitting informants. This is what I've learned…"

The prince listened patiently, without interrupting, as the witch spun a lurid tale of dark ambition, betrayal of trust, and a possible plot against his life.

"Have you any specific details?" Edwin asked.

"I do not. Have you noticed anything out of the ordinary in your daily routine?"

"Yes. Just this morning, when I went to the library, I saw the court physician loitering near the main entrance. He pretended it was a chance meeting, but he gave me an elixir to build up my strength. He said to take it at bedtime. I waited until the doctor was out of sight before entering the building. At my request, the librarian helped me locate an old history book, then he left me alone in a cubicle. As soon as I could, I slipped out the backdoor of the library and hurried over here."

"Did you bring the elixir?"

Edwin handed her a small vial containing a greenish liquid. She removed the stopper and sniffed. "It's a sleeping potion."

"Does this mean the doctor, either by accident or by design, is an active participant in the plot to deny me my rightful place on the throne?"

"I fear so. In future, do not imbibe any liquid he offers you, or partake of any solids from a questionable source. This development calls for a slight change in our plans. We will move up the onset of your pretend pox, and your departure, by a day. I'll call in a favour so friends of mine can escort you to Tarnia. But first, you must survive until morning. Be sure to bar your door tonight, though I doubt that will guarantee your safety."

"Why not? The sound of someone breaking down my bedchamber door would alert the guards and likewise wake the servants. They would come swarming to my rescue."

"Methinks the approach will be silent. There's a secret door somewhere in your private chambers. I know of its existence but, so far, I've been unable to determine any points of access to the passageway at either end. Whoever shows up will expect to find you asleep. I pray you can defend yourself. To do that, you must keep a constant vigil from dusk to dawn."

Alex sat on the ground. "Lie down. Put your head on my lap and rest."

The witch gently rubbed Edwin's temples with the tips of her fingers while she softly sang a lullaby in the language of the codex. Soon, he was fast asleep.

***

After sunset, Edwin lit two tall beeswax candles and placed them on opposite sides of his bedchamber. Although he thought they should burn through until morning, he had replacements ready if needed. The widely spaced night lights could not both be blown out with a single deep breath by a lone intruder.

He arranged pillows on his bed to fashion a crude facsimile of a human form. He covered his creation with a blanket.

There was nothing more to do but wait.

The prince sat in shadows in a highbacked chair pushed snug against the wall.

Nearly half the sand in the upper chamber of his

hourglass had run out—following its second turning since nightfall—when he heard a faint squeaking sound. A mouse? No. It was a wooden protest by the panel which concealed the opening to the secret passage. Perhaps the jam had warped. Whatever the reason, Edwin appreciated the advance warning. He knew where to look.

Edwin was puzzled by what he saw. Although the intruder held both hands in the air in front of his chest as he approached the bed, there was no glint of candlelight from a burnished blade. Could he have blackened his dagger for night fighting? Was it possible he had entered the room without any murderous intent? His fists were clinched. Was that significant? Did he plan to pummel the prince?

The intruder bent over the bed.

Edwin drew his dagger, rose silently from his chair, and took three stealthy steps forward. From where he stood, he could easily stab the man in the back. He hesitated. Too many questions were unanswered. Was he justified in making a sneak attack? Even if he were, would his efforts be successful. What if the man wore armour? Could he strike a mortal blow from behind? Should he?

"I'm here," Edwin said out loud.

The man whirled around with lightning speed. He

raised his hands. There was no longer any question of his intent. Between the dowels clutched in either hand there was a taut cord braided from strips of rawhide. The assassin had a garrotte.

The prince's reaction was swift and instinctive. He sliced cleanly through the cord with an upward swipe of his dagger. His weapon was still extended at arm's length and just above shoulder height when his attacker sprang forward. The assassin was impaled by his own unchecked momentum with the blade entering just below his chin. The fatal wound was well-placed. The man sank to the floor without emitting a sound.

Edwin dragged the body into the secret passage. In the process, he learned his assailant indeed wore armour beneath his tunic. He also discovered a dagger. Why hadn't the would-be killer used it? The prince thought he knew the answer to that question. *The thug was afraid if he stabbed me, I might cry out in my sleep.*

The prince tidied up his room and closed the panel that hid the secret passage.

Should he take further precautions? It seemed unlikely to him a second assassin would be sent to learn the fate of the first. Even so, he spent the remainder of the night in his chair. With two daggers at his disposal, he felt twice as safe as before.

At the break of dawn, Alex, disguised as a servant,

came to Edwin's quarters and tapped lightly on his door. He sensed who it was and let her in.

Edwin told her as succinctly as possible what had transpired in his room. "Should we change our plans again?"

"I think not. Your help is needed more than ever in the Northern Provinces. There's a troop of lancers in the palace guard with the essential skills needed to destroy the scaly beast. Late yesterday, the Regent of Gastonia refused the Tariq commander's request for their assistance."

Alex assumed the guise of an apothecary. Edwin posed as her patient with a pox. Their well thought out escape plan went off without a hitch.

"The Regent will most likely declare you dead," Alex commented, before they went their separate ways.

"Let him. Depending on how my encounter with the beast is resolved, I may well give truth to his lie."

"What if you survive? Will you seek the throne anon?"

"It's too soon to say. I prefer to deal with one challenge at a time."

"The key to a successful reign in a peaceful and secure kingdom is to forge strong alliances with other powerful rulers. Winning the trust of the Tariq commander will be a good start, an auspicious beginning—if you will—to your own future success. You can count on my continued support no matter what you decide but do keep in mind the boon I plan to ask of you."

***

On the first day of his stint in the largest stable in Tarnia, Edwin was not asked to identify himself. He answered to "hey, you."

Mostly with body language—nudging and pointing—the boisterous grooms adroitly steered the newcomer toward a dark corner of the stable. The final stall and its occupant—a stallion—both showed signs of neglect. All eyes, including those of the horse with its head turned to see what was causing such a commotion, were on the new guy as he approached the three-sided enclosure.

Edwin knew he was being tested. He paused just outside the entrance to the stall. Although the light was dim, he could make out the matted mane and tail of the horse and the broken kickboards along the sides of the stall.

One of the gawkers got too close. Jostled from behind by the press of observers, he was propelled within striking distance of the stallion's hindquarters.

In the blink of an eye, Edwin reached out, grabbed the off-balance groom's arm, and pulled him out of harm's way just before the stallion's hoof whizzed by. There was no contact, but the trajectory was way too close for comfort.

"You can thank your lucky stars that was a straight kick, Omar, and not a cow kick," the head groom told the man who'd stumbled. "A sideways kick could have killed you. This stall can be tended to later. It will take a while for Spirit to settle down."

Edwin acted as though he had not heard. He cleared his throat a couple of times. In between, he grunted out the word *listen* in the language of the codex. The stallion pricked up its ears. Taking that as a good sign, the prince hugged the edge of the stall and inched his way forward. When he got close enough, he began to talk in earnest. The horse listened.

The other grooms drifted away. The excitement was over, and they had work to do.

Once Edwin was completely satisfied, he and the stallion had reached an understanding; he picked up a curry comb, untied Spirit's lead rope, and escorted him outside to a duck pond. When he finished grooming the stallion, he returned him to the stable.

The corner stall was clean. A show of gratitude from the groom whose life he'd saved. Edwin had made two friends. One equine, one human.

In the days that followed, Omar proved he was a friend indeed. In his spare time, he taught Edwin, alias Nemo, the rudiments of horsemanship. The prince was a quick learner.

On the day of the hunt, Edwin held his breath for fear one of the warriors might select Spirit as his warhorse. He needn't have worried. The stallion's renegade reputation still lingered.

The prince did not ride with the main hunting party. He donned his leather helmet and followed from a distance.

Besides his short-bladed daggers, his only other weapon, fashioned from a broken pitchfork handle, was a wooden spear with a fire-hardened point.

The hunters were temporarily lost from view when they went over a hill. Shortly afterwards, as he approached the crest, Edwin heard a war cry. The beast had been sighted. He urged his mount to greater speed and topped the hill at a gallop.

From his high vantage point, the prince surveyed the scene with a critical eye. Apparently, any plan for an organised attack was quickly abandoned. The riders were preoccupied. All their attention was focused on controlling the panicked horses.

Edwin spotted a ravine to his left. He decided to

take a closer look. The narrow gorge with steep sides might serve as a physical barrier they could use to corner the beast.

His inspection was cut short. The earlier war cry was superseded by ululations. The commander had fallen from his mount and lay motionless on the ground. Edwin drove his stake into the ground so he would have both hands free.

The beast pawed the ground three times before it charged.

Edwin and Spirit were already in motion. They had nearly twice the distance to cover, but they moved like the wind. Meanwhile, the beast lumbered along like a giant armadillo with spikes on its back.

Would Spirit falter as they approached the beast? Edwin shouted words of encouragement loud enough to be heard over the thunder of hooves.

Coming to a sudden stop beside the fallen warrior, Spirit lowered his haunches. Otherwise, his rider could have been tossed over the stallion's head. Edwin hopped to the ground.

The commander stirred. He stared in wide-eyed wonder at the approaching beast. The two men wasted no time in scrambling onto the back of the waiting stallion. As soon as they were settled and had secure handholds, Edwin gave a command in the language of the codex.

"Were you talking to your horse or to me?" the commander asked, as they rode away from the beast.

"The horse. He's a good listener."

"Does he understand what you say?"

"I like to think so."

"I hope so because I didn't comprehend a single word. By the by, who are you?"

"Everyman. I doubt you know my family. We lived elsewhere for many years."

"You arrived at an opportune time. You saved my life, for now, at least. Any thoughts on how to defeat the scaly monstrosity that threatens our land?"

"I'd say the beast is best confronted head-on with a battering ram."

"We have no use for such an instrument of war. We have few foes and, for the most part, they live like outlaws in tents or caves. The nearest large trees are several days' ride from here."

"We'll find another way then," Edwin stated with greater confidence than he felt. A show of fear would only serve to demoralise the hunters even more than they were already. "Are your horses good jumpers?"

"They are."

"I suggest we reform on the other side of the ravine." He avoided use of the word retreat. "That beast has the bulk of a pachyderm and, like an elephant, is incapable of jumping. It cannot follow us there." *Unless the witch has lent enchantment to its feet.* "I'll let you give the command. Your men will listen to you."

Edwin retrieved his wooden stake. After a short run, even though he was carrying double, the stallion easily leaped over the ravine. The other riders followed.

The beast approached the edge of the gorge with caution, stopped short of the lip, and stared balefully at the men and horses on the other side.

"What now?"

"May I borrow a sword?"

Those nearest Edwin were quick to unsheathe their blades and proffer them hilt foremost for his inspection. He examined them closely, one by one.

"Too light… the balance is off… too heavy… there's a brittle section—take this to a swordsmith and have it properly tempered… too short…"

"Try mine," the commander said.

The prince scrutinised the entire length of the sword on both sides. He hefted the weapon several times before nodding his head slightly. He held out his left index finger—not quite halfway along its overall length—and placed the flat side of the blade on it. He let go of the hilt. The sword did not wobble.

"This one will do." He picked up the pitchfork handle. "Now, if we can somehow lash these two items together, we'll have an improvised lance. I have neither the skill nor the materials to do so. It must be a secure connection."

"Leave that to us," one of the hunters said. They moistened strips of rawhide with water from their canteens and wrapped the stretchy bands in place as tightly as they could. When they finished, they took turns slowly rotating the lance so the intense sunlight could dry the rawhide evenly to make the bond even stronger.

While that was going on, Edwin put on a show for the otherwise idle onlookers. Talking incessantly, he stood beside Spirit's neck and brandished another borrowed sword with his fully outstretched arm. When he completed his demonstration, he walked over to look at the lance.

"What did you say to that horse?" a hunter wondered. "It looked to me like you nearly talked its ear off."

"I was simply telling him he must not allow himself to be distracted by the waving of the lance. His job is to get me close enough to the beast to drive home the blade."

"Do you expect me to believe that?"

"Believe what you please. My message was for Spirit."

"Do you think he got it?"

"Why don't we ask him?"

"Is it safe?"

"I'll stand between you and the horse."

They approached Spirit. In a normal tone of voice, Edwin spoke in the Tariq tongue. "Did you understand what I said earlier?" He added a whispered command in the language of the codex.

Spirit bobbed his head twice.

"Do I need to repeat my instructions?"

Spirit moved his head from side to side a couple of times.

"Satisfied?"

The hunter did not answer.

"Your lance is ready," the commander said. He handed Edwin a gantlet. "This should improve your grip and protect your hand."

The beast continued to stand on the other side of the ravine directly opposite the hunters. Edwin rode what he considered a safe distance along the gorge before crossing. The stallion cleared the divide without any great effort.

The beast turned to face the challenger, lowered its

head, and advanced. Edwin remained in place. He reached inside his tunic and clasped the amulet in his left hand. While looking at the point of the commander's sword, he uttered an incantation designed to negate an opponent's protection spells. The steel tip appeared to glow. Was it the reflection of the sun? Perhaps. Perhaps not.

As ready as he would ever be, the prince nudged his mount with his foot. Spirit eagerly sprang forward nearly dislodging his rider then proceeded at a moderate pace.

To avoid bouncing, Edwin relaxed and became as one with the horse. The point of his lance rose and lowered as though being carried over gentle waves by an even-keeled boat.

With both adversaries moving, the distance between them closed rapidly. Edwin could clearly make out the scales on the beast. His hand was steady. He directed Spirit to pass by the oncoming leviathan on the left side. In response to his steed's subtle change in direction, the rider adjusted the angle of his lance so the point lined up with a seam between two large scales which—alternately bulging and receding at a regular rate—he perceived as shielding the creature's beating heart.

His aim was true. The sword glided through the miniscule unprotected space and the blade completely disappeared inside the beast. The broader hilt could not follow. It was abruptly halted by contact with the keratinous plates. The impact was greater than Edwin could have imagined. He released his grip on the handle, but not before a shockwave travelled up his arm and wrenched his shoulder within a razor's edge of dislocation.

The prince turned Spirit around in time to see the last stumbling steps of the dying beast. Soon the Tariq warriors crossed the ravine for a closer look.

"Why did you need to borrow a sword?" the commander asked.

"I have none of my own."

"Let me remedy that lack. I am in your debt so long as I shall live, and so are my people." The commander grabbed the pitchfork handle with both hands, put one foot on the chest of the beast, and withdrew the lance. After he wiped off the blood, he offered the weapon to Edwin. "In my service, this blade was nameless. Now, it is worthy of an honorific. Take this well-tested sword as a token of our gratitude and name it what you will."

Edwin accepted the present. "I dub this blade Fidelio."

"Where will you go now?"

"I will return to Tarnia to meet a trusted confidante."

***

"Have you made your decision?" Alex asked.

"I have," Prince Edwin replied. "I will assume my role as king, fight for the throne if necessary, but I do not wish to rule alone."

"Do you seek a consort?"

"Not a consort only, but a wife, an equal partner, and a sage advisor. Someone like you."

"Why not me?"

"Can a witch love?"

"I cannot speak for the others, but *I* can, and do."

"Will you marry me and share the throne with me?"

"I will."

They embraced.

"When should our nuptials be made official?"

"Soon. If you're amenable to the idea, we can ask the Tariq commander to perform a tribal wedding."

That's what they did. Following a brief but joyful ceremony, they spent their honeymoon in a tent.

Their idyllic interlude was brief.

Alex continued to receive sporadic reports from her network of spies. Much of the information was trivial. Some was not.

One forenoon, when she returned from the city marketplace, she was clearly agitated.

"What's wrong, my love?" her husband asked.

"I received troubling news today. The shapeshifted

scaly beast conjured up by the evil witch was intended to wreak havoc and spread panic throughout the Northern Provinces as a prelude to an invasion. I thought you thwarted her plans by slaying the beast, but I was sorely mistaken. She is raising an army."

"Who would serve such a tyrant?"

"Willingly? Very few. She emptied the prisons of able-bodied men and ensorcelled the murderers among them to serve as her minions. They stand guard on the spiral stairs of a lofty turret where she holds a king hostage in his own castle. Of late, she's threatened to torture the monarch unless his subjects enlist in her cause. The ranks of reluctant conscripts grow each day. With her death-dealing minions scattered among them, even an untrained, undisciplined mob of men could pose a serious threat."

"Do you think the Tariq capable of defending their border against the onslaught of such a horde?"

"I do, but at what cost?" She got a dreamy look on her face. "Would that you were already seated on the throne of Gastonia."

"Why do you wish that? What difference would it make?"

"I'd need wait no longer to ask you for a boon."

"I have not forgotten my promise. If you desire, I can fulfil my obligation to you sooner rather than later.

Provided, of course, it is within my power to carry out your request. What would you have me do?"

"If it were not so dangerous, I would have you lead a small band of warriors to remove the captive king from the clutches of the vindictive evil witch. She values him now as a means to an end. Once she has raised an army, her assessment of him will likely change. If war breaks out, I fear the monarch's life will be forfeit no matter which side wins."

"You care about him?"

"I do. And I also care about you. If you're successful in freeing the king, he will support you wholeheartedly, just as the Tariq commander does. With two armies at your back, I predict the Regent of Gastonia will not stand in your way. He is ambitious but not a fool."

Edwin sought fighters willing to accompany him on a perilous quest. Alex was the first to volunteer. "Although the first part of our journey will be under the cover of darkness, we will eventually have to pass through some lighted parts of town. I can use my witch's glamour to confuse the defenders regarding who we are and what we intend to do. The element of surprise will give us a decided advantage."

The Tariq commander was the second person to offer his assistance. He and the prince selected a dozen additional warriors. Omar was enlisted to look after their horses.

Before their departure, Edwin asked the recruits to present their weapons for inspection. In the blink of an eye, a wide variety of steel blades was on display.

Alex, wand in hand, stepped up to the first man in line. He quickly stepped back two paces. "Who are you?"

"My name is unimportant. All you need to know is I am a sorceress. Where you're going, you will not be fighting ordinary men. Although your opponents are not trained swordsmen, they have been imbued with magical powers. Black magic emanating from an evil witch. The sword you wield cannot harm them. I can change that if you will allow me to approach. Hold up your blade."

The man complied.

Alex touched the tip of her wand to the point of the sword. There was a brilliant flash of light.

"Did that hurt?" the next man in line asked.

"No. My arm tingles, but in a good way."

A series of flashes followed. Large flares for swords, smaller ones for daggers.

***

BEYOND THE REALM

With Alex casting spells to cloak their appearance—whenever they were in danger of being detected—the band of stealthy fighters reached the base of the turret without resistance. Most of them took up defensive positions around the entrance of a nearby barracks where the off-duty guards were housed. Those sleeping minions would awake and swarm out of their quarters at the first sound of an alarum.

Edwin paused near the portal at the foot of the tower. He turned to Alex and whispered. "Do you have any advice?"

"I do. The winding of the spiral stairs is designed to favour right-handed defenders and to present difficulties for right-handed attackers. You trained to be ambidextrous. Hold your sword in your left hand, your dagger in your right."

The prince shifted his sword to his sinister hand and drew his dagger with his dextral. He entered and began his ascent. Alex was right behind him.

At regular intervals, metal brackets set in the curved wall held burning torches.

As he rounded the second blind turn, Edwin confronted the first defender. The minion swung his scimitar with all his might. The prince parried by moving his blade the width of his hand. Accustomed perhaps to delivering a fatal blow with each swing of his enchanted blade, the minion hesitated. Edwin did not. He sank his dagger into his opponent's heart.

The clash of swords alerted the remaining minions.

Edwin continued his ascent, fighting each step of the way. He dispatched some of the turret defenders outright. Others he disarmed by slashing the muscle of their dominant arm, so they dropped their weapon. He left those for Alex to deliver a *coup de grâce*.

The prince experienced several close calls. In one encounter, a mortally wounded minion fell against him. With a restricted view of the next attacker, Edwin had to wrap his arm partway around the body of the dying man and thrust his blade forward. The point buried itself in a bone. Edwin struggled to dislodge his sword. The second wounded man struck back with his scimitar. Most of the impact was absorbed by the body of the man between them. The curved blade, however, extended beyond. Edwin felt a burning sensation in his left shoulder. Alex tapped him with her wand. With his vitality restored, he freed his sword with a powerful yank, cast the corpse aside, and finished off the minion who had wounded him.

When they reached the top of the stairs, Edwin and Alex were the only ones still standing. Uncertain of what danger they might face next, they entered the chamber side by side.

Inside, in the light of a new day, they found the king sitting on a wooden chair. He appeared to be alone.

"Where is the wicked witch?" Edwin asked.

"Gone. She could follow the tide of battle—as could I—by the sounds funnelled up the stairwell. When she apprehended all was lost, she tried to fly away on her enchanted besom. What she didn't realise was—during my long captivity, when she wasn't looking—I gradually loosened the bonds that held the twigs in place at the base of her stick. The effect was the same as clipping the wings of a bird of prey. When she picked up her broom, most of the twigs slipped out and cascaded quietly to the floor. In her haste to depart, she didn't notice. Look over the balcony and you'll see her body lies shattered on the cobblestones below."

When Edwin and Alex stepped out on the balcony and looked over the railing, they saw a crowd had gathered at the foot of the turret.

Before long, members of the crowd noticed the couple. Someone pointed upward and yelled, "Look! It's Princess Alexandra!"

Edwin was gobsmacked. "You're a princess?"

"Yes. You just saved my father's life."

The king stuck his head out through the archway.

"Help me get down from here, daughter. The steps are uneven. I don't want to fall when I'm this close to freedom."

The trio descended together.

The commander met them at the foot of the stairs. "I received a dispatch with good news. The Regent of Gastonia has fled. When you reach the palace, Prince Edwin, there will be no confrontation. Only your coronation."

BEYOND THE REALM

JOHN H. DROMEY grew up on a farm in northeast Missouri, USA. At first, he cultivated his imagination by thinking up songs and stories. After he learned to type, he really went to town with his writing. Later in life, he moved to the city. John enjoys reading—mysteries in particular—and writing in a variety of genres.

Bibliography

Angels, Black Hare Press, 2019
Apocalypse, Black Hare Press, 2019
Beyond the Realm, Black Hare Press, 2020
Beyond, Black Hare Press, 2019
Castles and Kimono, Insignia, 2020
Curses and Cauldrons, Blood Song Books, 2019
Dark Moments Year One, Black Hare Press, 2019
Hate, Black Hare Press, 2020
Japanese Fantasy Drabbles, Insignia, 2020
Lockdown Fantasy #1, Black Hare Press, 2020
Love, Black Hare Press, 2020
Lust, Black Hare Press, 2020
Monsters, Black Hare Press, 2019
Oceans, Black Hare Press, 2020
Sloth, Black Hare Press, 2020
Twenty Twenty, Black Hare Press, 2020
Unravel, Black Hare Press, 2019
Worlds, Black Hare Press, 2019

BLACK HARE PRESS

BEYOND THE REALM

VANYA'S NECKLET
By Rich Rurshell

Two sellswords embark on a quest with the king's daughter to stop a malevolent sorcerer from finding all the pieces of a powerful artifact and taking over the world.

"One moment. I'm going to be si…" Ernest ran to the side of the ship and expelled his breakfast into the sea below. Mavern laughed heartily.

"Seasick, mercenary?" she asked.

"Damn you, witch," said Ernest, wiping vomit from his chin. "It's your stinking army. Never in my life have I smelt such a stench." Ernest turned to me.

"Griffin, how can you stand it?"

The deck was crowded with Mavern's undead thralls. Ernest was right. The smell of rotting flesh and decay was overwhelming.

"I don't like it any more than you do," I said. "But these things will be useful when the fighting starts."

"They'd better be."

"They *will* be," chimed in Mavern.

"Yeah, we'll see," said Ernest, scowling.

Mavern sniggered and turned away, disappearing among her undead soldiers.

"You good?" I asked.

"I don't trust witches, Griffin."

"What about her?" I asked. Princess Jade stood alone at the front of the ship.

"I don't trust any witch. I don't care if she is King Lucas's daughter. I am only protecting her because that is what the king is paying us to do."

I shared Ernest's lack of trust when it came to Mavern. She was no doubt a powerful ally, and her army would indeed be useful, but I'm wary of anyone who practices necromancy, especially to the standard that Mavern does. As for the princess, she was quiet and kept to herself. I wasn't sure what to think about her.

"Why would the king need us to protect her

anyway?" I asked. "Why not just keep her safe in his castle? Why would he send his daughter into battle?"

"He is scared, Griffin. He knows the warlock Kredak is searching for the fragments of Vanya's Necklet. The princess has one of the fragments. As does the necromancer Mavern. By sending his daughter with his army to deal with Kredak overseas, his kingdom is no longer a direct target. Though, if we fail and Kredak gets all the pieces, he will attempt to conquer the entire world…and probably succeed."

"We have two of the fragments here on this ship?"

"Yes. Mavern has the necromancy fragment, hence her ability to raise and control an army of undead this size. I believe the princess holds the nature fragment."

"How many does Kredak have?"

"I don't know. I heard one of the king's men say that Kredak has already murdered Curo the pyromancer and Nahla the rainmaker. Kredak already owned the lightning fragment, so he has at least three of the eight fragments. He now has enhanced power in fire, water, and lightning magic."

"Then the warlock Tynis holds another fragment? That is why we are going to Canis Isle to aid him against Kredak?"

"Yes. Tynis has the fear fragment."

Something in Ernest's face when he mentioned the fear fragment concerned me. Ernest was not easily shaken. I changed the subject.

"So, who has the remaining fragments?" I asked.

"Selwynne, the head lecturer at the Mages' College in Guidon City has the soul fragment. That's the healing magic fragment. As for the earth fragment, I'm not sure."

"No wonder King Lucas didn't explain all of this to us. Being personal bodyguards for his daughter in the fight against Kredak is barely half of the story."

"Had you known the whole truth, would you have agreed on the same price for your sword? Would you have taken the job at all?"

I looked at Ernest and he paused and then smiled.

"Of course," we cried in unison. "Never turn a job down. Never have, never will." We laughed and clasped our sword hands together, reminiscent of the day we became brothers of blood. Brothers of the sword. Ernest breathed in deeply, then sighed.

"Oh. Not again…" He turned back to the side of the ship and was sick again.

***

I awoke to the sound of shouting. Ernest was

already out of his hammock and pulling on his clothes.

"Are we at Canis Isle already?" I asked.

"I don't think so. Come on, let's see what is happening."

As we arrived on the deck, we saw the few living crew members scrambling around the ship in a panic. Mavern's undead warriors stood where they had stood for the entire voyage, indifferent to what was going on around them.

"What's happening?" shouted Ernest to the captain.

"It's Nautametus! She's just taken down one of the ships."

"Nautametus exists?" I asked. "She's not just a myth?"

"Why don't you ask the people on that ship, Griffin?" replied Ernest.

I'd heard stories of Nautametus, the almighty sea serpent as a child, but had never spoken to anyone who had actually encountered her. Maybe for a good reason, most don't live to tell the tale.

"How far have we got to go until…"

Nautametus rose from the ocean some distance away. I shuddered. Even at the distance we were, her sheer size was terrifying. As quickly as she had appeared, Nautametus returned to the depths, taking another one of our ships with her.

"That was more of the king's men," cried out one of the crew from behind us. "Why can't it take the ships with those damned undead on?"

"Maybe she doesn't like the smell," answered Ernest.

Mavern and Princess Jade came out from below deck.

"What's all the fuss about," asked Mavern.

"Nautametus," I answered. "She's attacking us."

"If Nautametus was attacking us, we would already be dead," replied Mavern.

"A lot of the king's men are," said Ernest.

"How many?" asked the princess.

"It's taken two of the ships of the king's men, M'lady," answered the crew member securing the sails behind us. "It hasn't touched any of the ships with the undead on."

Mavern cackled away to herself. Ernest frowned at her.

The great sea serpent burst out of the water again, much closer to our ship than before, smashing one of the other ships to splinters as she climbed into the air. I watched in fear and awe as she arched over and came back down heavily, mouth open, devouring yet another ship as she entered the water again.

"We're being decimated," shouted the captain.

"At least it was two of the undead ships this time," said the crew member behind us. Mavern said nothing. I gripped the rail on the edge of the deck, waiting for Nautametus to pull us under. In all my years as a mercenary, I'd never felt so vulnerable and helpless. I glanced at the sword hanging at my side. It was pretty useless right now. All that I had learned and experienced in my line of work was worthless against a creature of this size. I looked at Ernest. He looked back at me, grimly. There was a good chance we wouldn't survive this voyage.

***

Nautametus took another seven ships before finally losing interest, leaving us with four ships of Mavern's undead and just two ships of the king's men. I don't think anyone slept for the rest of the journey. I know I certainly didn't. My mind replayed Nautametus's assault on our fleet. The fear of not knowing where she was in the ocean beneath us or where she would appear next. The way the black surface of her skin glistened, the ferocity of her roar. When we eventually arrived at Canis Isle, we were all exhausted.

Once we were on the land, I felt much safer. Nautametus had been a frightening experience, but I knew I had to put it behind me. The fight against Kredak was still ahead, and we didn't really know what to expect. Thanks to Nautametus, we no longer had the grand army we had set out with from Torvir, but it was what we had, so we would have to make do. Mavern's undead were quickly assembled on the beach into marching formation. Since they were dead, we were able to pack a lot of them onto each ship. We had just over two hundred undead warriors, forty of the king's men, Princess Jade, Mavern, Ernest, and myself.

The king's soldiers unloaded crates of weapons from the ships and distributed them among the undead. Spears, swords, shields, daggers. The king's soldiers each carried a longbow, and a sword on their hip. Ernest had his war hammer, and I had my sword and shield. Princess Jade and Mavern had their magic, and of course their fragments of Vanya's Necklet. We were still a force to be wary of.

On either side of the beach, the coastline became vertical cliffs. Ahead of us, the sandy beach gradually became forest. One of the king's men was sent into the forest to scout ahead.

Ernest nudged me and nodded towards the princess. She was headed to the forest edge. Charged with protecting her, we thought it best to stay by her side. We ran across the beach after her.

"Where are you going, M'lady?" asked Ernest.

"I can smell dragon fruit. I want to find some."

"Dragon fruit!" replied Ernest, smiling. "I love dragon fruit." We reached the edge of the forest and sure enough, dragon fruit sat in the upper branches of the trees.

"One moment," said Ernest, leaning his war hammer against the trunk of one of the trees. He was about to start climbing when the princess spoke.

"Wait." She closed her eyes and began forming shapes in the air in front of her with her hands. Gradually her arms moved in wider shapes and an aura of green surrounded her. I'd seen spells cast before, but it was still fascinating to watch. It was almost like a dance, and the princess had perfected the moves, graceful movements made all the more beautiful by the green light that emanated from her. Noises in the branches above us caused me to look up and see several small monkeys had appeared in the treetops and were picking the dragon fruit. They dropped the fruit onto the ground around us whilst bouncing from branch to branch. Ernest looked at me with a huge smile, then laughed to himself as he gathered up the dragon fruit. Princess Jade stopped her spellcasting, and the monkeys all disappeared into the forest again.

"Can you control any creature with your magic, M'lady?" I asked.

"I'm unsure. There was a time when I was just a child, that larger animals proved difficult for me. I tried to influence my father's horses, but it took me a lot of time and practice to finally achieve that. Even then, I could only influence one, or at best, two at a time. At least until I was given the fragment of Lady Vanya's Necklet. My power has been considerably stronger since then. One time, I encountered a large pack of wolves whilst out walking in the woods by my father's castle in Torvir. Perhaps as many as thirty wolves. The two soldiers my father had assigned to accompany me stood their ground and stood either side of me, ready to protect me if the wolves attacked. They were somewhat perplexed when the wolves began to dance around us in circles. I even ran to join in, much to my protectors' dislike." Princess Jade smiled. "That was a really nice day."

Ernest had taken off his shirt and filled it with the fruit the monkeys had picked for us. He joined us.

"How much do you know about the sorceress Vanya, M'lady?"

"Probably not much more than you. Only that she was born during the mage rebellion, and her parents sent her to the sorcerer Sarkus when she showed early signs of aptitude for magic. Sarkus was astounded by her abilities and took her in at the Guidon Mage College as his apprentice, where she quickly became an accomplished mage. By the time she was a young woman, she had surpassed Sarkus and was studying her own magical theory. Namely the enhancement of magical abilities by enchanting materials with magical properties."

"Of course, by this time, the mage rebellion had become an uprising and the mage armies were oppressing the kingdoms. A few attempts had already been made in the early days of the uprising to take the college at Guidon, which was still loyal to the king, but Sarkus, along with his followers and the king's army, had managed to successfully defend it. The rebel mage armies grew stronger and larger, and became experienced in magical warfare, having taken many cities and even entire kingdoms."

"Lady Vanya created her necklet from obsidian taken from Mount Blackfire and enchanted each fragment with runes to enhance her magical abilities she felt were necessary to quell the mage uprising. When the mage armies came to take Guidon City again, it became the beginning of the end of the mage uprising. After defeating the army at Guidon, Lady

Vanya left the college to rid the world of the mage rebels. It took her twelve years to return control of all the kingdoms back to the kings and queens, but her victory came at a cost. Although she had ended a bloody war that had seen the loss of many innocent lives, she became feared throughout all the kingdoms. Her fearsome armies of animals and undead warriors were infamous. Her control of the elements was unlike anything seen before. Sarkus had died by the end of the mage wars, and Lady Selwynne, the newly appointed head of the college, refused to let Lady Vanya return to the college. Lady Vanya divided her necklet into the eight fragments and entrusted them to mages throughout the kingdoms she had met during the war and come to trust. Then she disappeared."

"She just disappeared?" I said.

"Yes. Though she had allies and friends around the world, she could not stay in any of the cities for the common people feared her. And the monarchy feared her presence too."

"Do you know what happened to her?" asked Ernest.

"No. Nobody does for sure. There are rumours that whilst fighting in the mage wars, she had met and fallen in love with a soldier from Torvir and that they had disappeared together, perhaps to live out a peaceful life together after a decade of war. At least, I like to think that's what happened to Lady Vanya."

Ernest nodded, but said nothing.

"Come. We should return," said the princess.

***

We took the dragon fruit back to the beach and we sat in the sand together to eat. We sat in silence, just the sound of the waves breaking at the shoreline and the chatter of the king's men as they ate their rations. I thought about what Princess Jade had told us about Lady Vanya and the mage wars. I wondered if she was still out there somewhere with her soldier lover. Shortly after we'd finished eating, the scout returned.

Tynis's tower was just beyond the forest. The scout said there were bodies scattered around the tower, so we could assume Kredak had already arrived. He'd seen no sign of Kredak or Tynis. Or anyone else for that matter.

"We need to move now," cried the captain of the king's army. "Fall in line." The king's soldiers assembled behind the ranks of the undead.

"March!"

With a disinterested wave of her hand, Mavern commanded her undead army to move. The king's soldiers followed behind them and the two witches, Ernest, and I took the back. We headed into the forest and towards events that would change life as we knew it, forever.

***

"It has begun," cried Mavern as several claps of thunder echoed through the forest from somewhere farther ahead. "Charge, my warriors of the undead. Destroy Kredak!"

The undead warriors ahead of us suddenly changed from docile and indifferent, to animated and enraged. They charged off through the forest towards the tower. Mavern had a wild look on her face and broke into a run to keep up with her thralls.

"Advance and assemble at the forest edge and ready bows," commanded the king's captain.

"Stay close," said Ernest to the princess. He turned to me. "This is it, Griffin. Let's do this." He quickened his pace and began overtaking the king's men, and we followed behind him. Thunderclap after thunderclap rumbled around us. When we broke from the forest and the tower came into view, we saw the true nature of what we were up against.

Bolts of lightning hammered down from the sky

into the undead army, disintegrating anything in their path. A dozen stone golems charged at our front ranks. In the archway at the bottom of the tower stood Kredak. It had to be him. Each time he reached into the sky and clenched his fists, lightning bolts pounded the ground. His face was mostly obscured by the hood of his black robes which whipped around him as the winds of the storm he was evoking tore across the battlefield. Watching him in action chilled my blood. I'd never seen such power, even from a warlock.

"He has golems," said Ernest. "He must already have the earth fragment."

"And probably Tynis's fragment too," I replied.

"If that is the case, then we can't get close to him," said Princess Jade. Ernest turned to her, that unnerved look on his face again. "Powerful fear magic would be paralysing to the living. Mavern's army won't be affected by it, so they should be fine. Well, aside from the golems and lightning."

The stone golems ripped through the undead army. The king's men now charged into the battle, swords drawn as their bows were ineffective against stone and Kredak was too far away. The golems were making short work of the undead. For every golem that fell, nearly twenty undead were either crushed by the golems' stone limbs or burnt into ash by the unrelenting lightning bolts.

Princess Jade was young and slight of build, but she certainly had nerve. She appeared unfazed by what was happening before us, a determined look upon her face. She looked at me and nodded towards the battlefield as one of the golems left the main battle and lumbered towards us.

"Stay back," shouted Ernest as he raised his hammer and charged at the advancing golem. I nodded to the princess and followed Ernest. Ernest leapt at the golem and brought his hammer down onto the golem's head. He landed and brought the hammer up again for another strike. He smashed the hammer into the golem's chest, but the golem brought back its arm to counter. I ran with my shield braced against my shoulder into the path of the stone fist as the golem swung at Ernest. It crashed into my shield which was driven into my shoulder and ribs. I was thrown into Ernest and we were both sent flying through the air. We landed on the ground, dazed. I looked up just in time to see the golem striding towards us; its fists raised above its head. Somehow, I was able to roll out of the way as the golem's fists hammered down at me. Its fists struck the ground so hard; they sank into the mud. Ernest got to his feet and with gritted teeth, brought his hammer down on the back of the golem's head. The head smashed apart, and the golem fell to pieces. I looked at the tower and saw that Kredak had now made his way onto the battlefield.

"He's come for the fragments," screamed Mavern as she retreated past us. We were losing the battle. Most of the king's men were dead, and I watched hopelessly as the pockets of undead around each of the remaining five golems were being obliterated.

"Come on," cried Princess Jade. I turned to see her beckoning to us. She turned and ran towards a cave in the rocky slopes by the forest edge.

"You good?" I asked Ernest.

"I'm good. You?"

"Yeah," I lied. I wasn't physically hurt. A little bruised from the golem maybe, but my confidence had suffered. First the encounter with Nautametus, now this futile battle. Until today, I'd been confident in my skills as a mercenary warrior. Even cocky at times. Confident of winning each fight. Now I wasn't so sure.

"Stay with the princess, Griffin," cried Ernest.

Between us and the cave, Mavern stood casting a spell with deliberate but elegant arm movements. As we ran past her, we could hear her chanting quietly in a language I could not understand. I watched Ernest run into the cave after the princess. Before following them inside, I turned back to the battlefield. Mavern was reanimating the king's men who had fallen on the field. Just three of the golems remained.

That might have made it into more of a close battle had Kredak not cast a bolt of lightning onto Mavern, turning her to a charred heap on the ground. Instantly, all the undead warriors dropped to the ground, as dead as the day she had cursed their remains with her magic. The few surviving soldiers beat a hasty retreat, the golems giving close chase. Kredak moved across the battlefield towards the smoking remains of Mavern. I knew he was going for the necromancy fragment, but I had to find the princess. I turned and ran into the darkness of the cave, fearing what might come next.

***

I saw daylight ahead and made my way carefully towards it. I could hear cave spiders scuttling around in the darkness. I had to weave my way through several nets of their strong, sticky webbing. Cave spiders usually don't attack humans and prey on rats and other small animals. As I got closer to the cave exit, I saw one or two dead monkeys hanging in the webs, bound tightly in the silk. I quickened my pace, but my boot clipped one of the strands of web and became stuck. I hacked at the web with my sword and freed myself but shuffling in the darkness all around me alerted me to impending attack. A cave spider appeared in the passage before me, blocking my way. The coarse hair on its thick legs and abdomen was easy to make out, even silhouetted in the light from the cave exit. It was bigger than any cave spider I'd ever seen, standing easily as tall as me. I held up my sword ready to fight, but the spider didn't move. It stood perfectly still, blocking the exit. Something wasn't right. A noise above me caused me to look up in time to see another spider descending rapidly towards me on a cord of web. I leapt backwards and swung my sword at its legs, missing. It dropped off the web and landed before me, but quickly leapt at me again, fangs gaping open. I rammed my shield into its maw and hacked at its front legs with my sword, severing two of them. The spider hissed and disappeared into the darkness. The large spider barring my way started towards me until a flash of green light illuminated the cave.

"Griffin, this way," shouted Princess Jade, her hands held out in front of her, radiating the green light. The huge cave spider scuttled off deeper into the cave, no longer interested.

"Thank you, M'lady," I said, bowing.

"Come. There is not much time. Kredak is almost upon us."

I looked back into the darkness of the cave as the green light faded and Princess Jade made her way back out of the cave. I could hear explosions. Fire magic. The spiders were not giving Kredak much trouble.

I ran out of the cave to find myself on a wide ledge, sat high up in the cliff face, overlooking the ocean. Sheer rock faces surrounded us. Ernest stood by the cave entrance, and the princess stood by the edge, looking into the water.

"So, does anyone have a plan?" I asked.

"We're trapped, Griffin," replied Ernest. "The only thing we can do is fight Kredak by ourselves. We will either defeat him and save the world as we know it or die, and Kredak will have more fragments of the necklet." He was right. Everything depended on us now. No time for fear. Scared or not, we had to win.

"He has Mavern's fragment now," I said. "If he kills me and turns me against you, do not hesitate to strike me down, Ernest."

"It would be my pleasure, my friend. I wouldn't leave you that way."

"We've had some great adventures, Ernest. Should Kredak defeat us, know that I'm glad to have fought by your side."

"Likewise, Griffin. But he's not going to defeat us." Ernest smiled.

"He's here!" cried Princess Jade.

Flames shot out of the cave, narrowly missing me. The heat singed my face and hair as I sprawled backwards out of the way, falling to the ground. I jumped to my feet as Kredak appeared in the cave entrance. Up close, Kredak was far more terrifying. Within the hood, his face remained hidden, but I could feel his eyes on me and my skin crawled. Ernest leapt out from beside the cave entrance and swung his war hammer towards Kredak. The head of the hammer thumped loudly as it smashed into Kredak's torso, sinking into his chest and knocking him off his feet. Kredak landed on his back, a fine mist of blood slowly following him. He screamed and shot another plume of fire towards Ernest. Ernest fell backwards, shielding his face with his arms. I ran forward with my shield raised and pulled Ernest away from a gasping Kredak, back towards the cliff edge. Kredak held up his hand and white light cascaded over him. He slowly rose to his feet, his ascension unnatural. The war hammer dropped out of his chest and fell onto the ground at his feet.

"He has the soul fragment, Griffin," hissed Ernest through his clenched teeth, the skin on his arms blistered and cracked. "He is healing himself. He is unstoppable." I turned to the princess. She was standing with her eyes closed, her arms drawing wide shapes in the air before her.

"The spiders!" muttered Ernest. "She's calling the spiders."

The white light bathing Kredak slowly faded as he lowered his hand. I got to my feet and picked up my sword. I needed to give Princess Jade time to finish her spell. I lifted my shield up once again and prepared to charge at Kredak.

"Now, M'lady!" cried Ernest. "He is fully healed, he must be sto…"

Princess Jade fully extended her arms towards the sky and screamed out. The whole ledge shook as a deafening roar filled the air. Beyond her, Nautametus rose from the ocean. The great serpent loomed over us, drenching us in the salty water as it ran off her smooth scales. I fell to the ground in awe. Kredak raised his fist and a bolt of lightning erupted from the sky and hit Nautametus. She bellowed and recoiled, writhing around in the shallow waters by the cliff edge.

"Griffin!" Ernest pointed at Kredak.

I got up once again and hurled my sword at Kredak. He had to side step to avoid it as it flew past his head, interrupting whatever spell he was about the cast. I charged at him with my shield held up in front of me, intending to knock him down again. Nautametus had other ideas. As I was about to collide with Kredak, the colossal head of the sea serpent appeared before me, her jaws snapping shut around Kredak. I ran into the closed teeth and collapsed in a heap in the dust. I watched, trembling as Nautametus rose again, towering over us, opening and shutting her almighty jaws. Kredak's bloody boots sat on the ground a little way away from me, his feet still in them.

Princess Jade turned to Nautametus and held out her hands. The great serpent lowered her head until she was at eye level with the princess. Nautametus opened her mouth and we all saw the shredded remains of Kredak caught between her long, pointed teeth. Princess Jade reached inside the mouth and plucked something out of the chewed-up mess.

"Griffin, I don't like this," said Ernest.

We watched as she wiped the blood on her robes, then took off the cord from around her neck. She began threading the fragments of Vanya's necklet she'd taken from Kredak onto the cord with her own.

"Griffin, this isn't good."

"M'lady," I shouted. "What are you doing?"

Once she'd threaded all the fragments onto the cord, she returned it to her neck. The fragments glowed brightly and appeared to fuse together, tightening around her neck. She turned to us, but this was no longer the same girl we had travelled with.

"Kneel before your new ruler," she said calmly, "and in return for your assistance today, I shall offer you both a place in my army. Oppose me, and you shall die."

"What about your father?" I asked. "He is the king. Do you intend to overthrow him?"

"KNEEL!" she screamed. Her feet left the ground and she became suspended in the air as blackness infested the air around us. Ernest and I immediately fell to our knees. Not in submission. In absolute terror. Ernest and I huddled together like scared children and cried. Jade's fear magic was now unrivalled. She could reduce the bravest of warriors to a nervous wreck in an instant, and I had no doubt that over the coming months, she would use it to do just that, as she takes over the world, kingdom by kingdom.

"I am the most powerful being alive since the grand sorceress Vanya herself," cried out Jade. "Do you yield and pledge yourselves to me?"

Ernest and I leant forward, our hands and knees on the ground in worship of Jade, pledging ourselves to her through sobs. Jade came back down to the ground and the darkness around us dissipated. She seemed satisfied. She waved away Nautametus and started towards the cave as the serpent disappeared back into the waves.

"Come. There is much to do."

Ernest and I looked at one another. Although the fear magic had worn off, a terrible sense of foreboding remained. There was no magic causing this feeling. It was real.

"This is why I don't trust witches, Griffin," said Ernest.

We got to our feet and followed Jade into the cave.

BLACK HARE PRESS

RICH RURSHELL is a short story writer from Suffolk, England. Rich writes Horror, Sci-Fi, and Fantasy, and his stories can be found in various short story anthologies and magazines.
When Rich is not writing stories, he likes to write and perform music.

Bibliography
100 Word Zombie Bites, Reanimated Writers Press,2020
Angels, Black Hare Press,2019
Apocalypse, Black Hare Press,2019
Beyond, Black Hare Press,2019
Blaze, Clarendon House,2019
Curses and Cauldrons, Blood Song Books, 2019
Fated, Stormy Island Publishing
Fireburst, Clarendon House,2019
Flash Fiction Addiction, Zombie Pirate Publishing
Full Metal Horror 2, Zombie Pirate Publishing,2019
Full Metal Horror, Zombie Pirate Publishing, 2019
Gleam, Clarendon House,2019
Monsters, Black Hare Press,2019
Of Kami and Yokai, Fantasia Divinity,2019
Phuket Tattoo, Zombie Pirate Publishing,2019
Salty Tales, Stormy Island Publishing
Storming Area 51, Black Hare Press,2019
Treasure Chest, Zombie Pirate Publishing,2020
Unravel, Black Hare Press,2019
World War Four, Zombie Pirate Publishing,2019
Worlds, Black Hare Press,2019

BEYOND THE REALM

THE SEVENTH SOUL

By Carole de Monclin

After years spent fighting for the king, Erwin aspires to a peaceful life. Instead, he finds himself bound by a dark prophecy to a mysterious young woman. To protect Azeline, he will battle dragons, monsters, and a sorceress. But will he go as far as sacrificing his soul?

Twenty-two pairs of eager eyes followed me avidly. I squatted low to the children's eye level, my leather breeches stretching over my knees. For days, they had waited to hear the tale of my last battle.

"The sun slowly set in the West. Remember, the fighting started at dawn. Golden sunlight reflected on the white scales of the beast. We were exhausted, but the evil beast showed no sign of fatigue. Ten noble and courageous knights had succumbed one after the other to the flames. Then, Sir Emery roared he'd had enough of the Maiden Killer and charged on his destrier. But the dragon's formidable paw struck him like you would swat a fly. Emery was unhorsed, vulnerable on the ground. The beast was about to pounce."

I paused to let the tension build, my eyes tracking from wide eye to wide eye. Since the day I came back to Pendle, I'd entertained the children every night by the fire in the clearing just outside the village. After seven nights of practise, I was becoming quite the storyteller.

"I couldn't let my friend die. I yelled with all my might, managing to get the beast's attention. The dragon turned his fiery eyes towards me instead and attacked. Enraged, he surged but didn't breathe fire. He hadn't done so for some time. We suspected all his fire was spent. The dragon reared, ready to strike. I saw my opportunity and plunged my sword into his heart."

"Ooh!"

Here, I stood and unsheathed my sword, Fortitude, holding it high.

"But he wasn't dead. His enormous claws slashed out, cutting deep into my skin."

I sheathed Fortitude and lifted my shirt to show the five parallel scars that ran along my torso. With time, they would fade. For now, crimson and raised, they remained a dramatic sight. I wouldn't tell the children about the infection afterwards that almost killed me. That didn't sound very knightly.

"I stood my ground and drove the blade deeper until he breathed no more. The last of the snow dragons had been slain."

"Did you keep a tooth?" one little voice asked.

"The King's mages took them. I did not."

"Why?"

I let out a chuckle, "Why, a dragon's no small sheep. His claws are longer than your arm, but," one finger lifted the pendant I wore on a thin leather strap around my neck, "I did keep a scale."

Pearly white, it glimmered in the firelight. More sighs of wonder erupted.

"Are you a Sir like Sir Emery?"

I bowed. "Indeed, I am. But I prefer not to use the title in Pendle."

"Time for bed," interrupted the mothers who had stood beyond the circle of light during my tale. They gathered the children despite their offspring's protests.

But I wasn't looking at the children or their mothers anymore.

I watched her.

She drifted behind the row of villagers, at the edge of the woods, partly hidden behind a tree. I doubted anyone except me had noticed her presence. She moved quietly with catlike grace. I sensed unusual energy in her lithe form. The darkness enveloping her made it difficult to make out her features. Every night, she'd come to listen. But the minute my tale ended, she disappeared into the woods. Catching a glimpse of her during the day proved impossible.

Sleepy, quiet Pendle was nestled in the forest away from any main road. All its inhabitants were known to me. Nobody ever moved in or out of such places. Except for me. I went away to serve King Godefroy for five years. At twenty-one, the call of the outside world had been impossible to resist. A similar yearning, for home this time, had brought me back.

She was the other exception.

Tonight, I decided to meet her. As I finished the tale, I moved away from the children. On previous nights, I'd observed the path she used to make her escape. A few long strides brought me around a tree to block her way. We nearly collided.

I enjoyed her little surprised gasp. She recoiled, and before she could flee, I bowed. "I don't believe we've been introduced, mademoiselle. I'm Erwin."

She held herself stiffly, fingers intertwined in front of her. "I know."

"Who do I have the pleasure of addressing?" I asked gently.

She hesitated. "The villagers call me the girl."

"You're hardly a girl."

She was tall and slender. Now I stood close, I could see her delicate features. Almost twenty if I had to guess. She averted her eyes and didn't answer. I wondered if my comment had offended her.

In the silence, the words of one of the mothers floated towards us from the clearing, "Behave, or the Soulless will steal your soul."

I smiled at the familiar warning followed by a child's subdued assent.

"Do children really believe this nonsense?" the girl asked, searching my face, then looking away.

"A monster that steals your soul so he can devour it?" I curled the fingers of my right hand around my chin. "Worked on me when I was their age. Parents don't even need to mention the end of the story. When the Soulless has eaten seven souls, he'll destroy the world."

"Some say it's a prophecy."

"No. The Soulless is just a children's tale. He's a good way of keeping children in line."

She shrugged. "Why do all monsters have to be male?"

"I…"

She seemed to enjoy my puzzlement. "Do you know for a fact the dragon you slew was male?"

"I assumed."

"Are you an expert in dragon anatomy?"

I shook my head, and she smiled. When she did, the right side of the mouth curved higher in a manner I found charming.

"I have to go," she whispered so softly I almost didn't hear.

"Stay."

She cocked her head. "Why?"

"I'd like to know you better."

She put a hand on my arm. With a gentle push, she turned me around towards the village, murmuring in my ear, "Believe me, you don't. The village girls, on the other hand… See, they're all dying to talk to you."

Since my return, all the young women of marriageable age—and some too young to even think about such things—had tried to gain my attention and favour. They were pleasant and enjoyable company, but having grown up with them, they held no mystery.

When I looked back, my stranger had vanished into the forest.

BEYOND THE REALM

***

The tale of my adventures finished, it was now time to help my father plough the fields. I came home every night, exhausted. Agriculture required more stamina than soldiering.

In my spare time, I asked around about the stranger. In hushed whispers, villagers told me she'd settled in my uncle's household three years ago. But nobody could explain how she came to be under his care. They were reluctant to share more. Even if they didn't say so, I could sense they were afraid of her. A few mumbled something about her repulsive appearance, but from what I'd seen, it was everything pleasing. Only one woman thought she'd heard her name. Azeline. I liked it.

On a rainy day, when the fields were too sodden to be worked, I took RavenMane, my mare, out of the stable. She needed exercise, and a visit to my uncle was long overdue. He hadn't been in the village since my return, and I hadn't called on him. I had a familial duty to visit.

My uncle, Odemar, had always been a bit of a misanthrope, especially since the death of my mother. He lived alone in the woods in a small abandoned stone tower. Nobody knew who built it, but before my uncle took possession, rumours said the building had been forsaken for centuries. A childless man, my uncle always showed me affection. I looked forward to seeing him.

And her.

Ivy swallowed the austere tower's façade, diminishing its foreboding aspect. My uncle waited for me at the heavy wooden door. We hugged heartily. Time hadn't been kind to him. Deep grooves now lined his face. He showed me into the great circular hall where a fire burned in the expansive fireplace. What struck me in the room, even more than usual for my long absence, was the large circular stained glass window. Even with the overcast sky, the colours touched something deep inside me. Seven coloured circles all different, but all adorned with intricate patterns, surrounded a woman's silhouette. She had her arms extended. Light streamed from her in every direction. Somehow, the window felt personal, but it elicited chills rather than warmth.

My uncle placed a tankard of ale in front of me. The usual pleasantries were exchanged. We talked about my travels, and he appraised me of the new tomes he had added to his impressive library on the top floor. It was the work of his life. When I tried to broach the subject of his charge, his demeanour changed.

"I don't want you near her."

"Why?"

"The reasons are my own, nephew. I wouldn't be honouring your mother's memory if I let you grow close to her."

He looked at me with piercing blue eyes, so like my mother's, but didn't say more.

"What has happened to you, uncle?"

He brought his tankard to his lips and drained it. "Promise me you'll stay away."

I held his stare. "I'll promise no such thing."

"Foolish boy. I fear you've grown even more stubborn. I wished you'd never come back," he spat.

He stood to pour more ale in our tankards. We left the subject of the stranger behind and enjoyed the excellent beverage until the rain stopped. I rode back home, puzzled. I had almost reached the village when I saw her coming up on the mud path. Unlike other females who wore flowing skirts and tight bodices, she was clad, like my uncle, in a long, dull grey tunic over loose trousers. Those were splattered with mud. Thick black hair cascaded over her face, hiding half of it. She seemed not to care about the state of the path or the fact she'd been caught in the rain. Her clothes cling to her skin, leaving no doubt that "girl" was a totally inappropriate name for her.

"Greetings," I called before she noticed me.

She started, then she averted her eyes, which didn't surprise me.

I dismounted. "Can I walk you back home?"

She hurried past me. "Your uncle forbids me to talk to anyone."

Why did my uncle think he had the right to deprive her of the simple and natural pleasure of conversing?

I called from behind her, "I won't bother you today. Please agree to meet me tomorrow."

She froze, then resumed walking. Disappointment lodged in my stomach, but then she barely turned towards me, nodded, and whispered, "By the great oak at midday."

Before she spun around and skittered away, I could have sworn I saw two things: the ghost of a smile gracing her lips, and a strange green flash on her cheek when a gust of wind blew her hair away from her face.

***

At the appointed hour, I stood under the ancient tree. Its majestic trunk soared in the middle of a glade well known to all Pendle children. It presided in the forest long before men settled in these parts.

Some ridiculous impulse had made me wear my court clothes. No doubt I looked a fool. While I waited, I traced the markings carved around the bark by successive generations. I even discovered one I thought had been made by my parents.

I had almost lost hope she would come when an acorn fell square on my forehead. I looked up and found her perched high up in the branches.

"Hello there. Won't you come down?"

She tilted her head and gestured for me to join her. I sighed. My last foray in a tree must have dated from a decade ago. So much for my fine clothes.

"Good day, my fair lady," I puffed when my struggles to join her ended.

"Good day, valiant knight." She reclined against the trunk with her legs dangling on each side of a large limb, revealing her ankles. As I positioned myself carefully on the same branch, I ventured a peek at her face, but her mane still covered half of it.

"Why doesn't my uncle let you go into the village?"

Her face fell at those words. Her deep exhale seemed heavy with frustration and sadness. "I can't tell you. They don't like me anyway. And if they knew…"

Asking what she meant would be met with silence, so I said, "They know so little about you. It makes them wary. They have no clue where you come from."

"You know nothing of me. Yet, you don't appear wary."

"Ah, but I'm different. The unknown has always fascinated me."

"I'll never do them any harm. If I can avoid it."

I didn't remark on the odd phrasing of that sentiment.

She exhaled and ran a hand into her hair, pushing it away from her face. Mid movement, she stopped, her eyes wide. The gesture had been involuntary. She turned away, but I'd already seen the green swirls that adorned the side of her face. The motif covered the high cheekbone and grazed the side of her mouth. With the darkness, I had missed it the other night. I'd never seen anything like it. It didn't look like a tattoo. It made me think of a kiss of gem dust.

I saw another one on her hand, blood red. It started to glow as Azeline recoiled from me and climbed down the branch. I called after her.

She paused, her eyes searching. "You're not afraid?"

"Should I be?"

Her eyes considered me as if I were a strange creature. I thought she'd changed her mind, but she resumed her escape. Her feet touched the ground before

I could even descend three limbs. She looked up, mischief in her eyes and a green gleam on her cheek, and curtsied. "Until tomorrow."

Then she dashed into the woods.

***

The following day, I again found her atop the tree, lounging on a different limb. I sensed a mix of relief and apprehension in her features when I reached her. She no longer sheltered her face from view, but conscious of her discomfort, I didn't bring up the bizarre markings on her skin. We discussed inconsequential nothings until she left. Azeline possessed the talent of being entertaining without giving away anything about herself.

Arboreal meetings became our routine. Azeline often didn't talk for long stretches. I didn't mind her silences. It gave me more time to lose myself in the study of her eyes. I noticed another mysterious drawing peeking out her clothes behind her neck; this one yellow. I understood why the markings would scare superstitious villagers. Anything with a whiff of magic elicited fear from them. The drawings had the opposite effect on me.

On our seventh meeting, I couldn't help asking,

"What are those markings?"

As soon as the words passed my lips, I wished them back. Hurt and anger overtook her features. I had hoped to steal a kiss today. Instead, I watched helplessly as she alighted from our perch and fled into the forest. I was such an idiot.

***

She didn't come back for an entire week. I resolved to visit my uncle in hopes of finding news when I spotted her sitting higher than ever. I'd never thought I had a fear of heights, but that climb changed my mind. None of us mentioned the incident. We simply picked up where we left off.

One sunny day, I brought my sword. She'd requested to see it. For the first time, she waited for me at the base of the tree. "Let me see that blade of yours."

I unsheathed Fortitude and handed it, pommel directed towards her.

She examined the sword with interest. "King Godefroy gave it to you?"

"Yes. A horde of giants attacked us. I saved his life."

Her index finger brushed along the edge. "I wouldn't have thought King Godefroy to be so ungenerous."

"What do you mean?"

"You save his life, and your reward is a plain sword. Not even one gem set in the hilt."

"I wanted it this way. A sword isn't meant to be ornamented. Its purpose is to be faithful, robust, and powerful. Gems only distract from its true nature."

She weighed the blade. "It's too heavy for me, but it has amazing balance."

She swung Fortitude, giving it a few thrusts; her form perfect, and her pleasure evident. The swirls on the cheek glimmered intensely as she did.

"Where did you learn to handle a sword like that?"

Reluctantly, she extended Fortitude towards me, but I held my hands up. "Don't stop. Your fighting skills are just one more thing I'm curious about. I've heard many a fascinating account."

"Oh?"

I'd charmed the information out of the village girls. Using them wasn't one of my most gallant endeavours. But since they didn't perceive Azeline as a rival, they hadn't been as reluctant to speak as their parents.

"The villagers hardly ever see you, but somehow you come out every time they need help. A child is at death's door, and our healer is powerless. You approach Pendle just long enough to deliver a potion, then the child miraculously recovers. They say, even they didn't witness you do it, you've singlehandedly chased a pack of wolves, turned infertile fields into fruitful ones…Too many deeds over the last three years for me to remember."

Azeline shrugged and executed a perfect eight with the blade. "I try to help when I can."

"But you never want the credit. Don't mistake me, it's commendable. But my question is, where did you learn so much on so many subjects?"

Fortitude swished. "Books."

I shook my head. "Even my uncle's library isn't that large. Besides, one cannot learn to wield a sword this way without diligent practice. The villagers think sorcery."

Her head snapped up; her lips parted in surprise. The marking on her cheek dimmed.

I smiled. "I don't believe that. But you have to agree, it seems like you possess knowledge accumulated over several lifetimes."

She planted the sword in the dirt and backed away from me like a cornered animal.

My voice soft and caressing, I pleaded, "Tell me the truth for once."

"I can't."

She turned away from me. The yellow swirls on her nape had come to life. It appeared one, and only one of the markings glowed at any given time. What that meant eluded me. Was I condemned never to break through the walls behind which she hid? I thought Azeline would run off. Instead, she did the unexpected.

Standing straight, she walked up to me, took my face between her palms, and kissed me. The experience was nothing like the shy kisses I'd received from a few maidens during my time at court. These soft lips of hers didn't hesitate or lack skill. She made me feel like a green boy.

She pulled away. "So, that's what kissing is like."

Not one to be undone, I pulled her into my arms, all thoughts having deserted me.

***

Revelling in the felicity of her embrace and laughter, I didn't ask any more questions. I wanted to learn Azeline's secrets but was willing to wait until she was ready to reveal them. Our time together wasn't confined to the oak tree anymore. Azeline showed me places in the forest of my childhood I never suspect existed. We spent many hours secluded at a small waterfall, careful never to be discovered by anyone in the village. But my uncle came to the farm one afternoon to visit my father, and the piercing stare he gave me left me with no doubt he knew.

"We have to tell uncle," I told her the next day.

Her hand gripped mine tighter. "Never. He'd find a way to keep me from you."

"Why?"

"He only wants to protect me."

"From me?"

"Please, let's just enjoy our time together."

She grabbed my necklace to pull my head down to hers. I gladly obliged, fully aware it was a tactic to silence me. But before our lips touched, she cried in pain and jerked back. She looked down at her hand in disbelief.

"What is it?" I grabbed her fingers, angling her hand towards me.

On her palm, I found a burn the shape of my dragon scale. "How?"

Her eyes bore into mine, accusing. "You tell me."

"It doesn't burn me. See?" I demonstrated by closing my hand over the scale.

Her face paled. "Tell me more about that dragon."

Right below her collarbone, a blue glow became visible through her tunic. Another marking. It must have burned intensely to be noticeable. For a second, it distracted me.

"The dragon was roughly three times the size of my horse. White as snow. It came from the wildlands of the North."

"The wildlands? Why didn't you say before?"

"I didn't think it was important. I'd been delayed, so I joined the troops only for the final battle."

"Delayed?"

"The dragons had gotten close to the capital. King Godefroy wanted us to escort the Queen to safety farther South."

She stared at her injured palm. "How many dragons?"

I tried to pull her close, but she slipped away and started to pace, with her arms firmly folded in front of her.

"I'm not sure. Six? Seven, maybe."

I could tell Azeline's alarm was mounting, "What did they do? Burn houses?"

"That's the strange thing. Emery called them the Maiden Killers because in every village the monsters came across, they searched every house and snatched young women, only the young women, into their paws, sniffed, and then…"

That part had been too gruesome to mention in my tales to the children.

She closed her eyes. "Then what?"

The memory of the offensive stench still vivid in my mind, I said, "They burned them alive."

Azeline took a deep breath as if she was afraid to speak the next words. "Only young women?"

"Yes. But the King's knights killed every last one of the dragons. To my knowledge, no more has been spotted."

"No matter," her voice quivered. She glared at her palm. "All those women died because of me. The dragons were looking for me. They killed those women because they weren't me."

Disbelief warred with shock in my mind.

Azeline's injured hand closed into a fist. "She knows where I am."

"Who knows?"

She didn't answer. I could tell her mind was no longer with me. "I must warn Odemar."

Before I could protest, she ran into the forest. I wanted to go after her, but she turned around and said, "Bring Fortitude. Hurry."

I threw the dragon scale in the mud and dashed to the farm.

***

Raised voices escaped the tower when I reached it. From the door, I observed Azeline and my uncle standing in front of the fireplace in the great room. Above them, the setting sunlight streamed through the round stained-glass window. One of the seven coloured circles caught my eyes. I hadn't noticed before it contained a sword, plain like Fortitude, and a white rose with an oak tree for backdrop. The white petals particularly stood out. The design made me uneasy.

Odemar's thundering voice brought me back to the present. "Reckless child. You knew what's at stake."

"How could I have anticipated she had enchanted dragons? That even a scale would retain the magic?"

"Everything can be a threat. I told you to stay away from Erwin."

"You did." She looked down for a second, then put a hand on his shoulder, "I worry for you."

His tone changed. I saw a tenderness in his eyes I'd never witnessed before. "I always knew my time would come."

She nestled against him. "I never wanted to bring this on you."

"I know, child." His voice faltered.

"We will save you," she said, but I could hear doubt in her voice.

"Uncle?' I said.

Odemar started at my voice and stared at me in dismay. He turned back towards Azeline, but the anger had left him. "You told him?"

"No. But I think Erwin can help against whatever she will send. Do you think she'll come herself?"

"What enemy is coming? I need to understand what we're up against," I asked.

She still held Odemar, but I saw her fingers curl into fists. "I believe the dragons you fought were sent by a sorceress named Kalinka."

I'd heard that name mentioned several times at court, every time with dread. The King's mages had been afraid her powers were increasing, but since she never left the Wildlands, they'd advised Godefroy not to provoke her.

"Why is she looking for you?"

Azeline briefly glanced towards my uncle. He gave her his approval with a slight nod, "Kalinka's been hunting me my entire life."

She closed her eyes and took a deep breath. When she opened her eyes, they held a haunted look. The green marking gleamed.

Before she could say more, the stained glass window exploded. Shards fell everywhere. When the tinkling sound of the glass raining down stopped, it was replaced by a feral roar. Its vicious ring made my nape tingle uncomfortably.

Large and hideous, a head poked into the window. From a flat skull, two long antennae jutted forward. Eyes seemed absent, but a pair of curved black fangs caught the candlelight viciously. The creature slid inside the opening, fast and slippery. The monster's movements looked like water flowing along the wall. The long body descending in the eerie silence looked twice the width of my shoulders. It was made up of segments, each equipped with two legs ending with sharp claws. Dark red plating covered the segments.

I held Fortitude tighter. I would have to aim between the joints if I wanted to inflict harm to this creature. As the monster descended along the wall, new segments appeared, making it even longer. Or was it an illusion? The monster angled itself towards Azeline and my uncle, its claws crunching the broken glass.

I tried to charge, but my arm wouldn't lift Fortitude. My feet wouldn't budge. A fog had crawled into my mind. The creature's will, primal and crude, had invaded mine. It held me captive as I watched helplessly the monster's body twist in large loops.

Despite Azeline's efforts to step in front of Odemar, the creature slithered between them. She stood tall and fierce, looking unaffected by the crippling paralysis that imprisoned Odemar and I. But she was so small compared to the monster, her courage pointless when she had no weapon.

With surprising gentleness, the monster pushed her to the side, while one body loop drew behind Odemar. Myriads of legs closed on him, digging into his flesh, from his calves to his hips, his torso, all the way up to his neck. Odemar howled in pain. The contrast between the creature's actions towards Azeline and my uncle was disturbingly fascinating. A question invaded my mind, like claws sinking into my brain, prodding. The monster needed information, but I didn't understand what.

Azeline screamed and dropped to her knees, the head of the creature hovering over her. One antenna even touched her forehead. She didn't react to the disgusting touch. Instead, I saw her hand inch to the side, towards the fireplace.

The bottom loop of the creature came between us, blocking my view. It moved my way. I wouldn't be able to resist if it wanted to impale me with its claw-like legs like it had Odemar.

"I am the guardian," I heard my uncle say. His voice carried with surprising strength.

The creature halted as if it tried to make sense of my uncle's words. But the pause only lasted a few seconds before its progression towards me resumed.

"Don't kill him. The girl needs a new guardian," Odemar roared this time, panic in his voice.

The monster became immobile, then the loop retreated away from me, allowing me to spot Azeline. She had crawled to the side of the fireplace. A fire poker had found its way into her hand. She surged to her feet and swung the improvised weapon at the creature's head, hitting square between the antennae.

The monster squealed and retracted. The tight telepathic fist that encased my brain and body suddenly loosened. My limbs prickled. I ignored the sensation. Lurching forward, I raised Fortitude and slashed. My first blow rebounded on its armour, but the second one slipped between two segments of plating. The sharp edge cut all the way through.

The severed body section spasmed, but I barely paid it any mind. I was already running towards Odemar. One swing from Fortitude and the portion of the creature's body that restrained my uncle was separated from the rest. With each blow, I worked my way up to the long body, towards the head. Odemar collapsed forward, the section of the creature still attached to him. I'd hoped in death the legs would slacken their hold. I'd been wrong.

"Azeline!" I tried to reach her, but the flexible loops of the creature's body prevented me from approaching. She still fought with her fire poker. The monster wriggled to avoid her blows. I eyed the black fangs with dread, but the creature seemed unwilling to strike back. One antenna lay bloodied on the floor.

"Behind you," Azeline called.

I turned in time to block the lashing tail of the creature with my sword. The tail? But I had chopped it. The monstrous tail attacked again. By some unimaginable magic, the severed pieces had reattached themselves. With the segments looking identical, I couldn't even see where I had initially struck. How was one supposed to defeat such an enemy?

Azeline cried. I couldn't help glancing in her direction, earning a graze from one of the sharp legs as a reward for my lack of focus. Judging by what I glimpsed, Azeline hadn't been screaming in pain like I had imagined first, but in satisfaction. The poker was no longer in her hand but deeply embedded at the top of the creature's head, all the way down to its throat.

Shrieks of agony echoed in my head. The disgusting body convulsed. I lunged for the head and with a murderous swing and hacked it off. With the poker still sticking out, it fell to the ground with a clanging noise.

I didn't trust the monster to stay dead.

"Throw it in the fire," I ordered.

Without hesitation, Azeline grabbed the fleshy remains by the antennae and hauled them in the blazing flames. The skin blistered, wheezed, and a foul stench filled the room. But Azeline didn't spare a glance.

She dashed to my uncle's side. With the creature's demise, the claws had finally released his body. Blood oozed from Odemar's countless wounds. Azeline cradled his head in her lap, caressing his hair. He grabbed her hand, smearing blood on her.

"It's my fault," she sobbed.

"No. Even you cannot control fate, child." He turned towards me. "Erwin, come closer."

"Uncle, we must attend to your wounds."

Azeline lifted Odemar's tunic, studied his torso, and slowly shook her head.

"Nephew, come," my uncle repeated.

I kneeled next to him and took his other hand in mine.

"Erwin—"

"No." Azeline's head shot up. The expression on her face one I'd never seen before. Fury mixed with sadness. "Odemar, you can't do this to him."

He tilted his head in her direction with a sad smile. "There's no other choice."

Azeline screamed in response, "I forbid it."

She pinned me with a fierce stare. The green

markings flashed brighter than ever before. "Do not agree. I beg you."

His voice barely above a whisper, Odemar repeated, "I've no choice, child."

Clenching his hand in both of hers, she rested her head on his chest, pleading, "Entrust me to Kalinka if you have to. I'm strong enough."

His hand slid out of mine. He caressed Azeline's hair. "I'm afraid she'd destroy your other souls."

"I don't care. Erwin must live."

His fingers stopped moving. "If the Sorceress has her way. He won't be safe. No one will. Nothing can stop the fulfilment of the prophecy, but we can choose how it unfolds."

This talk of prophecy snapped me out the trance-like state I'd been in, numbly watching the life flood out of my uncle.

I growled, "Enough. Prophecies are for children and superstitious old crones."

Odemar ignored me. "Azeline, go fetch the purse."

She hesitated, her eyes frantically darting between my uncle and me. "I don't want to leave you two alone."

"For once, obey me."

She kissed Odemar's cheek and stood slowly. On the way out, she touched my shoulder. "Please. Say no."

"Say no to what?"

Between the trauma of the battle and my utter lack of understanding, I felt lost, useless. I also felt betrayed Azeline hadn't trusted me with her secrets. All this might have been avoided had I known, and she was still speaking in riddles.

A palm leaning on the door jamb, she peered at me over her shoulder. "Sometimes monsters are female." Her fingers tensed. "I am the Soulless. You said it yourself, I devour souls," she paused, "I don't want yours."

She left the room, leaving me mute with incomprehension.

Odemar moaned, his face contorted. He'd been maintaining a brave face for Azeline's benefit. I took off my coat and slid it under his head. "The Soulless? She's delirious. It's just a bedtime story."

With difficulties, Odemar shook his head. "A prophecy."

"I don't believe in prophecies."

Odemar snorted, "Prophecies don't care how one feels about them. They just march on." He closed his eyes and heaved a few shallow breaths. Then, he sucked in a deep breath and shut his eyes tighter, making the deep furrows that lined his face even more pronounced. "I want you to take care of her when I'm gone. She'll need protection, a new guardian."

"I'd do anything."

The answer came in a strangled whisper, "Anything? You sure?"

As he scrutinised my face behind half-open lids, I searched my soul. I didn't fully grasp what was asked of me, but I wanted to be with Azeline. No matter what. I didn't believe she was the Soulless, but that didn't change the fact others did, putting her in danger.

"I am."

His hand was cold on my face. "Nephew, I'm asking for the greatest sacrifice. I wanted to spare you, but I should have seen it was impossible. Fate can't be stopped. I don't have enough time to explain the details. Know it's the greatest responsibility a man can be asked to fulfil. You'll have to offer your protection and love. Ultimately, your life and soul. The day will come when she'll go on without you. You'll be but a step in her destiny. According to the prophecy, she'll have seven guardians. I was the fifth. Do you accept becoming the next guardian?"

"Yes."

Odemar nodded with a sad smile. "Very well." His features relaxed. "Leave right away. Kalinka will send other creatures after you. She must never become the last guardian. You hear me?"

I nodded. "I'll do anything to make sure that never happens."

"My money's yours. Go."

Odemar was slipping away. His mission accomplished, he could leave satisfied. I gathered him in my arms and held him carefully. His breathing whizzed. His chest went up and down, but the movements grew fainter.

To my surprise, he spoke again, "I need to say the words. Erwin, I entrust the Soulless to you."

A hot wave washed over my body, making the world turn black.

I didn't know how long I lay unconscious. I came to Azeline's scream. I sensed she wasn't in danger. Her scream hadn't been one of fear or pain, at least not physical pain. Her scream carried her heartbreak. I had fallen on my side but still held my uncle. I lowered his body. Nothing more could be done for him, but Azeline needed me.

I rushed up the stairs and found her in the library on the stone floor, curled into a ball. When I kneeled to brush hair out of her face, she didn't react. Her eyes were open, but she stared unseeing. Sapphire blue swirls had appeared on the right side of her forehead. I stroke them gently.

The purse Odemar had mentioned lay toppled beside her. I never suspected my uncle owned so much wealth. I pocketed it before I slid my arms under Azeline's small body, lifted her, and hurried to RavenMane. How could this slip of a girl be the Soulless? A legendary monster? The supposed destroyer of all that lived?

Whatever Azeline was, something inside me had changed. My link to her had taken an almost tangible quality. I couldn't deny Odemar's death had marked her skin. Powerful magic was afoot. As to its nature, I was ignorant.

Dwelling on this would wait. Fleeing was our priority. I sat Azeline on the saddle, worried she would fall while I mounted. But I slid behind her easily and encircled her waist with my left arm, holding the reins in my right hand.

I didn't stop to say goodbye, not even to my father. Shame gripped me at the thought of leaving Odemar's body without proper care, but I knew the villagers would do all that was needed. With Azeline huddled in front of me, I directed RavenMane towards the woods, away from any travelled paths, away from the life I'd known

***

For three days, we followed game trails, riding in silence, only stopping to allow RavenMane some well-deserved rest, to hunt for our sustenance, or to catch a few hours of restless sleep. I didn't question Azeline's need for silence. She would speak when she was ready. None of the markings on her skin glowed. It worried me, but I understood so little about them.

We needed new clothes. Ours were caked with Odemar's blood. My left arm had to be kept bandaged. The monster hadn't left me with a graze as I'd thought at first, still fresh from the battle, but with a gash that ran deep into the muscle.

For now, I was satisfied with putting as much distance as possible between us, Pendle, and whatever evil loomed there. My concern for my family and the inhabitants left behind proved difficult to quiet down. But I couldn't help them.

Dawning sunlight streamed through the trees bordering the clearing where we had stopped late the night before. Azeline sat in front of the small fire I had lit, her arms around her knees, staring at the flames while I checked RavenMane's hoofs.

"I told you to say no." Her voice was low but determined.

Those first words in almost four days caught me

off guard.

"She'll hunt us relentlessly. Erwin, you're the sixth guardian. She'll want to be last by any means." She lifted her gaze to me, the anguish plain in her eyes. "I didn't want this for you."

"Nobody forced me," I said, stroking the mare.

"You don't know what you agreed to."

I sat next to her, put an arm around her, and pulled her body to me. When she rested her head on my shoulder, warmth filled me. She'd been avoiding my touch since Odemar died.

I spoke softly, "Then, tell me about the prophecy."

"The cursed prediction was made centuries ago by a clairvoyant queen. The prophecy says, 'A Soulless child shall arise and be placed under the care of seven successive guardians. One after the other, the guardians' lives will end with the completion of their watch. Their souls will be offered freely to gather into the Soulless' depths. The demise of the seventh guardian will herald a new cycle as the Soulless' implacable fingers close on the fragile world.'"

"It doesn't really say the Soulless will destroy the world, then?"

"What more do you want than a hand crushing the world?"

I shook my head. "You would never do that." I

traced the swirls on her forehead. For the first time, they'd come to life. My skin tingled at the touch. "It could be interpreted as you ruling everything."

Azeline curled up against me. "Kalinka agrees with you. That's why she wants the power of the Soulless."

"How would she get it? She'd be dead."

"She believes she can work on me while she's the guardian to destroy all my souls one after the other until there's only a husk for her soul to take over. Kalinka will force you to make her the last guardian. Then she'll kill you."

I kissed the top of her head. "I won't let her."

"Whatever happens, you will die."

"I know. I'm only a mortal after all." She buried herself deeper against me. "I'm the reason Kalinka found you. Without that dragon scale, you'd be in Pendle, and Odemar would be alive. It's only fair I should be the one protecting you."

With a finger, I lifted her head so I could look into her eyes. I rested my forehead against hers. We just stared, inhaling each other's breaths.

"I might be the source—" Azeline trailed off when I winced. She'd squeezed my injured arm. As if it were the first time she noticed it, she glared at the bandage. "What happened?"

"It's nothing. One of the monster's claws caught me."

Carefully she undid the dressing. The wound oozed a light streak of greenish pus.

Her brow furrowed. The glow under her tunic had returned. "Kalinka can use this to track us."

Azeline glanced around as if she expected some creature hidden behind the trees to pounce. "Build a bigger fire. We need to cauterise that wound."

Already Azeline was gathering branches, but the idea didn't appeal to me at all. "Are you sure?"

"The woman had a direct hand in killing three of my guardians. Kalinka doesn't like to leave the Wildlands, but she's an expert at enchanting objects and living beings so she can hunt her prey from the comfort of her castle. She's never bothered to come herself, but now there's only one guardian left, she will come to claim the position."

Azeline retrieved Fortitude from my saddlebags. "I know how it's done."

The phrasing didn't sound reassuring. "But have you ever done it?"

"No." She smiled. "Like I had never kissed anyone before you or held a sword before Fortitude. The knowledge of several lifetimes, you called it. You didn't realise how true that was. I steal souls. They come to me brimming with memories and abilities. One of my guardians was a healer; therefore, so am I."

Azeline used all the contents of the waterskin to clean my wound. To distract me, she spoke of her second guardian, Iricha, a soldier of fortune who named Azeline after her late sister. Iricha gave her life helping Azeline escape Kalinka.

Before placing a piece of wood between my teeth, Azeline ran a hand on my cheek. Next, Fortitude was plunged into the flames until it glowed red.

"I owe my sword skills to Iricha," Azeline continued as if she wasn't about to burn my skin. "She died when I was seven."

I felt no shame at looking away when she pressed the hot metal to my wound. Biting down, I almost passed out from the mix of agony and burnt flesh's stench. To distract me, Azeline explained it was too soon for her to have absorbed Odemar's knowledge, but she managed to glean from his memories several scrapes I'd been involved in as a child.

As soon as I could stand, despite the pain, I forced myself back into the saddle, so we could leave this clearing and the possibility we'd been followed behind. For days, we let RavenMane wander, only redirecting her when she got too close from main roads or villages. I wasn't even sure we were in Godefroy's kingdom anymore. One morning, RavenMane brought us to a large sunny glade. A stream ran not far. When I crumpled a handful of fertile soil between my fingers, I knew farming here would be easy. We could finally rest.

***

The soft sound of drops of water falling into a pot woke me. Azeline must have placed it while I slept. The roof badly needed repairs, but I always forgot until the next rain.

I rolled carefully in the bed to check if she was still asleep. I enjoyed watching Azeline in deep slumber, the only time when no anxiety was etched in her features, and the markings stayed dormant. She tried to hide it, but she was afraid for me, afraid of what she might unconsciously do to me. Her hand rested open palm up. Even after three years, the scar left by the dragon scale still marred her delicate skin.

In the time Azeline and I spent hidden deep in the glade, a more serious side of my beloved had emerged. I supposed I had the influence of my uncle's soul to thank for that. Also, for her quoting poetry at every turn. My gaze left her sleeping form to roam around the cabin we built together, small but comfortable, apart from some minor defects like a leaky roof.

I dared to believe she'd been happy with me despite everything. Secluded as we were, we pretended the prophecy didn't exist. It was even tempting to wonder if prophecies always came true. I accepted my fate, but a sliver of hope endured. Maybe the world would never find us here, and the Soulless would live her life in peace. I preferred to remain on the side of optimism, although Azeline would have called it denial. Maybe my mark would never grace her skin. Each drawing represented a guardian. One was always alive and glowing. I could anticipate how Azeline would react depending on which one.

I coughed as quietly as I could. The rainy weather had caught me unawares two or three times lately.

I hadn't been quiet enough. Azeline's eyes shot open. "Are you feeling unwell?"

I whispered, stroking her arm, "No, love. It was just a cough. I'm well. Go back to sleep."

"Just a cough? You're sure?"

I nodded, but I could tell by her frown she was worried. Every time I showed signs of sickness or weakness, she fretted. The only way to alleviate her concern was for me to be in good health.

I pulled the cover up to her chin and kissed her brow. "You haven't killed me yet."

"Don't you dare joke about this."

"I'm just trying to show you how ridiculous you are."

She shook her head, looking heavenward. "I'm not."

"I have to pick up supplies. I'll come back in the afternoon."

I silently left the cabin and rode out. The sun hadn't yet risen, but RavenMane and I knew all the best trails. We varied our route each time we ventured out to replenish our stocks. I always went alone, pretending to be a misanthrope hoping to avoid unnecessary contacts with other human beings. But that morning, I headed towards a market town I normally avoided. It was bigger than the village I usually patronised. I had a deer strapped to RavenMane's back to sell, and some of our savings in my purse.

Azeline would be turning twenty-one soon. I wanted something special. A fine dress for my love. She'd never worn one. Since leaving Pendle, she wore only male clothing. It proved more practical when living in the wilderness. It didn't attract unwanted attention when I bought it, and it had the added benefit of looking good on her. In the last three years, Azeline had not met a single human being.

The deer fetched a good price. As I wandered amid

the small crowd, my gaze left the stalls to study the people. I envied their ordinary lives. Couples held hands, smiling and laughing. I particularly noticed a young woman gazing at her husband, the love in her eyes, simple, unencumbered, free of fear.

Since the day I became her guardian, Azeline had stopped looking at me this way. She was terrified illness would consume me because of her. Two of her guardians had died from a mysterious one. She believed it hadn't been natural, but the prophecy at work, and she was the disease.

Part of her already mourned me.

I banished those dreary thoughts and concentrated on the wares, but it seemed there were no dresses to be had. However, among the many stalls, I selected a pretty necklace as well as a small dagger. Both would make a suitable gift for my fierce Azeline. But I chose the necklace. For once, things in her life would be about beauty and not battle or fear. The necklace drew me with its seven encrusted gemstones, each a different colour. Each beautiful in its own right like the various facets of my love.

The necessary coins exchanged hands. The merchant handed me the piece of jewellery on a crimson velvet cloth. Before I folded the fabric, I couldn't resist the temptation of stroking the necklace.

As soon as I brushed the cold metal, I realised my mistake. I yanked back my hand, but the damage was already done. My fingertips where they had touched the metal had been burned in a way I recognised only too well. Kalinka had found me.

I desperately looked around. I didn't know if I was expecting soldiers closing in on me or some kind of beast attacking me. For the people nearby, nothing had changed. They went about their lives as they had seconds before, laughing, arguing, bargaining.

I had no idea how the enchantment worked. Did Kalinka know only where I was or did she know Azeline's position too? Should I run away from Azeline or to her? What a guardian I made, bringing her enemy to her doorstep, twice.

I jumped on RavenMane and galloped towards the forest. My mare guided us among the trees while my eyes never left what I could make out of the sky through the leaves. I expected to discover a dragon flying over the forest, or another monster like the one who attacked us back at Odemar's tower. Who knew what other horrors Kalinka could summon?

I hoped I wouldn't arrive too late because of my hesitation to rush back. When I reached our little glade, a short middle-aged woman stood in front of our cabin. Her dark red brocade dress threaded with gold was as sophisticated as anything I had seen at Godefroy's court. Her dark hair was pinned up in a convoluted arrangement. Azeline was nowhere in sight. I took heart she might have already escaped.

At the sound of hoofbeats, the woman turned towards me and inclined her head gracefully. If I hadn't known who she was or what she was capable of, I would never have thought this was the woman who had made Azeline's life hell.

She opened her arms. "Erwin, welcome. You have my sincerest gratitude. You've proven more valuable than all my creatures. Not once, but twice have you showed me where to find the Soulless. Especially today, at the most crucial moment." She placed a hand over her heart. "I believe it my destiny to become the seventh guardian. The last. The most important of all. The one who will guide her to become the great power she's meant to be. Under my tutelage, she'll grow into a mighty sorceress fit to rule over all the kingdoms."

I dismounted and unsheathed Fortitude. "I'll never entrust Azeline to you."

Kalinka raised a dubious eyebrow. "Do you see anyone else around here?"

"My lady, I assume you're familiar with the particulars of the prophecy. Does it say anything about the chosen guardian being close? I might as well appoint the cobbler from the closest village."

"You must see I'm the best choice for her."

Kalinka's calm and poised tone made me even more uncomfortable than if she'd been screaming. I kept my distance, my sword in my hand, but she stared at me with amused patience.

"Erwin's time isn't over," Azeline's voice came from the threshold of the cabin.

Kalinka whirled with a broad grin. "I've waited for so long to meet you, my dear. More than two decades is a long time. I always thought we would meet in the Wildlands."

"I can't say the same, witch." Azeline took a few steps on the grass.

Kalinka brushed a crease in her skirts, "You have fire. I like that, but you're wrong. His time's over."

An elegant curl of Kalinka's finger, and I found myself lifted off the ground. Against my will, all my muscles relaxed. Fortitude clattered into the dirt. Kalinka closed her right hand into a fist. I floated towards the sorceress, stopping inches in front of her. Then with a tilt of her head, she opened her hand, fingers straight and pressed together. From her palm and enveloping her fingers, light surged, forming what looked like a blade.

"Release him," Azeline shouted. She had my

sword aimed at the side of Kalinka's throat. She must have picked it up after I dropped it. The sorceress didn't even flinch. Her eyes stayed fixed on me, but she waved her left hand. Like me, Azeline was lifted off the ground, unable to hold on to Fortitude. She should have struck when she had the opportunity. Although I wondered if Kalinka hadn't let her get close on purpose.

Kalinka smiled. "However this day plays out, I win. If you don't make me her guardian, I'll kill her. She's just a girl for now. I cannot let her enter into her powers if I don't control her. So, you see, knight, you don't have a choice. Make me her guardian."

I looked at my love. The tears streaming down her face were for me. I had failed my mission, but I still had to protect her. Our eyes met. I tried to convey all my feelings for her in one look. Azeline's green marking shone, and, despite the tears, I saw a deep resolve etched in her features.

"I'm not a patient woman." Kalinka's thrust her weapon deep into my stomach. She sliced horizontally before removing the blade.

Pain radiated through my body as if the weapon had shattered into a thousand pieces now rushing along my veins. But Azeline's anguished exhale hurt me even more than the wound.

"Erwin. Don't entrust me to her," she paused, staring at my midsection, "Please. Let me go with you."

I didn't peer down. No need to see the blood when I felt a hot liquid flowing along my legs. My heart beat frantically. So little time remained. I'd long known I'd die for Azeline, but I couldn't do as she said, and let her die with me, nor could I let Kalinka win. Azeline had a destiny. I didn't want the sorceress to take that away from her. But what could I do?

My vision was getting blurry. Kalinka squinted at me, then faced Azeline. I was afraid she would stab Azeline with her blade but saw it had vanished. Instead, she twirled her fingers. Fortitude levitated until it was level with Azeline's throat. My own sword. Kalinka meant to use my own sword to kill my love.

"Wait," I managed to utter against the lump in my throat.

"Yes?" I could tell by the satisfied smirk on her face, Kalinka thought I had surrendered.

"Very well," I whispered, "You'll become the next guardian."

Azeline shook her head frantically, but my mind was made up.

I didn't rush despite the weakness seeping into my body. "Every guardian must pay the ultimate price. We're only stepping stones towards her destiny."

Kalinka snorted.

"You'll be no different," I added.

Kalinka might think her soul would dominate the others, she was wrong. I sensed it. She'd just become a part of a whole like my own soul would. No amount of dark magic could ever change that.

"Every guardian wakes up different."

Azeline's eyes widened at those words. I prayed she understood my meaning. My next words would bind her irremediably to the loathsome woman but hopefully only for a short time. I wished I could tell her goodbye. I said the words, "Kalinka, I entrust the Soulless to you."

My gaze locked with Azeline's for the last seconds before I felt myself start to dissolve. My body fell face first in the dirt with a thud, but it didn't hurt. I was beyond pain. As I hoped, Kalinka's immaterial grip had vanished.

When I became Azeline's guardian, I lost consciousness before waking up possessed by a new energy. That energy now flowed out of me, escaping towards the sorceress. It didn't matter anymore. What mattered was Kalinka had passed out as I had hoped.

The day I became her guardian, I had come to Azeline's scream, but I never asked her if she'd collapsed too. Today I gambled she didn't. I gambled she'd been paralyzed by grief, not incapacitated. With difficulty, my eyelids lifted slightly. I couldn't keep them open for long, but I'd seen what I wanted. My love picking up Fortitude, ready to slay her enemy.

Behind closed eyes, I heard the thrust. The culmination of twenty years of hunt concluded with Kalinka being the guardian for a few mere seconds.

I had but one regret. That I wouldn't see Azeline fulfil her potential. My last thoughts went to her. When my soul became hers, she'd find them among my memories.

"Farewell. I'd hoped to stay longer with you, my love. But I know I'll become part of you forever. Whatever strength I possessed will be yours. I knew you would prevail. The world is now yours."

***

I expected the void.

Instead, I found myself swirling round and round in a blinding light.

Others spun with me, bright colourful glows twisting in intricate patterns, their meanings now intelligible. Characters, feelings, and abilities translated into sinuous coils.

At the centre, the light source stood. A human

shape. A woman. A disturbing sense of familiarity gripped me. Just like in the stained glass window in Odemar's tower, we were orbiting a goddess.

I tried to reach out to Azeline. She had to be the woman. When no answer came, I feared some treachery. But Kalinka was revolving with me, along with Odemar and the others. The green marking, Iricha, had always been the most active of all. I wanted to get close to her, but we whirled too fast.

The prophecy was about to be fulfilled.

Happiness filled me.

My love would reign fairly over an enlightened kingdom.

But when I looked at the woman again, I saw her true nature, a shell filled with one compulsion. Hunger. Limitless. Irresistible.

I understood.

Azeline wasn't the Soulless. The shell was.

The shell knew no emotions. It drew from stolen souls to counterfeit humanity.

Both vessel and lure, Azeline had attracted the required souls, inspired the devotion necessary for our sacrifices. But Azeline never really existed.

Only the shell.

My love had been an artefact created by borrowed souls, and she was no more.

I refused to believe Azeline knew.

She'd been an ignorant accomplice in our downfall. Seven souls offered willingly to a monstrosity, putting the world between its fingers.

Why did my consciousness linger? Why was I forced to witness the mockery made of my sacrifice?

The light swallowed everything, fulfilling the prophecy.

I felt the collective cry when all lives in the kingdoms disappeared.

But, pain and sorrow didn't last.

When it claimed me, I welcomed nothingness.

BEYOND THE REALM

CAROLE DE MONCLIN writes Science-Fiction and Fantasy. Her tales invite you on a journey.

Without the support of her amazing husband, her stories would still be floating around in her head. Many of them still are, but she plans on catching them one after the other. Although, she expects it will be an endless endeavour. The sneaky things tend to multiply on her.

The 7th Soul is a special tale for her. The idea stayed nestled into notebooks for decades. Sleeping, but not forgotten. It has become darker, and changed languages along the way, but her teenage self would still approve.

Bibliography
ANGELS, Black Hare Press, 2019
APOCALYSPE, Black Hare Press, 2019
BEYOND THE REALM, Black Hare Press, 2020
BEYOND, Black Hare Press, 2019
C is for Cosmic Wanderer, Exoplanet Magazine, 2019
DEEP SPACE, Black Hare Press, 2019
ETERNITY Ltd., The Arcanist, 2019
HATE, Black Hare Press, 2020
LOVE, Black Hare Press, 2020
MONSTERS, Black Hare Press, 2019
OCEANS, Black Hare Press, 2020
UNRAVEL, Black Hare Press, 2019
WORLDS, Black Hare Press, 2019

Connect
Website: CaroledeMonclin.com
Twiter: @CaroledeMonclin
Amazon: amazon.com/-/e/B07SW7DNP5

BLACK HARE PRESS

BEYOND THE REALM

SEEKER
By Stuart West

Since the investigation commenced, the slumber of the Order's greatest Seeker was fitful, and he became acutely aware of a familiar ancient malevolence, lurking just out of sight, presenting itself only for an instant when he stepped between worlds...can Garven maintain his perfect record without revealing his own forbidden secrets?

The tree was massive. Garven could imagine clouds snagging upon the uppermost reaches of its crown. The russet bark had occasional purple tones, which peeled like paper when his delicate fingers brushed against it, and the needle-like spines protruding from the twigs of its great bows, arching high above, seemingly bore tiny scarlet fruits or berries. Unsurprisingly, there was still no visible entrance about its cyclopean roots. Garven sighed as he turned his back towards the prodigious trunk. The luscious grasses of the meadows that stretched down the hillside from his viewpoint ended a league to the west where the ocean could be heard slowly eating the sandstone cliffs. *Something wasn't right.* The tree was impenetrable. It always ended this way—with a feeling of frustration and then a flashing vision of cold reptilian eyes and a vicious, serrated beak.

He flinched and shook his head slightly, glancing feverishly around to make sure nobody had noticed his shudder, his hand reflexively jerking towards the fetish about his neck. Everyone's attention was on the Witch as she reassured the committee once more that her preferred location for the tower was a result of her inheritance of land rather than anything untoward. She sat alone at the ornate table opposite Garven; one alabaster hand hidden from view on her lap and the other placed flat upon the oaken surface with a single finger brushing the base of a pewter goblet. Since the case officer had introduced the proposal earlier in the week, she remained composed and answered the queries of the regional elders with admirable eloquence.

"…the land was bequeathed to me by my aunt, Sir," she continued as she carefully tucked a strand of raven hair behind her ear, "it has little value and I have no means to acquire an alternative site."

On the surface it seemed like a superficial matter; a Witch sought to establish herself in a new region and a number of the locals had objected. But there was more to it than that. Garven looked to his right beyond the parish officials towards the Chairman at the front of the chamber. The Regional Magus observed proceedings with the same detached impartiality as was expected, and indeed required, of an official representing the Order. Disgruntled murmuring from the gallery to the left in response to the Witch's comments fought for Garven's attention but he maintained focus on Magus Reedbank whose lips began to purse beneath his impeccably groomed beard.

"I believe we have established the extent of the land, Councillor." Reedbank's eyes narrowed. "Now is there anything else before we move on to the objectors?" The portly elder swallowed hard and adjusted his spectacles as he shook his head.

"N-nothing more," he said, looking at his hands.

"Very well, we'll reconvene after noon," said the Magus. He stood, straightened his dress robes mechanically with the palms of his hands, and walked from the Chair to his antechamber, passing through the ornate doorway without a so much as a glance at the congregation. The heavy door closed with a solid thud and the room erupted with raised voices and the scrape of furniture as the gathering broke for lunch.

The noise began to recede as people filtered from the Council Chamber, and Garven exhaled slowly. He pinched the bridge of his nose. Breathing slowly through his mouth, he waited for the room to become still before he finally opened his eyes. *What was going on here?* The Witch seemed to be speaking the truth… He was focused enough not to be seduced by her attractiveness; the necessary rituals had been undertaken to prevent his bewitchment; and both his mind and his heart told him that she practised within all parameters set out by the Order under the terms of the Act. He looked around the chamber and up at the empty public gallery to his left. He rubbed his eyes and fought to stifle a yawn. Since arriving in the townstead, his slumber was fitful and he was acutely aware that he was being shadowed by a familiar ancient malevolence, lurking just out of sight, presenting itself only for an instant when he moved from the Other World to this.

***

Like the case, the townstead of Baccataburg was unremarkable. Garven smiled politely at the maiden as she leaned across him to place the wooden bowl on the coarse, heavy table. She held the position for a moment too long with a smile that didn't reach her eyes.

"Can I get you anything else darling?" she asked placing a hand softly on his chest.

"No, no, that'll do just fine," he replied, holding up a hand. She gave an exaggerated curtsey and retreated to the kitchen with a flick of her hair. He tore a chunk from the cob and began to stir the broth. The meat certainly looked like rabbit, but you could never be sure. As a stranger to these parts he may well be served rodents; he never did understand why in the provinces they paid a bounty solely on tails, it was just asking for trouble in the hostelries. Garven retrieved a generous pinch of salt from his pouch and crumbled it into his supper.

The broth took the edge off the cob, which could easily have lacerated the roof of his mouth if he weren't careful. As he slurped the hot fluid from the bread, he tried once more to piece things together. Upon arriving, Reedbank had briefed him on the matter. The Magus had initially believed that it was just bigotry that had caused the furore. Afterall, there had been no practising Witches in Baccataburg since the "Times of Strife," before the creation of the Order. If he hadn't been shown the ancient scrolls, Garven too would have believed this to be the case given the testimonies of the afternoon session where the townsfolk were permitted to raise their concerns.

At their first meeting, Reedbank had carefully lifted the scrolls from a leaden chest in his antechamber and laid them on his desk. They had been dispatched to him from the Citadel when a date for the hearing had been set. The ancient vellum parchments bore maps in faded ink and across each sheet, the crisscrossing Jinmalian Channels were depicted. Garven quickly leaned forward to examine the maps with widening eyes.

"Are they real," he stood upright and looked the old Magus in the eye, pulse racing.

"They are authentic," he confirmed.

The meridian lines detailed on the ancient maps had underpinned the theological structure and ritual practices of the Witches for generations. With the establishment of the Order, all knowledge of their whereabouts had been subverted and to common folk they had almost been lost to mythology.

"This Witch proposes to build her tower directly upon a convergence point of three separate channels," Reedbank advised as he inserted a monocle and gripped it within his right eye socket "look." He traced a finger across the parchment to a point where three of the green lines met. Garven noted the familiar square and cross symbol for a settlement a little way from the old Magus's finger and could barely make out the word "Baccataburg" in italicised script.

"Is there any evidence that she is in league with the forbidden powers?"

"That is where you come in, Seeker."

Since that discussion, fourteen moons previous, Garven had resided at the "Baccataburg Inn," working in partnership with the local authorities to investigate the Witch and her claims on behalf of the Order. To date, no evidence had been uncovered to indicate that the Witch was colluding with anyone suspected of defying the Act or that she was aware of the "sensitive" nature of her site. Indeed, the claims that the land was inherited seemed to be perfectly in order and she did seem to be trying to establish herself as the resident Witch of the region through the legitimate channels. As one of the most successful Seekers employed by the Order, Garven had never before failed to close a case in less than eight moons. But this was different, and the presence of the familiar evil was unsettling.

***

The bedroom was situated at the back of the inn so the sound from the bar below was muted. Having a private room had made Garven something of a talking point amongst the staff and regulars. His attendance at the hearing each day, and links with the Order, dissuaded all but the most inebriated from engaging him in conversation though. This was fine; Garven enjoyed socialising and meeting new people but work was work—the less distractions that he had to deal with whilst he was in town the better.

Despite the high-end nature of the room in comparison with others at the inn, it was still basic compared to those in the cities and it was not particularly large. It boasted a straw-filled mattress in the cot, a lockable trunk, a writing desk with a heavy beeswax candle that cast dancing shadows across the whitewashed walls, and a small stool. There was a modest sash and casement window beside the desk and a pot for pissing in the corner. All in all, it was a good room and such comfort was not lost on Garven who had endured periods of his life wanting for even the most basic provisions and accommodation. He spent a moment looking from the window at the empty cobbled square below. The main public areas in Baccataburg were lighted by slow-burning, oil-soaked wicks set in iron lanterns that flickered gently within their housings of orange-tinted glass. He pushed his face closer to the glass and craned his neck to catch a glimpse of the empty stocks a short distance away, beside the imposing gallows for perpetrators of more serious crimes.

Having drawn the hessian sheet across the window, the Seeker moved over to the trunk and retrieved a folded blanket and a small tin box. He carefully set the box upon the writing desk. The golden thread woven through the geometric shapes on the fabric twinkled by the light of the candle as he unfurled the blanket that he lay neatly between the cot and the desk. Content that the blanket was free of wrinkles, Garven returned to the desk and opened the hinged lid of the box. He gently removed the contents and placed them upon the desk: a small clay bowl with ropework pattern around its rim, a length of wick, a glass bottle with a cork stopper, a flint and steel, and a tarnished silver snuff box with small holes drilled into the lid.

Garven placed the snuff box onto the blanket and used his rolled travelling cloak to cover the gap at the foot of his door. Satisfied that the heavy iron key was in the locked position, he returned to the desk and assembled the lamp, adding the cedarwood oil from the stoppered bottle. Preparing for the ritual had become second nature over the years. Once the wick had soaked up enough of the pungent oil, he efficiently lit it before sitting cross-legged on the blanket with a hand placed on either side of the snuff box.

Garven opened his eyes to see the familiar tree looming before him at the crest of the hill. He was vaguely aware of the rich scent of the oil in his room at the Baccataburg Inn where his corporeal form now sat motionless. The sound of the waves continued to crash against the cliffs in the distance, and the thick grass beneath his hands felt warm under the midday sun. The Seeker sat cross-legged and was tempted to lay back and watch the high clouds skimming past for a while; but he knew there would be plenty of time for such luxuries once the case was closed. He sat for a few moments listening to the waves in the distance until he felt a tickling on the back of his right hand as a small scarlet ladybird with six black spots emerged from the grass. Garven lifted the tiny creature up to eye level and smiled.

"Good day little one," Garven carefully rose to his feet keeping his hand as level as possible in the process. "Thank you very much for your help." He held his hand high in the air and the insect flew into the sky. He watched it for a moment until it disappeared from view and then he closed his eyes and began to breath slowly:

in through his nose and out through his mouth. As he felt his feet slowly lift from the grass, Garven extended his arms to keep his balance. Once his breathing had become regular, he opened his eyes and looked at the floor a few feet below. If there wasn't an entrance at the roots of the tree, perhaps there was an access point higher up?

With each exhalation, Garven lowered his hands slightly and, as he did, he rose slowly into the air beside the mighty trunk. Whilst not the most proficient flyer, Garven could manoeuvre himself in a similar way to treading water if he were careful. He gradually ascended and took care to avoid the bows of the tree and its many needles. From this vantage point, the small red berries were clearly visible; glistening in the sunlight, they appeared ripe to the point that they would soon drop earthward. For what seemed like an age, Garven examined the upper reaches of the tree and its gnarled branches; yet there was no sign of any access point. The trunk was solid without even the smallest fissure or hollow to gain entry.

With a sigh, he turned from the tree and surveyed the surrounding landscape. From his position high above the ground, he could see the crystal azure waters of the ocean to the west and the rolling emerald hills to the north, east, and south. It was a beautiful place. His eyes widened and he felt his stomach clench. In the distance to the south, Garven caught sight of another tree, and to the east, another. It was hard to gauge their size, but they were certainly a long way distant, their forms mirroring the original beside which he hovered. Hopefully, this was the breakthrough he had sought.

With exhaustion fast approaching, Garven slowly descended towards the ground. Waves of energy seemed to rush from his toes, through his body and into his ears—each one causing his muscles to contract, prompting spells of vertigo and uncomfortable pressure on the back of his eyes. He dropped into a crouch as the balls of his feet made landfall before losing his balance and laying on the grass as the waves continued to pulse through him. As he felt his grip on the Other World faltering, he saw it again. An inky darkness flooded his view. All that was visible were two piercing amber eyes with black vertical slashes for irises. The imposing beak was dark orange, fading to yellow and then darkening once more to pitch at its extremities. A great head emerged from the blackness and moved swiftly towards him—its serrated beak opening wide with silent rage.

***

BEYOND THE REALM

Garven's eyes snapped open and he slowly rolled his shoulders with a wince. The clay lamp had long since burned out and rays of early morning light streamed from beneath the hessian window drape. He took the snuff box and pushed himself from the blanket to his feet with an involuntary grunt. The old window opened with a squeal under force and the odour of Baccataburg assaulted his senses like smelling salts, bringing his thoughts into sharp relief. Garven thumbed the lid from the box and held it out of the window.

"Thank you little one," he murmured to the ladybird as it thrummed its wings for a long moment before flying to freedom. He smiled and closed the window with a jolt.

Having stowed his blanket and personal effects in the chest at the foot of his bed, Garven visited the washroom at the end of the corridor to pour cold water through his ruffled hair, splashing it onto the back of his neck in an attempt to reinvigorate himself before leaving the inn. It was too early for breakfast but too late to make any effort to catch any real sleep before the day started. He resolved to survey the proposed site of the Witch's tower once more. As the door of the inn swung closed behind him, he turned up the collar on his cloak—more to obscure his features than to protect against the wind. Although many townspeople were yet to awaken, some early risers were visible in side streets, including the young street cleaners that were busy utilising their besoms to clear all traces of the discarded contents of chamber pots that had been used during the night. Garven stepped around the lamplighter's ladder, which was propped precariously against a merchant's house on the main square; having already extinguished the streetlamps, the watchman would have until nightfall to replenish the oil supplies and he was no doubt taking some well-earned rest before he set about his task.

Once away from the dense burgage plots at the heart of the town, the arrangement of buildings became less regimented and the multi-storey merchants' houses gave way to informal shacks and stores. The cobbled street ended abruptly at the town boundary and a dirt track stretched away to the north into the open countryside. The lack of a defensive wall spoke volumes of the poor agricultural quality of the surrounding moorland and, if not for the silver ore a day's ride into the mountains, it would be unlikely that the town would ever have grown from the small hamlet evident on the ancient maps that Garven carried in his knapsack, which he had retrieved from the Town House upon his arrival.

Although currently very much a peripheral

BEYOND THE REALM

province, historically, these lands had held some degree of strategic importance. Baccataburg had presumably been founded as a resting place for people travelling into the mountains to the west and as a market post for the surrounding community to peddle their wares. Indeed, the Town's Records Office held detailed accounts of meetings for over 120 winters and there were dockets of sales and notes of transfer of deeds stretching back almost as long. Looking back at the modest settlement, and the wisps of smoke that curled skyward from the myriad chimneys, Garven found it hard to comprehend that it was largely unchanged since before the establishment of the Order. Those buildings and streets had existed in a time before the Magi had risen to power, when the Witches had held free reign and engaged unchecked with ruinous powers.

In the Age of Strife, it was common knowledge that Witches held society firmly in their grasp, controlling the masses through fear, with those that challenged them meeting grisly ends or being cursed to a fate worse than death. For thousands of years, the Witches had provided counsel to rulers, healed the sick, and assisted peasants with their problems—for a price. They isolated themselves from society, building towers on the edge of communities or amongst nature at sites where their unearthly masters could more easily commune with them. The actions of one particular Witch had been the catalyst for the change that society had craved. Despite having pledged herself to the Goddess of the Moon and the Horned Master, the Witch fell in love with the son of the King. When their relationship failed, she ended the royal lineage in an act of rage that prompted an uprising amongst the masses. The powers released upon the family of the King, and upon his subjects, were so unspeakable that all Witches were forbidden to commune with, or draw power from, their masculine deity any longer. From that day, Witches could continue as specialists in herbalism and were permitted to engage with the Mother Goddess, but any proven to have pledged themselves to the Horned One were executed.

The Order had been founded to oversee the Witches and to ensure they did not break the terms of the Act. Magi were trained in the ways of Witches and were required to undertake years researching ancient wisdom and the movements of the stars. Whereas the Witches drew their knowledge from their matrons and their power from the supernatural, the Magi drew their knowledge from restricted tomes and their power from the heavens. Despite the initial bloodshed, this arrangement had proven successful for over a hundred years. From the Citadel, the Order governs the Heartlands and the Provinces, providing Magi to determine the outcome of hearings and trials. The Witches, although dwindling in numbers, were licensed and regulated so that they could act in an official capacity, primarily as healers and soothsayers.

In recent times, the relationship between the two factions had become more fraught. Greater numbers of Witches were being convicted of breaking the terms of the Act each season. Usually they were found to have murdered loved ones—this sacrifice being a demand of the Horned One before he would impart his powers on his children. Others were proven to have bewitched common folk, or of having used forbidden spells or charms, to compel people to seek to undermine the Order.

A weathered signpost bearing the recently repainted words "Baccataburg: 2" and "Argentrix: 19" prompted Garven to leave the dusty trail and pick his way slowly through the heather towards a hill to the north. The sun had risen higher in the sky behind Garven's left shoulder. He halted for long enough to stow his cloak in his knapsack and retrieve some twice-baked sweet oats in the process. He broke his fast with the golden crumbling discs as he made his way up the gentle incline towards the site, continuing his meditation on the relationship between Witches and the Order as he went.

Although broadly feared by society, Garven had no issues with Witches as a whole. He had grown up in a provincial town where one of the more respected schools of witchcraft operated and had befriended many from amongst their ranks as a boy, occasionally taking that friendship further than the matrons would have allowed. The honest and earthly nature of the girls he had known in his hometown meant that he did not automatically distrust or fear them, but instead approached each of his cases on its merits, objectively considering the facts. He had of course come across cruel and lost souls over the course of his career: ambitious witches that had slain their closest relatives to taste the forbidden powers, and those so worn down by discrimination and isolation that they ultimately became what they had been accused of for so long, lashing out at those that shunned and persecuted them.

In recent years, instances of Witches breaking the terms of the Act had become so numerous that the Order had to draft the services of freelance Seekers such as Garven, as their own ranks lacked the resources or specialisations to undertake investigations and uncover the truth. Having worked on over a score of cases on behalf of the Order, he had become familiar with their methods of operation and their organisational idiosyncrasies. Their lack of tolerance for non-Order members being acquainted with any ancient knowledge or rituals was of grave concern, especially given Garven's own background. He sighed and paused to catch his breath having reached the midway point between the track and the hilltop.

Looking to the south, Baccataburg was a vague grey smear on the horizon, surrounded by a modest patchwork of yellow and green fields that had been laid to crop. Ahead, the land sloped gently towards a natural plateau upon which could now be seen a small cairn of stones and a sharp upright monolith. Garven loosened the stopper in the small goatskin that hung from his belt. He sipped the ale conservatively so that it quenched his thirst but did not dull his wits; the liquid consumables on offer in Baccataburg seemed particularly adept at numbing the senses and had to be imbibed in strict moderation.

There had been a time when Garven wouldn't care about dulled senses or conservatism. Upon completing his compulsory education in the Order-sponsored school in his township, he had set out to explore all the lands between the Western Mountains and the Blackwater in the East. Having socialised with spice traders from across the southern fens and travelled for a year with a dancing troupe from the frozen north, he had thrived on adventure and recklessness. He smiled for a moment, eyes fixed on no particular point in the distance, as he recalled some of his antics and the bizarre company he had kept. All these experiences made him who he was; they allowed him not to be startled and to empathise with people regardless of their creed, culture, or beliefs. His mouth narrowed and he took in a deep breath. It had been when he had been at his most reckless, when he was beginning to lose who he was and what he really believed, that he had met the Shaman from the Steppes and he found his path.

Whilst he understood and respected the beliefs of both the Witches and the Magi, as an animist, Garven had his own distinct worldview. He respected all things and regularly communed with natural spirits and entities when he stepped between worlds. He saw patterns and order where others only saw coincidences, and he worked with all living things to preserve the natural balance. Of course, once his training had progressed so far, his teacher had sought to impose a hierarchical order on the followers of the path where none naturally existed—as he had seen with all other belief structures. Having cleared his mind and shed his demons, Garven left his mentor and returned to the

Heartlands where he picked up his old life and forged his current identity.

It was almost noon when Garven reached the crest of the hill. He set down his knapsack and took a longer draught from the goatskin before reinserting the stopper and dropping it beside his other effects. It was a fine day; the heather was flowering, and the moorland was more lilac than brown. Bees clumsily made their way from here to there and unseen skylarks sang high above. A beautiful spot. A plume of dust in the distance below marked the passage of a caravan that slowly made its way towards Baccataburg from parts unknown, probably taking metal ware, highfalutin textiles, or spices as trade for honey or beeswax, the main exports of the settlement.

The flat plateau was ideal for construction and the outlook from the hilltop was breath taking. Garven knelt and unfastened his knapsack. He rummaged within for a few moments and withdrew the maps, the site plan, and his brass telescope. He glanced around in search of a stone to unfurl the map upon and noticed the jagged upright of the shattered monolith a short distance away. He walked over to the ancient stone and laid a hand upon its face. As he did, he closed his eyes and slowed his breathing, opening himself to any energies that may lie within. Nothing. The shattered remnants of its upper section lay half buried on the ground. As he looked sorrowfully at the defiled monument, Garven noticed a patch of striking red a few paces beyond the stone. Carefully piled upon a large flat stone was a small pyramid of around a dozen bright red berries. Garven stooped to examine the berries; they were identical in size and hue to those on the impregnable tree in the Other World. Standing, Garven searched the surrounding landscape for any evidence of the soul responsible for depositing the fruit but there was nothing to be seen.

From this position on the site, the similarity between the morphology of the landscape surrounding the application site and the location of the great tree in Other World was uncanny. Of course, there was no ocean in the physical world. Looking westward, instead of seeing a low horizon where the otherworldly cliffs were located, Garven saw instead a lea in the hillside, reminiscent of an old quarry, and the great Western Mountains in the distance. Comparing these features with the site plan, Garven could see that the lea was in fact the entrance to the baron silver mine that prompted the acquisition of the land several generations previous.

Garven orientated the ancient maps northwards and laid them to rest on the large flat rock beside the berries, pinning them beneath a number of weighty stones. Recalling the positions of the other trees he had observed in the Other World, he referred to the maps and sought to plot their locations. Garven's brows furrowed as he traced lines to the south and the east. Each of these lines intersected distant settlements, contemporary with Baccataburg—one long since abandoned and another now nothing more than a modest inn for travellers named "The Hanged Man," within which Garven had spent a night en route to Baccataburg. The inn stood amongst crumbling ruins where much of the building stone had long since been robbed to build drystone dykes to contain livestock.

An ancient grass-domed tomb with a frontage of dressed white limestone stood sentry over the trackway from the inn to Baccataburg, and Garven had marvelled that it appeared to have never been pillaged. The one-armed barkeep at The Hanged Man had explained that nobody was foolish enough to disturb the spirits of the mound, which he claimed destroyed the town once the sentinel stones had been crippled.

The Provinces were a relict landscape, littered with the evidence of past civilisations that had been lost in the Heartlands, either through salvage of materials, the redevelopment of sites, or erosion by the plough. Efforts had been made by an ancient King, Harriden the

Third, to destroy the sacred places of his ancestors and usher in a new era. He has sent crews of mercenaries the length and breadth of his kingdom to cast down the monumental architecture of his ancestors. These "stone killers" had travelled during the winter months and had shattered the frozen stones with boiling water. Within the course of a few years, a whole chapter of history had been expunged: the king careful to purge all written records of the beliefs of his heretical forebears. Such attempts to reset the collective beliefs and worldview of the subjects seemed to Garven to occur on a cyclical basis, with the Order having arguably undertaken a similar process over recent generations.

***

The scent of sandalwood filled the room and Garven sat once more upon his blanket beside the cot. Although his on-site investigations had shown that the entrance to the abandoned mine had entirely collapsed, he was keen to investigate further.

Upon opening his eyes, the now familiar tree stood steadfastly before him. Garven's mind was clearer than it had been in recent memory. The need to break the case pressed upon him and the internal fluttering of excitement as he drew closer to his goal had prompted the consumption of some precious Fenris Root from his emergency supply. The effects of imbibing the root in its unrefined state had been instantaneous; his metabolism had increased, and all feelings of tiredness had been brushed away. He would have a period of great focus and productivity that should be long enough to conclude his dealings in Baccataburg before the inevitable crash that followed, where he would feel as though the world had ended for at least three moons, unable to wake or function in any productive way.

His sharpened senses were even more enhanced in the Other World, and the vivid colours that surrounded him fed his excitement and spurred him onwards. He fought to maintain control and to remain still: concentrating on the feeling of the thick grasses brushing and stroking his hands until he felt the light footfall of the moth. Bounding to his feet with his arm outstretched, he looked at the cream fur of the creature and the distinct chestnut arcs on its wings.

"Thank you," he whispered, and the moth flew from his hand into the cobalt sky. Eagerly, Garven took flight without his normal trepidation and he soared towards the cliffs and the roar of the waves as they crashed into the landmass. As the land dropped away beneath him, the frothing ocean and rich orange-brown cliffs came into view. He remembered for a moment how he had lived for years with this same exhilaration as a youth—almost constantly imbibing flora of one kind or another on a day to day basis, fighting off the inevitable plunge towards melancholy as the powerful substances left his system. This would certainly not become a habit again. It would be difficult to shake off, but Garven had become strong and he could meditate through the challenging days that would follow.

Swooping around, the tree came back into view. As he flew back towards the land with the salt of the spray below on his lips, he saw what he had been searching for. The cave sat around three-quarters of the way up the cliff face, a gentle trickle of water running from its open mouth. He carefully adjusted his trajectory and manoeuvred himself to set down just beyond the opening. The aperture was certainly large enough for Garven to fit without stooping; in fact, he would have trouble reaching the dark roof that glistened with moisture if he tried. Underfoot, shallow water lapped around the soles of his boots and the slippery green algal growth on either side of the water appeared to thin within the gloom of the corridor ahead.

Within the Other World, Garven could wield powers akin to the greatest sorcerers of the physical realm. With a murmured incantation, a small bright light manifested and bobbed gently in the air beside his shoulder. It took the merest thought for the orb to move ahead and light the blackness of the cave. Garven followed carefully in the wake of his mage light as he sought to investigate what lay ahead.

The tunnel was long, but the consistent pace of the water confirmed to Garven that it was as level as it felt. The cave was natural, with rough surfaces betraying no evidence of being worked by tools or other means. The fact that its gaping mouth was no longer visible indicated that the route had been slightly curved. As the Seeker began to feel niggling doubts of whether it was indeed the access point he had been looking for, his mage light illuminated a series of steps carved into the stone ahead. The steps were steep and spiralled withershins out of view. With a thought, the orb dimmed and floated to a point beside the Shaman's left knee. Garven slowly ascended the ancient-looking, and well-worn staircase, ignoring the tunnel that continued into the distance.

Despite the steepness and sheer number of steps, he proceeded without pause until light was visible above. The mage light flickered and blinked from existence as the summit was reached. Garven found himself in a large circular chamber with a high ceiling of great oaken beams, which was filled with hunched wretches silently poring over large black cauldrons.

The walls of the vast room were hewn from stone to a point twice the height of a man before giving way to smooth timber of russet and purple. Multiple light sources illuminated the space: torches on the walls and flames flickering within candelabras suspended from the ceiling. The creatures either didn't see the shaman enter the room or else they chose to ignore him. They toiled with large wooden ladles over the heavy iron pots. It was unclear if those silently tending the contents of the vessels were human or not, their thin grey skin and white wispy hair unnatural in so many ways, yet unsettlingly familiar.

There was a clear path between the doorway and a raised dais at the far side of the chamber, upon which stood a figure clad in flowing white robes of silk or satin. Ignoring the grimy, unkempt souls that continued to stir the contents of their cauldrons, Garven slowly walked across the room. After a few moments, the figure on the platform, a woman with golden hair, beckoned him forward with a smile. He joined the woman and noted the ornate copper vessel beside her that bubbled and glowed with a faint light the colour of under-ripe limes. She spread her arms in welcome and he noted that the light passing through the fabric of her robes highlighted her curved form and his loins constricted involuntarily.

Narrowing his eyes and furrowing his brow, Garven made to speak.

"Who—" he began but stopped as she pressed a finger to her lips. She motioned with her hands at her toiling subjects and smiled at him contentedly. Garven relaxed and a mild serenity began to wash over him, suppressing the Fenris root and bringing him to a state of almost dazed calm. Instinctively, the shaman reached and touched the cylinder that hung from a cord about his neck and a level of awareness flashed from his fingertips to every extremity. He began to walk around the enchantress and her face turned to follow him with a serene smile. Despite the reassurance that he felt, he gripped his talisman tighter and continued to circle her, passing the bubbling cauldron as he went. He had almost completed his circuit when she lurched for him with clawed hands, eyes flashing amber. Her snarling mouth revealed wooden pegs in the place of teeth, and for an instant, her glamour dropped, and her hair was replaced with a rough, patchy stubble.

***

Garven bounded to his feet, clutching for his necklace, flailing backwards into his cot. The oil lamp still smouldered, and he could feel the effects of the

Fenris root burning within his heart. It took only moments for the shaman to recover his wits and re-orientate himself. He snatched up the snuff box and released the moth through the window into the night with a bow of his head and the thanks it deserved before hastily gathering up his effects and bundling them into the chest.

Things had become clear at last and it was essential that the Magus was warned. A greater evil than he had feared was at work and the Witch must be stopped at any cost. Garven had first encountered the avian demon during his initial journeys to the Other World when an aspect of it had sought to gain control of him as it presented itself as his guide. Without the teachings of his mentor, he would surely have been led down a path from which there would be no return. He had been warned, however, of the need to walk full circle around any entity that presents itself when you journey to other realms to see it for what it really is. The true nature of the great bird was revealed, and it had attacked—its fierce beak snapping—and it released a gout of unnatural flames in an attempt to immolate his vulnerable soul. In the years that followed, the shaman had developed strong defences and had managed to elude the being. His latest journey had revealed it was at work here and there was some link between the ancient culture that had erected the megaliths in forgotten times and the Jinmalian Channels of the Witches. If this horror had seduced the Witches and was actively empowering them, the Order would have to respond.

The hurried journey across Baccataburg was uneventful although it seemed to Garven that shrouded figures flitted within the shadows and darkened streets. The Magus would be within his quarters at the administrative building where the case was being heard. The shaman rattled the polished knocker continuously glancing left and right, peering into the gloom to ensure he had not been followed. Reedbank's retainer answered the door with a frown, which turned into a scowl as the door was unceremoniously pushed from his hands as the dishevelled Seeker marched into the hallway.

"Fetch the Magus, now," Garven insisted, striding towards the antechamber where the Magus would attend visitors. It was late and this was a grave breach of etiquette, but the Seeker was within his rights to call a meeting at any time should circumstance dictate it.

He paced the room, glancing from each of the windows in turn. The sight of the leaden chest beside the Magus's desk caused him to pause for a moment to consider once more what he had uncovered... A malevolent being from an alien dimension was in league with the Witches, guiding them to ancient points of power and opposing the Order. It seemed that the nexus points along the Jinmalian Channels, where the veil between worlds was at its thinnest, were known in forgotten times as places of power also. Garven paused for a moment to consider the implications. If such nexus points existed in the heartlands, where the remains of the shattered megaliths and contemporary structures had long since been cleared, how many of these places had already fallen into the hands of those that would use them for their own nefarious means?

Magus Reedbank entered the chamber and closed the door gently behind him, seemingly undisturbed by the lateness of the call, with his beard and hair well-groomed and his amethyst robes impeccable as ever. The sight of the Seeker clutching his midriff whilst rocking slowly on the balls of his feet caused him to crease his brow and tilt his head slightly to the side with only the a slightest of smiles.

"Is all well, Seeker? You appear ill at ease."

"Magus, I have grave news. I have uncovered evidence that the Witches are indeed attempting to gain control of the site for improper means." Magus Reedbank frowned and moved towards his desk, placing his hands upon the leather surface and leaning forward slightly.

"Go on Seeker. What have you learned?"

"The nexus points of the Witches' channels align with the ancient sites of the Lost People." Garven moved forward and stood on the opposite side of the desk. "They are in league with a demon." Magus Reedbank's eyes narrowed slightly, and he sat down on his chair.

"Tell me, how can you know this?" He took a decanter and some goblets from the drawer to his left. Garven hesitated; he must be careful not to implicate himself in any wrongdoing.

"There was a trail, offerings on the plateau. There are also records. If we could study the maps, I am sure we could show the lines converge on the ancient megaliths and tombs." The Magus poured a rich red wine from the crystal decanter and offered a glass to his guest. "I can't believe it hadn't been noticed before…" The Magus stood carefully and walked to the heavy chest. He glanced up and gestured towards the seat before the desk.

"Sit, sit. You need a moment," said Reedbank softly. Garven sat down and savoured the delicate bouquet of the wine, swilling it slowly around his mouth as the Magus withdrew the maps and laid them on the desk. The Magus began to unfurl the maps and paused.

"But the daemon, how can you be sure they are in league with it?"

"I have my methods…" Garven smiled satisfactorily before realising the implication of the words he had uttered. His left hand went instinctively to the protection about his neck and his eyes bulged as he stared at the drink in his hand. His head swam. He was half aware of the glass falling to the floor and of the Magus standing over him. Was he speaking? It was hard to be sure. The room and its furniture lurched sideways, and the cool, polished floorboards seemed to caress his hot cheek.

The robed figure of the Magus was joined by another, wearing riding boots of soft leather. It was impossible to see above the ankles of the two individuals. Garven lay stunned and helpless, unable to move; his left hand frozen claw-like before his breast and his right somewhere beneath him. Without the Fenris root, he would surely be unconscious.

"Drug the Witch. Then, take them to his room, strip them, and slit his throat." This was the familiar voice of the Magus but he sounded distant and cruel. "That should be enough to get a conviction and get us out of the damned place." It wasn't until he was being dragged by his arm towards the Council Chamber that the Seeker realised his mistake. It had never been the Witches that were in league with his otherworldly foe, but Reedbank. He couldn't know if the entire Order had been compromised or if the Magus was acting alone. How many of the Witches executed in recent times had been innocent?

As he was pulled through the doorway, with blurred vision, he caught a final glimpse of the Magus sneering towards him with cold satisfaction and piercing amber eyes.

"Goodbye, Seeker."

BLACK HARE PRESS

STUART WEST is a qualified archaeologist and chartered town planner living on an island archipelago within the hinterland of Thule. In his spare time, Stuart plays tabletop wargames for fun and competitively for his country; writes speculative fiction; and paints. Stuart has no cats—nor does he want any.

Writing mainly Sci-fi, Stuart has been published in a variety of short story anthologies, magazines and journals—one day he'll finish the novel!

Bibliography
ANCIENTS, Black Hare Press, 2019
Flash Fiction Addiction, Zombie Pirate Publishing, 2019
Lovecraftiana Candlemas, Rogue Planet Press, 2020
Relationship AddVice, Zombie Pirate Publishing, 2019
The Collapsar Directive, Zombie Pirate Publishing, 2019
WORLDS, Black Hare Press, 2019

Connect
instagram: northerninvasion
Twiter: @aosbatrep

BEYOND THE REALM

VESTAL SCARLET
By Jacqueline Moran Meyer

Empowered with the mark of the Vestals, Scarlet rises under unsurmountable odds—will she save her friend, Sage, and the Kingdom from the ominous mystic-god Leiden and his Faceless army?

Many people fear trolls, but I have never met one I didn't like. Yes, they are snarky, but trolls are always honest. No one ever needs to guess what a troll is thinking. I met my troll friend one morning, while coming back from a meeting with Her Majesty, the queen.

While crossing the Jory Bridge, I heard a terrible

moaning and two angry voices coming from below. Tales of a troll residing under the bridge had been told, but I had crossed the Jory bridge at least a hundred times and never saw a sign of the creature.

I dismounted my horse, crept to the edge and hung my head over the side to see what was going on. The stench made me gag: skunk weed, urine and vomit. Trolls are not known for their cleanliness. I did my best to breathe through my mouth.

A troll lay on his back in the mud, groaning and slurring words to a song about the lies of what happens to trolls at sunrise and turning things to stone. Two men hovered over him. One reed-thin man with a strange green eyepatch stood about two inches taller than me, I guessed, at six feet tall. He grabbed the troll by his dishevelled silver hair. The other man, dressed in ripped homespun trousers, had a scabbard set neatly on his waist.

"Ye must 'ave a silver coin or two, ye drunken freak!" Eyepatch snarled.

I doubted the troll had as much as a crumb of mouldy bread to spare based on his pitiful surroundings.

The second man was not much taller than the troll. His body resembled the shape of an egg. He kicked the poor creature about his chest, enjoying himself, giggling like a little boy watching his first sorcery show.

I feared the troll had little chance of surviving to the end of their abuse, so I unsheathed my sword and held it in my right hand, grabbed my hatchet knife from a pants pocket and held it in my left. I filled my lungs with air and steadied my shaking hands. I am known to suffer from a bit of stage fright.

Jumping from the bridge, I screamed the Vestal Cry. My Vestal sister Sage, may the fire god rest her soul, used to say my scream sounded like an owl being murdered. The men peered up at me, mouths agape, shielding their eyes from the sun. I'm not adept at judging heights. Although the marsh softened my landing, my knee buckled, and a feeling of fire shot through my thigh. Recovering quickly, I nicked the tip of my sword into Eyepatch's neck. Blood trickled down his shirt. I continued screaming, hoping I was the only one who recognised the Vestal War Cry had turned into a cry of pain.

The two men, stunned, said nothing and took in the sight of me, a tall young woman with long black hair, dressed in leather, wielding an axe and a sword. Coupled with the jumping off the bridge and my scream, I was a lot to take in.

"Morning, gentlemen," I said, breathing heavily,

my confidence in high gear now.

The egg-shaped man drew his dagger.

"No, stay away! She aims to skewer me!" Eyepatch squealed. "That scream—the woman's a warrior!"

Egg-shape Man inched toward me, anyway, tossing his dagger from one hand to the next. I bared my teeth and narrowed my eyes to slits. When Egg-shape Man lunged at me, I flung my hatchet at his hand, going easy on him by only slicing his wrist a third of the way through. He might be able to save it this way, if he lived.

"Damn you, girl!" he screamed, dropping his weapon.

"I think you mean, 'Damn you, Vestal,'" I corrected. "Say it...now!"

He screamed, clutching his wrist. "Damn you, Vestal!"

"Better," I said. I moved to kick Eyepatch toward his wounded friend. "Give your friend your shirt."

eyepatch removed his shirt and tied it tightly around the bleeding man's wrist.

I focused on the two men in front of me. "What should I do with you?"

All colour drained from Eyepatch's face.

"The devil 'imself killed ye all," Eyepatch said. His

lips quivered. "You're a Vestal! I thought you were all dead. Leiden stormed your temple."

"I live," I said. I moved my vest to expose my shoulder, revealing my Vestal mark. All Vestals are born with the mark of the flame. Anyone who looks upon the mark can see what their future holds. "What do you see beside the flame, thief?"

"Shackles."

"I believe you have jail to look forward to," I laughed. I covered my shoulder. "But you're not dead yet. Change your ways, Eyepatch. If we ever meet again, there may be a different image on my shoulder."

"May the gods and crown forgive me. I repent." He swallowed with some difficulty. "If you would be so kind as to let me be on my way, you can keep my friend."

"Shut ye hole, ye arse. I'm the one who'll lose me feckin' hand. 'Twas your idea t'bother the 'lil troll!" his companion bellowed. "Can I view your mark, Miss Vestal?"

"No need for you to view the mark. Had you any skill or wits, you'd have gladly killed me *and* the troll. The executioner waits for you." I peered deep into his eyes. "What's this troll done to you?"

"Nothin'. 'E's but a troll," Egg-shape Man said.

"Remove your weapons," I ordered and pointed to

the marsh. They removed their scabbards and threw them near the river, where they sank in the mud.

I glanced around and saw one large brown and one small black mare grazing nearby.

"Are the poor horses yours?"

Looking at the ground, Eyepatch nodded.

"Walk over to the brown mare. Take everything off her."

The mare wore many scars on her old thin body. I stroked her before shooing the horse off, and she ran off to a better life without the thieves.

"Take this black mare over to the troll," I instructed.

"No 'fense to ye, Vestal, I dun tink trolls ride 'orses," Eyepatch said. "Prubly why day live under bridges. Ain't known for their usefulness." He started talking faster. "For all I know if 'e waran't a drunk'd, he would'a been robbin' me first! Or worse, turned me to stone."

"I've never heard of a useful thief, so you and trolls have more in common than you realise, according to your foolishness."

I ordered him to pick up the troll and lay him over the horse.

The troll's bleeding nose bent at an unnatural angle. A jagged gash crossed his forehead, and blood gushed into his eyes.

As I led the mare holding the troll out from under the bridge to Trixie, my horse, I spoke gently. "What's your name, new friend?"

He groaned and answered in the softest voice I would ever hear leave his lips again. "Grisden."

"Thank you for my life, Vestal!" Eyepatch yelled.

"It won't happen again," I called back.

Grisden has been my companion since that morning.

***

The sound of Trixie's hooves and breathing were hypnotic, the grass and wildflowers a blur beneath me. The rush of wind cooled the sweat draining from my body and blew Trixie's mane into my sunburned face. I slowed to a trot, glancing behind me. Grisden was keeping up at a steady pace. He flung his hand up and scowled, insulted to be checked on, which amused me.

"Scarlet, keep your eyes on your own business! You'll fall, and don't expect me to tend to you!"

We were travelling north, through the countryside, having left Ixlar before dawn. By noon, we were riding through farmland and soon reached the gate of Noras, a small village. Grisden was soon next to me.

"What do you think, Gris?" I asked, breathless, my mouth dry.

Grisden patted his horse, Rex, and took a few minutes to catch his breath before speaking. He tapped his index finger on his temple, contemplating his answer. Still winded, Grisden stroked his long black beard for several minutes.

"My prediction?" Grisden grunted. "This town will stink of manure and stale beer, not of Leiden." The troll puffed up his chest and ran a hand through his hair.

In Ixlar, we were told Noras was still free. We'd been travelling for two weeks with not much rest. Three more days remained before we would reach our destination and I would face Leiden, the sorcerer who killed my Vestal sisters and created chaos in the realm. Each mile twisted my insides into tighter knots.

We entered Noras. The main cobblestone street was filled with vendors selling food and wares under the shade of colourful tents. We bought four meat pies and walked our horses down to the river.

The villagers stared at us. We were quite a sight, of course. A tall, muscular woman accompanied by a troll. My leather attire stood out from the clothing in Noras, which was spun from wool. I wore a black leather vest, loose nubuck pants containing many pockets, and a thick leather scabbard held my sword.

Grisden, wildly hairy, stood at half my height but twice my width. His scraggly black beard trailed down to his ample belly, and his thick silver hair made him appear three inches taller because he teased it upwards for hours on end with his fingers. He had remained sober. And in his sober health, he had grown stronger. He wore a clean, burly sheepskin tunic and wool pants, a thin scabbard housing his small sword.

I tried to reset his nose after he sobered up, the day we met, but it didn't heal well and hung now to the left. His heavy eyes were as green as the giant winter pines growing on the hills surrounding the town of my birthplace, and our destination, Agora.

"Is something troubling you?" I teased. Grisden's face was usually in a perpetual scowl.

"Never! Nothing ever bothers me. Happy as willow tree by a stream, I am."

We sat in the shade of a tree by the river, watching our horses drink. I ate my first pie in the time it took Grisden to eat both of his.

"Mouse food," he said. "I'm off. Got coins to spend, I do. There must be heartier, troll-worthy grub. Scream if you need me."

"I will, kind sir," I said.

"Don't call me *kind*. I hate words like *kind*, and you know it. I'm a troll. Don't ruin my unusual tolerance for your company." He walked off, grumbling.

It was a relief to be alone and rest. I watched the townspeople live their lives. Children played while parents shopped and gossiped. Couples walked arm-in-arm. I guessed that to be what normal life looked like. I finished my second pie, and, knowing Grisden was keeping an eye on me, I let myself fall asleep.

"Scarlet?" A deep familiar voice woke me. The sun blurred my vision, obscuring the features of the man saying my name. My hand hovered above my sword.

"Scarlet. It's Malachoir. Am I unrecognisable?"

I felt like it was a dream. "Malachoir?" I sputtered as my eyes adjusted to the light. I could make out the features of the man's face. Yes, Malachoir, my old friend! The sight of him, someone who knew me when I was one among many Vestals, drew unexpected tears. He had changed in the four years since I last saw him. When I knew Malachoir, his gentle hands did little more than turn pages in books or grace my cheek with brotherly affection. Now he wore a clean white tunic and cloth pants tied at his waist with burlap rope. His silky brown hair had grown long, gracing his broad shoulders. Nothing remained soft about him as he stood before me with rough hands and a rugged, tanned face.

"Malachoir!" I said, still seated, looking up at him.

BEYOND THE REALM

Clapping his hands together, Malachoir threw his head back and laughed. "May I sit?"

I smiled and patted the grass next to me. Other people may have embraced, but with my being brought up as a Vestal, that kind of greeting was inappropriate, uncomfortable.

Malachoir turned and leaned his back on the tree. He groaned while he eased his body next to mine, and his head turned to me.

"I spend my time differently than I did in Azar," he said. "Farm life and hide tanning are destroying my spine."

"I never thought to see you again."

"Fate's brought us together."

Not many people are alive who knew me as a child, but Malachoir is one of them. He and I spent nine years living in Azar at Temple Tine. I, as a Vestal—a great honour, bestowed by the fire god Tine—tended to the great eternal fire at the temple with my Vestal sisters. Malachoir lived in Azar as an apprentice mage, like many wealthy second-born sons who displayed promise in sorcery. I rarely saw him without a spell or sorcery book pressed to his nose. He and the other apprentices accompanied the Vestals to games and events. He dressed in fine robes of purple velvet, often wearing a gold wreath upon his glossy soft brown hair.

Given a chance, Malachoir would have made a fine mage.

"What is news of Leiden?" I asked.

"Nothing good. I knew you'd be back to finish—"

Thwack! A dagger landed above his head, lodging into the tree.

"Don't move a muscle," Grisden growled, hovering over the seated Malachoir.

Grisden's greatest skill was his stealth. He appeared out of thin air, whether needed or not. Malachoir's eyes darted toward me, then my sword. Because it was just Grisden, I merely smiled back at my old friend. Malachoir's confusion mounted.

"Miserable tall man. Don't let my size fool you. I can use this dagger with as much force as any human," Grisden said, spewing spit in Malachoir's face with every syllable. He reached for the dagger stuck in the trunk of the tree. But the blade would not dislodge.

"Malachoir, move a bit to your left so my friend can get a better grip," I said.

Grisden's face reddened. Malachoir scrambled further away than needed.

Grisden grabbed the dagger with two hands and pulled. It didn't budge.

"Arghhh! Just a bit more muscle it needs is all, I say," Grisden said.

He pressed both feet against the tree for more leverage. On the third heave, he ejected the knife from the tree, only to tumble unceremoniously to the ground. But, like a dancer, with one leap, Grisden stood, quickly dusting himself off. He crossed his arms, shifted his hips, so he leaned on one leg. He avoided eye contact with me.

"Thank you, Grisden, but Malachoir is an old friend," I said. "Toys can be packed away now, Gris."

He grumbled as he walked toward the market before a proper introduction could be made, his voice disappearing with his distance. "Always treating me like a child. I'm a solitary creature, I am. She should be singing with joy to the gods for the pleasure of my company...*hmpff*."

Malachoir's mouth hung open.

"You've just met my companion, Grisden. We're like an old married couple, aren't we?" I said.

"You're married?" His mouth widened.

"We're friends," I assured him. "Not married. I'm a Vestal, don't forget."

"I can't understand why you like having him around."

"He's protective and amuses me."

"But quite a grump. You'd agree with that, right?"

"He's a troll. It's his nature. He lets me be me, and

doesn't expect anything from me."

Malachoir gave me a sad smile. I continued.

"To be truthful, I don't know his story. It must be a sad one, he almost died under a bridge. I've told him my story, though."

"Our story," Malachoir corrected me. We shared another glance, and I nodded in agreement.

"What do you know of Leiden? Her Royal Highness has sent me to kill him. I hear he took over Agora, where we were both born."

"The queen? I'm not surprised, she recognised your skill."

"My anger too"

Malachoir nodded.

"Leiden has taken Agora. I work on a farm near there. Did you know both my parents died in the Vildoma pandemic in Agora, after the fall of Azar?" Malachoir asked.

"I'm sorry. We all lost loved ones, didn't we?" I thought of Sage. How I loved her.

"Her Royal Highness is aware of my time in Azar, being a Vestal, surviving the siege, the ultimate fall of the city, and the end of the flame "I continued.

"You've deservedly risen again."

"The queen wants me to investigate Leiden's movements. Signs from her mage, Palundro, have led her to believe Leiden has broken the treaty and is heading to our birthplace. Agora is a stronghold."

Malachoir's body stiffened. He ran the back of his chapped hand across his wrinkled brow. "No easy way to say this...Agora has been taken."

My stomach twisted, again. "Leiden himself?"

"Leiden, along with his court and his new army." He placed a hand on my shoulder.

"What army?"

"He has figured out a way to change people who aren't useful to him into faceless drones. They all look the same and can communicate somehow. If you're caught by one of them, they rip you to shreds. Or worse...turn you."

I stood and paced for several silent moments.

"We must contact the queen to request archers and cannons," I said, bending over trying to ease the fire burning in my belly.

"The bishop regent who escaped Agora sent a rider to the palace two weeks ago."

My pacing speed increased. I bit my nails, ripping the ends off my fingers. "They'll be on their way, assuming she gets the message. I didn't take the common roads, so she may have tried to find me to give word." I stopped and stared at Malachoir. "Do you know a trusted courier to send word of my arrival to the palace?"

"Yes. My niece, Aspael. A seasoned equestrian, brave and loyal to the crown. She reminds me of you."

My pacing commenced. "Why are you here?"

"I was travelling south to meet with a skilful mage. My skills are not what they were in Azar. I want to be useful, but I'm not anymore." He stood next to me now, his eyes following my movements. "But now I believe the gods sent me this way to meet you. There are no coincidences. This reunion is a sign from Tine. We should work together to reclaim the flame. You're the strongest person I've ever met."

Malachoir always gave me too much credit. I was so sure of the world when I was younger. While I don't believe our meeting was destined, I loved that Malachoir still believed in destiny and the goodness of the gods. I agreed we would make a good team; we always did. I trusted Malachoir, and I don't trust many. He still wanted to right wrongs. I wanted revenge.

"The flame, Malachoir. What was, or is, the point of the flame?"

"It protected the kingdom, and now we're in danger again."—he paused a moment—"I need to tell you something else."

I stopped pacing and stared at him. Somehow, I knew what he was about to share.

"Sage is with Leiden," he said.

"She's...she's *alive*?"

"She is. And...they have a daughter."

My stomach churned at the thought of Sage and what we went through together. I loved Sage like I've loved no other. Everything she did, she did well. The best sword fighter, lute player, singer, spell creator, sorceress. Kind, strong, wise—aptly named Sage. "*They*? What do you mean *they*?!"

"Sage has been by his side these four years. She has changed, appears meek, fearful. The villagers believe she loves him."

"I won't believe that! Fearing him, yes. Not...*love*! Maybe he put a spell on her. Or, most likely, she loves her child and fears for her safety."

"I don't know."

"Do you think Leiden would recognise me?"

"Unfortunately, I do. You're hard to forget, Scarlet. You also escaped Azar."

I shuddered. "I'm loyal to the crown, Mal, but I want him. I want him to suffer."

"Of course you do. But there are more important things than our feelings in this, Scarlet. His power and sickness have increased, and his Featureless army grows every day. Don't play around. Kill him."

I sat down again, leaning against the tree.

"Leiden has trapped the town within its walls," Malachoir said. "No one can leave."

"How do you know what's happened?"

"A boy escaped two weeks ago. They threw the dead from the wall into the river. He crawled into the burlap bag of his deceased neighbour. Although badly beaten up by the drop, he somehow survived. He crawled for miles before reaching his aunt and uncle's farm, which is where I work now."

Grisden walked toward us, his arms filled with food and supplies, enough to sustain us for the next three days of travelling.

"We'll go to Agora together. Be warned...Grisden won't be happy with your company."

"Can he be any less happy?"

I nodded. "He can."

***

We reached the farmlands near Agora.

Grisden and I waited outside the cottage where the boy lived with his aunt and uncle while Malachoir entered to explain why he had brought us.

"Your friend is no good. He eats with a metal weapon with four points, and always has his face in a book. He'll trick us, he will," Grisden warned.

"What he uses to eat is called a fork. We ate with them at the Temple. He's studying magic, this is true, but he's on our side."

"I trust *you*, think so."

"Fair enough." I said. "I'll watch him carefully, too. I trust your concerns."

Malachoir emerged with a man and a woman. The bearded young man stood a few inches shorter than Malachoir. His skin was deeply tanned and rough on his boyish face. The woman was thin, pale, and walked toward us, wringing her hands.

"Welcome, Vestal Scarlet," the man said. "I'm Seb, this is my wife, Katherine." Seb wrapped one arm around the frail woman as if to keep her from blowing away.

"Good day. Thank you for letting me speak to your nephew," I said.

Katherine's eyes darted at her husband. She wrung her hands together and balanced her weight on one foot and her other, and back again.

"Vestal, my brother-in-law is a baker in Agora," Katherine said. "He and my two nieces remain there. You'll be speaking to his son, Elias. He carried water to the cooks for Leiden's court. He's experienced...terrible things."

"I aim to help, Katherine."

Katherine's face turned red, and she clenched her fists. "Will you, Vestal? My sister, rest her sweet soul with the gods, died of vildoma a few years back. Was it so difficult to keep the fire going?"

"Kath!" Seb said.

The young woman pushed her husband's arm away and stomped off.

"She-she's in agony over the girls," Seb stammered. "Forgive her, Vestal."

Occasionally, I encounter an honest person in the kingdom. Someone who verbalises what I believe everyone is thinking. The Vestals let the fire go out, and Leiden took over Azar, the religious capital of the realm. We had failed. Although the words stung, it was the truth. We Vestals let the fire go out, and as a result, people died.

Seb invited us in. After we ate meat and drank fresh milk, he led me and Grisden out the back door. The boy sat in a wooden chair, swaddled in a blanket. His eyes were closed. His thin face pointed toward the sun.

"Hello, Elias. I'm Scarlet."

He opened his eyes. Dark circles around them made him look bruised.

"Aunt Kath explained who you are."

"Who am I?"

"You were a Vestal of privilege...more interested in sporting events and plays...than protecting the flame." Elias spoke in a soft monotone whisper. His down-turned mouth and drooping eyes gave me the impression he wanted to sink into the blanket he wore and disappear.

Grisden cleared his throat loudly and stamped one foot like a bull about to charge.

"May I speak with Elias alone?" I asked.

"*Hrmmmph*," Grisden snorted and walked around to the front of the house.

I sat crossed legged in front of Elias and peered up into his expressionless face.

"Yes, it's true, I'm a Vestal. And I was there when the flame went out. I feel shame and regret about failing everyone. I want to make things right. May I tell you my story?"

"I don't care," the boy said.

"I'll tell you. When I was seven, I moved hundreds of miles away from Agora to the Temple in Azar. My chaperone for the journey was the Vestal Sage, who became my closest friend.

When we arrived in Azar, thousands of villagers lined the street leading up the hill to my new home, Temple Tine, created by the fire god at the beginning of time. I asked Sage if there was a parade.

"'Yes. *You* are the parade!' she laughed kindly at me.

"We passed through the gates and were welcomed with cheers and songs. So many flowers were showered upon us. We were buried in roses and daisies. I felt loved as the villagers shouted their welcomes. Sage gave me no instructions, but she held my hand. That gesture comforted me so much because I feared making a mistake and disappointing everyone. I felt like an impostor. I always have..."

Elias took the blanket off his head and rested it on his slight shoulders. His hair was light brown, thick and curly. The boy leaned in closer.

"The Vestal sisters were ten years apart. We wore robes the colour of our names. My name being Scarlet, I wore crimson, rose and red. We were committed to serving the god Tine, to tending the flame and protecting the kingdom. We would never marry or bear children. If the sacred fire burned out, destruction and chaos would reign. While the older Vestals tended to the flame, we younger ones trained for hours in hand-to-hand combat, sword fighting and war strategy. We became fierce warriors, but we also were involved in politics.

"At the time, Jon Von Leiden, was a young, rich and respected cloth merchant. He sat on the town council. But he would ridicule and berate anyone for the slightest

BEYOND THE REALM

disagreement. I often accompanied Sage to the meetings. She sat on the council, too. Leiden became obsessed with Sage, but she tossed his love letters away, unopened. Leiden tried to change the laws in Azar so Vestals could marry. Still, Sage showed no interest in him—and would never marry—but Leiden convinced himself he could make her love him.

"Leiden began to grow a faithful following among the villagers through a doctrine of fear. He used his sorcery to trick them into believing the apocalypse was near, claiming he could speak directly to Tine. He was a powerful sorcerer: he created lightning on sunny days, and birds dropped dead from the trees, with the snap of his fingers. The villagers believed the world was ending and Leiden was a god."

"This sounds like what happened here," Elias said, eyes wide.

"Leiden deemed himself a god and instructed the villagers to destroy the temple. The town cannons brought the whole stone building down, extinguishing the flame. Chaos and darkness came upon the city, and every Vestal, mage and priest was to be enslaved or killed. Except for Sage—he wanted her."

Elias began to speak. "Vestal. There are women with him always. He brings them to the centre of town, every morning for his sermons. He also spews black smoke from his mouth and covers people with it. They either die or are changed into beasts. Grey-skinned beings without a face."

"I'm here to get revenge, Elias."

Elias nodded before saying, "May I see your Vestal mark? You haven't mentioned it."

"Ah... I left out the most important part. The mark that started the course of my life! I was born with the Vestal mark, as you may know. Every ten years in our kingdom, a female child is born with this mark. Everyone can see the flame, which glows an orange-red, but I can't describe the complete mark because everyone sees something different. When I see my reflection in rivers and lakes, next to the flame rests a small red sword. Others have told me it's a green heron, a blue antelope horn, or a hand. Whatever sign you see on a Vestal will be of importance to your life. The mark can be anywhere on the body. Mine is on my shoulder. I hide it under my vest."

I moved my vest, exposing my shoulder.

"What do you see?"

"Bread."

"A baker," I said. "Like your father."

Elias gasped. I could see a faint light in his eyes. He sat up a little taller. "I'll tell you what I know, Vestal."

BEYOND THE REALM

***

Two days after speaking with Elias, I stood in view of Agora's wall, planning on entering, alone. After much arguing, Grisden and Malachoir agreed: I was to assess the situation before the queen's army arrived and Leiden was put on high alert.

The queen had gifted me three tiny glass vials of crushed opaline. The powder is made from a stone only found in the outer kingdom, where the forever storm rages and the gods fight amongst themselves. Only one out of every ten thousand people who go there to search for the stone survives. When the powder is ingested, it cloaks the person in invisibility for one hour. I was to swim the moat, climb the wall and find Elias' house in one hour. I needed to do everything fast.

Grisden, Malachoir and I had spent these past two days out in the fields mapping the town. We hatched a plan. Although my fingernails were down to bloody nubs from me biting them so much, I was ready. As ready as I would ever be.

When Vestals go to live at the Temple, we lose most of our memory about our past lives. I have shadowy images of holding a woman's hand and being carried on the shoulders of a man. Of feeling safe. But I wouldn't be safe now, here again in my hometown, because I could only hope the opaline would hide me from the Featureless. It was thus crucial, after entering Agora, that I didn't startle the baker and have him draw attention to me. That could mean my capture. And who knew what else?

I stood at the base of the tree line which bled into a field, the moat and finally, the wall. I took a vial out of a pants pocket, ingested it, and counted to ten, as instructed by the queen. I raised my hand to my face. I was told I would still be able to see myself...I hoped no one else could.

I cricked my neck and shook out my limbs. I ran through the field before tiptoeing into the wretched moat, which smelled of rot and death. I swam through the water as silently as I could. Once on the shore, I glanced up to the sky.

The wall was a mountain!

My wet, heavy clothes clung to my body. My fingers were stiff, frozen. I blew on my fingertips until I could feel them again. I climbed. The exertion warmed me.

When I reached the top, I hopped over the wall, my arms shaking. I glided to the nearest stairwell.

Featureless!

I froze in place, holding my breath longer than I ever had. I slowly exhaled and knew I couldn't stay here. Shaking—from cold or fear, or probably both—I crept silently past the Featureless, not daring to look at their horrid bodies, as if somehow, they'd see me in return.

There was a curfew, according to Elias, so no one walked the streets. I hugged the walls of the buildings as I glided down the streets. I passed a house, which caused me to have a flashback, an urge to run into the small cottage with the whitewashed walls and thatched roof.

I lived here?

I pictured a man and a woman, their faces blurred, standing arm-in-arm in the doorway. I am seven and being put in an emerald carriage. Sage helps me in. The man and woman wave and fall to their knees, clinging to each other before I lose sight of them.

Each Vestal was renamed upon entry to the Temple. A spell was cast to make us forget our original name. If someone who knew us as a child mistakenly called us by our old name, we wouldn't understand it. If someone wrote our old name on a scroll and put it in front of us, we wouldn't be able to read it. We were no longer anything but Vestals. I cannot remember my parents' faces or their names. I will never remember the name given to me at birth. My head ached.

I was wasting time. I had no room in my life to be sentimental. I focused my attention on Elias' directions to reach the baker's home. *Bakery* was written on the sideways metal sign hanging by one rusty chain, the other having broken.

I crept to the back window, but the shutters were closed. I used my fingers and dagger to unlatch it. *Grmph*...if I hadn't bitten off all my nails, I could get a better grip. I heard scratching as the latch gave way. The shutter opened. Grasping the ledge, I somersaulted in, landing in a crouch.

This was a breeze, I thought before something grabbed each of my legs and pulled me down. I guessed an hour was up, and I was no longer invisible. I thrashed wildly in the blind dark, managing to fling a creature off me. I grabbed one by the neck and put them in a headlock.

"Light a candle. Don't scream. I have a knife," I said to the other creature I could not see.

The thing in my arms stopped moving and whimpered.

"If anyone screams or tries to leave, the knife goes in this neck."

I heard a scratching sound, detected the smell of sulphur, and there was light showing me that I held a knife to a girl's throat. She'd felt like a monster but was a girl, no more than eleven years of age. I loosened my grip around her head and neck.

A tall girl had lit the candle. Her long hair was clean and plaited, her green eyes brimmed with tears. She was thin. Too thin—her collarbones jutted out, leaving deep caverns in her neck. She was sweating from the sheer exhaustion of the fight.

Elias's sisters? There was no baker in sight.

The room was small and tidy, and two pillows on the bed showed indents. The sisters slept in here together, it was clear. There was a stool by a basin and a wooden chair by the window. I asked the older girl to get them and put them in the centre of the room. They sat quietly, and I stood in front of them.

"What are your names?"

The older girl answered. "Estela. This is my sister Madralena."

"Where's your father?"

Estela turned sickly white and began to shake. "He's a Featureless."

"Oh no. When?" I studied the girls, their black rings under pitiful eyes.

"Two nights now," Estela said, lips quivering.

"I'm sorry."

The sisters glanced at each other, trying to figure out what I was doing here.

"Is there anyone else in the house?"

"Me, my sister and our dog, Molly."

"I bring word from your brother, Elias. To prove I'm a friend, he has written a letter. I'm sorry about the knife, but I didn't want you to scream. I needed time to explain."

"Our brother is a traitor—a *devil*. He didn't listen to King Leiden. We spit on his memory!"

"Leiden calls himself king, does he? Listen. This isn't a trick." I pulled a scroll from my vest and handed it to Estela.

Dear Father,

I am well. Trust Vestal Scarlet. Let her help you. I need you all. To prove this is me, remember when I buried Hersula, Estela's doll, and you made me sweep the street for three months.

With love,

Elias

The girls' shoulders relaxed, and they wiped away tears.

"Elias is alive?" Madralena cried.

"Yes. And I'm here for Leiden. To end all this. How can I find him?"

"Leiden gathers everyone in the town square," Estela said. "He gives a sermon in the town square every morning. We must all attend. They're often violent, Vestal."

I slept on the floor, next to their bed. I kept my

boots on and held my sword.

I decided to wait till morning and learn more about what I was up against.

The next morning, Estela gave me her father's old cloak with a large hood to disguise myself. I could save the second invisibility vial for that night—both would help me would break into the church where Leiden and Sage lived.

"Come, it's time to go and see this 'god-king'." When both girls hesitated, I said, "Girls, you've been very brave. Brave enough to help me, I think."

Estela opened her arms and hugged me. I stood awkwardly with my arms at my side. I had never been used to being hugged, touched. I didn't hug back. I patted her head, not knowing what else to do. She let go and dried her tears.

"Vestal Scarlet, I-I don't want to marry an old man!"

"Marry? You're a child."

"The god-king says we must marry. The women outnumber the men, now. He has sixteen wives."

I thought I might vomit. "I will stop him."

We walked to the town centre, where the villagers had gathered for Leiden's sermon. There was a plain wooden platform the people circled around, leaving the street which led to the church clear.

"Leiden will be coming from there," Estela pointed to the church. The church had two stories, and an enormous maple tree stood next to it.

The women did outnumber the men. The condition these people were in was wretched. Sickly thin. Sores all over their bodies. Bald or scratching their lice-filled hair. Children beating a small child for the crust of bread he clutched in his hand. Old men stood next to young women with dead eyes and dirty clothes. People fought to not stand in the front row.

I saw Leiden appear in the distance.

Clip-clop...clip-clop...

The crowd fell silent.

Not a bird chirped, no babies cried; it seemed as if the trees were frozen with fear in his presence. He rode down the worn cobblestone street, perched, back straight, atop a regal, well-fed black horse and dressed all in black. The sun lent a dramatic whiteness to his blonde hair.

A woman riding sidesaddle on a cream-coloured horse rode close behind him. She dressed in a long white gown that covered every inch of her body but her hands and face. A wreath of fresh lilies sat atop the hair I would never forget.

Sage! My dear friend.

Her auburn hair gleamed in the sun, radiating

shades of warmth; copper, reds, orange. I wanted to shout, "I'm here, let's fight!" and scream the Vestal Cry. I fantasied about her presenting a sword and racing her horse toward Leiden, ready to swing.

Behind her marched a parade of women in single file. Leiden's other wives. One looked as young as eleven.

"Children of Agora live the righteous path," Leiden began, his voice deep, his words deliberate. "The end is near, but we will not fear death. Those who believe in me are eternal."

He opened his mouth wide, and black smoke billowed out, snaking menacingly around his brides and into the crowd.

"Those who don't believe in me have no place to hide. You see, I listen to your evil thoughts." The smoke settled on one of his wives, no older than sixteen. The girl wore a white dress with a red sash. Pink roses adorned her loose chestnut hair. Upon closer inspection, one of her eyes was swollen and bruised shut.

"She publicly defied him yesterday," Estela said, "rejecting his gift of jewellery. It was taken from an elderly neighbour he recently made a Featureless."

The girl closed her eyes as the smoke encircled her. Tears streamed down her cheeks, but she did not cry out.

"Open your eyes, Zelda!" Leiden said. My stomach ached.

I'm a Vestal, I can defeat him. Perhaps. But not here and now.

She opened her eyes and brazenly glared at Leiden. His face turned red at her sign of insolence. He began to dance. The smoke mimicked his movements, enveloping the girl and lifting her off the ground. She rose past the height of the wall, her arms and legs splayed. She began to scream.

The noise stopped when she burst apart.

A blood mist rained down upon the crowd, but the villagers made no sound.

"I create and I take. The wrath is coming. Who will be left standing with me?"

Everyone exclaimed, "Aye!!" and cheered.

The smoke circled his body and re-entered his mouth, and when he extended his hand up to the sky, hundreds of doves appeared and flew around the courtyard.

"He's lightening the mood," Estela whispered, with no hint of humour.

I tried to stop my hands from shaking as I pulled the girls behind me. "This will be over for good," I said. "Tonight."

This would be the last day of Leiden's life, even if it were to be my last day, too.

I spent the rest of the day in hiding while the girls did their chores and scrounged for food.

Night fell.

***

Estela and Madralena stood silently as I placed the two vials of opaline on their dining table.

"To fight Leiden, I need a little sorcery of my own. I'm ingesting one of these vials tonight. It will make me invisible for one hour."

"Your clothes, too?" Madralena asked.

"Yes, anything that I am wearing as well. I'm leaving the other one for the two of you."

The girls turned pale.

"Aren't you coming back?" Estela asked.

"Maybe, if Tine protects me. But I'm ready to defend the kingdom—at any cost. If I don't return by morning, or if the town turns into a battleground, promise me you'll split the vial between the two of you. Each of you ingest half. Hold hands, you'll have more power."

"But won't you need the extra vial? What if you need more time to come back to us?" Estela insisted.

"I'll manage. I have a secret trick up my sleeve. A vial of liquid to use in case of an emergency," I said, half-heartedly. "Do you know of a way out of the village?"

"There's a drainage pipe by the south wall," Estela said.

"But the Featureless are always guarding it," Madralena added.

"But...it's there." Estela sounded a little hopeful.

"After taking the vial, you'll not be seen by the Featureless, but you will need to walk among them. Will you both have the courage to walk past them without making a sound?"

Madralena tugged on her sister's dress. Estela bent down, and Madralena whispered into her ear.

Estela said to her little sister, "Yes, you can. For our brother, who sent Vestal Scarlet to us." Estela glanced up at me. "The Featureless frighten her but also make her sad—they were our friends and neighbours. One of them was once our father."

I nodded.

"Madralena, it's alright to be frightened, but you can't make a sound. Not one sound," I said, my voice firm.

I ingested the powder and counted to ten.

"She's gone!" Madralena gasped. "I hope she

comes back." Their eyes darted around their cottage for some sign of me.

"Still here, but I'm leaving now. Be safe."

***

I ran across the street, through the courtyard, and approached the maple tree by the church, which was illuminated by the torches of the Featureless protecting it. Unsure which room Leiden would be in when I arrived, I needed to be even faster tonight than when scaling the wall one long night ago. Soft light escaped through the second-floor windows. The grey creatures moved about erratically. Every noise had them skittering about. Unlike the stone wall, the church was made from wood and not scalable. The tree was my way in.

With the Featureless standing only a few feet away, I stopped at the base of the tree and peered upward to see that the lowest branches were out of my reach. I jumped, but my hands slipped from the branch. Several Featureless turned their faceless heads in my direction and raced toward the tree to investigate. I threw a stone in the direction of the church. The Featureless turned, running in the direction of the rock hitting the earth.

Creepy little creatures, but not the smartest critters in the litter.

Knots in the trunk of the tree helped me to climb to the lowest branch as the Featureless settled and continued to guard the perimeter of the church. When I snapped a twig or rustled too many leaves, although eyeless, their heads tilted upward, and I rested for a few moments, until something else caught their attention, Eventually, I jumped softly to the roof and scrambled to the back of the church.

I slid a thin, strong rope and metal hook from my pants pocket and anchored the hook to the chimney. Pulling on it several times, I convinced myself it would bear my weight. I rappelled down the church wall to the open window, which, as Elias had explained, would lead me to the upper hallway. Easily climbing in, I threw the rope back on the roof so no one would see it if they walked down the hall.

Several brass sconces lined the long hallway, casting a soft yellow glow. The plush rugs beneath my feet muffled my footsteps. I reached a stairwell at the end of the hallway; I heard many voices below me. I walked up the stairs to Leiden's sleeping quarters. It was difficult for me to judge how much time had passed. My internal clock stopped at survival mode.

The steps led to a small white-walled landing. A

bright-blue door stood closed to my right. Turning the crystal doorknob, I found the door unlocked, but, to my dismay, the old door creaked and groaned.

I stepped into a white room with a heavy black iron chandelier holding at least one hundred lit white candles. I felt as if I had entered heaven. The temple was comfortable, the room resplendent. The rich textured furniture, tufted and covered in silk and velvet, dotted the room. I imagined Leiden pilfering the finest items from the doomed villagers. At the end of the room stood a four-poster oak bed decorated with fur pillows and cashmere blankets. Cheese and wine sat on a small table.

Next to the bed was a vanity, with a mirror, and a beautiful woman seated in front of it.

Sage...

I held my breath. She faced me, startled by the opened door, but didn't see me. I had a little more time. Sage placed her hairbrush on the vanity, stood, and walked to the door. She looked about, body tense. Suspicious.

I wanted to say something, but I was unsure of her reaction. I also did not know where Leiden was.

She closed the door and went back to her mirror to resume brushing her hair, and she began to hum.

I crept behind her and grabbed her, placing one

hand firmly over her mouth and drawing her head toward me while wrapping my arm around her body, anchoring her firmly in her chair.

Sage's eyes grew wild, and she tried to break free. I could feel her thin bones beneath my grasp.

"Sage, it's Scarlet!" I cooed. "Don't be afraid."

I let go of her mouth.

"Is this a trick, Jon? Are you testing me again? You have my love and devotion. Scarlet is dead." Her breathing was heavy, her voice shaky. Other than her appearance, I recognised nothing of the confident Sage I once knew.

"There's not much time," I whispered. "I *am* Scarlet. Ask me something only I would know."

"What was my secret nickname for you?"

An easy question. "Star," I told her.

She started to cry. I had never seen her cry.

"No, no, no. Scarlet, no. Leave me alone—you must!" she pleaded.

Stung, Disgusted. I let go of her, my body recoiling from her words. "No, what? Sage. I'm going to kill him." I didn't have much time before becoming visible again.

"How do you plan to kill him? He'll trick you."

Sage rose from her chair. She felt for me, found me and fell to her knees, clutching my legs. "You must leave. We've lost, Star. I have a child—and he'll *hurt* her. Do you understand? Leave, *please.*"

"No," I hissed through clenched teeth.

"Leave, or I'll scream—and he'll come!" Sage said.

I grabbed her and turned her around, pushing her back to the floor. I lay on top of her, facing her. With one hand covering her mouth, I took off my scabbard and threw it under a chair. I grabbed the vial of liquid, which Palundro, the queen's mage, had given me as I left the palace. I opened the vial and pressed the bitter pink liquid to my lips.

"Is he coming here soon? Shake your head if he is."

He was coming soon.

"I don't know what you've been through, but we're Vestals. We can't fail the kingdom again. You'll help me whether you want to or not."

She gasped. "I see you." The opaline powder had worn off.

I drew my face close to Sage, released my hand from her mouth and kissed her lips. She sputtered and licked her lips. It was done.

The room spun. The candles blurred. I shut my eyes, dizzy from the sudden rush of movement. When I opened them, I was staring into my own face.

"What did you do to me?" my image cried. We

both stood. I felt my new arms. No muscles.

"I haven't felt this strong since fencing class at Temple Azar," my image said with a smirk.

"Sage. You may look like me, but you're not. When Leiden walks in here, who do you think he'll kill first?" I asked.

She frowned.

"You think he'll believe you? I can see you—the opaline's worn off. Do you want to rely on Leiden believing we've traded bodies, leading him to kill me in yours?" I asked.

The door started to open. She snuck behind the dark, thick drapes framing a window.

He walked in and saw me, pretending to be Sage, sitting at the vanity brushing my hair. Leiden was taller and broader than I remembered him. He stood still, staring at me for a full minute, while shaking his head. Could he see I wasn't really Sage? I didn't know how they greeted each other.

He stomped over to the vanity, grabbed Sage's hair and threw me to the ground by the chair my scabbard lay beneath. Well, now I knew how he greeted her, the bastard.

"How dare you not rise when I enter the room? What game are you playing?"

He loomed above me, laughing.

Sage, in my image, came out from behind the drapes. "Jon," she said.

He snapped his head toward her. "Scarlet?"

He glanced at Sage's face—my face. "I was trying to give you a sign, Jon," I said. "Scarlet surprised and frightened me, threatening to harm you. I was trying to act differently, so you'd know something was wrong."

"No, please," my image begged.

Black smoke shot out of Leiden's mouth and covered Sage. I watched her trapped within my body, rise. As he threw Sage across the room, where she landed in a heap, I grabbed my sword.

He turned to see me, looking like Sage, standing with my sword ready to strike. I thrust the sword into his stomach and sliced upwards. He fell backward to the floor. I stood over him and plunged my sword into his heart and skewered him to the floorboard. The black smoke disappeared out the door. I pulled out the sword and wiped Leiden's blood on Sage's white gown.

I ran to the crumpled body in the corner and took the pink liquid from the pants pocket I'd left it in. I pressed the liquid to my lips. Sage, in my body, opened her eyes. She raised her hand and buried my hatchet into the chest I inhabited—Sages chest.

"No! Sage, what have you done?" Blood spilled over the white gown. I fell on top of her, making sure our lips pressed together.

Outside, I heard cannons and commotion. The queen's guard had arrived.

My world went black.

***

Six weeks had passed since the day the kingdom took back Agora. It was time for me and Grisden to go back to the palace. I rested at Malachoir's while my broken leg and wrist healed. I'm a terrible patient. Standing when I should be sitting, getting things others should get for me, and irritable at being so well tended to.

Kath sewed my deep cuts and cleaned my wounds. Grisden made sure to entertain me with his stories of bravely battling the Featureless army.

"They all surrounded me, they did. I stood in the centre of them, I did. Ten Featureless at a time came at me!" He acted out the scene for me, which involved complicated kicks and sword fighting moves. "Those creepy, grey things are no more. I killed them all, I did. With some help from the queen's army, of course."

Malachoir, on the other hand, said it was an easy victory since the Featureless died quickly. We guessed they had lost their direction because of the death of

Leiden and his sorcery.

I'm back in my body. Sage and Leiden are dead. I feel tremendous sorrow and guilt that I could not save Sage.

"She died at the fall of Azar. You aren't the one who killed her, Sage was already dead." Malachoir tried to console me.

I will always see events differently, though.

The fate of Leiden's black smoke is unclear. My hope is that it died with Leiden.

Malachoir helped me get on my horse. Out of the corner of my eye, I saw Grisden grumbling as he mounted his own.

"Are you sure you're up to this? I can come with you," Malachoir said. He rested his hand upon my cheek. I didn't recoil at his touch, which had begun to feel less brotherly. But I was not ready for him to have any expectations of me.

Grisden coughed and cleared his throat.

"I'm sure," I said. "I'll be back. You're needed here, and I don't know where I'm needed next." I gave him a brief smile. He picked up my hand and kissed it. Yes, I would be back, I was sure.

Elias, Estela and Madralena stood in front of Seb and Kath. They had eaten well over the past weeks, and their fuller faces now had rosy glows. Kath held a chubby one-year-old girl with auburn hair—Sage and Leiden's child, Lyra. Kath was apprehensive about taking in the baby, but Lyra's smiles and giggles quickly changed her mind.

Kath walked toward me, "You're always welcome, Vestal Scarlet."

We'd come a long way since our first meeting.

"Thank You, Kath. Call me Scarlet. There are no more Vestals."

They all glanced at each other and shared a laugh between themselves.

"What is it? You have a secret?" I asked.

The children walked forward, standing next to Kath and Lyra.

"There was something that I—we all—kept from you. My parents said they always feared a child of theirs would be born with the Vestal mark and be sent away." Elias said. He pushed Madralena closer to me and Trixie, unrecognisable with clean hair and new livery.

Madralena lifted her skirt, and below the knee, she bore the Vestal mark. I stared at the flame and saw my sword next to it.

"Vestal Madralena, my sister." We smiled at each other.

"Will you change my name?"

"No, Madralena suits you, and it's *your* name. You won't be taken away, either, but I'll train you."

Kath pulled Lyra's dress to her belly, "She wears one, too. Please don't take her away."

"She'll live here, of course. What would I do with a baby?"

I glanced at Malachoir, who was the only one who didn't laugh at the comment.

"People can always change their minds, Scarlet," he said.

I nodded and felt my face get hot as I turned, displaying a grin.

Grisden, the troll, my friend who has never asked anything of me that I could not give, and I travelled home.

BLACK HARE PRESS

JACQUELINE MORAN MEYER is a writer, artist and small business owner living in New York, where she received her master's degree from Teachers College, Columbia University. Jacqueline enjoys writing speculative fiction and mysteries. Her favorite author is Alice Munro and her favorite film...is...anything horror related. Jacqueline also enjoys hiking with her dog Molly and the company of her husband Bruce and daughters; Julia, Emma and Lauren.

Bibliography
101 WORDS, 2019
APOCALYPSE, Black Hare Press 2019
BEWILDWERING STORIES ISSUE #831, 2019
BEYOND THE REALM, Black Hare Press,2020
BEYOND, Black Hare Press, 2019
FLASH FICTION MAGAZINE, 2020
HATE, Black Hare Press,2019
LOVE, Black Hare Press,2019
MONSTERS, Black Hare Press, 2019
OCEANS, Black Hare Press,2020
SCARY STUFF, Oddity Prodigy
TEACH.WRITE.A WRITING TEACHERS' LITERARY JOURNAL
THE DRABBLE, 2019
THE SEVEN DEADLY SINS: LUST, Black Hare Press, 2020
THE SEVEN DEADLY SINS: PRIDE, Black Hare Press, 2020
THE SIRENS CALL eZINE, 2019
TWENTY TWENTY, 2020
UNRAVEL, Black Hare Press 2019

Connect
Website: www.jmoranmeyer.net
Amazon: amazon.com/author/jacquelinemoranmeyer
Twitter: @jmmeyer64

BEYOND THE REALM

A KNIGHT OF MANY PIECES

By Derek Dunn

A knight is met with a gruesome death while travelling through a cursed land, his body ripped apart and dispersed among the deranged villagers; but with the help of a reclusive enchantress, the dead man is pieced back together for another chance at life....and revenge.

No one knew who threw the first stone. It didn't matter. The whole village joined in, from the oldest cripple to the wee toddlers barely able to walk. Some of the stones bounced off with little harm done; but others—the large ones thrown with brute force and calculated aim—shattered the man's bones.

He fell to his knees within seconds. A haze of grimy faces floated around, sneering and shouting obscenities. He didn't know them. He'd never been to their tiny village before. But the barrage of rocks continued. The feral mob had pounced on him like a vicious cat. They didn't care who he was or why he was there. All they saw was the king's coat of arms draped over his breastplate.

He'd been asking for someone, but no one gave him any heed. His inquiries were soon drowned out by the clanking of stones against armour. In a fair fight, the knight could have taken any one of the deranged villagers. He wasn't a coward. He'd achieved great victories on the battlefield and would be seen as a hero in most villages. But this wasn't a normal village. These peasants despised the king and his men. They'd been left on this cursed land for centuries, unable to leave its wretched boundaries.

Years ago, the villagers had protested the king's authority. The details of the dispute had been lost with time, but as a result, the king's mage had cursed the land and its people. No peasant born in the village would ever be able to leave. An invisible barrier had been placed around a twenty-mile radius from the market square. No one could leave. Those who tried

BEYOND THE REALM

were met with a sturdy brick wall that was felt but not seen. Markers had been placed on the roadside to warn speedy riders of the upcoming barricade. Otherwise, a hard hit and a swift fall awaited them—and oftentimes a lost horse, for even the animals yearned to leave.

The king had all but forgotten them, and the peasants' resentment towards all nobility had festered in their hearts for generations. Once a year, their lord sent an army of men to collect taxes; but this wasn't one of his men, nor was it tax collection day. So, when Sir Jacobus arrived this morning, the villagers didn't hesitate to give him a hostile welcome.

He didn't even have time to draw his sword before the onslaught overpowered him. The knight clutched a gold medallion in his hand and ripped it from his neck as he fell to the ground. The sky blurred above him. A deafening ring filled his ears. The chants of his executioners faded into oblivion. With his fate decided, Sir Jacobus closed his eyes and drew his last breath.

***

The woman's frail legs carried her up the dirt road to the market square. It was a path she had taken many times from her cottage in the forest. Although recently, Dorcas rarely left the comforts of her own home. To the younger children, she would appear a stranger. But to the old timers, she was known as a witch. Though they'd never accused her of such, everyone knew of the evil enchantress in the woods. She could grow plants beyond their natural limits and make animals do her bidding—or so the rumours went. Few had experienced her powers first-hand, but they all claimed she was responsible for their failed crops, illnesses, and all other misfortune. Yet, no one had ever confronted her. For none of their claims could be proven, and if she did indeed have magical powers, they dared not hasten their demise.

As Dorcas entered the village, an uncustomary excitement greeted her. People were parading in the streets. Children danced while their parents shouted for joy. She wandered from group to group, listening to the chatter. She heard something about a man. A knight had been here. He'd been stoned.

Dorcas reached for someone's arm. "What have they done with him?"

An old woman turned to her with a toothless grin. "He's not in one place now." She spoke in Dorcas's direction, but her white glassy eyes looked past her.

"What do you mean?"

"He's here. He's there. He's everywhere." She laughed from the back of her throat until a cough erupted.

"No, this can't be." Dorcas took a step back and almost collapsed. "Why did he come? Did he say?"

"Who knows? Looking for trouble I suspect." The woman laughed again, even though it pained her to do so. "And that's exactly what he got." Dorcas retreated just as the woman cleared her throat and spat a wad of phlegm to the ground.

She drifted through the crowd until finding the place where he'd been killed. The knight's blood stained the once dry earth. A mess of stones lay scattered about. Dorcas scanned the area. Something glistened in the dirt. She reached down and dusted off the gold medallion. It reflected a brilliant light as she raised it to her face. Dorcas recognised the engraved symbols. She dropped to her knees and wept. This was the same medallion she'd given her son many years ago.

The old woman had never forgotten her little boy. Though he was just a babe when she'd given him up, the child had remained in her heart and mind ever since.

She was so young then. Her family had tended the fruit trees in the forest. The lord of the land came to visit one day. He was a tall and graceful man. He ate of their fruit and praised them for their efforts. Never had he tasted such fine berries. Dorcas blushed at his every word. His smile revealed a full set of teeth unlike any she'd ever seen.

He wasn't unaware of her beauty either. The young Dorcas had caught his eye from the moment he arrived. Her golden locks flowed past her shoulders and rested on her maturing breasts. Innocence radiated from her spotless skin. It was the purest form of beauty he'd ever seen, and the lord couldn't resist. His guards restrained her parents while he took her inside and forced himself upon her. She screamed for mercy, but none was granted.

Dorcas vowed to get her revenge and commenced a study of the dark arts. However, the lord never returned, and due to the village's curse, she couldn't reach him. The magic that bound her to this land was more powerful than anything she could learn. It could not be broken.

Months later, Dorcas gave birth to a son. She loved and cared for the boy deeply, but she knew his future was dim. So, when the opportunity came to offer him something greater, she took it.

When the boy was still an infant, a knight and his lady were passing through the village when their carriage was ambushed. A group of angry villagers deployed a flood of arrows upon them. The horses carried them frantically down the road until crashing into a tree. Dorcas heard the commotion as she picked berries nearby.

She rushed through the woods and found the carriage on its side, wrapped around the tree's trunk. Dorcas stumbled over the wreckage. The horses were nowhere in sight. Splintered remains lay scattered on the roadside. She tiptoed around the jagged pieces until a moan resounded from the carriage. She hurried on and gasped at the gruesome sight. The driver lay on the ground with an arrow through his skull. Blood trickled down the back of his head and bathed the dirt beneath him. He was most definitely dead. She stepped over the poor fellow and climbed up the wagon. The moaning continued from inside. Dorcas pulled on the door, but it wouldn't budge.

"Please help us," said a soft, raspy voice from below. A woman's face appeared in the shadows. Her pale skin had been scratched and bruised, but she moved as though nothing was broken. She reached a hand upward and pushed.

Dorcas tugged on the door with all her strength, but still nothing happened. "Who else is down there?"

"My husband. He's badly injured. Please help."

Dorcas took a deep breath. She had only performed magic in secret, but the woman's pleas could not be ignored. She closed her eyes and stretched a hand over the door. Energy flowed through her veins. A look of impenetrable concentration filled her face. More and more energy gathered and flowed into her fingers. They tingled with an electric force. The glowing digits grew brighter until she thrust her hand down and expelled a fiery bolt to the door. The wood shattered on impact.

The woman looked up with wide eyes. Dorcas extended a hand, and she took it. As the woman climbed out, Dorcas saw the man below. He had passed out. An arrow protruded from his chest, and blood covered his garments.

"Please, can you help him?" The woman's tone had changed. Her trusting eyes swelled with tears—not from fear or pain, but with a sincere supplication. Dorcas knew she sought the use of her powers. "I can," she said, "but will you do something for me in return?"

"Yes, anything, as long as you save my husband."

Dorcas wiped the tears from the woman's face and rubbed them over his wound. He gave no reaction as she kneaded her fingers deep into the flesh.

She removed her hand, and the lady gasped. Her husband's skin had sealed itself over the wound. Not even a scar remained. She reached for him, and the knight stirred awake. He looked up to his wife. She lunged forward before he could speak and embraced him. Then she turned to Dorcas.

"Thank you. Whatever you wish shall be granted."

Dorcas reached for the woman's hand. "Please, take my son." Her voice broke as tears began to fall. The woman narrowed her eyes and squeezed the girl's hand. "He has no future here," Dorcas continued. "None of us do. I pray thee, give him the life I cannot."

The lady brushed the hair from Dorcas's face. "My sweet girl. Oh, that I could. But is this land not cursed? He won't make it past the boundary with us."

"Yes, but he is not a peasant. Noble blood runs through his veins."

The knight and his wife shared a confused look.

"Please trust me."

The woman smiled. "You've given my husband a second chance at life. For that, I am eternally grateful. Bring your boy hither, and I will take him. He shall be raised as a knight in the king's palace. I promise you; he will have the life he deserves."

Dorcas brought her son to the lady, along with a gold medallion her father had given her. It was a family heirloom, engraved with the genealogy of her ancestors. Though they were not noble, their heritage was great, and Dorcas wanted her son to have something of hers, so that he could always keep her close.

The old woman had never forgotten that day. After all these years of solitude, her heart still yearned for the little boy. As she wrapped her fingers around the medallion, questions raced through her mind. Had he returned? Had he come to see her? The man who wore this was now dead. His blood lay before her. His body had disappeared.

Dorcas clutched the medallion to her chest. The swelling beat of her heart grew louder as pain turned to anger. She squeezed the gold emblem till her knuckles turned white. The people would pay for this.

***

The villagers continued their celebration well into the night. Dorcas searched high and low for any clue of the knight's whereabouts and finally made headway when she spotted Peter walking down the street in a suit of armour. She weaved through the crowd until cornering the young troublemaker in an alley. The armour he wore was dented and much too large for his scrawny frame.

"Where's the body?" she said.

"What are you talking about, you old hag?"

"The armour, it belonged to the knight, did it not?"

"So?"

"What happened to him?"

"Didn't you see? The fool got what he deserved."

Dorcas pushed him against the stone wall with surprising strength.

"And the body?"

"I don't know." His voice shook as her thumbs dug into his shoulders.

"Yet you don the armour he wore this very day."

"I found it."

"Don't lie to me you boorish boy."

She pulled his face within inches of her own and poked a finger against his sweaty temple.

"Do you know who I am?" she said.

"Yes." His breath smelled of rancid meat.

"Then you know I can push this finger right through your skull and pull your feeble brain out in tiny pieces."

"Uh…" He trembled in her grasp. She poked harder. The fingernail pricked his skin.

"Okay, okay. Some of the men…" He paused, looked over her shoulder, and took a deep breath. In a low voice, he said, "They cut him up. They took pieces as trophies or something. They left the armour behind, and I took it."

"Who were they?"

Peter looked down, avoiding the witch's stern gaze. Dorcas threw his shoulders into the wall. His head flung back and hit the stones with a loud thud.

"Ouch!"

She grabbed his head between her palms and squeezed. Without further delay, he listed off the names of the perpetrators.

"See, that wasn't too bad." She released her grip. "And now the armour."

"What?"

"I'll be taking it."

"No, it's mine. I didn't do anything."

She reared back a fist and punched him in the face. The boy fell to the ground. Blood dribbled from his nose as he crawled away. Dorcas stretched out her arm. Peter froze in place, bound by the witch's spell. With a flick of the wrist, she lifted him from the ground and turned him towards her.

"You fools never learn," she said, drawing him closer. She ripped the leg harnesses off then flipped him upside down. Peter wailed like a baby, begging to be released. His long, dingy hair almost reached the ground.

Dorcas yanked the breastplate over his head, and the remaining pieces fell from his limbs. After collecting each fragment, she released the spell. Peter dropped. His head crashed against the dirt road, sending a wave of dust into the air. Dorcas left the naked boy behind. The first rays of twilight were painting the sky, and she still had to make the trek home.

***

The witch knew exactly where to find Henfrey, the first victim on her list. Like many of the deadbeat youth, he could always be found at the pub—not just because he was a drunk, but because he lived there. Henfrey called the small loft above the Headless Bear his home. While the majority of the room was used for storage, one little nook in the corner housed a bed of straw where Henfrey lay his head each night. The boy had been orphaned at a young age and was found hiding in the loft shortly after his parents' passing. Geoff, the owner of the tavern, pitied the boy and let him stay. If Henfrey wasn't at the bar drinking, then he would be passed out in bed.

Dorcas strolled into the bar. It smelled of sweat and urine. The day was young, but several bums had already gathered, ignoring their duties in the field. Even during the day, the place remained dark. A few candles lit the corners of the room, casting a wave of shadows across the walls.

Young Henfrey was nowhere in sight. Dorcas passed Geoff on her way to the back. He stared from behind the bar and tried to speak, but nothing came out. The witch had silenced him. He knew better than to provoke her further. Geoff was one of the few who had experienced her powers first-hand. As a much younger man, he had tried to seduce her many times, but Dorcas never fell for his whimsy. After several bouts for her affection, the witch finally agreed to meet him. They took a walk by the river, and as expected, he got a little handsy. Dorcas pulled his filthy paws from her body and stuck them to a cow's rear end. There they remained until the spell wore off a few hours later. By then, the cow had done her business, and Geoff had received it all.

Dorcas proceeded up the ladder to the loft. Henfrey's snores reached her before she even entered the room. It reeked worse than the bar below. Light seeped through the poorly thatched roof, revealing the boy on his bed of straw. He cradled something in his arms. The mysterious object, wrapped in a blood-stained cloth, stretched from his head to his hip. Dorcas prodded at the ragged, cocoon-like mass. It gave in a few inches but seemed solid enough. She lifted one of his arms. Henfrey stirred and shifted onto his side.

Dorcas froze, watching his dormant eyes. She didn't fear the boy, but she hoped not to disturb him. A hand rose to his mouth and wiped the drool away. Then it fell limp to the bed, and the snoring resumed.

Dorcas exhaled a sigh of relief. She slid the thing from his grasp and laid it on the hardwood floor beside him. The cloth unravelled as she rolled it out. It was a leg, badly bruised and bloodied but still intact. Dorcas glanced back at the sick freak who'd cradled it like a loving child. He slept like a baby, but his deeds were far from innocent. She could have conjured any number of spells on the unsuspecting brute, but she resisted. In time, justice would be served.

***

Dorcas found the pig farmer, Barnabus, slouched against a rotting tree trunk, watching his animals play in the mud. The fat slob was almost indistinguishable from the dirty swine, but Dorcas identified him from his annoying chuckle. Only a man could make such a heinous sound.

She leaned against the wooden fence and cleared her throat. "What a fine day it is," she said.

"Fine, indeed."

"Your swine are looking mighty fat this year.

What have you been feeding them?"

"This and that. They got a special treat today, though."

Dorcas searched the pigsty. Amongst all the mud and pink flesh, she caught a glimpse of something else. The pigs nibbled at a mud-soaked object. It too had flesh, but the skin was blackened and bruised. White bone protruded from one end.

"Can I have a closer look at your animals? I might be needing one myself," she said.

"Be my guest."

Dorcas slid under the top rung of the fence and entered the muddied pen.

"Just be careful," he added. "The little buggers are quite excited. I took a leg off that darned knight and greased it up for them."

There was nothing little about them. The pigs were at least twice her size. They squealed as Dorcas approached, and Barnabus threw his head back in laughter.

"That fool thought he was tough stuff," he said, "but we showed him, didn't we?"

"We sure did."

Dorcas reached for the leg and chucked it at him. The pigs bolted for it, breaking down the fence en route. They trampled over the man. His laughs turned to cries and then drowned away as his face sunk into the mud. Dorcas swiped the leg. She roped the leanest swine and dragged it away, leaving the others in a frenzy.

***

It was a half-day's journey from the pigsty to the cornfields. Sampson tended the land on the opposite side of the village. Dorcas trekked all afternoon on her donkey Ewart. The old animal's energy had waned over the years, but his legs were still durable. The recently acquired pig followed behind at a steady pace.

The trio arrived before sunset. The dirt road leading to Sampson's ramshackle hut was lined with tall stalks of corn. He and his family had cultivated the land for centuries. It was all they'd ever known and all they ever would. Dorcas spotted several scarecrows along the path. Their straw arms stretched high over the waving tassels. A gentle breeze nudged them to and fro, as though swaying in a synchronised dance. Their tattered faces had been worn by the wind and the rain and now sported blank canvases of white.

Ewart led them farther into Sampson's field. Dorcas could see the roof of his house just over the stalks. But then she noticed another scarecrow. Its face was like the others, but its arms held a legion of crows. Instead of frightening the wretched creatures, the scarecrow had attracted them.

Dorcas dismounted the donkey and fetched a rock from the side of the road. She heaved it at the birds and sent them flying. The scarecrow's arms drooped from their weight. That wasn't straw in those sleeves. The old woman produced a knife from her purse and cut the thing down. Its fleshy arms plopped to the ground. A swarm of flies buzzed around them. The skin had been ripped from the birds' incessant pecking, but the muscle and bones remained.

Dorcas removed each one from the sackcloth shirt and added them to her bag with the two legs. She hadn't seen Sampson or anyone else. They most likely hadn't seen her either. She mounted Ewart and headed back home.

It was late when Dorcas arrived. Her cottage was larger than many of the peasants' huts. Nestled around the base of a large oak tree, the wooden walls rose into the lower branches that held the roof in place. The wide trunk served as a centrepiece for the single, circular room.

Dorcas cleared off a long wooden table, stained with years of juices and potions. She retrieved the four limbs from her bag and laid them across its surface.

Shelves of glass bottles and flasks lined the walls. The witch searched the elixirs. She removed a bottle and tossed it into the fire. Flames rose from the dying embers and sparked life into the unlit candles around the room.

She sewed the decaying skin back together where the birds and pigs had ripped it apart. The stitches were rudimentary, but they would suffice. Where larger portions of skin were missing, Dorcas attached slices of pig flesh. Then she fetched another bottle. Its cork popped off with a twist, and Dorcas applied the clear gel to the sutured body parts. She rubbed it between her fingers, massaging every inch of the skin. The ointment further sealed the fragments together.

Dorcas covered the four appendages with a clean white sheet and placed the gold medallion over it. Night was upon her, and the old woman needed to rest. The excitement of the day had left her drained. The job was far from finished, and she would need to recover her strength. She bade goodnight to her partial son and went to bed.

***

Lucian, the blacksmith, was hard at work when Dorcas entered his shop the next morning. He was a large man with tough, leathery skin. His bulging head hung below his shoulders from years of ducking under low ceilings. The shop sat on the square, and Dorcas had come early, hoping to catch him before other customers arrived.

The heat from the forge was almost unbearable. Dorcas remained in the doorway while Lucian hammered away on the anvil. Most of the feeling in his face and arms had already been lost, and the heat made no difference to him.

Dorcas knocked on the open door. The man turned to face her, but she no longer appeared in her old age. She'd taken the form of a beautiful youth. The spell was effective, but it wouldn't last.

"Can I help you?" the man said, his low gravelly voice not much more than a whisper.

"I missed all the excitement the other day, but everyone says you took that knight out with one blow."

Lucian lowered the hammer. His already reddened cheeks appeared to blush. "I can't take all the credit," he said.

"But surely your blow did him in."

The man smiled, unable to find suitable words.

"Only a strong man like you could have taken out a knight."

"Perhaps you're right."

"You must have kept a trophy. A helmet or sword?"

"There was a lot of fighting over the sword. So, in the end, I took the trunk."

"The trunk?"

"I wanted the man's heart. His life source."

"I see. What do you plan to do with it?"

"I'm not sure yet. I put it in the cellar. Perhaps it will make a good stew."

"Well, I hope you'll invite me to dinner." She flashed him a beaming smile. The man's cheeks turned a deep crimson. "While I'm here, I was hoping you could fix my armour." Dorcas handed him the pieces of metal.

"Of course, I'll get right on that." He set his current project aside and went to work.

"Thanks, I'll be right back."

Dorcas found the cellar behind the shop. She lifted the heavy metal door and was greeted with a whiff of spices and aged meat. A gust of cold air pierced her skin. She eased down the steps. The worn wood creaked under her weight. Darkness filled the damp air. Dorcas pulled a stone from her purse and pressed it against her forefinger. The smooth rock glowed bright orange.

On a table in the middle of the room lay the torso.

She shoved it into the bag and returned for the armour. The blacksmith had the job done in no time. Dorcas thanked him again and left the man with false hopes and promises.

***

The cockfights were underway in the village stadium. Dorcas knew Joaquin would be there and headed straight for his chancery. The man was driven by money. He was a power-hungry gambling addict who was seen as a leader amongst the peasants. Though he held no official office, Joaquin collected the taxes each year and presented them to the lord's servants.

He housed himself in the old chapel. No one went to church anymore. The few men who tried to spread God's word, were met with a similar fate to Sir Jacobus. The front door of the building led to the nave, which had been used as a meeting place and hall where games and festivities were held. On the back side of the building was a separate door that led to the former apse. The room had been partitioned from the nave for Joaquin's private quarters.

Dorcas unlocked the door and entered the man's dwelling. The place was full of scrolls and strange objects, including jars with fingers and toes floating in oils, most likely collected from those who'd crossed him. There amongst them was the knight's head. His dark hair floated in the heavy liquid. The eyes had been gouged, and deep scars stretched across the cheeks and forehead. Dorcas reached in and pulled it out. The oil dripped on the floor and clung to her skin. It smelled of death. After stashing the head in her bag, Dorcas withdrew the pig's head and placed it in the jar. She was about to leave when she noticed a battered helmet sitting on the desk. It must have been the knight's, so she grabbed it and made for the door.

***

Before heading home, Dorcas stopped at the Headless Bear. She'd heard rumours that the knight's sword hung on Geoff's wall of fame. She'd missed it before, but there it was, hanging between the signature grizzly head and the dubious mermaid tail.

"Are you going to silence me again?" the bartender said.

"I would never do such a thing." She laughed as if they were old friends. Geoff cracked a grin. "Is that the knight's sword?" she said, pointing to the blade over his head.

"It sure is."

"It looks good up there with all your trophies."

"It's not just mine. It was a community victory."

"May I see it then?"

Geoff shook his head and turned away.

"It's mine as much as yours, is it not?"

"Perhaps, but I think we should keep it up there. If we start letting folks play with it, someone could get hurt."

"Do you not trust me?" A sly smile curved her lips.

"I've never trusted you. Why should I now?"

"Well, can you at least pour me a drink?"

He grabbed two mugs from below the bar. "You still take a mead?"

"You know me so well." Though she had aged significantly, the woman's eyes still sparkled as Geoff remembered. He poured them both a drink, and then another and another until the booze got the best of him. The bartender rarely got drunk, but Dorcas had a way of messing with him. She slammed her empty mug on the bar and walked out the door. Geoff watched her leave once again, the one prize he'd failed to conquer.

He turned to his wall of souvenirs, but the sword was gone.

***

The tired woman rested her head on the table's edge. The pieces of her son lay before her. She hoped he'd had a good life. She never wanted it to end this way. With only a few hours left in the day, Dorcas stitched all the pieces together. It wasn't a pretty job, but at least he was whole.

She carried a ladle of boiling frothy liquid she'd produced from her cauldron and poured it over his body. The dark green sludge bubbled and foamed over the flesh before dissolving into its pores. She continued until every part of the skin had been covered.

The witch recited a chant in an ancient tongue. She repeated the incantation over and over until finally the knight's skin regained colour. It wasn't a natural skin tone, but life had been restored. The bluish hue spread throughout. Then his fingers twitched. The entire body convulsed in erratic spasms. It moved as though lightning had shot through its withered veins and recharged his dead heart. After a few seconds, the body fell back to the table, unmoving and silent. Dorcas leaned forward. Her heart raced. She reached for her son but flinched as the chest suddenly rose. A breath of life exhaled from his lungs, and the chest gently fell.

A smile stretched across the old woman's face. Her son was alive. After all these years, they'd been reunited. She grabbed his hand. His cold, stiff fingers wrapped around hers. His head turned to face her. The white glassy eyes she'd created looked into hers. His features showed no expression, but she knew he saw her. His mouth trembled, struggling to open, but the jaw was locked in place. Still, the message came through. Warmth returned to his fingers as they held each other tighter.

Dorcas pulled on his arm, and the knight rose. He sat up and slid his legs over the edge of the table. The old woman wrapped her arms around him as tears fell down her face. The man reached around and put a hand on her back. Though it was heavy, his tender touch felt like that of a child. A tear trickled down his decayed cheek and rested on her shoulder.

The two held each other for what seemed an eternity. Neither spoke. Neither moved. The silence wasn't broken till the cock crowed.

***

The village awoke to towers of smoke rising from the fields. The flames had spread so fast, there was nothing they could do. Everyone gathered in the square. The fire hadn't reached the village yet, but all the surrounding land was ablaze. A smoky haze engulfed them. Rays of sunlight filtered through, illuminating a figure approaching from the east.

A large man sat atop a horse, slowly riding towards them. As the figure neared, the villagers saw they were mistaken. It wasn't a horse, but a donkey. Murmurings swelled throughout the crowd. Some laughed at the sight. Others screamed. They were pointing at something he held. The man had lifted a long pole over his head. Atop it sat a smaller figure, motionless with outstretched arms. It appeared to be a scarecrow.

The rider was badly disfigured, but he wore the armour of a knight. In fact, he bore an eerie resemblance to the knight they'd killed just days before. He came to a halt and threw the pole to the ground. It landed with a hard thud. The head popped off the scarecrow and rolled towards the crowd, stopping at a woman's feet.

Sampson's dead eyes glared up at her.

The woman shrieked and ran. As others realised what it was, they too ran, pushing and shoving, trampling over their own children to find cover.

The knight drew his sword. He moved with deliberation, slashing the peasants who'd taken his life. Screams of terror filled the air. They had nowhere to run. The flames were upon them. Sir Jacobus slaughtered everyone in his path until none were left and the wailing ceased.

He fell to the ground, gasping for air. The body had rewarded him with vengeance, but its strength was spent. In the cloud of smoke, Dorcas appeared. Her presence repelled the fire. She placed a hand on her son's chest.

"I'm sorry," she said, clutching the medallion that hung from his neck. "I'm sorry I couldn't save you."

"It's okay," he said. His voice cracked on the broken words. "I'm home now." He fell into his mother's arms.

Dorcas looked to the sky and shouted. The earth trembled beneath her. As tears flowed freely, a drop of water hit her face. Within seconds, a downpour fell upon the cursed land.

The village had burned, and all who dwelled there perished. Dorcas alone remained. She lifted her son onto Ewart's back and guided him home.

The mother buried her son in the forest. While the fire had destroyed most of the land, Dorcas had protected her sacred trees. She planted a bed of flowers over the grave and passed the rest of her days in that small oasis.

Nothing ever grew on that cursed land again, except for a few trees where a loving mother once lived. Those who passed by were astonished at the beautiful flowers that covered the ground. No matter the season, the blooms remained, reaching ever upward to the heavens above.

BLACK HARE PRESS

DEREK DUNN is an author of dark fiction whose works have appeared in anthologies by Black Hare Press, Blood Song Books, Reanimated Writers Press, and Eerie River Publishing. He's been a musician and film enthusiast for many years and received a bachelor's degree in Media Arts Studies. Derek lives in the American northwest with his family, dog, and fish.

Bibliography
100 Word Bigger Zombie Bites, Reanimated Writers Press, 2020
100 Word Zombie Bites, Reanimated Writers Press, 2019
Angels, Black Hare Press, 2019
Apocalypse, Black Hare Press, 2019
Beyond, Black Hare Press, 2019
Eerie Christmas, Black Hare Press, 2019
Forest Of Fear: Volume 1, Blood Song Books, 2019
Forgotten Ones, Eerie River Publishing, 2020
Monsters, Black Hare Press, 2019
Oceans, Black Hare Press, 2020
Twenty Twenty, Black Hare Press, 2020

Connect
Twitter: @DerekTDunn

BEYOND THE REALM
ACKNOWLEDGEMENTS

When we embarked on our Black Hare Press journey back in late 2018, we never envisioned the huge support we'd get from the writing community. We have been truly humbled by the number of submissions we've received (around 5,000 over ten publications!) and have loved reading every single one.

So, thank you to everyone who crafted tales just for us—from the tiny tales in our Dark Drabbles series to these magical beauties you have read here in Beyond the Realm—we thank you from the bottom of our hearts.

To our families and friends, collaborators, random strangers who took pity on us, and everyone who has helped us on the way: we couldn't have done it without you.

And to you, our discerning reader, we and these fifteen talented writers did it all for you. We hope you enjoyed these magical tales of quests and conquerors. If you did, don't forget to leave a review.

Thank you all, and see you next time.

Love & kisses
Ben Thomas & Dean Kershaw

www.blackharepress.com

BLACK HARE PRESS

Lightning Source UK Ltd.
Milton Keynes UK
UKHW021832180920
370090UK00003B/16/J